Dorothy Vernon of Haddon Hall

BY

CHARLES MAJOR

GROSSET & DUNLAP, *Publishers*

NEW YORK

c. 51

To My Wife

A TOUCH OF BLACK MAGIC

I DRAW the wizard's circle upon the sands, and blue flames spring from its circumference. I describe an inner circle, and green flames come responsive to my words of magic. I touch the common centre of both with my wand, and red flames, like adders' tongues, leap from the earth. Over these flames I place my caldron filled with the blood of a new-killed doe, and as it boils I speak my incantations and make my mystic signs and passes, watching the blood-red mist as it rises to meet the Spirits of Air. I chant my conjurations as I learned them from the Great Key of Solomon, and while I speak, the ruddy fumes take human forms. Out of the dark, fathomless Past — the Past of near four hundred years ago — comes a goodly company of simple, pompous folk all having a touch of childish savagery which shows itself in the fierceness of their love and of their hate.

The fairest castle-château in all England's great domain, the walls and halls of which were builded in the depths of time, takes on again its olden form quick with quivering life, and from the gates of Eagle Tower issues my quaint and radiant company. Some are clad in gold lace, silks, and taffetas ; some wear leather, buckram and clanking steel. While the caldron boils, their cloud-forms grow ever more distinct and definite, till at length I can trace their every feature. I see the color of their eyes. I discern the shades of their hair. Some heads are streaked with gray; others are glossy with the sheen of youth.

As a climax to my conjurations I speak the word of all words magical, "Dorothy," and lo! as though God had said, "Let there be light," a fair, radiant girl steps from the portals of Haddon Hall and illumines all my ancient company so that I may see even the workings of their hearts.

They, and the events of their lives, their joys and sorrows, their virtues and sins, their hatreds, jealousies, and loves — the seven numbers in the total sum of life — pass before me as in a panorama, moving when I bid them move, pausing when I bid them pause, speaking when I bid them speak, and alas! fading back into the dim gray limbo of the past long, long ere I would have them go.

But hark! my radiant shades are about to speak. The play is about to begin.

Dorothy Vernon of Haddon Hall

CHAPTER I

I RIDE DOWN TO HADDON

SINCE I play no mean part in the events of this chronicle, a few words concerning my own history previous to the opening of the story I am about to tell you will surely not be amiss, and they may help you to a better understanding of my narrative.

To begin with an unimportant fact — unimportant, that is, to you — my name is Malcolm François de Lorraine Vernon. My father was cousin-german to Sir George Vernon, at and near whose home, Haddon Hall in Derbyshire, occurred the events which will furnish my theme.

Of the ancient lineage of the house of Vernon I need not speak. You already know that the family is one of the oldest in England, and while it is not of the highest nobility, it is quite gentle and noble enough to please those who bear its honored name. My mother boasted nobler blood than that of the Vernons. She was of the princely French house of Guise — a niece and ward to the Great Duke, for whose sake I was named.

My father, being a younger brother, sought adventure in the land of France, where his handsome person and engaging manner won the smiles of Dame Fortune and my mother at one and the same cast. In due time I was born, and upon the day following that great event my

3

father died. On the day of his burial my poor mother, unable to find in me either compensation or consolation for the loss of her child's father, also died, of a broken heart, it was said. But God was right, as usual, in taking my parents ; for I should have brought them no happiness, unless perchance they could have moulded my life to a better form than it has had — a doubtful chance, since our great virtues and our chief faults are born and die with us. My faults, alas! have been many and great. In my youth I knew but one virtue : to love my friend; and that was strong within me. How fortunate for us it would be if we could begin our life in wisdom and end it in simplicity, instead of the reverse which now obtains!

I remained with my granduncle, the Great Duke, and was brought up amid the fighting, vice, and piety of his sumptuous court. I was trained to arms, and at an early age became Esquire in Waiting to his Grace of Guise. Most of my days between my fifteenth and twenty-fifth years were spent in the wars. At the age of twenty-five I returned to the château, there to reside as my uncle's representative, and to endure the ennui of peace. At the château I found a fair, tall girl, fifteen years of age : Mary Stuart, Queen of Scotland, soon afterward Queen of France and rightful heiress to the English throne. The ennui of peace, did I say? Soon I had no fear of its depressing effect, for Mary Stuart was one of those women near whose fascinations peace does not thrive. When I found her at the château, my martial ardor lost its warmth. Another sort of flame took up its home in my heart, and no power could have turned me to the wars again.

Ah! what a gay, delightful life, tinctured with bitterness, we led in the grand old château, and looking back at it how heartless, godless, and empty it seems. Do not from these words conclude that I am a fanatic, nor that I shall pour into your ears a ranter's tale; for cant is more to be despised

even than godlessness; but during the period of my life of
which I shall write I learned — but what I learned I shall
in due time tell you.

While at the court of Guise I, like many another man,
conceived for Mary Stuart a passion which lay heavy upon
my heart for many years. Sweethearts I had by the scores,
but she held my longings from all of them until I felt the
touch of a pure woman's love, and then — but again I am
going beyond my story.

I did not doubt, nor do I hesitate to say, that my passion
was returned by Mary with a fervor which she felt for no
other lover; but she was a queen, and I, compared with her,
was nobody. For this difference of rank I have since had
good cause to be thankful. Great beauty is diffusive in
its tendency. Like the sun, it cannot shine for one alone.
Still, it burns and dazzles the one as if it shone for him and
for no other; and he who basks in its rays need have no
fear of the ennui of peace.

The time came when I tasted the unutterable bitterness
of Mary's marriage to a simpering fool, Francis II., whom
she loathed, notwithstanding absurd stories of their sweet
courtship and love.

After her marriage to Francis, Mary became hard and
callous of heart, and all the world knows her sad history.
The stories of Darnley, Rizzio, and Bothwell will be rich
morsels, I suppose, for the morbid minds of men and
women so long as books are read and scandal is loved.

Ah, well, that was long ago; so long ago that now as
I write it seems but a shadow upon the horizon of time.

And so it happened that Francis died, and when the
queen went back to Scotland to ascend her native throne,
I went with her, and mothlike hovered near the blaze that
burned but did not warm me.

Then in the course of time came the Darnley tragedy.
I saw Rizzio killed. Gods! what a scene for hell was that!

Then followed the Bothwell disgrace, the queen's imprisonment at Lochleven, and my own flight from Scotland to save my head.

You will hear of Mary again in this history, and still clinging to her you will find that same strange fatality which during all her life brought evils upon her that were infectious to her friends and wrought their ruin.

One evening, in the autumn of the year 1567, I was sitting moodily before my fire in the town of Dundee, brooding over Mary's disgraceful liaison with Bothwell. I had solemnly resolved that I would see her never again, and that I would turn my back upon the evil life I had led for so many years, and would seek to acquire that quiescence of nature which is necessary to an endurable old age. A tumultuous soul in the breast of an old man breeds torture, but age, with the heart at rest, I have found is the best season of life.

In the midst of my gloomy thoughts and good resolves my friend, Sir Thomas Douglas, entered my room without warning and in great agitation.

"Are you alone?" he asked hurriedly, in a low voice.

"Save for your welcome presence, Sir Thomas," I answered, offering my hand.

"The queen has been seized," he whispered, "and warrants for high treason have been issued against many of her friends—you among the number. Officers are now coming to serve the writ. I rode hither in all haste to warn you. Lose not a moment, but flee for your life. The Earl of Murray will be made regent to-morrow."

"My servant? My horse?" I responded.

"Do not wait. Go at once. I shall try to send a horse for you to Craig's ferry. If I fail, cross the firth without one. Here is a purse. The queen sends it to you. Go! Go!"

I acted upon the advice of Sir Thomas and hurried into the street, snatching up my hat, cloak, and sword as I went. Night had fallen, and darkness and rain, which at first I was inclined to curse, proved to be my friends. I sought the back streets and alleys and walked rapidly toward the west gates of the city. Upon arriving at the gates I found them closed. I aroused the warden, and with the artful argument of gold had almost persuaded him to let me pass. My evident eagerness was my undoing, for in the hope of obtaining more gold the warden delayed opening the gates till two men approached on horseback, and, dismounting, demanded my surrender.

I laughed and said: "Two against one! Gentlemen, I am caught." I then drew my sword as if to offer it to them. My action threw the men off their guard, and when I said, "Here it is," I gave it to the one standing near me, but I gave it to him point first and in the heart.

It was a terrible thing to do, and bordered so closely on a broken parole that I was troubled in conscience. I had not, however, given my parole, nor had I surrendered; and if I had done so — if a man may take another's life in self-defence, may he not lie to save himself?

The other man shot at me with his fusil, but missed. He then drew his sword; but he was no match for me, and soon I left him sprawling on the ground, dead or alive, I knew not which.

At the time of which I write I was thirty-five years of age, and since my fifteenth birthday my occupations had been arms and the ladies — two arts requiring constant use if one would remain expert in their practice.

I escaped, and ran along the wall to a deep breach which had been left unrepaired. Over the sharp rocks I clambered, and at the risk of breaking my neck I jumped off the wall into the moat, which was almost dry. Dawn was breaking when I found a place to ascend from the moat, and I hastened to the fields and forests, where all day and all night long I wandered without food or drink. Two hours before sunrise next morning I reached Craig's Ferry. The horse sent by Douglas awaited me, but the ferry-master had been prohibited from carrying passengers across the firth, and I could not take the horse in a small boat. In truth, I was in great alarm lest I should be unable to cross, but I walked up the Tay a short distance, and found a fisherman, who agreed to take me over in his frail craft. Hardly had we started when another boat put out from shore in pursuit of us. We made all sail, but our pursuers overtook us when we were within half a furlong of the south bank, and as there were four men in the other boat, all armed with fusils, I peaceably stepped into their craft and handed my sword to their captain.

I seated myself on one of the thwarts well forward in the boat. By my side was a heavy iron boat-hook. I had noticed that all the occupants of the boat, except the fisherman who sailed her, wore armor; and when I saw the boat-hook, a diabolical thought entered my mind and I immediately acted upon its suggestion. Noiselessly I grasped the hook, and with its point pried loose a board in the bottom of the boat, first having removed my boots, cloak, and doublet. When the board was loosened I pressed my heel against it with all the force I could muster, and through an opening six inches broad and four feet long came a flood of water that swamped the boat before one could utter twenty words. I heard a cry from one of the men: "The dog has scuttled the boat. Shoot him!" At the same instant the blaze and noise of two fusils broke the still blackness of the night, but I was overboard and the powder and lead were wasted. The next moment the boat sank in ten fathoms of water, and with it went the men in armor. I hope the fisherman saved himself. I have often wondered if even the law of self-preservation justified my act. It is an awful thing to inflict death, but it is worse to endure it, and I feel sure that I am foolish to allow my conscience to trouble me for the sake of those who would have led me back to the scaffold.

I fear you will think that six dead men in less than as many pages make a record of bloodshed giving promise of terrible things to come, but I am glad I can reassure you on that point. Although there may be some good fighting ahead of us, I believe the last man has been killed of whom I shall chronicle — the last, that is, in fight or battle.

In truth, the history which you are about to read is not my own. It is the story of a beautiful, wilful girl, who was madly in love with the one man in all the world whom she should have avoided — as girls are wont to be. This perverse tendency, philosophers tell us, is owing to the fact that the unattainable is strangely alluring to woman-kind. I, being a man, shall not, of course, dwell upon the foibles of my own sex. It were a foolish candor.

As I said, there will be some good fighting ahead of us, for love and battle usually go together. One must have warm, rich blood to do either well; and, save religion, there is no source more fruitful of quarrels and death than that passion which is the source of life.

You, of course, know without the telling, that I reached land safely after I scuttled the boat, else I should not be writing this forty years afterwards.

The sun had risen when I waded ashore. I was sword-less, coatless, hatless, and bootless; but I carried a well-filled purse in my belt. Up to that time I had given no thought to my ultimate destination; but being for the moment safe, I pondered the question and determined to make my way to Haddon Hall in Derbyshire, where I was sure a warm welcome would await me from my cousin, Sir George Vernon. How I found a peasant's cottage, purchased a poor horse and a few coarse garments, and how in the disguise of a peasant I rode southward to

the English border, avoiding the cities and the main high-
ways, might interest you; but I am eager to come to my
story, and I will not tell you of my perilous journey.

One frosty morning, after many hairbreadth escapes, I
found myself well within the English border, and turned
my horse's head toward the city of Carlisle. There I
purchased a fine charger. I bought clothing fit for a
gentleman, a new sword, a hand-fusil, a breastplate, and a
steel-lined cap, and feeling once again like a man rather
than like a half-drowned rat, I turned southward for Derbyshire and Haddon Hall.

When I left Scotland I had no fear of meeting danger
in England; but at Carlisle I learned that Elizabeth held
no favor toward Scottish refugees. I also learned that the
direct road from Carlisle to Haddon, by way of Buxton,
was infested with English spies who were on the watch
for friends of the deposed Scottish queen. Several Scotch-
men had been arrested, and it was the general opinion
that upon one pretext or another they would be hanged. I
therefore chose a circuitous road leading to the town of
Derby, which lay south of Haddon at a distance of six or
seven leagues. It would be safer for me to arrive at Haddon travelling from the south than from the north. Thus,
after many days, I rode into Derby-town and stabled my
horse at the Royal Arms.

I called for supper, and while I was waiting for my joint
of beef a stranger entered the room and gave his orders
in a free, offhand manner that stamped him a person of
quality.

The night outside was cold. While the stranger and
I sat before the fire we caught its infectious warmth, and
when he showed a disposition to talk, I gladly fell in with
his humor. Soon we were filling our glasses from the
same bowl of punch, and we seemed to be on good terms
with each other. But when God breathed into the human

body a part of himself, by some mischance He permitted the devil to slip into the tongue and loosen it. My tongue, which ordinarily was fairly well behaved, upon this occasion quickly brought me into trouble.

I told you that the stranger and I seemed to be upon good terms. And so we were until I, forgetting for the moment Elizabeth's hatred of Mary's friends, and hoping to learn the stranger's name and quality, said : —

"My name is Vernon — Sir Malcolm Vernon, knight by the hand of Queen Mary of Scotland and of France." This remark, of course, required that my companion should in return make known his name and degree; but in place of so doing he at once drew away from me and sat in silence. I was older than he, and it had seemed to me quite proper and right that I should make the first advance. But instantly after I had spoken I regretted my words. I remembered not only my danger, being a Scottish refugee, but I also bethought me that I had betrayed myself. Aside from those causes of uneasiness, the stranger's conduct was an insult which I was in duty bound not to overlook. Neither was I inclined to do so, for I loved to fight. In truth, I loved all things evil.

"I regret, sir," said I, after a moment or two of embarrassing silence, "having imparted information that seems to annoy you. The Vernons, whom you may not know, are your equals in blood, it matters not who you are."

"I know of the Vernons," he replied coldly, "and I well know that they are of good blood and lineage. As for wealth, I am told Sir George could easily buy the estates of any six men in Derbyshire."

"You know Sir George?" I asked despite myself.

"I do not know him, I am glad to say," returned the stranger.

"By God, sir, you shall answer —"

"At your pleasure, Sir Malcolm."

"My pleasure is now," I retorted eagerly.

I threw off my doublet and pushed the table and chairs against the wall to make room for the fight; but the stranger, who had not drawn his sword, said:—

"I have eaten nothing since morning, and I am as hungry as a wolf. I would prefer to fight after supper; but if you insist—"

"I do insist," I replied. "Perhaps you will not care for supper when I have—"

"That may be true," he interrupted; "but before we begin I think it right to tell you, without at all meaning to boast of my skill, that I can kill you if I wish to do so. Therefore you must see that the result of our fight will be disagreeable to you in any case. You will die, or you will owe me your life."

His cool impertinence angered me beyond endurance. He to speak of killing me, one of the best swordsmen in France, where the art of sword-play is really an art! The English are but bunglers with a gentleman's blade, and should restrict themselves to pike and quarterstaff.

"Results be damned!" I answered. "I can kill you if I wish." Then it occurred to me that I really did not wish to kill the handsome young fellow toward whom I felt an irresistible attraction.

I continued: "But I prefer that you should owe me your life. I do not wish to kill you. Guard!"

My opponent did not lift his sword, but smilingly said:—

"Then why do you insist upon fighting? I certainly do not wish to kill you. In truth, I would be inclined to like you if you were not a Vernon."

"Damn your insolence! Guard! or I will run you through where you stand," I answered angrily.

"But why do we fight?" insisted the stubborn fellow, with a coolness that showed he was not one whit in fear of me.

"You should know," I replied, dropping my sword-point to the floor, and forgetting for the moment the cause of our quarrel. "I — I do not."

"Then let us not fight," he answered, "until we have discovered the matter of our disagreement."

At this remark neither of us could resist smiling. I had not fought since months before, save for a moment at the gates of Dundee, and I was loath to miss the opportunity, so I remained in thought during the space of half a minute and remembered our cause of war.

"Oh! I recall the reason for our fighting," I replied, "and a good one it was. You offered affront to the name of Sir George Vernon, and insultingly refused me the courtesy of your name after I had done you the honor to tell you mine."

"I did not tell you my name," replied the stranger, "because I believed you would not care to hear it; and I said I was glad not to know Sir George Vernon because — because he is my father's enemy. I am Sir John Manners. My father is Lord Rutland."

Then it was my turn to recede. "You certainly are right. I do not care to hear your name."

I put my sword in its scabbard and drew the table back to its former place. Sir John stood in hesitation for a moment or two, and then said: —

"Sir Malcolm, may we not declare a truce for to-night? There is nothing personal in the enmity between us."

"Nothing," I answered, staring at the fire, half regretful that we bore each other enmity at all.

"You hate me, or believe you do," said Manners, "because your father's cousin hates my father; and I try to make myself believe that I hate you because my father hates your father's cousin. Are we not both mistaken?"

I was quick to anger and to fight, but no man's heart

was more sensitive than mine to the fair touch of a kind word.

"I am not mistaken, Sir John, when I say that I do not hate you," I answered.

"Nor do I hate you, Sir Malcolm. Will you give me your hand?"

"Gladly," I responded, and I offered my hand to the enemy of my house.

"Landlord," I cried, "bring us two bottles of your best sack. The best in the house, mind you."

After our amicable understanding, Sir John and myself were very comfortable together, and when the sack and roast beef, for which the Royal Arms was justly famous, were brought in, we sat down to an enjoyable meal.

After supper Sir John lighted a small roll or stick made from the leaves of tobacco. The stick was called a cigarro, and I, proud not to be behind him in new-fashioned, gentlemanly accomplishments, called to the landlord for a pipe. Manners interrupted me when I gave the order and offered me a cigarro which I gladly accepted.

Despite my effort to reassure myself, I could not quite throw off a feeling of uneasiness whenever I thought of the manner in which I had betrayed to Sir John the fact that I was a friend to Mary Stuart. I knew that treachery was not native to English blood, and my knowledge of mankind had told me that the vice could not live in Sir John Manners's heart. But he had told me of his residence at the court of Elizabeth, and I feared trouble might come to me from the possession of so dangerous a piece of knowledge by an enemy of my house.

I did not speak my thoughts upon the matter, and we sat the evening through discussing many subjects. We warmed toward each other and became quite confidential. I feel ashamed when I admit that one of my many sins was an excessive indulgence in wine. While I was not a drunkard, I was given to my cups sometimes in a degree both dangerous and disgraceful; and during the evening of which I have just spoken I talked to Sir John with a freedom that afterward made me blush, although my indiscretion brought me no greater trouble.

My outburst of confidence was prompted by Sir John's voluntary assurance that I need fear nothing from having told him that I was a friend of Queen Mary. The Scottish queen's name had been mentioned, and Sir John had said : —

"I take it, Sir Malcolm, that you are newly arrived in England, and I feel sure you will accept the advice I am about to offer in the kindly spirit in which it is meant. I deem it unsafe for you to speak of Queen Mary's friendship in the open manner you have used toward me. Her friends are not welcome visitors to England, and I fear evil will befall those who come to us as refugees. You need have no fear that I will betray you. Your secret is safe with me. I will give you hostage. I also am Queen Mary's friend. I would not, of course, favor her against the interest of our own queen. To Elizabeth I am and always shall be loyal; but the unfortunate Scottish queen has my sympathy in her troubles, and I should be glad to help her. I hear she is most beautiful and gentle in person."

Thus you see the influence of Mary's beauty reached from Edinburgh to London. A few months only were to pass till this conversation was to be recalled by each of us, and the baneful influence of Mary's beauty upon all whom it touched was to be shown more fatally than had appeared even in my own case. In truth, my reason for speaking so fully concerning the Scottish queen and myself will be apparent to you in good time.

When we were about to part for the night, I asked Sir John, "What road do you travel to-morrow ?"

"I am going to Rutland Castle by way of Rowsley," he answered.

"I, too, travel by Rowsley to Haddon Hall. Shall we not extend our truce over the morrow and ride together as far as Rowsley?" I asked.

"I shall be glad to make the truce perpetual," he replied laughingly.

"So shall I," was my response.

Thus we sealed our compact and knitted out of the warp and woof of enmity a friendship which became a great joy and a sweet grief to each of us.

That night I lay for hours thinking of the past and wondering about the future. I had tasted the sweets—all flavored with bitterness — of court life. Women, wine, gambling, and fighting had given me the best of all the evils they had to offer. Was I now to drop that valorous life, which men so ardently seek, and was I to take up a browsing, kinelike existence at Haddon Hall, there to drone away my remaining days in fat'ning, peace, and quietude? I could not answer my own question, but this I knew: that Sir George Vernon was held in high esteem by Elizabeth, and I felt that his house was, perhaps, the only spot in England where my head could safely lie. I also had other plans concerning Sir George and his household which I regret to say I imparted to Sir John in the sack-prompted out-pouring of my confidence. The plans of which I shall now speak had been growing in favor with me for several months previous to my enforced departure from Scotland, and that event had almost determined me to adopt them. Almost, I say, for when I approached Haddon Hall I wavered in my resolution.

At the time when I had last visited Sir George at Haddon, his daughter Dorothy — Sir George called her Doll — was a slipshod girl of twelve. She was exceedingly plain, and gave promise of always so remaining. Sir George,

who had no son, was anxious that his vast estates should
remain in the Vernon name. He had upon the occasion
of my last visit intimated to me that when Doll should
become old enough to marry, and I, perchance, had had
my fill of knocking about the world, a marriage might be
brought about between us which would enable him to leave
his estates to his daughter and still to retain the much-loved
Vernon name for his descendants.

Owing to Doll's rusty red hair, slim shanks, and freckled
face, the proposition had not struck me with favor, yet to
please Sir George I had feigned acquiescence, and had
said that when the time should come, we would talk it
over. Before my flight from Scotland I had often thought
of Sir George's proposition made six or seven years
before. My love for Mary Stuart had dimmed the light
of other beauties in my eyes, and I had never married.
For many months before my flight, however, I had not
been permitted to bask in the light of Mary's smiles to
the extent of my wishes. Younger men, among them
Darnley, who was but eighteen years of age, were preferred to me, and I had begun to consider the advisability
of an orderly retreat from the Scottish court before my
lustre should be entirely dimmed. It is said that a man is
young so long as he is strong, and I was strong as in the
days of my youth. My cheeks were fresh, my eyes were
bright, and my hair was red as when I was twenty, and
without a thread of gray. Still, my temperament was
more exacting and serious, and the thought of becoming
settled for life, or rather for old age and death, was growing in favor with me. With that thought came always
a suggestion of slim, freckled Dorothy and Sir George's
offer. She held out to me wealth and position, a peaceful
home for my old age, and a grave with a pompous, pious
epitaph at Bakewell church, in death.

When I was compelled to leave Scotland, circumstances

c

forced me to a decision, and my resolution was quickly taken. I would go to Derbyshire and would marry Dorothy. I did not expect ever again to feel great love for a woman. The fuse, I thought, had burned out when I loved Mary Stuart. One woman, I believed, was like another to me, and Dorothy would answer as well as any for my wife. I could and would be kind to her, and that alone in time would make me fond. It is true, my affection would be of a fashion more comfortable than exciting; but who, having passed his galloping youth, will contemn the joys that come from making others happy? I believe there is no person, past the age of forty, at all given to pondering the whys of life, who will gainsay that the joy we give to others is our chief source of happiness. Why, then, should not a wise man, through purely selfish motives, begin early to cultivate the gentle art of giving joy?

But the fates were to work out the destinies of Dorothy and myself without our assistance. Self-willed, arrogant creatures are those same fates, but they save us a deal of trouble by assuming our responsibilities.

CHAPTER II

THE IRON, THE SEED, THE CLOUD, AND THE RAIN

THE morning following my meeting with Manners, he and I made an early start. An hour before noon we rode into the town of Rowsley and halted at The Peacock for dinner.

When we entered the courtyard of the inn we saw three ladies warmly wrapped in rich furs leave a ponderous coach and walk to the inn door, which they entered. One of them was an elderly lady whom I recognized as my cousin, Lady Dorothy Crawford, sister to Sir George Vernon. The second was a tall, beautiful girl, with an exquisite ivory-like complexion and a wonderful crown of fluffy red hair which encircled her head like a halo of sunlit glory. I could compare its wondrous lustre to no color save that of molten gold deeply alloyed with copper. But that comparison tells you nothing. I can find no simile with which to describe the beauties of its shades and tints. It was red, but it also was golden, as if the enamoured sun had gilded every hair with its radiance. In all my life I had never seen anything so beautiful as this tall girl's hair. Still, it was the Vernon red. My cousin, Sir George, and many Vernons had hair of the same color. Yet the girl's hair differed from all other I had ever seen. It had a light and a lustre of its own which was as distinct from the ordinary Vernon red, although that is very good and we are proud of it, as the sheen of gold is from

the glitter of brass. I knew by the girl's hair that she
was my cousin, Dorothy Vernon, whom I reluctantly had
come to wed.

I asked myself, "Can this be the plain, freckled girl I
kne v seven years ago?" Compared with her beauty even
Mary Stuart's was pale as the vapid moon at dawn. The
girl seemed to be the incarnated spirit of universal life
and light, and I had condescendingly come to marry this
goddess. I felt a dash of contemptuous pity for my com-
placent self.

In my cogitations concerning marriage with Dorothy
Vernon, I had not at all taken into consideration her personal inclination. A girl, after all, is but the chattel of
her father, and must, perforce, if needs be, marry the man
who is chosen for her. But leaving parental authority out
of the question, a girl with brick-red hair and a multitude
of freckles need not be considered when an agreeable,
handsome man offers himself as a husband. She usually
is willing to the point of eagerness. That is the manner
in which I had thought about Dorothy Vernon, if I considered her at all. But when a man is about to offer himself to a goddess, he is apt to pause. In such a case
there are always two sides to the question, and nine
chances to one the goddess will coolly take possession
of both. When I saw Dorothy in the courtyard of The
Peacock, I instantly knew that she was a girl to be
taken into account in all matters wherein she was personally concerned. Her every feature, every poise and gesture, unconsciously bore the stamp of "I will" or "I will
not."

Walking by Dorothy's side, holding her hand, was a fair
young woman whose hair was black, and whose skin was
of the white, clear complexion such as we see in the faces
of nuns. She walked with a hesitating, cautious step, and
clung to Dorothy, who was gentle and attentive to her.

But of this fair, pale girl I have so much to say in the pages to come that I shall not further describe her here.

When the ladies had entered the inn, my companion and I dismounted, and Manners exclaimed : —

"Did you see the glorious girl who but now entered the inn door?   Gods! I never before saw such beauty."

"Yes," I replied, "I know her."

"How fortunate I am," said Sir John.   "Perhaps I may induce you to present me to her.   At least you will tell me her name, that I may seek her acquaintance by the usual means.   I am not susceptible, but by my faith, I — I — she looked at me from the door-steps, and when I caught her eyes it seemed — that is, I saw — or I felt a stream of burning life enter my soul, and — but you will think I am a fool.   I know I am a fool.   But I feel as if I were — as if I had been bewitched in one little second of time, and by a single glance from a pair of brown eyes.   You certainly will think I am a fool, but you cannot understand —"

"Why can't I understand?" I asked indignantly.   "The thing you have seen and felt has been in this world long enough for every man to understand.   Eve used it upon Adam.   I can't understand?   Damme, sir, do you think I am a clod?   I have felt it fifty times."

"Not —" began Sir John, hesitatingly.

"Nonsense!" I replied.   "You, too, will have the same experience fifty times again before you are my age."

"But the lady," said Sir John, "tell me of her.   Will you — can you present me to her?   If not, will you tell me who she is?"

I remained for a moment in thought, wondering if it were right for me to tell him that the girl whom he so much admired was the daughter of his father's enemy.   I could see no way of keeping Dorothy's name from him, so I determined to tell him.

"She is my cousin, Mistress Dorothy Vernon," I said.

"The eldest is Lady Dorothy Crawford. The beauti-ful, pale girl I do not know."

"I am sorry," returned Sir John ; "she is the lady whom you have come to marry, is she not?"

"Y-e-s," said I, hesitatingly.

"You certainly are to be congratulated," returned Man-ners.

"I doubt if I shall marry her," I replied.

"Why?" asked Manners.

"For many reasons, chief among which is her beauty."

"That is an unusual reason for declining a woman," responded Sir John, with a low laugh.

"I think it is quite usual," I replied, having in mind the difficulty with which great beauties are won. But I con-tinued, "A woman of moderate beauty makes a safer wife, and in the long run is more comforting than one who is too attractive."

"You are a philosopher, Sir Malcolm," said Manners, laughingly.

"And a liar," I muttered to myself. I felt sure, how-ever, that I should never marry Dorothy Vernon, and I do not mind telling you, even at this early stage in my history, that I was right in my premonition. I did not marry her.

"I suppose I shall now be compelled to give you up to your relatives," said Manners.

"Yes," I returned, "we must say good-by for the present; but if we do not meet again, it shall not be for the lack of my wishing. Your father and Sir George would feel deeply injured, should they learn of our friendship, therefore —"

"You are quite right," he interrupted. "It is better that no one should know of it. Nevertheless, between you and me let there be no feud."

"The secrecy of our friendship will give it zest," said I.

"That is true, but 'good wine needs no bush.' You will not mention my name to the ladies?"

"No, if you wish that I shall not."

"I do so wish."

When the stable boys had taken our horses, I gave my hand to Sir John, after which we entered the inn and treated each other as strangers.

Soon after I had washed the stains of travel from my hands and face, I sent the maid to my cousins, asking that I might be permitted to pay my devotions, and Dorothy came to the tap-room in response to my message.

When she entered she ran to me with outstretched hands and a gleam of welcome in her eyes. We had been rare friends when she was a child.

"Ah, Cousin Malcolm, what a fine surprise you have given us!" she exclaimed, clasping both my hands and offering me her cheek to kiss. "Father's delight will be beyond measure when he sees you."

"As mine now is," I responded, gazing at her from head to foot and drinking in her beauty with my eyes. "Doll! Doll! What a splendid girl you have become. Who would have thought that — that — " I hesitated, realizing that I was rapidly getting myself into trouble.

"Say it. Say it, cousin! I know what is in your mind. Rusty red hair, angular shoulders, sharp elbows, freckles thickly set as stars upon a clear night, and so large and brown that they fairly twinkled. Great staring green eyes. Awkward! — " And she threw up her hands in mimic horror at the remembrance. "No one could have supposed that such a girl would have become — that is, you know," she continued confusedly, "could have changed. I haven't a freckle now," and she lifted her face that I might prove the truth of her words by examination, and perhaps that I might also observe her beauty.

Neither did I waste the opportunity. I dwelt longingly upon the wondrous red golden hair which fringed her low broad forehead, and upon the heavy black eyebrows, the pencilled points of whose curves almost touched across the nose. I saw the rose-tinted ivory of her skin and the long jet lashes curving in a great sweep from her full white lids, and I thought full sure that Venus herself was before me. My gaze halted for a moment at the long eyes which changed chameleon-like with the shifting light, and varied with her moods from deep fathomless green to violet, and from violet to soft voluptuous brown, but in all their tints beaming forth a lustre that would have stirred the soul of an anchorite. Then I noted the beauty of her clean-cut saucy nose and the red arch of her lips, slightly parted for the purpose of showing her teeth. But I could not stop long to dwell upon any one especial feature, for there were still to be seen her divine round chin, her large white throat, and the infinite grace in poise and curve of her strong young form. I dared not pause nor waste my time if I were to see it all, for such a girl as Dorothy waits no man's leisure — that is, unless she wishes to wait. In such case there is no moving her, and patience becomes to her a delightful virtue.

After my prolonged scrutiny Dorothy lowered her face and said laughingly : —

"Now come, cousin, tell me the truth. Who would have thought it possible ? "

"Not I, Doll, not I, if you will pardon me the frankness."

"Oh, that is easily done." Then with a merry ripple of laughter, "It is much easier, I fancy, for a woman to speak of the time when she was plain than to refer to the time when — when she was beautiful. What an absurd speech that is for me to make," she said confusedly.

"I certainly did not expect to find so great a change," said I. "Why, Doll, you are wondrous, glorious, beautiful. I can't find words — "

"Then don't try, Cousin Malcolm," she said with a smile

that fringed her mouth in dimples. "Don't try. You will make me vain."

"You are that already, Doll," I answered, to tease her.

"I fear I am, cousin — vain as a man. But don't call me Doll. I am tall enough to be called Dorothy."

She straightened herself up to her full height, and stepping close to my side, said: "I am as tall as you. I will now try to make you vain. You look just as young and as handsome as when I last saw you and so ardently admired your waving black mustachio and your curling chin beard."

"Did you admire them, Doll — Dorothy?" I asked, hoping, though with little faith, that the admiration might still continue.

"Oh, prodigiously," she answered with unassuring candor. "Prodigiously. Now who is vain, Cousin Malcolm François de Lorraine Vernon?"

"I," I responded, shrugging my shoulders and confessing by compulsion.

"But you must remember," she continued provokingly, "that a girl of twelve is very immature in her judgment and will fall in love with any man who allows her to look upon him twice."

"Then I am to believe that the fire begins very early to burn in the feminine heart," I responded.

"With birth, my cousin, with birth," she replied; "but in my heart it burned itself out upon your curling beard at the mature age of twelve."

"And you have never been in love since that time, Doll — Dorothy?" I asked with more earnestness in my heart than in my voice.

"No, no; by the Virgin, no! Not even in the shadow of a thought. And by the help of the Virgin I hope I never shall be; for when it comes to me, mark my word, cousin, there will be trouble in Derbyshire."

"By my soul, I believe you speak the truth," I answered,

little dreaming how quickly our joint prophecy would come true.

I then asked Dorothy to tell me about her father.

"Father is well in health," she said. "In mind he has been much troubled and disturbed. Last month he lost the lawsuit against detestable old Lord Rutland. He was much angered by the loss, and has been moody and morose in brooding over it ever since. He tries, poor father, to find relief from his troubles, and — and I fear takes too much liquor. Rutland and his friends swore to one lie upon another, and father believes that the judge who tried the case was bribed. Father intends to appeal to Parliament, but even in Parliament he fears he cannot obtain justice. Lord Rutland's son — a disreputable fellow, who for many years has lived at court — is a favorite with the queen, and his acquaintance with her Majesty and with the lords will be to father's prejudice."

"I have always believed that your father stood in the queen's good graces?" I said interrogatively.

"So he does, but I have been told that this son of Lord Rutland, whom I have never seen, has the beauty of — of the devil, and exercises a great influence over her Majesty and her friends. The young man is not known in this neighborhood, for he has never deigned to leave the court; but Lady Cavendish tells me he has all the fascinations of Satan. I would that Satan had him."

"The feud still lives between Vernon and Rutland?" I asked.

"Yes, and it will continue to live so long as an ounce of blood can hold a pound of hatred," said the girl, with flashing eyes and hard lips. "I love to hate the accursed race. They have wronged our house for three generations, and my father has suffered greater injury at their hands than any of our name. Let us not talk of the hateful subject."

We changed the topic. I had expected Dorothy to invite me to go with her to meet Lady Crawford, but the girl seemed disinclined to leave the tap-room. The Peacock was her father's property, and the host and hostess were her friends after the manner of persons in their degree. Therefore Dorothy felt at liberty to visit the tap-room quite as freely as if it had been the kitchen of Haddon Hall.

During our conversation I had frequently noticed Dorothy glancing slyly in the direction of the fireplace; but my back was turned that way, and I did not know, nor did it at first occur to me to wonder what attracted her attention. Soon she began to lose the thread of our conversation, and made inappropriate, tardy replies to my remarks. The glances toward the fireplace increased in number and duration, and her efforts to pay attention to what I was saying became painful failures.

After a little time she said: "Is it not cool here? Let us go over to the fireplace where it is warmer."

I turned to go with her, and at once saw that it was not the fire in the fireplace which had attracted Dorothy, but quite a different sort of flame. In short, much to my consternation, I discovered that it was nothing less than my handsome new-found friend, Sir John Manners, toward whom Dorothy had been glancing.

We walked over to the fireplace, and one of the fires, Sir John, moved away. But the girl turned her face that she might see him in his new position. The movement, I confess, looked bold to the point of brazenness; but if the movement was bold, what shall I say of her glances and the expression of her face? She seemed unable to take her eager eyes from the stranger, or to think of anything but him, and after a few moments she did not try. Soon she stopped talking entirely and did not even hear what I was saying. I, too, became silent, and after a long pause the girl asked: —

"Cousin, who is the gentleman with whom you were travelling?"

I was piqued by Dorothy's conduct, and answered rather curtly: "He is a stranger. I picked him up at Derby, and we rode here together."

A pause followed, awkward in its duration.

"Did you — not — learn — his — name?" asked Dorothy, hesitatingly.

"Yes," I replied.

Then came another pause, broken by the girl, who spoke in a quick, imperious tone touched with irritation: —

"Well, what is it?"

"It is better that I do not tell you," I answered. "It was quite by accident that we met. Neither of us knew the other. Please do not ask me to tell you his name."

"Oh, but you make me all the more eager to learn. Mystery, you know, is intolerable to a woman, except in the unravelling. Come, tell me! Tell me! Not, of course, that I really care a farthing to know — but the mystery! A mystery drives me wild. Tell me, please do, Cousin Malcolm."

She certainly was posing for the stranger's benefit, and was doing all in her power, while coaxing me, to display her charms, graces, and pretty little ways. Her attitude and conduct spoke as plainly as the spring bird's song speaks to its mate. Yet Dorothy's manner did not seem bold. Even to me it appeared modest, beautiful, and necessary. She seemed to act under compulsion. She would laugh, for the purpose, no doubt, of showing her dimples and her teeth, and would lean her head to one side pigeon-wise to display her eyes to the best advantage, and then would she shyly glance toward Sir John to see if he was watching her. It was shameless, but it could not be helped by Dorothy nor any one else. After a few moments of mute pleading by the girl, broken now and then by, " Please, please," I said : —

"If you give to me your promise that you will never speak of this matter to any person, I will tell you the gentleman's name. I would not for a great deal have your father know that I have held conversation with him even for a moment, though at the time I did not know who he was."

"Oh, this is delightful! He must be some famous, dashing highwayman. I promise, of course I promise — faithfully." She was glancing constantly toward Manners, and her face was bright with smiles and eager with anticipation.

"He is worse than a highwayman, I regret to say. The gentleman toward whom you are so ardently glancing is — Sir John Manners."

A shock of pain passed over Dorothy's face, followed by a hard, repellent expression that was almost ugly.

"Let us go to Aunt Dorothy," she said, as she turned and walked across the room toward the door.

When we had closed the door of the tap-room behind us Dorothy said angrily : —

"Tell me, cousin, how you, a Vernon, came to be in his company ? "

"I told you that I met him quite by accident at the Royal Arms in Derby-town. We became friends before either knew the other's name. After chance had disclosed our identities, he asked for a truce to our feud until the morrow; and he was so gentle and open in his conduct that I could not and would not refuse his proffered olive branch. In truth, whatever faults may be attributable to Lord Rutland, — and I am sure he deserves all the evil you have spoken of him, — his son, Sir John, is a noble gentleman, else I have been reading the book of human nature all my life in vain. Perhaps he is in no way to blame for his father's conduct. He may have had no part in it."

"Perhaps he has not," said Dorothy, musingly.

It was not a pleasant task for me to praise Sir John, but my sense of justice impelled me to do so. I tried to make myself feel injured and chagrined because of Dorothy's manner toward him; for you must remember I had arranged with myself to marry this girl, but I could not work my feelings into a state of indignation against the heir to Rutland. The truth is, my hope of winning Dorothy had evaporated upon the first sight of her, like the volatile essence it really was. I cannot tell you why, but I at once seemed to realize that all the thought and labor which I had devoted to the arduous task of arranging with myself this marriage was labor lost. So I frankly told her my kindly feelings for Sir John, and gave her my high estimate of his character.

I continued: " You see, Dorothy, I could not so easily explain to your father my association with Sir John, and I hope you will not speak of it to any one, lest the news should reach Sir George's ears."

"I will not speak of it," she returned, sighing faintly. "After all, it is not his fault that his father is such a villain. He doesn't look like his father, does he ?"

"I cannot say. I never saw Lord Rutland," I replied.

"He is the most villanous-looking—" but she broke off the sentence and stood for a moment in revery. We were in the darkened passage, and Dorothy had taken my hand. That little act in another woman of course would have led to a demonstration on my part, but in this girl it seemed so entirely natural and candid that it was a complete bar to undue familiarity. In truth, I had no such tendency, for the childish act spoke of an innocence and faith that were very sweet to me who all my life had lived among men and women who laughed at those simple virtues. The simple conditions of life are all that are worth striving for. They come to us fresh from Nature and from Nature's God. The complex are but concoctions of man after recipes in the devil's alchemy. So much gold, so much ambition, so much lust. Mix well. Product : so much vexation.

"He must resemble his mother," said Dorothy, after a long pause. "Poor fellow! His mother is dead. He is like me in that respect. I wonder if his father's villanies trouble him?"

"I think they must trouble him. He seems to be sad," said I, intending to be ironical.

My reply was taken seriously.

"I am sorry for him," she said, "it is not right to hate even our enemies. The Book tells us that."

"Yet you hate Lord Rutland," said I, amused and provoked.

Unexpected and dangerous symptoms were rapidly developing in the perverse girl, and trouble was brewing "in Derbyshire."

The adjective perverse, by the way, usually is superfluous when used to modify the noun girl.

"Yet you hate Lord Rutland," I repeated.

"Why, y-e-s," she responded. "I cannot help that, but you know it would be very wrong to — to hate all his family. To hate him is bad enough."

I soon began to fear that I had praised Sir John overmuch.

"I think Sir John is all there is of Lord Rutland's family," I said, alarmed yet amused at Dorothy's search for an excuse not to hate my new-found friend.

"Well," she continued after a pause, throwing her head to one side, "I am sorry there are no more of that family not to hate."

"Dorothy! Dorothy!" I exclaimed. "What has come over you? You surprise me."

"Yes," she answered, with a little sigh, "I certainly have surprised myself by — by my willingness to forgive those who have injured my house. I did not know there was so much — so much good in me."

"Mistress Pharisee," thought I, "you are a hypocrite."

Again intending to be ironical, I said, "Shall I fetch him from the tap-room and present him to you?"

Once more my irony was lost upon the girl. Evidently that sort of humor was not my strong point.

"No, no," she responded indignantly, "I would not speak to him for — " Again she broke her sentence abruptly, and after a little pause, short in itself but amply long for a girl like Dorothy to change her mind two score times, she continued: "It would not be for the best. What think you, Cousin Malcolm?"

"Surely the girl has gone mad," thought I. Her voice was soft and conciliating as if to say, "I trust entirely to your mature, superior judgment."

My judgment coincided emphatically with her words, and I said: "I spoke only in jest. It certainly would not be right. It would be all wrong if you were to meet him."

"That is true," the girl responded with firmness, "but — but no real harm could come of it," she continued, laughing nervously. "He could not strike me nor bite me. Of course it would be unpleasant for me to meet him, and as there is no need — I am curious to know what one of his race is like. It's the only reason that would induce me to consent. Of course you know there could be no other reason for me to wish — that is, you know — to be willing to meet him. Of course you know."

"Certainly," I replied, still clinging to my unsuccessful irony. "I will tell you all I know about him, so that you may understand what he is like. As for his personal appearance, you saw him, did you not?"

I thought surely that piece of irony would not fail, but it did, and I have seldom since attempted to use that form of humor.

"Yes — oh, yes, I saw him for a moment."

"But I will not present him to you, Dorothy, however much you may wish to meet him," I said positively.

"It is almost an insult, Cousin Malcolm, for you to say that I wish to meet him," she answered in well-feigned indignation.

The French blood in my veins moved me to shrug my shoulders. I could do nothing else. With all my knowledge of womankind this girl had sent me to sea.

But what shall we say of Dorothy's conduct? I fancy I can hear you mutter, "This Dorothy Vernon must have been a bold, immodest, brazen girl." Nothing of the sort. Dare you of the cold blood — if perchance there be any with that curse in their veins who read these lines — dare you, I say, lift your voice against the blessed heat in others which is but a greater, stronger, warmer spark of God's own soul than you possess or than you can comprehend? "Evil often comes of it," I hear you say. That I freely admit; and evil comes from eating too much bread, and from hearing too much preaching. But the universe, from the humblest blade of grass to the infinite essence of God, exists because of that warmth which the mawkish world contemns. Is the iron immodest when it creeps to the lodestone and clings to its side? Is the hen bird brazen when she flutters to her mate responsive to his compelling woo-song? Is the seed immodest when it sinks into the ground and swells with budding life? Is the cloud bold when it softens into rain and falls to earth because it has no other choice? or is it brazen when it nestles for a time on the bosom of heaven's arched dome and sinking into the fathomless depths of a blue black infinity ceases to be itself? Is the human soul immodest when, drawn by a force it cannot resist, it seeks a stronger soul which absorbs its ego as the blue sky absorbs the floating cloud, as the warm earth swells the seed, as the magnet draws the iron? All these are of one quality. The iron, the seed, the cloud, and the soul of man are *what* they are, do *what* they do, love as they love, live as they live, and die as they die because they must — because they have no other choice. We think we are free because at times we act as we please, forgetting that God gives us the "please," and that every act of our being is but the result of a dictated motive. Dorothy was not immodest. This was her case. She was the iron, the seed, the cloud, and the rain. You, too, are the iron, the seed, the cloud, and the rain. It is only human vanity which prompts you to believe that you are yourself and that you are free. Do you find any freedom in this world save that which you fondly believe to exist within yourself? Self! There is but one self, God. I have been told that the people of the East call Him Brahma. The word, it is said, means "Breath," "Inspiration," "All." I have felt that the beautiful pagan thought has truth in it; but my conscience and my priest tell me rather to cling to truths I have than to fly to others that I know not of. As a result, I shall probably die orthodox and mistaken.

CHAPTER III

The Pitcher goes to the Well

DOROTHY and I went to the inn parlors, where I received a cordial welcome from my cousin, Lady Crawford. After our greeting, Dorothy came toward me leading the fair, pale girl whom I had seen in the courtyard.

"Madge, this is my cousin, Malcolm Vernon," said Dorothy. "He was a dear friend of my childhood and is much beloved by my father. Lady Magdalene Stanley, cousin," and she placed the girl's soft white hand in mine. There was a peculiar hesitancy in the girl's manner which puzzled me. She did not look at me when Dorothy placed her hand in mine, but kept her eyes cast down, the long, black lashes resting upon the fair curves of her cheek like a shadow on the snow. She murmured a salutation, and when I made a remark that called for a response, she lifted her eyes but seemed not to look at me. Unconsciously I turned my face toward Dorothy, who closed her eyes and formed with her lips the word "blind."

I retained the girl's hand, and she did not withdraw it. When I caught Dorothy's unspoken word I led Lady Madge to a chair and asked if I might sit beside her.

"Certainly," she answered smilingly; "you know I am blind, but I can hear and speak, and I enjoy having persons I like sit near me that I may touch them now and then while we talk. If I could only see!" she exclaimed,

Still, there was no tone of complaint in her voice and very little even of regret.   The girl's eyes were of a deep blue and were entirely without scar or other evidence of blindness, except that they did not seem to see.   I afterward learned that her affliction had come upon her as the result of illness when she was a child.   She was niece to the Earl of Derby, and Dorothy's mother had been her aunt. She owned a small estate and had lived at Haddon Hall five or six years because of the love that existed between her and Dorothy.   A strong man instinctively longs to cherish that which needs his strength, and perhaps it was the girl's helplessness that first appealed to me.   Perhaps it was her rare, peculiar beauty, speaking eloquently of virtue such as I had never known, that touched me.   I cannot say what the impelling cause was, but this I know: my heart went out in pity to her, and all that was good within me — good, which I had never before suspected — stirred in my soul, and my past life seemed black and barren beyond endurance.   Even Dorothy's marvellous beauty lacked the subtle quality which this simple blind girl possessed.   The first step in regeneration is to see one's faults; the second is to regret them; the third is to quit them.   The first and second steps constitute repentance; the second and third regeneration. One hour within the radius of Madge Stanley's influence brought me to repentance.   But repentance is an everyday virtue.   Should I ever achieve regeneration?   That is one of the questions this history will answer.   To me, Madge Stanley's passive force was the strongest influence for good that had ever impinged on my life.   With respect to her, morally, I was the iron, the seed, the cloud, and the rain, for she, acting unconsciously, moved me with neither knowledge nor volition on my part.

Soon after my arrival at the ladies' parlor dinner was served, and after dinner a Persian merchant was ushered in, closely followed by his servants bearing bales of rare Eastern fabrics. A visit and a dinner at the inn were little events that made a break in the monotony of life at the Hall, and the ladies preferred to visit the merchant, who was stopping at The Peacock for a time, rather than to have him take his wares to Haddon.

While Lady Crawford and Dorothy were revelling in Persian silks, satins, and gold cloths, I sat by Lady Madge and was more than content that we were left to ourselves. My mind, however, was as far from thoughts of gallantry as if she had been a black-veiled nun. I believe I have not told you that I was of the Holy Catholic Faith. My religion, I may say, has always been more nominal and political than spiritual, although there ran through it a strong vein of inherited tendencies and superstitions which were highly colored by contempt for heresy and heretics. I was Catholic by habit. But if I analyzed my supposed religious belief, I found that I had none save a hatred for heresy. Heretics, as a rule, were low-born persons, vulgarly moral, and as I had always thought, despisedly hypocritical. Madge Stanley, however, was a Protestant, and that fact shook the structure of my old mistakes to its foundation, and left me religionless.

After the Persian merchant had packed his bales and departed, Dorothy and Lady Crawford joined Madge and me near the fireplace. Soon Dorothy went over to the window and stood there gazing into the courtyard.

After a few minutes Lady Crawford said, "Dorothy, had we not better order Dawson to bring out the horses and coach?" Will Dawson was Sir George's forester.

Lady Crawford repeated her question, but Dorothy was too intently watching the scene in the courtyard to hear. I went over to her, and looking out at the window discovered the object of Dorothy's rapt attention. There is no need for me to tell you who it was. Irony, as you know, and as I had learned, was harmless against this thick-skinned nymph. Of course I had no authority to scold her, so I laughed. The object of Dorothy's attention was about to mount his horse. He was drawing on his gauntleted gloves and held between his teeth a cigarro. He certainly presented a handsome figure for the eyes of an ardent girl to rest upon while he stood beneath the window, clothed in a fashionable Paris-made suit of brown, doublet, trunks, and hose. His high-topped boots were polished till they shone, and his broad-rimmed hat, of soft beaver, was surmounted by a flowing plume. Even I, who had no especial taste nor love for masculine beauty, felt my sense of the beautiful strongly moved by the attractive picture my new-found friend presented. His dress, manner, and bearing, polished by the friction of life at a luxurious court, must have appeared god-like to Dorothy. She had never travelled farther from home than Buxton and Derby-town, and had met only the half-rustic men belonging to the surrounding gentry and nobility of Derbyshire, Nottingham, and Stafford. She had met but few even of them, and their lives had been spent chiefly in drinking, hunting, and gambling — accomplishments that do not fine down the texture of a man's nature or fit him for a lady's bower. Sir John Manners was a revelation to Dorothy; and she, poor girl, was bewildered and bewitched by him.

When John had mounted and was moving away, he looked up to the window where Dorothy stood, and a light came to her eyes and a smile to her face which no man who knows the sum of two and two can ever mistake if he but once sees it.

When I saw the light in Dorothy's eyes, I knew that all the hatred that was ever born from all the feuds that had ever lived since the quarrelling race of man began its feuds in Eden could not make Dorothy Vernon hate the son of her father's enemy.

" I was — was — watching him draw smoke through the — the little stick which he holds in his mouth, and — and blow it out again," said Dorothy, in explanation of her attitude. She blushed painfully and continued, "I hope you do not think — "

" I do not think," I answered. "I would not think of thinking."

"Of course not," she responded, with a forced smile, as she watched Sir John pass out of sight under the arch of the innyard gate. I did not think. I knew. And the sequel, so full of trouble, soon proved that I was right.

After John had passed through the gate, Dorothy was willing to go home; and when Will Dawson brought the great coach to the inn door, I mounted my horse and rode beside the ladies to Haddon Hall, two miles north from Rowsley.

I shall not stop to tell you of the warm welcome given me by Sir George Vernon, nor of his delight when I briefly told him my misfortunes in Scotland — misfortunes that had brought me to Haddon Hall. Nor shall I describe the great boar's head supper given in my honor, at which there were twenty men who could have put me under the table. I thought I knew something of the art of drinking, but at that supper I soon found I was a mere tippler compared with these country guzzlers. At that feast I learned also that Dorothy, when she had hinted concerning Sir George's excessive drinking, had told the truth. He, being the host, drank with all his guests. Near midnight he grew distressingly drunk, talkative, and violent, and when toward morning he was carried from the room by his servants, the company broke up. Those who could do so reeled home; those who could not walk at all were put to bed by the retainers at Haddon Hall. I had chosen my bedroom high up in Eagle Tower. At table I had tried to remain sober. That, however, was an impossible task, for at the

upper end of the hall there was a wrist-ring placed in the
wainscoting at a height of ten or twelve inches above the
head of an ordinary man, and if one refused to drink as
much as the other guests thought he should, his wrist was
fastened above his head in the ring, and the liquor which
he should have poured down his throat was poured down
his sleeve.   Therefore to avoid this species of rustic sport
I drank much more than was good for me.   When the
feast closed I thought I was sober enough to go to my
room unassisted; so I took a candle, and with a great show
of self-confidence climbed the spiral stone stairway to the
door of my room.   The threshold of my door was two or
three feet above the steps of the stairway, and after I had
contemplated the distance for a few minutes, I concluded
that it would not be safe for me to attempt to climb into
my sleeping apartments without help.   Accordingly I sat
down upon the step on which I had been standing, placed
my candle beside me, called loudly for a servant, received no
response, and fell asleep only to be awakened by one of Sir
George's retainers coming downstairs next morning.

After that supper, in rapid succession, followed hunting
and drinking, feasting and dancing in my honor.   At the
dances the pipers furnished the music, or, I should rather
say, the noise.   Their miserable wailings reminded me of
Scotland.   After all, thought I, is the insidious, polished
vice of France worse than the hoggish, uncouth practices
of Scotland and of English country life?   I could not endure the latter, so I asked Sir George, on the pretext of
ill health, to allow me to refuse invitations to other houses,
and I insisted that he should give no more entertain-
ments at Haddon Hall on my account.   Sir George eagerly
acquiesced in all my wishes.   In truth, I was treated like
an honored guest and a member of the family, and I congratulated myself that my life had fallen in such pleasant
lines.   Dorothy and Madge became my constant com-

panions, for Sir George's time was occupied chiefly with his estates and with his duties as magistrate. A feeling of rest and contentment came over me, and my past life drifted back of me like an ever receding cloud.

Thus passed the months of October and November.

In the meantime events in Scotland and in England proved my wisdom in seeking a home at Haddon Hall, and showed me how great was my good fortune in finding it.

Queen Mary was a prisoner at Lochleven Castle, and her brother Murray had beheaded many of her friends. Elizabeth, hating Mary as only a plain, envious woman can hate one who is transcendently beautiful, had, upon different pretexts, seized many of Mary's friends who had fled to England for sanctuary, and some of them had suffered imprisonment or death.

Elizabeth, in many instances, had good cause for her attitude toward Mary's friends, since plots were hatching thick and fast to liberate Mary from Lochleven; and many such plots, undoubtedly, had for their chief end the deposition of Elizabeth, and the enthronement of Mary as Queen of England.

As a strict matter of law, Mary was rightful heir to the English throne, and Elizabeth was an usurper. Parliament, at Henry's request, had declared that Elizabeth, his issue by Anne Boleyn, was illegitimate, and that being true, Mary was next in line of descent. The Catholics of England took that stand, and Mary's beauty and powers of fascination had won for her friends even in the personal household of the Virgin Queen. Small cause for wonder was it that Elizabeth, knowing all these facts, looked with suspicion and fear upon Mary's refugee friends.

The English queen well knew that Sir George Vernon was her friend, therefore his house and his friendship were my sanctuary, without which my days certainly would have been numbered in the land of Elizabeth, and their number would have been small. I was dependent on Sir George not only for a roof to shelter me, but for my very life. I speak of these things that you may know some of the many imperative reasons why I desired to please and conciliate my cousin. In addition to those reasons, I soon grew to love Sir George, not only because of his kindness to me, but because he was a lovable man. He was generous, just, and frank, and although at times he was violent almost to the point of temporary madness, his heart was usually gentle, and was as easily touched by kindness as it was quickly moved to cruelty by injury, fancied or actual. I have never known a more cruel, tender man than he. You will see him in each of his natures before you have finished this history. But you must judge him only after you have considered his times, which were forty years ago, his surroundings, and his blood.

During those two months remarkable changes occurred within the walls of Haddon, chief of which were in myself, and, alas! in Dorothy.

My pilgrimage to Haddon, as you already know, had been made for the purpose of marrying my fair cousin; for I did not, at the time I left Scotland, suppose I should need Sir George's protection against Elizabeth. When I met Dorothy at Rowsley, my desire to marry her became personal, in addition to the mercenary motives with which I had originally started. But I quickly recognized the fact that the girl was beyond my reach. I knew I could not win her love, even though I had a thousand years to try for it; and I would not accept her hand in marriage solely at her father's command. I also soon learned that Dorothy was the child of her father, gentle, loving, and tender beyond the naming, but also wilful, violent, and fierce to the extent that no command could influence her.

First I shall speak of the change within myself. I will soon be done with so much " I " and "me," and you shall have Dorothy to your heart's content, or trouble, I know not which.

Soon after my arrival at Haddon Hall the sun ushered in one of those wonderful days known only to the English autumn, when the hush of Nature's drowsiness, just before her long winter's sleep, imparts its soft restfulness to man, as if it were a lotus feast. Dorothy was ostentatiously busy with her household matters, and was consulting with butler, cook, and steward. Sir George had ridden out to superintend his men at work, and I, wandering aimlessly about the hall, came upon Madge Stanley sitting in the chaplain's room with folded hands.

"Lady Madge, will you go with me for a walk this beautiful morning?" I asked.

"Gladly would I go, Sir Malcolm," she responded, a smile brightening her face and quickly fading away, "but I — I cannot walk in unfamiliar places. I should fall. You would have to lead me by the hand, and that, I fear, would mar the pleasure of your walk."

"Indeed, it would not, Lady Madge. I should enjoy my walk all the more."

"If you really wish me to go, I shall be delighted," she responded, as the brightness came again to her face. "I sometimes grow weary, and, I confess, a little sad sitting alone when Dorothy cannot be with me. Aunt Dorothy, now that she has her magnifying glasses, — spectacles, I think they are called, — devotes all her time to reading, and dislikes to be interrupted."

"I wish it very much," I said, surprised by the real eagerness of my desire, and unconsciously endeavoring to keep out of the tones of my voice a part of that eagerness.

"I shall take you at your word," she said. "I will go to my room to get my hat and cloak."

She rose and began to grope her way toward the door, holding out her white, expressive hands in front of her. It was pitiful and beautiful to see her, and my emotions welled up in my throat till I could hardly speak.

"Permit me to give you my hand," I said huskily. How I longed to carry her! Every man with the right sort of a heart in his breast has a touch of the mother instinct in him; but, alas! only a touch. Ah, wondrous and glorious womanhood! If you had naught but the mother instinct to lift you above your masters by the hand of man-made laws, those masters were still unworthy to tie the strings of your shoes.

"Thank you," said the girl, as she clasped my hand, and moved with confidence by my side. "This is so much better than the dreadful fear of falling. Even through these rooms where I have lived for many years I feel safe only in a few places, — on the stairs, and in my rooms, which are also Dorothy's. When Dorothy changes the position of a piece of furniture in the Hall, she leads me to it several times that I may learn just where it is. A long time ago she changed the position of a chair and did not tell me. I fell against it and was hurt. Dorothy wept bitterly over the mishap, and she has never since failed to tell me of such changes. I cannot make you know how kind and tender Dorothy is to me. I feel that I should die without her, and I know she would grieve terribly were we to part."

I could not answer. What a very woman you will think I was! I, who could laugh while I ran my sword through a man's heart, could hardly restrain my tears for pity of this beautiful blind girl.

"Thank you; that will do," she said, when we came to the foot of the great staircase. "I can now go to my rooms alone."

When she reached the top she hesitated and groped for

a moment; then she turned and called laughingly to me while I stood at the bottom of the steps, "I know the way perfectly well, but to go alone in any place is not like being led."

"There are many ways in which one may be led, Lady Madge," I answered aloud. Then I said to myself, "That girl will lead you to Heaven, Malcolm, if you will permit her to do so."

But thirty-five years of evil life are hard to neutralize. There is but one subtle elixir that can do it — love; and I had not thought of that magic remedy with respect to Madge.

I hurriedly fetched my hat and returned to the foot of the staircase. Within a minute or two Madge came down stairs holding up the skirt of her gown with one hand, while she grasped the banister with the other. As I watched her descending I was enraptured with her beauty. Even the marvellous vital beauty of Dorothy could not compare with this girl's fair, pale loveliness. It seemed to be almost a profanation for me to admire the sweet oval of her face. Upon her alabaster skin, the black eyebrows, the long lashes, the faint blue veins and the curving red lips stood in exquisite relief. While she was descending the stairs, I caught a gleam of her round, snowy forearm and wrist; and when my eyes sought the perfect curves of her form disclosed by the clinging silk gown she wore, I felt that I had sinned in looking upon her, and I was almost glad she could not see the shame which was in my face.

"Cousin Malcolm, are you waiting?" she asked from midway in the staircase.

"Yes, I am at the foot of the steps," I answered.

"I called you 'Cousin Malcolm,'" she said, holding out her hand when she came near me. "Pardon me; it was a slip of the tongue. I hear 'Cousin Malcolm' so frequently from Dorothy that the name is familiar to me."

"I shall be proud if you will call me 'Cousin Malcolm' always. I like the name better than any that you can use."

"If you wish it," she said, in sweet, simple candor, "I will call you 'Cousin Malcolm,' and you may call me 'Cousin Madge' or 'Madge,' just as you please."

"'Cousin Madge' it shall be; that is a compact," I answered, as I opened the door and we walked out into the fresh air of the bright October morning.

"That will stand for our first compact; we are progressing famously," she said, with a low laugh of delight.

Ah, to think that the blind can laugh. God is good.

We walked out past the stables and the cottage, and crossed the river on the great stone bridge. Then we took our way down the babbling Wye, keeping close to its banks, while the dancing waters and even the gleaming pebbles seemed to dimple and smile as they softly sang their song of welcome to the fair kindred spirit who had come to visit them. If we wandered from the banks for but a moment, the waters seemed to struggle and turn in their course until they were again by her side, and then would they gently flow and murmur their contentment as they travelled forward to the sea, full of the memory of her sweet presence. And during all that time I led her by the hand. I tell you, friends, 'tis sweet to write of it.

When we returned we crossed the Wye by the stone footbridge and entered the garden below the terrace at the corner postern. We remained for an hour resting upon the terrace balustrade, and before we went indoors Madge again spoke of Dorothy.

"I cannot tell you how much I have enjoyed this walk, nor how thankful I am to you for taking me," she said.

I did not interrupt her by replying, for I loved to hear her talk.

"Dorothy sometimes takes me with her for a short

walk, but I seldom have that pleasure. Walking is too slow for Dorothy. She is so strong and full of life. She delights to ride her mare Dolcy. Have you seen Dolcy?"

"No," I responded.

"You must see her at once. She is the most beautiful animal in the world. Though small of limb, she is swift as the wind, and as easy as a cradle in her gaits. She is mettlesome and fiery, but full of affection. She often kisses Dorothy. Mare and rider are finely mated. Dorothy is the most perfect woman, and Dolcy is the most perfect mare. 'The two D's,' we call them. But Dorothy says we must be careful not to put a — a dash between them," she said with a laugh and a blush.

Then I led Madge into the hall, and she was blithe and happy as if the blessed light of day were in her eyes. It was in her soul, and that, after all, is where it brings the greatest good.

After that morning, Madge and I frequently walked out when the days were pleasant. The autumn was mild, well into winter time, and by the end of November the transparent cheeks of the blind girl held an exquisite tinge of color, and her form had a new grace from the strength she had acquired in exercise. We had grown to be dear friends, and the touch of her hand was a pleasure for which I waited eagerly from day to day. Again I say thoughts of love for her had never entered my mind. Perhaps their absence was because of my feeling that they could not possibly exist in her heart for me.

One evening in November, after the servants had all gone to bed, Sir George and I went to the kitchen to drink a hot punch before retiring for the night. I drank a moderate bowl and sat in a large chair before the fire, smoking a pipe of tobacco, while Sir George drank brandy toddy at the massive oak table in the middle of the room.

Sir George was rapidly growing drunk. He said:

"Dawson tells me that the queen's officers arrested another of Mary Stuart's damned French friends at Derbytown yesterday, — Count somebody; I can't pronounce their miserable names."

"Can you not remember his name?" I asked. "He may be a friend of mine." My remark was intended to remind Sir George that his language was offensive to me.

"That is true, Malcolm," responded Sir George. "I beg your pardon. I meant to speak ill only of Mary's meddlesome friends, who are doing more injury than good to their queen's cause by their plotting."

I replied: "No one can regret these plots more than I do. They certainly will work great injury to the cause they are intended to help. But I fear many innocent men are made to suffer for the few guilty ones. Without your protection, for which I cannot sufficiently thank you, my life here would probably be of short duration. After my misfortunes in Scotland, I know not what I should have done had it not been for your generous welcome. I lost all in Scotland, and it would now be impossible for me to go to France. An attempt on my part to escape would result in my arrest. Fortune certainly has turned her capricious back upon me, with the one exception that she has left me your friendship."

"Malcolm, my boy," said Sir George, drawing his chair toward me, "that which you consider your loss is my great gain. I am growing old, and if you, who have seen so much of the gay world, will be content to live with us and share our dulness and our cares, I shall be the happiest man in England."

"I thank you more than I can tell," I said, careful not to commit myself to any course.

"Barring my quarrel with the cursed race of Manners," continued Sir George, "I have little to trouble me; and if you will remain with us, I thank God I may leave the feud

in good hands. Would that I were young again only for
a day that I might call that scoundrel Rutland and his
imp of a son to account in the only manner whereby an
honest man may have justice of a thief. There are but
two of them, Malcolm, — father and son, — and if they
were dead, the damned race would be extinct."

I believe that Sir George Vernon when sober could not
have spoken in that fashion even of his enemies.

I found difficulty in replying to my cousin's remarks,
so I said evasively : —

"I certainly am the most fortunate of men to find so
warm a welcome from you, and so good a home as that
which I have at Haddon Hall. When I met Dorothy at
the inn, I knew at once by her kindness that my friends
of old were still true to me. I was almost stunned by
Dorothy's beauty."

My mention of Dorothy was unintentional and unfortunate. I had shied from the subject upon several previous
occasions, but Sir George was continually trying to lead
up to it. This time my lack of forethought saved him
the trouble.

"Do you really think that Doll is very beautiful — so
very beautiful? Do you really think so, Malcolm?" said
the old gentleman, rubbing his hands in pride and pleasure.

"Surprisingly beautiful," I answered, seeking hurriedly
through my mind for an excuse to turn the conversation. I
had within ... months learned one vital fact : beautiful as
Dorothy was, I did not want her for my wife, and I could
not have had her even were I dying for love. The more
I learned of Dorothy and myself during the autumn
through which I had just passed — and I had learned more
of myself than I had been able to discover in the thirty-
five previous years of my life — the more clearly I saw the
utter unfitness of marriage between us.

"In all your travels," asked Sir George, leaning his

4

elbows upon his knees and looking at his feet between
his hands, "in all your travels and court life have you ever
seen a woman who was so beautiful as my girl Doll?"

His pride in Dorothy at times had a tinge of egotism
and selfishness. It seemed to be almost the pride of
possession and ownership. "My girl!" The expression
and the tone in which the words were spoken sounded as if
he had said: "My fine horse," "My beautiful Hall," or
"My grand estates." Dorothy was his property. Still, he
loved the girl passionately. She was dearer to him than
all his horses, cattle, halls, and estates put together, and he
loved even them to excess. He loved all that he possessed; whatever was his was the best of the sort. Such
a love is apt to grow up in the breasts of men who have
descended from a long line of proprietary ancestors, and
with all its materialism it has in it possibilities of great
good. The sturdy, unflinching patriotism of the English
people springs from this source. The thought, "That
which I possess is the best," has beauty and use in it,
though it leads men to treat other men, and, alas! women,
as mere chattels. All this was passing through my mind,
and I forgot to answer Sir George's question.

"Have you ever seen a woman more beautiful than
Doll?" he again asked.

"I certainly have never seen one whose beauty may
even be compared with Dorothy's," I answered.

"And she is young, too," continued Sir George; "she
is not yet nineteen."

"That is very young," I answered, not knowing what
else to say.

"And she will be rich some day. Very rich. I am called
'King of the Peak,' you know, and there are not three estates in Derbyshire which, if combined, would equal mine."

"That is true, cousin," I answered, "and I rejoice in
your good fortune."

"Dorothy will have it all one of these days — all, all," continued my cousin, still looking at his feet.

After a long pause, during which Sir George took several libations from his bowl of toddy, he cleared his throat and said, "So Dorothy is the most beautiful girl and the richest heiress you know?"

"Indeed she is," I responded, knowing full well what he was leading up to. Realizing that in spite of me he would now speak his mind, I made no attempt to turn the current of the conversation.

After another long pause, and after several more draughts from the bowl, my old friend and would-be benefactor said: "You may remember a little conversation between us when you were last at Haddon six or seven years ago, about — about Dorothy? You remember?"

I, of course, dared not pretend that I had forgotten.

"Yes, I remember," I responded.

"What do you think of the proposition by this time?" asked Sir George. "Dorothy and all she will inherit shall be yours — "

"Stop, stop, Sir George!" I exclaimed. "You do not know what you say. No one but a prince or a great peer of the realm is worthy of aspiring to Dorothy's hand. When she is ready to marry you should take her to London court, where she can make her choice from among the nobles of our land. There is not a marriageable duke or earl in England who would not eagerly seek the girl for a wife. My dear cousin, your generosity overwhelms me, but it must not be thought of. I am utterly unworthy of her in person, age, and position. No! no!"

"But listen to me, Malcolm," responded Sir George. "Your modesty, which, in truth, I did not know you possessed, is pleasing to me; but I have reasons of my own for wishing that you should marry Dorothy. I want my estates to remain in the Vernon name, and one day you or your children will make my house and my name noble. You and Dorothy shall go to court, and between you — damme! if you can't win a dukedom, I am no prophet. You would not object to change your faith, would you?"

"Oh, no," I responded, "of course I should not object to that."

"Of course not. I knew you were no fool," said Sir George. "Age! why, you are only thirty-five years old — little more than a matured boy. I prefer you to any man in England for Dorothy's husband."

"You overwhelm me with your kindness," I returned, feeling that I was being stranded on a very dangerous shore, amidst wealth and beauty.

"Tut, tut, there's no kindness in it," returned my cousin. "I do not offer you Dorothy s hand from an unselfish motive. I have told you one motive, but there is another, and a little condition besides, Malcolm." The brandy Sir George had been drinking had sent the devil to his brain.

"What is the condition?" I asked, overjoyed to hear that there was one.

The old man leaned toward me and a fierce blackness overclouded his face. "I am told, Malcolm, that you have few equals in swordsmanship, and that the duello is not new to you. Is it true?"

"I believe I may say it is true," I answered. "I have fought successfully with some of the most noted duellists of —"

"Enough, enough! Now, this is the condition, Malcolm, —a welcome one to you, I am sure; a welcome one to any brave man." His eyes gleamed with fire and hatred. "Quarrel with Rutland and his son and kill both of them."

I felt like recoiling from the old fiend. I had often

quarrelled and fought, but, thank God, never in cold blood and with deliberate intent to do murder.

"Then Dorothy and all I possess shall be yours," said Sir George. "The old one will be an easy victim. The young one, they say, prides himself on his prowess. I do not know with what cause, I have never seen him fight. In fact, I have never seen the fellow at all. He has lived at London court since he was a child, and has seldom, if ever, visited this part of the country. He was a page both to Edward VI. and to Queen Mary. Why Elizabeth keeps the damned traitor at court to plot against her is more than I can understand. Do the conditions suit you, Malcolm?" asked Sir George, piercing me with his eyes.

I did not respond, and he continued: "All I ask is your promise to kill Rutland and his son at the first opportunity. I care not how. The marriage may come off at once. It can't take place too soon to please me."

I could not answer for a time. The power to speak and to think had left me. To accept Sir George's offer was out of the question. To refuse it would be to give offence beyond reparation to my only friend, and you know what that would have meant to me. My refuge was Dorothy. I knew, however willing I might be or might appear to be, Dorothy would save me the trouble and danger of refusing her hand. So I said: —

"We have not consulted Dorothy. Perhaps her inclinations — "

"Doll's inclinations be damned. I have always been kind and indulgent to her, and she is a dutiful, obedient daughter. My wish and command in this affair will furnish inclinations enough for Doll."

"But, Sir George," I remonstrated, "I would not accept the hand of Dorothy nor of any woman unless she desired it. I could not. I could not."

"If Doll consents, I am to understand that you accept?" asked Sir George.

I saw no way out of the dilemma, and to gain time I said, "Few men in their right mind would refuse so flattering an offer unless there were a most potent reason, and I — I — "

"Good! good! I shall go to bed happy to-night for the first time in years. The Rutlands will soon be out of my path."

There is a self-acting retribution in our evil passions which never fails to operate. One who hates must suffer, and Sir George for years had paid the penalty night and day, unconscious that his pain was of his own making.

Before we parted I said, "This is a delicate matter, with reference to Dorothy, and I insist that you give me time to win, if possible, her kindly regard before you express to her your wish."

"Nonsense, nonsense, Malcolm! I'll tell the girl about it in the morning, and save you the trouble. The women will want to make some new gowns and — "

"But," I interrupted emphatically, "I will not have it so. It is every man's sweet privilege to woo the woman of his choice in his own way. It is not a trouble to me; it is a pleasure, and it is every woman's right to be wooed by the man who seeks her. I again insist that I only shall speak to Dorothy on this subject. At least, I demand that I be allowed to speak first."

"That's all damned nonsense," responded Sir George; "but if you will have it so, well and good. Take your own course. I suppose it's the fashion at court. The good old country way suits me. A girl's father tells her whom she is to marry, and, by gad, she does it without a word and is glad to get a man. English girls obey their parents. They know what to expect if they don't — the lash, by God, and the dungeon under the keep. Your roundabout method is all right for tenants and peasants; but among people who possess estates and who control vast interests, girls are — girls are — Well, they are born and brought up to obey and to help forward the interests of their houses." The old man was growing very drunk, and after a long pause he continued: " Have your own way, Malcolm, but don't waste time. Now that the matter is settled, I want to get it off my hands quickly."

"I shall speak to Dorothy on the subject at the first favorable opportunity," I responded; "but I warn you, Sir George, that if Dorothy proves disinclined to marry me, I will not accept her hand."

"Never fear for Doll; she will be all right," and we parted.

Doll all right! Had he only known how very far from "all right" Dorothy was, he would have slept little that night.

This brings me to the other change of which I spoke — the change in Dorothy. Change? It was a metamorphosis.

A fortnight after the scene at The Peacock I accidentally discovered a drawing made by Dorothy of a man with a cigarro in his mouth. The girl snatched the paper from my hands and blushed convincingly.

"It is a caricature of — of him," she said. She smiled, and evidently was willing to talk upon the subject of "him." I declined the topic.

This happened a month or more previous to my conversation with Sir George concerning Dorothy. A few days after my discovery of the cigarro picture, Dorothy and I were out on the terrace together. Frequently when she was with me she would try to lead the conversation to the topic which I well knew was in her mind, if not in her heart, at all times. She would speak of our first meeting at The Peacock, and would use every artifice to induce me to bring up the subject which she was eager to discuss, but I always failed her. On the day mentioned when we were together on the terrace, after repeated failures to induce me to speak upon the desired topic, she said, "I suppose you never meet — meet — him when you ride out?"

"Whom, Dorothy?" I asked.

"The gentleman with the cigarro," she responded, laughing nervously.

"No," I answered, "I know nothing of him."

The subject was dropped.

At another time she said, "He was in the village — Overhaddon — yesterday."

Then I knew who "him" was.

"How do you know?" I asked.

"Jennie Faxton, the farrier's daughter, told me. She often comes to the Hall to serve me. She likes to act as my maid, and is devoted to me."

"Did he send any word to you?" I asked at a venture. The girl blushed and hung her head. "N-o," she responded.

"What was it, Dorothy?" I asked gently. "You may trust me."

"He sent no word to me," the girl responded. "Jennie said she heard two gentlemen talking about me in front of the farrier's shop, and one of them said something about — oh, I don't know what it was. I can't tell you. It was all nonsense, and of course he did not mean it."

"Tell me all, Dorothy," I said, seeing that she really wanted to speak.

"Oh, he said something about having seen Sir George Vernon's daughter at Rowsley, and — and — I can't tell you what he said, I am too full of shame." If her cheeks told the truth, she certainly was "full of shame."

"Tell me all, sweet cousin; I am sorry for you," I said.

She raised her eyes to mine in quick surprise with a look of suspicion.

"You may trust me, Dorothy. I say it again, you may trust me."

"He spoke of my beauty and called it marvellous," said the girl. "He said that in all the world there was not another woman — oh, I can't tell you."

"Yes, yes, go on, Dorothy," I insisted.

"He said," she continued, "that he could think of nothing else but me day or night since he had first seen me at Rowsley — that I had bewitched him and — and — Then the other gentleman said, 'John, don't play with fire; it will burn you. Nothing good can come of it for you.'"

"Did Jennie know who the gentleman was?" I asked.

"No," returned Dorothy.

"How do you know who he was?"

"Jennie described him," she said.

"How did she describe him?" I asked.

"She said he was — he was the handsomest man in the world and — and that he affected her so powerfully she fell in love with him in spite of herself. The little devil, to dare! You see that describes him perfectly."

I laughed outright, and the girl blushed painfully.

"It does describe him," she said petulantly. "You know it does. No one can gainsay that he is wonderfully, dangerously handsome. I believe the woman does not live who could refrain from feasting her eyes on his noble beauty. I wonder if I shall ever again — again." Tears were in her voice and almost in her eyes.

"Dorothy! My God, Dorothy!" I exclaimed in terror.

"Yes! yes! My God, Dorothy!" she responded, covering her face with her hands and sighing deeply, as she dropped her head and left me.

Yes, yes, my God, Dorothy! The helpless iron and the

terrible loadstone! The passive seed! The dissolving
cloud and the falling rain!

Less than a week after the above conversation, Dorothy,
Madge, and I were riding from Yulegrave Church up to
the village of Overhaddon, which lies one mile across the
hills from Haddon Hall. My horse had cast a shoe, and
we stopped at Faxton's shop to have him shod. The town
well is in the middle of an open space called by the villagers "The Open," around which are clustered the half-
dozen houses and shops that constitute the village. The
girls were mounted, and I was standing beside them in
front of the farrier's, waiting for my horse. Jennie Faxton,
a wild, unkempt girl of sixteen, was standing in silent admiration near Dorothy. Our backs were turned toward
the well. Suddenly a light came into Jennie's face, and
she plucked Dorothy by the skirt of her habit.

"Look, mistress, look! Look there by the well!" said
Jennie in a whisper. Dorothy looked toward the well. I
also turned my head and beheld my friend, Sir John, holding a bucket of water for his horse to drink. I had not
seen him since we parted at The Peacock, and I did not
show that I recognized him. I feared to betray our friendship to the villagers. They, however, did not know Sir
John, and I need not have been so cautious. But Dorothy
and Madge were with me, and of course I dared not make
any demonstration of acquaintanceship with the enemy of
our house.

Dorothy watched John closely, and when he was ready
to mount she struck her horse with the whip, and boldly
rode to the well.

"May I ask you to give my mare water?" she said.

"Certainly. Ah, I beg pardon. I did not understand,"
answered Sir John, confusedly. John, the polished, self-
poised courtier, felt the confusion of a country rustic in
the presence of this wonderful girl, whose knowledge of

life had been acquired within the precincts of Haddon Hall.
Yet the inexperienced girl was self-poised and unconfused,
while the wits of the courtier, who had often calmly flat-
tered the queen, had all gone wool-gathering.

She repeated her request.

"Certainly," returned John, "I — I knew what you said
— but — but you surprise me."

"Yes," said brazen Dorothy, "I have surprised myself."

John, in his haste to satisfy Dolcy's thirst, dashed the
water against the skirt of Dorothy's habit, and was profuse
in his apologies.

"Do not mention it," said Dorothy. "I like a damp
habit. The wind cannot so easily blow it about," and she
laughed as she shook the garment to free it of the water.
Dolcy refused to drink, and Dorothy having no excuse to
linger at the well, drew up her reins and prepared to
leave. While doing so, she said : —

"Do you often come to Overhaddon ?" Her eager eyes
shone like red coals, and looking at John, she awaited
smilingly his response.

"Seldom," answered John; "not often. I mean every
day — that is, if I may come."

"Any one may come to the village whenever he wishes
to do so," responded Dorothy, laughing too plainly at Sir
John's confusion. "Is it seldom, or not often, or every
day that you come ?" In her overconfidence she was
chaffing him. He caught the tone, and looked quickly
into the girl's eyes. Her gaze could not stand against
John's for a moment, and the long lashes drooped to shade
her eyes from the fierce light of his.

"I said I would come to Overhaddon every day," he
returned; "and although I must have appeared very foolish in my confusion, you cannot misunderstand the full
meaning of my words."

In John's boldness and in the ring of his voice Dorothy felt the touch of her master, against whom she well knew all the poor force she could muster would be utterly help-less. She was frightened, and said:—

"I — I must go. Good-by."

When she rode away from him she thought: "I believed because of his confusion that I was the stronger. I could not stand against him for a moment. Holy Virgin! what have I done, and to what am I coming?"

You may now understand the magnitude of the task which Sir George had set for me when he bade me marry his daughter and kill the Rutlands. I might perform the last-named feat, but dragon fighting would be mere child's play compared with the first, while the girl's heart was filled with the image of another man.

I walked forward to meet Dorothy, leaving Madge near the farrier's shop.

" Dorothy, are you mad? What have you been doing?" I asked.

" Could you not see?" she answered, under her breath, casting a look of warning toward Madge and a glance of defiance at me. "Are you, too, blind? Could you not see what I was doing?"

" Yes," I responded.

"Then why do you ask?"

As I went back to Madge I saw John ride out of the village by the south road. I afterward learned that he rode gloomily back to Rutland Castle cursing himself for a fool. His duty to his father, which with him was a strong motive, his family pride, his self love, his sense of caution, all told him that he was walking open-eyed into trouble. He had tried to remain away from the vicinity of Haddon Hall, but, despite his self-respect and self-restraint, he had made several visits to Rowsley and to Overhaddon, and at one time had ridden to Bakewell, passing Haddon Hall on his way thither. He had as much business in the moon as at Overhaddon, yet he told Dorothy he would be at the village every day, and she, it seemed, was only too willing to give him opportunities to transact his momentous affairs.

As the floating cloud to the fathomless blue, as the seed to the earth, as the iron to the lodestone, so was Dorothy unto John.

Thus you see our beautiful pitcher went to the well and was broken.

CHAPTER IV

The Golden Heart

THE day after Dorothy's first meeting with Manners at Overhaddon she was restless and nervous, and about the hour of three in the afternoon she mounted Dolcy and rode toward Bakewell. That direction, I was sure, she took for the purpose of misleading us at the Hall, and I felt confident she would, when once out of sight, head her mare straight for Overhaddon. Within an hour Dorothy was home again, and very ill-tempered.

The next day she rode out in the morning. I asked her if I should ride with her, and the emphatic "No" with which she answered me left no room for doubt in my mind concerning her desire for my company or her destination. Again she returned within an hour and hurried to her apartments. Shortly afterward Madge asked me what Dorothy was weeping about; and although in my own mind I was confident of the cause of Dorothy's tears, I, of course, did not give Madge a hint of my suspicion. Yet I then knew, quite as well as I now know, that John, notwithstanding the important business which he said would bring him to Overhaddon every day, had forced himself to remain at home, and Dorothy, in consequence, suffered from anger and wounded pride. She had twice ridden to Overhaddon to meet him. She had done for his sake that which she knew she should have left undone, and he had refused the offering. A smarting conscience, an aching heart, and a breast full of anger were Dorothy's rewards for her evil doing. The day after her second futile trip to Overhaddon, I, to test her, spoke of John. She turned upon me with the black look of a fury, and hurled her words at me.

"Never again speak his despised name in my hearing. Curse him and his whole race."

"Now what has he been doing?" I asked.

"I tell you, I will not speak of him, nor will I listen to you," and she dashed away from me like a fiery whirl-wind.

Four or five days later the girl rode out again upon Dolcy. She was away from home for four long hours, and when she returned she was so gentle, sweet, and happy that she was willing to kiss every one in the household from Welch, the butcher, to Sir George. She was radiant. She clung to Madge and to me, and sang and romped through the house like Dorothy of old.

Madge said, "I am so glad you are feeling better, Doro-thy." Then, speaking to me: "She has been ill for several days. She could not sleep."

Dorothy looked quickly over to me, gave a little shrug to her shoulders, bent forward her face, which was red with blushing, and kissed Madge lingeringly upon the lips.

The events of Dorothy's trip I soon learned from her.

The little scene between Dorothy, Madge, and myself, after Dorothy's joyful return, occurred a week before the momentous conversation between Sir George and me con-cerning my union with his house. Ten days after Sir George had offered me his daughter and his lands, he brought up the subject again. He and I were walking on the ridge of Bowling Green Hill.

"I am glad you are making such fair progress with

Doll," said Sir George. "Have you yet spoken to her upon the subject?"

I was surprised to hear that I had made any progress. In fact, I did not know that I had taken a single step. I was curious to learn in what the progress consisted, so I said : —

"I have not spoken to Dorothy yet concerning the marriage, and I fear that I have made no progress at all. She certainly is friendly enough to me, but — "

"I should say that the gift from you she exhibited would indicate considerable progress," said Sir George, casting an expressive glance toward me.

"What gift?" I stupidly inquired.

"The golden heart, you rascal. She said you told her it had belonged to your mother."

"Holy Mother of Truth!" thought I, "pray give your especial care to my cousin Dorothy. She needs it."

Sir George thrust at my side with his thumb and continued : —

"Don't deny it, Malcolm. Damme, you are as shy as a boy in this matter. But perhaps you know better than I how to go at her. I was thinking only the other day that your course was probably the right one. Doll, I suspect, has a dash of her old father's temper, and she may prove a little troublesome unless we let her think she is having her own way. Oh, there is nothing like knowing how to handle them, Malcolm. Just let them think they are having their own way and — and save trouble. Doll may have more of her father in her than I suspect, and perhaps it is well for us to move slowly. You will be able to judge, but you must not move too slowly. If in the end she should prove stubborn, we will break her will or break her neck. I would rather have a daughter in Bakewell churchyard than a wilful, stubborn, disobedient huzzy in Haddon Hall."

Sir George had been drinking, and my slip concerning the gift passed unnoticed by him.

"I am sure you well know how to proceed in this matter, but don't be too cautious, Malcolm; the best woman living loves to be stormed."

"Trust me," I answered, "I shall speak—" and my words unconsciously sank away to thought, as thought often, and inconveniently at times, grows into words.

"Dorothy, Dorothy," said the thoughts again and again, "where came you by the golden heart?" and "where learned you so villanously to lie?"

"From love," was the response, whispered by the sighing winds. "From love, that makes men and women like unto gods and teaches them the tricks of devils." "From love," murmured the dry rustling leaves and the rugged trees. "From love," sighed the fleecy clouds as they floated in the sweet restful azure of the vaulted sky. "From love," cried the mighty sun as he poured his light and heat upon the eager world to give it life. I would not give a fig for a woman, however, who would not lie herself black in the face for the sake of her lover, and I am glad that it is a virtue few women lack. One who would scorn to lie under all other circumstances would— but you understand. I suppose that Dorothy had never before uttered a real lie. She hated all that was evil and loved all that was good till love came a-teaching.

I quickly invented an excuse to leave Sir George, and returned to the Hall to seek Dorothy. I found her and asked her to accompany me for a few minutes that I migh* speak with her privately. We went out upon the terrace and I at once began:—

"You should tell me when I present you gifts that I may not cause trouble by my ignorance nor show surprise when I suddenly learn what I have done. You see when a man gives a lady a gift and he does not know it, he is apt to—"

F

"Holy Virgin!" exclaimed Dorothy, pale with fear and consternation. "Did you—"

"No, I did not betray you, but I came perilously near it."

"I — I wanted to tell you about it. I tried several times to do so — I did so long to tell somebody, but I could not bring myself to speak. I was full of shame, yet I was proud and happy, for all that happened was good and pure and sacred. You are not a woman; you cannot know—"

"But I do know. I know that you saw Manners the other day, and that he gave you a golden heart."

"How did you know? Did any one—"

"Tell me? No. I knew it when you returned after five hours' absence, looking radiant as the sun."

"Oh!" the girl exclaimed, with a startled movement.

"I also knew," I continued, "that at other times when you rode out upon Dolcy you had not seen him."

"How did you know?" she asked, with quick-coming breath.

"By your ill-humor," I answered.

"I knew it was so. I felt that everybody knew all that I had been doing. I could almost see father and Madge and you — even the servants — reading the wickedness written upon my heart. I knew that I could hide it from nobody." Tears were very near the girl's eyes.

"We cannot help thinking that our guilty consciences, through which we see so plainly our own evil, are transparent to all the world. In that fact lies an evil-doer's greatest danger," said I, preacher fashion; "but you need have no fear. What you have done I believe is suspected by no one save me."

A deep sigh of relief rose from the girl's heaving breast.

"Well," she began, "I will tell you all about it, and I am only too glad to do so. It is heavy, Malcolm, heavy on my conscience. But I would not be rid of it for all the kingdoms of the earth."

"A moment since you told me that your conduct was good and pure and sacred, and now you tell me that it is heavy on your conscience. Does one grieve, Dorothy, for the sake of that which is good and pure and sacred?"

"I cannot answer your question," she replied. "I am no priest. But this I know: I have done no evil, and my conscience nevertheless is sore. Solve me the riddle, Malcolm, if you can."

"I cannot solve your riddle, Dorothy," I replied; "but I feel sure it will be far safer for each of us if you will tell me all that happens hereafter."

"I am sure you are right," she responded; "but some secrets are so delicious that we love to suck their sweets alone. I believe, however, your advice is good, and I will tell you all that has happened, though I cannot look you in the face while doing it." She hesitated a moment, and her face was red with tell-tale blushes. She continued, "I have acted most unmaidenly."

"Unmaidenly perhaps, but not unwomanly," said I.

"I thank you," she said, interrupting my sentence. It probably was well that she did so, for I was about to add, "To act womanly often means to get yourself into mischief and your friends into as much trouble as possible." Had I finished my remark, she would not have thanked me.

"Well," said the girl, beginning her laggard narrative, "after we saw — saw him at Overhaddon, you know, I went to the village on each of three days —"

"Yes, I know that also," I said.

"How did you — but never mind. I did not see him, and when I returned home I felt angry and hurt and — and — but never mind that either. One day I found him, and I at once rode to the well where he was standing by his horse. He drew water for Dolcy, but the perverse mare would not drink."

"A characteristic of her sex," I muttered.

"What did you say?" asked the girl.

"Nothing."

She continued: "He seemed constrained and distant in his manner, but I knew, that is, I thought — I mean I felt — oh, you know — he looked as if he were glad to see me and I — I, oh, God! I was so glad and happy to see him that I could hardly restrain myself to act at all maidenly. He must have heard my heart beat. I thought he was in trouble. He seemed to have something he wished to say to me."

"He doubtless had a great deal he wished to say to you," said I, again tempted to futile irony.

"I was sure he had something to say," the girl returned seriously. "He was in trouble. I knew that he was, and I longed to help him."

"What trouble?" I inquired.

"Oh, I don't know. I forgot to ask, but he looked troubled."

"Doubtless he was troubled," I responded. "He had sufficient cause for trouble," I finished the sentence to myself with the words, "in you."

"What was the cause of his trouble?" she hastily asked, turning her face toward me.

"I do not know certainly," I answered in a tone of irony which should have pierced an oak board, while the girl listened and looked at me eagerly; "but I might guess."

"What was it? What was it? Let me hear you guess," she asked.

"You," I responded laconically.

"I!" she exclaimed in surprise.

"Yes, you," I responded with emphasis. "You would bring trouble to any man, but to Sir John Manners—well, if he intends to keep up these meetings with you it would be better for his peace and happiness that he should get him a house in hell, for he would live there more happily than on this earth."

"That is a foolish, senseless remark, Malcolm," the girl replied, tossing her head with a show of anger in her eyes. "This is no time to jest." I suppose I could not have convinced her that I was not jesting.

"At first we did not speak to each other even to say good day, but stood by the well in silence for a very long time. The village people were staring at us, and I felt that every window had a hundred faces in it, and every face a hundred eyes."

"You imagined that," said I, "because of your guilty conscience."

"Perhaps so. But it seemed to me that we stood by the well in silence a very long time. You see, Cousin Malcolm, I was not the one who should speak first. I had done more than my part in going to meet him."

"Decidedly so," said I, interrupting the interesting narrative.

"When I could bear the gaze of the villagers no longer, I drew up my reins and started to leave The Open by the north road. After Dolcy had climbed halfway up North Hill, which as you know overlooks the village, I turned my head and saw Sir John still standing by the well, resting his hand upon his horse's mane. He was watching me. I grew angry, and determined that he should follow me, even if I had to call him. So I drew Dolcy to a stand. Was not that bold in me? But wait, there is worse to come, Malcolm. He did not move, but stood like a statue looking toward me. I knew that he wanted to come, so after a little time I — I beckoned to him and — and then he came like a thunderbolt. Oh! it was delicious. I put Dolcy to a gallop, for when he started toward me I was frightened.

Besides I did not want him to overtake me till we were out of the village. But when once he had started, he did not wait. He was as swift now as he had been slow, and my heart throbbed and triumphed because of his eagerness, though in truth I was afraid of him. Dolcy, you know, is very fleet, and when I touched her with the whip she soon put half a mile between me and the village. Then I brought her to a walk and — and he quickly overtook me.

"When he came up to me he said: 'I feared to follow you, though I ardently wished to do so. I dreaded to tell you my name lest you should hate me. Sir Malcolm at The Peacock said he would not disclose to you my identity. I am John Manners. Our fathers are enemies.'

"Then I said to him, 'That is the reason I wish to talk to you. I wished you to come to meet me because I wanted to tell you that I regret and deplore the feud between our fathers.' — 'Ah, you wished me to come?' he asked. — 'Of course I did,' I answered, 'else why should I be here?' — 'No one regrets the feud between our houses so deeply as I,' replied Sir John. 'I can think of nothing else by day, nor can I dream of anything else by night. It is the greatest cause for grief and sorrow that has ever come into my life.' You see, Cousin Malcolm," the girl continued, "I was right. His father's conduct does trouble him. Isn't he noble and broad-minded to see the evil of his father's ways?"

I did not tell the girl that Sir John's regret for the feud between the houses of Manners and Vernon grew out of the fact that it separated him from her; nor did I tell her that he did not grieve over his "father's ways."

I asked, "Did Sir John tell you that he grieved because of his father's ill-doing?"

"N-o, not in set terms, but — that, of course, would have been very hard for him to say. I told you what he said, and there could be no other meaning to his words."

"Of course not," I responded.

"No, and I fairly longed to reach out my hand and clutch him, because — because I was so sorry for him."

"Was sorrow your only feeling?" I asked.

The girl looked at me for a moment, and her eyes filled with tears. Then she sobbed gently and said, "Oh, Cousin Malcolm, you are so old and so wise." ("Thank you," thought I, "a second Daniel come to judgment at thirty-five; or Solomon and Methuselah in one.") She continued: "Tell me, tell me, what is this terrible thing that has come upon me. I seem to be living in a dream. I am burning with a fever, and a heavy weight is here upon my breast. I cannot sleep at night. I can do nothing but long and yearn for — for I know not what — till at times it seems that some frightful, unseen monster is slowly drawing the heart out of my bosom. I think of — of him at all times, and I try to recall his face, and the tones of his voice until, Cousin Malcolm, I tell you I am almost mad. I call upon the Holy Virgin hour by hour to pity me; but she is pure, and cannot know what I feel. I hate and loathe myself. To what am I coming? Where will it all end? Yet I can do nothing to save myself. I am powerless against this terrible feeling. I cannot even resolve to resist it. It came upon me mildly that day at The Peacock Inn, when I first saw him, and it grows deeper and stronger day by day, and, alas! night by night. I seem to have lost myself. In some strange way I feel as if I had sunk into him — that he had absorbed me."

"The iron, the seed, the cloud, and the rain," thought I.

"I believed," continued the girl, "that if he would exert his will I might have relief; but there again I find trouble, for I cannot bring myself to ask him to will it. The feeling within me is like a sore heart: painful as it is, I must keep it. Without it I fear I could not live."

After this outburst there was a long pause during which

she walked by my side, seemingly unconscious that I was near her. I had known for some time that Dorothy was interested in Manners; but I was not prepared to see such a volcano of passion. I need not descant upon the evils and dangers of the situation. The thought that first came to me was that Sir George would surely kill his daughter before he would allow her to marry a son of Rutland. I was revolving in my mind how I should set about to mend the matter when Dorothy again spoke.

"Tell me, Cousin Malcolm, can a man throw a spell over a woman and bewitch her?"

"I do not know. I have never heard of a man witch," I responded.

"No?" asked the girl.

"But," I continued, "I do know that a woman may bewitch a man. John Manners, I doubt not, could also testify knowingly on the subject by this time."

"Oh, do you think he is bewitched?" cried Dorothy, grasping my arm and looking eagerly into my face. "If I could bewitch him, I would do it. I would deal with the devil gladly to learn the art. I would not care for my soul. I do not fear the future. The present is a thousand-fold dearer to me than either the past or the future. I care not what comes hereafter. I want him now. Ah, Malcolm, pity my shame."

She covered her face with her hands, and after a moment continued: "I am not myself. I belong not to myself. But if I knew that he also suffers, I do believe my pain would be less."

"I think you may set your heart at rest upon that point," I answered. "He, doubtless, also suffers."

"I hope so," she responded, unconscious of the selfish wish she had expressed. "If he does not, I know not what will be my fate."

I saw that I had made a mistake in assuring her that

John also suffered, and I determined to correct it later on, if possible.

Dorothy was silent, and I said, "You have not told me about the golden heart."

"I will tell you," she answered. "We rode for two hours or more, and talked of the weather and the scenery, until there was nothing more to be said concerning either. Then Sir John told me of the court in London, where he has always lived, and of the queen whose hair, he says, is red, but not at all like mine. I wondered if he would speak of the beauty of my hair, but he did not. He only looked at it. Then he told me about the Scottish queen whom he once met when he was on an embassy to Edinburgh. He described her marvellous beauty, and I believe he sympathizes with her cause — that is, with her cause in Scotland. He says she has no good cause in England. He is true to our queen. Well — well he talked so interestingly that I could have listened a whole month — yes, all my life."

"I suppose you could," I said.

"Yes," she continued, "but I could not remain longer from home, and when I left him he asked me to accept a keepsake which had belonged to his mother, as a token that there should be no feud between him and me." And she drew from her bosom a golden heart studded with diamonds and pierced by a white silver arrow.

"I, of course, accepted it, then we said 'good-by,' and I put Dolcy to a gallop that she might speedily take me out of temptation."

"Have you ridden to Overhaddon for the purpose of seeing Manners many times since he gave you the heart?" I queried.

"What would you call 'many times'?" she asked, drooping her head.

"Every day?" I said interrogatively. She nodded.

"Yes. But I have seen him only once since the day when he gave me the heart."

Nothing I could say would do justice to the subject, so I remained silent.

"But you have not yet told me how your father came to know of the golden heart," I said.

"It was this way: One morning while I was looking at the heart, father came upon me suddenly before I could conceal it. He asked me to tell him how I came by the jewel, and in my fright and confusion I could think of nothing else to say, so I told him you had given it to me. He promised not to speak to you about the heart, but he did not keep his word. He seemed pleased."

"Doubtless he was pleased," said I, hoping to lead up to the subject so near to Sir George's heart, but now farther than ever from mine.

The girl unsuspectingly helped me.

"Father asked if you had spoken upon a subject of great interest to him and to yourself, and I told him you had not. 'When he does speak,' said father most kindly, 'I want you to grant his request' — and I will grant it, Cousin Malcolm." She looked in my face and continued: "I will grant your request, whatever it may be. You are the dearest friend I have in the world, and mine is the most loving and lovable father that girl ever had. It almost breaks my heart when I think of his suffering should he learn of what I have done — that which I just told to you." She walked beside me meditatively for a moment and said, "To-morrow I will return Sir John's gift and I will never see him again."

I felt sure that by to-morrow she would have repented of her repentance; but I soon discovered that I had given her much more time than she needed to perform that trifling feminine gymnastic, for with the next breath she said : —

"I have no means of returning the heart. I must see

him once more and I will give — give it — it — back to —
to him, and will tell him that I can see him never again."
She scarcely had sufficient resolution to finish telling her
intention. Whence, then, would come the will to put it in
action? Forty thieves could not have stolen the heart
from her, though she thought she was honest when she
said she would take it to him.

"Dorothy," said I, seriously but kindly, "have you and
Sir John spoken of — "

She evidently knew that I meant to say "of love," for
she interrupted me.

"N-o, but surely he knows. And I — I think — at
least I hope with all my heart that — "

"I will take the heart to Sir John," said I, interrupting
her angrily, "and you need not see him again. He has
acted like a fool and a knave. He is a villain, Dorothy,
and I will tell him as much in the most emphatic terms I
have at my command."

"Dare you speak against him or to him upon the subject!" she exclaimed, her eyes blazing with anger; "you —
you asked for my confidence and I gave it. You said I
might trust you and I did so, and now you show me that
I am a fool indeed. Traitor!"

"My dear cousin," said I, seeing that she spoke the
truth in charging me with bad faith, "your secret is safe
with me. I swear it by my knighthood. You may trust
me. I spoke in anger. But Sir John has acted badly.
That you cannot gainsay. You, too, have done great evil.
That also you cannot gainsay."

"No," said the girl, dejectedly, "I cannot deny it; but
the greatest evil is yet to come."

"You must do something," I continued. "You must
take some decisive step that will break this connection, and
you must take the step at once if you would save yourself
from the frightful evil that is in store for you. Forgive

me for what I said, sweet cousin. My angry words sprang from my love for you and my fear for your future."

No girl's heart was more tender to the influence of kindness than Dorothy's. No heart was more obdurate to unkindness or peremptory command.

My words softened her at once, and she tried to smother the anger I had aroused. But she did not entirely succeed, and a spark remained which in a moment or two created a disastrous conflagration. You shall hear.

She walked by my side in silence for a little time, and then spoke in a low, slightly sullen tone which told of her effort to smother her resentment.

"I do trust you, Cousin Malcolm. What is it that you wish to ask of me? Your request is granted before it is made."

"Do not be too sure of that, Dorothy," I replied. "It is a request your father ardently desires me to make, and I do not know how to speak to you concerning the subject in the way I wish."

I could not ask her to marry me, and tell her with the same breath that I did not want her for my wife. I felt I must wait for a further opportunity to say that I spoke only because her father had required me to do so, and that circumstances forced me to put the burden of refusal upon her. I well knew that she would refuse me, and then I intended to explain.

"Why, what is it all about?" asked the girl in surprise, suspecting, I believe, what was to follow.

"It is this: your father is anxious that his vast estates shall not pass out of the family name, and he wishes you to be my wife, so that your children may bear the loved name of Vernon."

I could not have chosen a more inauspicious time to speak. She looked at me for an instant in surprise, turning to scorn. Then she spoke in tones of withering contempt.

"Tell my father that I shall never bear a child by the name of Vernon. I would rather go barren to my grave. Ah! that is why Sir John Manners is a villain? That is why a decisive step should be taken? That is why you come to my father's house a-fortune-hunting? After you have squandered your patrimony and have spent a dissolute youth in profligacy, after the women of the class you have known will have no more of you but choose younger men, you who are old enough to be my father come here and seek your fortune, as your father sought his, by marriage. I do not believe that my father wishes me to—to marry you. You have wheedled him into giving his consent when he was in his cups. But even if he wished it with all his heart, I would not marry you." Then she turned and walked rapidly toward the Hall.

Her fierce words angered me; for in the light of my real intentions her scorn was uncalled for, and her language was insulting beyond endurance. For a moment or two the hot blood rushed to my brain and rendered me incapable of intelligent thought. But as Dorothy walked from me I realized that something must be done at once to put myself right with her. When my fit of temper had cooled, and when I considered that the girl did not know my real intentions, I could not help acknowledging that in view of all that had just passed between us concerning Sir John Manners, and, in fact, in view of all that she had seen and could see, her anger was justifiable.

I called to her: "Dorothy, wait a moment. You have not heard all I have to say."

She hastened her pace. A few rapid strides brought me to her side. I was provoked, not at her words, for they were almost justifiable, but because she would

not stop to hear me.   I grasped her rudely by the arm
and said : —

"Listen till I have finished."

"I will not," she answered viciously.   "Do not touch
me."

I still held her by the arm and said : "I do not wish to
marry you.   I spoke only because your father desired me to
do so, and because my refusal to speak would have offended
him beyond any power of mine to make amends.   I could
not tell you that I did not wish you for my wife until you
had given me an opportunity.   I was forced to throw the
burden of refusal upon you."

"That is but a ruse — a transparent, flimsy ruse," responded the stubborn, angry girl, endeavoring to draw her
arm from my grasp.

"It is not a ruse," I answered.   "If you will listen to
me and will help me by acting as I suggest, we may between us bring your father to our way of thinking, and
I may still be able to retain his friendship."

"What is your great plan ?" asked Dorothy, in a voice
such as one might expect to hear from a piece of ice.

"I have formed no plan as yet," I replied, "although I
have thought of several.   Until we can determine upon
one, I suggest that you permit me to say to your father
that I have asked you to be my wife, and that the subject
has come upon you so suddenly that you wish a short time
— a fortnight or a month — in which to consider your
answer."

"That is but a ruse, I say, to gain time," she answered
contemptuously.   "I do not wish one moment in which to
consider.   You already have my answer.   I should think
you had had enough.   Do you desire more of the same
sort?   A little of such treatment should go a long way
with a man possessed of one spark of honor or self-respect."

Her language would have angered a sheep.

"If you will not listen to me," I answered, thoroughly aroused and careless of consequences, "go to your father. Tell him I asked you to be my wife, and that you scorned my suit. Then take the consequences. He has always been gentle and tender to you because there has been no conflict. Cross his desires, and you will learn a fact of which you have never dreamed. You have seen the manner in which he treats others who oppose him. You will learn that with you, too, he can be one of the cruelest and most violent of men."

"You slander my father. I will go to him as you advise and will tell him that I would not marry you if you wore the English crown. I, myself, will tell him of my meeting with Sir John Manners rather than allow you the pleasure of doing so. He will be angry, but he will pity me."

"For God's sake, Dorothy, do not tell your father of your meetings at Overhaddon. He would kill you. Have you lived in the same house with him all these years and do you not better know his character than to think that you may go to him with the tale you have just told me, and that he will forgive you? Feel as you will toward me, but believe me when I swear to you by my knighthood that I will betray to no person what you have this day divulged to me."

Dorothy made no reply, but turned from me and rapidly walked toward the Hall. I followed at a short distance, and all my anger was displaced by fear for her. When we reached the Hall she quickly sought her father and approached him in her old free manner, full of confidence in her influence over him.

"Father, this man"—waving her hand toward me—"has come to Haddon Hall a-fortune-hunting. He has asked me to be his wife, and says you wish me to accept him."

"Yes, Doll, I certainly wish it with all my heart," returned Sir George, affectionately, taking his daughter's hand.

"Then you need wish it no longer, for I will not marry him."

"What?" demanded her father, springing to his feet.

"I will not. I will not. I will not."

"You will if I command you to do so, you damned insolent wench," answered Sir George, hoarsely. Dorothy's eyes opened in wonder.

"Do not deceive yourself, father, for one moment," she retorted contemptuously. "He has come here in sheep's clothing and has adroitly laid his plans to convince you that I should marry him, but —"

"He has done nothing of the sort," answered Sir George, growing more angry every moment, but endeavoring to be calm. "Nothing of the sort. Many years ago I spoke to him on this subject, which is very dear to my heart. The project has been dear to me ever since you were a child. When I again broached it to Malcolm a fortnight or more since I feared from his manner that he was averse to the scheme. I had tried several times to speak to him about it, but he warded me off, and when I did speak, I feared that he was not inclined to it."

"Yes," interrupted the headstrong girl, apparently bent upon destroying both of us. "He pretended that he did not wish to marry me. He said he wished me to give a sham consent for the purpose of gaining time till we might hit upon some plan by which we could change your mind. He said he had no desire nor intention to marry me. It was but a poor, lame ruse on his part."

During Dorothy's recital Sir George turned his face from her to me. When she had finished speaking, he looked at me for a moment and said: —

"Does my daughter speak the truth? Did you say —"

"**Yes**," I promptly replied, "I have no intention of marrying your daughter." Then hoping to place myself before Sir George in a better light, I continued: "I could not accept the hand of a lady against her will. I told you as much when we conversed on the subject."

"What?" exclaimed Sir George, furious with anger. "You too? You whom I have befriended?"

"I told you, Sir George, I would not marry Dorothy without her free consent. No gentleman of honor would accept the enforced compliance of a woman."

"But Doll says that you told her you had no intention of marrying her even should she consent," replied Sir George.

"I don't know that I spoke those exact words," I replied, "but you may consider them said."

"You damned, ungrateful, treacherous hound!" stormed Sir George. "You listened to me when I offered you my daughter's hand, and you pretended to consent without at the time having any intention of doing so."

"That, I suppose, is true, Sir George," said I, making a masterful effort against anger. "That is true, for I knew that Dorothy would not consent; and had I been inclined to the marriage, I repeat, I would marry no woman against her will. No gentleman would do it."

My remark threw Sir George into a paroxysm of rage. "I did it, you cur, you dog, you — you traitorous, ungrateful — I did it."

"Then, Sir George," said I, interrupting him, for I was no longer able to restrain my anger, "you were a cowardly poltroon."

"This to me in my house!" he cried, grasping a chair with which to strike me. Dorothy came between us.

"Yes," said I, "and as much more as you wish to hear." I stood my ground, and Sir George put down the chair.

"Leave my house at once," he said in a whisper of rage. "If you are on my premises in one hour from now I will have you flogged from my door by the butcher."

"What have I done?" cried Dorothy. "What have I done?"

"Your regrets come late, Mistress Vernon," said I.

"She shall have more to regret," said Sir George, sullenly. "Go to your room, you brazen, disobedient huzzy, and if you leave it without my permission, by God, I will have you whipped till you bleed. I will teach you to say 'I won't' when I say 'you shall.' God curse my soul, if I don't make you repent this day!"

As I left the room Dorothy was in tears, and Sir George was walking the floor in a towering rage. The girl had learned that I was right in what I had told her concerning her father's violent temper.

I went at once to my room in Eagle Tower and collected my few belongings in a bundle. Pitifully small it was, I tell you.

Where I should go I knew not, and where I should remain I knew even less, for my purse held only a few shillings—the remnant of the money Queen Mary had sent to me by the hand of Sir Thomas Douglas. England was as unsafe for me as Scotland; but how I might travel to France without money, and how I might without a pass evade Elizabeth's officers who guarded every English port, even were I supplied with gold, were problems for which I had no solution.

There were but two persons in Haddon Hall to whom I cared to say farewell. They were Lady Madge and Will Dawson. The latter was a Scot, and was attached to the cause of Queen Mary. He and I had become friends, and on several occasions we had talked confidentially over Mary's sad plight.

When my bundle was packed, I sought Madge and

found her in the gallery near the foot of the great
staircase. She knew my step and rose to greet me with
a bright smile.

"I have come to say good-by to you, Cousin Madge,"
said I. The smile vanished from her face.

"You are not going to leave Haddon Hall?" she
asked.

"Yes, and forever," I responded. "Sir George has
ordered me to go."

"No, no," she exclaimed. "I cannot believe it. I supposed that you and my uncle were friends. What has
happened? Tell me if you can—if you wish. Let me
touch your hand," and as she held out her hands, I gladly
grasped them.

I have never seen anything more beautiful than Madge
Stanley's hands. They were not small, but their shape,
from the fair, round forearm and wrist to the ends of the
fingers was worthy of a sculptor's dream. Beyond their
physical beauty there was an expression in them which
would have belonged to her eyes had she possessed the
sense of sight. The flood of her vital energy had for so
many years been directed toward her hands as a substi-
tute for her lost eyesight that their sensitiveness showed
itself not only in an infinite variety of delicate gestures and
movements, changing with her changing moods, but they
had an expression of their own, such as we look for in
the eyes. I had gazed upon her hands so often, and
had studied so carefully their varying expression, discerni-
ble both to my sight and to my touch, that I could read
her mind through them as we read the emotions of others
through the countenance. The "feel" of her hands, if I
may use the word, I can in no way describe. Its effect on
me was magical. The happiest moments I have ever
known were those when I held the fair blind girl by the
hand and strolled upon the great terrace or followed the

babbling winding course of dear old Wye, and drank in
the elixir of all that is good and pure from the cup of her
sweet, unconscious influence.

Madge, too, had found happiness in our strolling. She
had also found health and strength, and, marvellous to say,
there had come to her a slight improvement in vision.
She had always been able to distinguish sunlight from
darkness, but with renewed strength had come the power
dimly to discern dark objects in a strong light, and even
that small change for the better had brought unspeakable
gladness to her heart. She said she owed it all to me.
A faint pink had spread itself in her cheeks and a plump-
ness had been imparted to her form which gave to her
ethereal beauty a touch of the material. Nor was this to
be regretted, for no man can adequately make love to a
woman who has too much of the angel in her. You must
not think, however, that I had been making love to Madge.
On the contrary, I again say, the thought had never entered my mind. Neither at that time had I even suspected
that she would listen to me upon the great theme. I had
in my self-analysis assigned many reasons other than love
for my tenderness toward her; but when I was about to
depart, and she impulsively gave me her hands, I, believing
that I was grasping them for the last time, felt the conviction come upon me that she was dearer to me than all else
in life.

"Do you want to tell me why my uncle has driven you
from Haddon?" she asked.

"He wished me to ask Dorothy to be my wife," I
returned.

"And you?" she queried.

"I did so."

Instantly the girl withdrew her hands from mine and
stepped back from me. Then I had another revelation. I
knew what she meant and felt. Her hands told me all,

even had there been no expression in her movement and in her face.

"Dorothy refused," I continued, "and her father desired to force her into compliance. I would not be a party to the transaction, and Sir George ordered me to leave his house."

After a moment of painful silence Madge said : —

"I do not wonder that you should wish to marry Dorothy. She — she must be very beautiful."

"I do not wish to marry Dorothy," said I. I heard a slight noise back of me, but gave it no heed. "And I should not have married her had she consented. I knew that Dorothy would refuse me, therefore I promised Sir George that I would ask her to be my wife. Sir George had always been my friend, and should I refuse to comply with his wishes, I well knew he would be my enemy. He is bitterly angry against me now ; but when he becomes calm, he will see wherein he has wronged me. I asked Dorothy to help me, but she would not listen to my plan."

" — and now she begs your forgiveness," cried Dorothy, as she ran weeping to me, and took my hand most humbly.

"Dorothy! Dorothy!" I exclaimed.

"What frightful evil have I brought upon you?" said she. "Where can you go? What will you do?"

"I know not," I answered. "I shall probably go to the Tower of London when Queen Elizabeth's officers learn of my quarrel with Sir George. But I will try to escape to France."

"Have you money?" asked Madge, tightly holding one of my hands.

"A small sum," I answered.

"How much have you? Tell me. Tell me how much have you," insisted Madge, clinging to my hand and speaking with a force that would brook no refusal.

"A very little sum, I am sorry to say; only a few shil lings," I responded.

She quickly withdrew her hand from mine and began to remove the baubles from her ears and the brooch from her throat. Then she nervously stripped the rings from her fingers and held out the little handful of jewels toward me, groping for my hands.

"Take these, Malcolm. Take these, and wait here till I return." She turned toward the staircase, but in her confusion she missed it, and before I could reach her, she struck against the great newel post.

"God pity me," she said, as I took her hand. "I wish I were dead. Please lead me to the staircase, Cousin Malcolm. Thank you."

She was weeping gently when she started up the steps, and I knew that she was going to fetch me her little treasure of gold.

Madge held up the skirt of her gown with one hand while she grasped the banister with the other. She was halfway up when Dorothy, whose generous impulses needed only to be prompted, ran nimbly and was about to pass her on the staircase when Madge grasped her gown.

"Please don't, Dorothy. Please do not. I beg you, do not forestall me. Let me do this. Let me. You have all else to make you happy. Don't take this from me only because you can see and can walk faster than I."

Dorothy did not stop, but hurried past her. Madge sank upon the steps and covered her face with her hands. Then she came gropingly back to me just as Dorothy returned.

"Take these, Cousin Malcolm," cried Dorothy. "Here are a few stones of great value. They belonged to my mother."

Madge was sitting dejectedly upon the lowest step of

the staircase. Dorothy held her jewel-box toward me, and in the midst of the diamonds and gold I saw the heart John Manners had given her. I did not take the box.

"Do you offer me this, too — even this?" I said, lifting the heart from the box by its chain. — "Yes, yes," cried Dorothy, "even that, gladly, gladly." I replaced it in the box.

Then spoke Madge, while she tried to check the falling tears: —

"Dorothy, you are a cruel, selfish girl."

"Oh, Madge," cried Dorothy, stepping to her side and taking her hand. "How can you speak so unkindly to me?"

"You have everything good," interrupted Madge. "You have beauty, wealth, eyesight, and yet you would not leave to me the joy of helping him. I could not see, and you hurried past me that you might be first to give him the help of which I was the first to think."

Dorothy was surprised at the outburst from Madge, and kneeled by her side.

"We may both help Cousin Malcolm," she said.

"No, no," responded Madge, angrily. "Your jewels are more than enough. He would have no need of my poor offering."

I took Madge's hand and said, "I shall accept help from no one but you, Madge; from no one but you."

"I will go to our rooms for your box," said Dorothy, who had begun to see the trouble. "I will fetch it for you."

"No, I will fetch it," answered Madge. She arose, and I led her to the foot of the staircase. When she returned she held in her hands a purse and a little box of jewels. These she offered to me, but I took only the purse, saying: "I accept the purse. It contains more money than I shall need. From its weight I should say there are twenty gold pounds sterling."

"Twenty-five," answered Madge. "I have saved them, believing that the time might come when they would be of great use to me. I did not know the joy I was saving for myself."

Tears came to my eyes, and Dorothy wept silently.

"Will you not take the jewels also?" asked Madge.

"No," I responded; "the purse will more than pay my expenses to France, where I have wealthy relatives. There I may have my mother's estate for the asking, and I can repay you the gold. I can never repay your kindness."

"I hope you will never offer to repay the gold," said Madge.

"I will not," I gladly answered.

"As to the kindness," she said, "you have paid me in advance for that many, many times over."

I then said farewell, promising to send letters telling of my fortune. As I was leaving I bent forward and kissed Madge upon the forehead, while she gently pressed my hand, but did not speak a word.

"Cousin Malcolm," said Dorothy, who held my other hand, "you are a strong, gentle, noble man, and I want you to say that you forgive me."

"I do forgive you, Dorothy, from my heart. I could not blame you if I wished to do so, for you did not know what you were doing."

"Not to know is sometimes the greatest of sins," answered Dorothy. I bent forward to kiss her cheek in token of my full forgiveness, but she gave me her lips and said: "I shall never again be guilty of not knowing that you are good and true and noble, Cousin Malcolm, and I shall never again doubt your wisdom or your good faith when you speak to me." She did doubt me afterward, but I fear her doubt was with good cause. I shall tell you of it in the proper place.

Then I forced myself to leave my fair friends and went to the gateway under Eagle Tower, where I found Will Dawson waiting for me with my horse.

"Sir George ordered me to bring your horse," said Will. "He seemed much excited. Has anything disagreeable happened? Are you leaving us? I see you wear your steel cap and breastplate and are carrying your bundle."

"Yes, Will, your master has quarrelled with me and I must leave his house."

"But where do you go, Sir Malcolm? You remember that of which we talked? In England no place but Haddon Hall will be safe for you, and the ports are so closely guarded that you will certainly be arrested if you try to sail for France."

"I know all that only too well, Will. But I must go, and I will try to escape to France. If you wish to communicate with me, I may be found by addressing a letter in care of the Duc de Guise."

"If I can ever be of help to you," said Will, "personally, or in that other matter, — Queen Mary, you understand, — you have only to call on me."

"I thank you, Will," I returned, "I shall probably accept your kind offer sooner than you anticipate. Do you know Jennie Faxton, the ferrier's daughter?"

"I do," he responded.

"I believe she may be trusted," I said.

"Indeed, I believe she is true as any steel in her father's shop," Will responded.

"Good-by, Will, you may hear from me soon."

I mounted and rode back of the terrace, taking my way along the Wye toward Rowsley. When I turned and looked back, I saw Dorothy standing upon the terrace. By her side, dressed in white, stood Madge. Her hand was covering her eyes. A step or two below them on the terrace staircase stood Will Dawson. They were three stanch friends, although one of them had brought my troubles upon me. After all, I was leaving Haddon Hall well garrisoned. My heart also was well garrisoned with a faithful troop of pain. But I shall write no more of that time. It was too full of bitterness.

CHAPTER V

MINE ENEMY'S ROOF-TREE

I RODE down the Wye to Rowsley, and by the will of my horse rather than by any intention of my own took the road up through Lathkil Dale. I had determined if possible to reach the city of Chester, and thence to ride down into Wales, hoping to find on the rough Welsh coast a fishing boat or a smuggler's craft that would carry me to France. In truth, I cared little whether I went to the Tower or to France, since in either case I felt that I had looked my last upon Haddon Hall, and had spoken farewell to the only person in all the world for whom I really cared. My ride from Haddon gave me time for deliberate thought, and I fully agreed with myself upon two propositions. First, I became thoroughly conscious of my real feeling toward Madge, and secondly, I was convinced that her kindness and her peculiar attitude toward me when I parted from her were but the promptings of a tender heart stirred by pity for my unfortunate situation, rather than what I thought when I said farewell to her. The sweet Wye and the beautiful Lathkil whispered to me as I rode beside their banks, but in their murmurings I heard only the music of her voice. The sun shone brightly, but its blessed light only served to remind me of the beautiful girl whom I had left in darkness. The light were worthless to me if I could not share it with her. What a moaning lout was I!

All my life I had been a philosopher, and as I rode from
Haddon, beneath all my gloominess there ran a current of
amusement which brought to my lips an ill-formed, half-
born laugh when I thought of the plight and condition in
which I, by candid self-communion, found myself. Five
years before that time I had left France, and had cast
behind me all the fair possibilities for noble achievement
which were offered to me in that land, that I might follow
the fortunes of a woman whom I thought I loved. Before
my exile from her side I had begun to fear that my idol
was but a thing of stone; and now that I had learned to
know myself, and to see her as she really was, I realized
that I had been worshipping naught but clay for lo, these
many years. There was only this consolation in the
thought for me: every man at some time in his life is a
fool — made such by a woman. It is given to but few
men to have for their fool-maker the rightful queen of
three kingdoms. All that was left to me of my life of
devotion was a shame-faced pride in the quality of my fool-
maker. "Then," thought I, "I have at last turned to be
my own fool-maker." But I suppose it had been written
in the book of fate that I should ride from Haddon a love-
lorn youth of thirty-five, and I certainly was fulfilling my
destiny to the letter.

I continued to ride up the Lathkil until I came to a fork
in the road. One branch led to the northwest, the other
toward the southwest. I was at a loss which direction to
take, and I left the choice to my horse, in whose wisdom
and judgment I had more confidence than in my own.
My horse, refusing the responsibility, stopped. So there
we stood like an equestrian statue arguing with itself until
I saw a horseman riding toward me from the direction of
Overhaddon. When he approached I recognized Sir John
Manners. He looked as woebegone as I felt, and I could
not help laughing at the pair of us, for I knew that his

trouble was akin to mine. The pain of love is ludicrous to all save those who feel it. Even to them it is laughable in others. A love-full heart has no room for that sort of charity which pities for kinship's sake.

"What is the trouble with you, Sir John, that you look so downcast?" said I, offering my hand.

"Ah," he answered, forcing a poor look of cheerfulness into his face, "Sir Malcolm, I am glad to see you. Do I look downcast?"

"As forlorn as a lover who has missed seeing his sweetheart," I responded, guessing the cause of Sir John's despondency.

"I have no sweetheart, therefore missing her could not have made me downcast," he replied.

"So you really did miss her?" I queried. "She was detained at Haddon Hall, Sir John, to bid me farewell."

"I do not understand—" began Sir John, growing cold in his bearing.

"I understand quite well," I answered. "Dorothy told me all to-day. You need keep nothing from me. The golden heart brought her into trouble, and made mischief for me of which I cannot see the end. I will tell you the story while we ride. I am seeking my way to Chester, that I may, if possible, sail for France. This fork in the road has brought me to a standstill, and my horse refuses to decide which route we shall take. Perhaps you will direct us."

"Gladly. The road to the southwest—the one I shall take—is the most direct route to Chester. But tell me, how comes it that you are leaving Haddon Hall? I thought you had gone there to marry—" He stopped speaking, and a smile stole into his eyes.

"Let us ride forward together, and I will tell you about it," said I.

While we travelled I told Sir John the circumstances of my departure from Haddon Hall, concealing nothing save that which touched Madge Stanley. I then spoke of my dangerous position in England, and told him of my great desire to reach my mother's people in France.

"You will find difficulty and danger in escaping to France at this time," said Sir John, "the guard at the ports is very strong and strict, and your greatest risk will be at the moment when you try to embark without a passport."

"That is true," I responded; "but I know of nothing else that I can do."

"Come with me to Rutland Castle," said Sir John. "You may there find refuge until such time as you can go to France. I will gladly furnish you money which you may repay at your pleasure, and I may soon be able to procure a passport for you."

I thanked him, but said I did not see my way clear to accept his kind offer.

"You are unknown in the neighborhood of Rutland," he continued, "and you may easily remain incognito."

Although his offer was greatly to my liking, I suggested several objections, chief among which was the distaste Lord Rutland might feel toward one of my name. I would not, of course, consent that my identity should be concealed from him. But to be brief—an almost impossible achievement for me, it seems—Sir John assured me of his father's welcome, and it was arranged between us that I should take my baptismal name, François de Lorraine, and passing for a French gentleman on a visit to England, should go to Rutland with my friend. So it happened through the strange workings of fate that I found help and refuge under my enemy's roof-tree.

Kind old Lord Rutland welcomed me, as his son had foretold, and I was convinced ere I had passed an hour under his roof that the feud between him and Sir George was of the latter's brewing.

The happenings in Haddon Hall while I lived at Rutland

I knew, of course, only by the mouth of others; but for convenience in telling I shall speak of them as if I had seen and heard all that took place. I may now say once for all that I shall take that liberty throughout this entire history.

On the morning of the day after my departure from Haddon, Jennie Faxton went to visit Dorothy and gave her a piece of information, small in itself, but large in its effect upon that ardent young lady. Will Fletcher, the arrow-maker at Overhaddon, had observed Dorothy's movements in connection with Manners; and although Fletcher did not know who Sir John was, that fact added to his curiosity and righteous indignation.

"It do be right that some one should tell the King of the Peak as how his daughter is carrying on with a young man who does come here every day or two to meet her, and I do intend to tell Sir George if she put not a stop to it," said Fletcher to some of his gossips in Yulegrave churchyard one Sunday afternoon.

Dorothy notified John, Jennie being the messenger, of Will's observations, visual and verbal, and designated another place for meeting, — the gate east of Bowling Green Hill. This gate was part of a wall on the east side of the Haddon estates adjoining the lands of the house of Devonshire which lay to the eastward. It was a secluded spot in the heart of the forest half a mile distant from Haddon Hall.

Sir George, for a fortnight or more after my disappearance, enforced his decree of imprisonment against Dorothy, and she, being unable to leave the Hall, could not go to Bowling Green Gate to meet Sir John. Before I had learned of the new trysting-place John had ridden thither several evenings to meet Dorothy, but had found only Jennie bearing her mistress's excuses. I supposed his journeyings had been to Overhaddon; but I did not press his confidence, nor did he give it.

Sir George's treatment of Dorothy had taught her that the citadel of her father's wrath could be stormed only by gentleness, and an opportunity was soon presented in which she used that effective engine of feminine warfare to her great advantage.

As I have told you, Sir George was very rich. No man, either noble or gentle, in Derbyshire or in any of the adjoining counties, possessed so great an estate or so beautiful a hall as did he. In France we would have called Haddon Hall a grand château.

Sir George's deceased wife had been a sister to the Earl of Derby, who lived at the time of which I am now writing. The earl had a son, James, who was heir to the title and to the estates of his father. The son was a dissipated, rustic clown — almost a simpleton. He had the vulgarity of a stable boy and the vices of a courtier. His associates were chosen from the ranks of gamesters, ruffians, and tavern maids. Still, he was a scion of one of the greatest families of England's nobility.

After Sir George's trouble with Dorothy, growing out of his desire that I should wed her, the King of the Peak had begun to feel that in his beautiful daughter he had upon his hands a commodity that might at any time cause him trouble. He therefore determined to marry her to some eligible gentleman as quickly as possible, and to place the heavy responsibility of managing her in the hands of a husband. The stubborn violence of Sir George's nature, the rough side of which had never before been shown to Dorothy, in her became adroit wilfulness of a quality that no masculine mind may compass. But her life had been so entirely undisturbed by opposing influences that her father, firm in the belief that no one in his household would dare to thwart his will, had remained in dangerous ignorance of the latent trouble which pervaded his daughter from the soles of her shapely feet to the top of her glory-crowned head.

Sir George, in casting about for a son-in-law, had hit upon the heir to the house of Derby as a suitable match for his child, and had entered into an alliance offensive and defensive with the earl against the common enemy, Dorothy. The two fathers had partly agreed that the heir to Derby should wed the heiress of Haddon. The heir, although he had never seen his cousin except when she was a plain, unattractive girl, was entirely willing for the match, but the heiress — well, she had not been con- sulted, and everybody connected with the affair instinc- tively knew there would be trouble in that quarter. Sir George, however, had determined that Dorothy should do her part in case the contract of marriage should be agreed upon between the heads of the houses. He had fully resolved to assert the majesty of the law vested in him as a father and to compel Dorothy to do his bidding, if there were efficacy in force and chastisement. At the time when Sir George spoke to Dorothy about the Derby marriage, she had been a prisoner for a fortnight or more, and had learned that her only hope against her father lay in cunning. So she wept, and begged for time in which to consider the answer she would give to Lord Derby's request. She begged for two months, or even one month, in which to bring herself to accede to her father's com- mands.

"You have always been so kind and good to me, father, that I shall try to obey if you and the earl eventually agree upon terms," she said tearfully, having no intention whatever of trying to do anything but disobey.

"Try!" stormed Sir George. "Try to obey me! By God, girl, I say you shall obey!"

"Oh, father, I am so young. I have not seen my cousin for years. I do not want to leave you, and I have never thought twice of any man. Do not drive me from you."

Sir George, eager to crush in the outset any disposition

H

to oppose his will, grew violent and threatened his daughter with dire punishment if she were not docile and obedient.

Then said rare Dorothy : —

"It would indeed be a great match."   Greater than ever will happen, she thought.   "I should be a countess."   She strutted across the room with head up and with dilating nostrils.   The truth was, she desired to gain her liberty once more that she might go to John, and was ready to promise anything to achieve that end.   "What sort of a countess would I make, father?"

"A glorious countess, Doll, a glorious countess," said her father, laughing.   "You are a good girl to obey me so readily."

"Oh, but I have not obeyed you yet," returned Dorothy, fearing that her father might be suspicious of a too ready acquiescence.

"But you will obey me," answered Sir George, half in command and half in entreaty.

"There are not many girls who would refuse the coronet of a countess."   She then seated herself upon her father's knee and kissed him, while Sir George laughed softly over his easy victory.

Blessed is the man who does not know when he is beaten.

Seeing her father's kindly humor, Dorothy said : —

"Father, do you still wish me to remain a prisoner in my rooms?"

"If you promise to be a good, obedient daughter," returned Sir George, "you shall have your liberty."

"I have always been that, father, and I am too old to learn otherwise," answered this girl, whose father had taught her deception by his violence.   You may drive men, but you cannot drive any woman who is worth possessing.   You may for a time think you drive her, but in the end she will have her way.

Dorothy's first act of obedience after regaining liberty was to send a letter to Manners by the hand of Jennie Faxton.

John received the letter in the evening, and all next day he passed the time whistling, singing, and looking now and again at his horologue. He walked about the castle like a happy wolf in a pen. He did not tell me there was a project on foot, with Dorothy as the objective, but I knew it, and waited with some impatience for the outcome.

Long before the appointed time, which was sunset, John galloped forth for Bowling Green Gate with joy and anticipation in his heart and pain in his conscience. As he rode, he resolved again and again that the interview toward which he was hastening should be the last he would have with Dorothy. But when he pictured the girl to himself, and thought upon her marvellous beauty and infinite winsomeness, his conscience was drowned in his longing, and he resolved that he would postpone resolving until the morrow.

John hitched his horse near the gate and stood looking between the massive iron bars toward Haddon Hall, whose turrets could be seen through the leafless boughs of the trees. The sun was sinking perilously low, thought John, and with each moment his heart also sank, while his good resolutions showed the flimsy fibre of their fabric and were rent asunder by the fear that she might not come. As the moments dragged on and she did not come, a hundred alarms tormented him. First among these was a dread that she might have made resolves such as had sprung up so plenteously in him, and that she might have been strong enough to act upon them and to remain at home. But he was mistaken in the girl. Such resolutions as he had been making and breaking had never come to her at all. The difference between the man and the woman was this: he resolved in his mind not to see her and failed in keeping to his resolution; while she resolved in her heart to see him —resolved that nothing in heaven or earth or the other place could keep her from seeing him, and succeeded in carrying out her resolution. The intuitive resolve, the one that does not know it is a resolution, is the sort before which obstacles fall like corn before the sickle.

After John had waited a weary time, the form of the girl appeared above the crest of the hill. She was holding up the skirt of her gown, and glided over the earth so rapidly that she appeared to be running. Beat! beat! oh, heart of John, if there is aught in womanhood to make you throb; if there is aught in infinite grace and winsomeness; if there is aught in perfect harmony of color and form and movement; if there is aught of beauty, in God's power to create that can set you pulsing, beat! for the fairest creature of His hand is hastening to greet you. The wind had dishevelled her hair and it was blowing in fluffy curls of golden red about her face. Her cheeks were slightly flushed with joy and exercise, her red lips were parted, and her eyes — but I am wasting words. As for John's heart it almost smothered him with its beating. He had never before supposed that he could experience such violent throbbing within his breast and live. But at last she was at the gate, in all her exquisite beauty and winsomeness, and something must be done to make the heart conform to the usages of good society. She, too, was in trouble with her breathing, but John thought that her trouble was owing to exertion. However that may have been, nothing in heaven or earth was ever so beautiful, so radiant, so graceful, or so fair as this girl who had come to give herself to John. It seems that I cannot take myself away from the attractive theme.

"Ah, Sir John, you did come," said the girl, joyously.

"Yes," John succeeded in replying, after an effort, "and you — I thank you, gracious lady, for coming. I do not deserve —" the heart again asserted itself, and Dorothy stood by the gate with downcast eyes, waiting to learn what it was that John did not deserve. She thought he deserved everything good.

"I fear I have caused you fatigue," said John, again thinking, and with good reason, that he was a fool.

The English language, which he had always supposed to be his mother tongue, had deserted him as if it were his step-mother. After all, the difficulty, as John subsequently said, was that Dorothy's beauty had deprived him of the power to think. He could only see. He was entirely disorganized by a girl whom he could have carried away in his arms.

"I feel no fatigue," replied Dorothy.

"I feared that in climbing the hill you had lost your breath," answered disorganized John.

"So I did," she returned. Then she gave a great sigh and said, "Now I am all right again."

All right? So is the morning sun, so is the arching rainbow, and so are the flitting lights of the north in midwinter. All are "all right" because God made them, as He made Dorothy, perfect, each after its kind.

A long, uneasy pause ensued. Dorothy felt the embarrassing silence less than John, and could have helped him greatly had she wished to do so. But she had made the advances at their former meetings, and as she had told me, she "had done a great deal more than her part in going to meet him." Therefore she determined that he should do his own wooing thenceforward. She had graciously given him all the opportunity he had any right to ask.

While journeying to Bowling Green Gate, John had formulated many true and beautiful sentiments of a personal nature which he intended expressing to Dorothy; but when the opportunity came for him to speak, the weather, his horse, Dorothy's mare Dolcy, the queens of England and

Scotland were the only subjects on which he could induce his tongue to perform, even moderately well.

Dorothy listened attentively while John on the opposite side of the gate discoursed limpingly on the above-named themes; and although in former interviews she had found those topics quite interesting, upon that occasion she had come to Bowling Green Gate to listen to something else and was piqued not to hear it. After ten or fifteen minutes she said demurely : —

"I may not remain here longer. I shall be missed at the Hall. I regained my liberty but yesterday, and father will be suspicious of me during the next few days. I must be watchful and must have a care of my behavior."

John summoned his wits and might have spoken his mind freely had he not feared to say too much. Despite Dorothy's witchery, honor, conscience, and prudence still bore weight with him, and they all dictated that he should cling to the shreds of his resolution and not allow matters to go too far between him and this fascinating girl. He was much in love with her; but Dorothy had reached at a bound a height to which he was still climbing. Soon John, also, was to reach the pinnacle whence honor, conscience, and prudence were to be banished.

"I fear I must now leave you," said Dorothy, as darkness began to gather.

"I hope I may soon see you again," said John.

"Sometime I will see you if — if I can," she answered with downcast eyes. "It is seldom I can leave the Hall alone, but I shall try to come here at sunset some future day." John's silence upon a certain theme had given offence.

"I cannot tell you how greatly I thank you," cried John.

"I will say adieu," said Dorothy, as she offered him her hand through the bars of the gate. John raised the hand gallantly to his lips, and when she had withdrawn it there seemed no reason for her to remain. But she stood for a moment hesitatingly. Then she stooped to reach into her pocket while she daintily lifted the skirt of her gown with the other hand and from the pocket drew forth a great iron key.

"I brought this key, thinking that you might wish to unlock the gate — and come to — to this side. I had great difficulty in taking it from the forester's closet, where it has been hanging for a hundred years or more."

She showed John the key, returned it to her pocket, made a courtesy, and moved slowly away, walking backward.

"Mistress Vernon," cried John, "I beg you to let me have the key."

"It is too late, now," said the girl, with downcast eyes "Darkness is rapidly falling, and I must return to the Hall."

John began to climb the gate, but she stopped him. He had thrown away his opportunity.

"Please do not follow me, Sir John," said she, still moving backward. "I must not remain longer."

"Only for one moment," pleaded John.

"No," the girl responded, "I — I may, perhaps, bring the key when I come again. I am glad, Sir John, that you came to meet me this evening." She courtesied, and then hurried away toward Haddon Hall. Twice she looked backward and waved her hand, and John stood watching her through the bars till her form was lost to view beneath the crest of Bowling Green Hill.

"'I brought this key, thinking that you might wish to unlock the gate and come to this side,'" muttered John, quoting the girl's words. "Compared with you, John Manners, there is no other fool in this world." Then meditatively: "I wonder if she feels toward me as I feel toward her? Surely she does. What other reason could bring her here to meet me unless she is a brazen, wanton creature who is for every man." Then came a jealous thought that hurt him like the piercing of a knife.   It lasted but a moment, however, and he continued muttering to himself: "If she loves me and will be my wife, I will — I will. . . .   In God's name what will I do?   If I were to marry her, old Vernon would kill her, and I — I should kill my father."

Then John mounted his horse and rode homeward the unhappiest happy man in England.   He had made perilous strides toward that pinnacle sans honor, sans caution, sans conscience, sans everything but love.

That evening while we were walking on the battlements, smoking, John told me of his interview with Dorothy and extolled her beauty, grace, and winsomeness which, in truth, as you know, were matchless.   But when he spoke of "her sweet, shy modesty," I came near to laughing in his face.

"Did she not write a letter asking you to meet her?" I asked.

"Why — y-e-s," returned John.

"And," I continued, "has she not from the first sought you?"

"It almost seems to be so," answered John, "but notwithstanding the fact that one might say — might call — that one might feel that her conduct is — that it might be — you know, well — it might be called by some persons not knowing all the facts in the case, immodest — I hate to use the word with reference to her — yet it does not appear to me to have been at all immodest in Mistress Vernon, and, Sir Malcolm, I should be deeply offended were any of my friends to intimate — "

"Now, John," I returned, laughing at him, "you could not, if you wished, make me quarrel with you; and if you desire it, I will freely avow my firm belief in the fact that my cousin Dorothy is the flower of modesty.   Does that better suit you?"

I could easily see that my bantering words did not suit him at all; but I laughed at him, and he could not find it in his heart to show his ill-feeling.

"I will not quarrel with you," he returned; "but in plain words, I do not like the tone in which you speak of her. It hurts me, and I do not believe you would wilfully give me pain."

"Indeed, I would not," I answered seriously.

"Mistress Vernon's conduct toward me," John continued, "has been gracious. There has been no immodesty nor boldness in it."

I laughed again and said: "I make my humble apologies to her Majesty, Queen Dorothy. But in all earnestness, Sir John, you are right: Dorothy is modest and pure. As for her conduct toward you, there is a royal quality about beauty such as my cousin possesses which gives an air of graciousness to acts that in a plainer girl would seem bold. Beauty, like royalty, has its own prerogatives."

For a fortnight after the adventures just related, John, in pursuance of his oft-repeated resolution not to see Dorothy, rode every evening to Bowling Green Gate; but during that time he failed to see her, and the resolutions, with each failure, became weaker and fewer.

One evening, after many disappointments, John came to my room bearing in his hands a letter which he said Jennie Faxton had delivered to him at Bowling Green Gate.

"Mistress Vernon," said John, "and Lady Madge Stanley will ride to Derby-town to-morrow. They will go in the Haddon Hall coach, and Dawson will drive. Mistress Vernon writes to me thus: —

"'To Sir John Manners: —

"'My good wishes and my kind greeting. Lady Madge Stanley, my good aunt, Lady Crawford, and myself do intend journeying to Derby-town to-morrow. My aunt,

Lady Crawford, is slightly ill, and although I should much regret to see her sickness grow greater, yet if ill she must be, I do hope that her worst day will be upon the morrow, in which case she could not accompany Lady Madge and me. I shall nurse my good aunt carefully this day, and shall importune her to take plentifully of physic that she may quickly recover her health — after to-morrow. Should a gentleman ask of Will Dawson, who will be in the tap-room of the Royal Arms at eleven o'clock of the morning, Dawson will be glad to inform the gentleman concerning Lady Crawford's health. Let us hope that the physic will cure Lady Crawford — by the day after to-morrow at furthest. The said Will Dawson may be trusted. With great respect,   DOROTHY VERNON.'"

" I suppose the gentleman will be solicitous concerning Lady Crawford's health to-morrow morning at eleven o'clock," said I.

"The gentleman is now solicitous concerning Lady Crawford's health," answered John, laughingly. "Was there ever a lady more fair and gracious than Mistress Vernon?"

I smiled with a superior air at John's weakness, being, as you know, entirely free from his complaint myself, and John continued : —

" Perhaps you would call Mistress Dorothy bold for sending me this letter?"

"It is redolent with shyness," I answered. " But would you really wish poor Lady Crawford to be ill that you might witness Mistress Dorothy's modesty?"

" Please don't jest on that subject," said John, seriously. " I would wish anything, I fear, that would bring me an opportunity to see her, to look upon her face, and to hear her voice. For her I believe I would sacrifice every one who is dear to me. One day she shall be mine — mine at whatever cost — if she will be. If she will be. Ah, there is the rub! If she will be. I dare not hope for that."

"I think," said I, "that you really have some little cause to hope."

"You speak in the same tone again. Malcolm, you do not understand her. She might love me to the extent that I sometimes hope; but her father and mine would never consent to our union, and she, I fear, could not be induced to marry me under those conditions. Do not put the hope into my heart."

"You only now said she should be yours some day," I answered.

"So she shall," returned John, "so she shall."

"But Lady Madge is to be with her to-morrow," said I, my own heart beating with an ardent wish and a new-born hope, "and you may be unable, after all, to see Mistress Dorothy."

"That is true," replied John. "I do not know how she will arrange matters, but I have faith in her ingenuity."

Well might he have faith, for Dorothy was possessed of that sort of a will which usually finds a way.

"If you wish me to go with you to Derby-town, I will do so. Perhaps I may be able to entertain Lady Madge while you have a word with Dorothy. What think you of the plan?" I asked.

"If you will go with me, Malcolm, I shall thank you with all my heart."

And so it was agreed between us that we should both go to Derby-town for the purpose of inquiring about Lady Crawford's health, though for me the expedition was full of hazard.

CHAPTER VI

A DANGEROUS TRIP TO DERBY-TOWN

THE next morning broke brightly, but soon clouds began to gather and a storm seemed imminent. We feared that the gloomy prospect of the sky might keep Dorothy and Madge at home, but long before the appointed hour John and I were at the Royal Arms watching eagerly for the Haddon coach. At the inn we occupied a room from which we could look into the court-yard, and at the window we stood alternating between exaltation and despair.

When my cogitations turned upon myself — a palpitating youth of thirty-five, waiting with beating heart for a simple blind girl little more than half my age; and when I remembered how for years I had laughed at the tenderness of the fairest women of the French and Scottish courts — I could not help saying to myself, "Poor fool! you have achieved an early second childhood." But when I recalled Madge in all her beauty, purity, and helplessness, my cynicism left me, and I, who had enjoyed all of life's ambitious possibilities, calmly reached the conclusion that it is sometimes a blessed privilege to be a fool. While I dwelt on thoughts of Madge, all the latent good within me came uppermost. There is latent good in every man, though it may remain latent all his life. Good resolves, pure thoughts, and noble aspirations — new sensations to me, I blush to confess — bubbled in my heart, and I made a mental prayer, "If this is folly, may God banish wisdom." What is there, after all is said, in wisdom, that men should seek it? Has it ever brought happiness to its possessor? I am an old man at this writing. I have tasted all the cups of life, and from the fulness of my experience I tell you that the simple life is the only one wherein happiness is found. When you permit your heart and your mind to grow complex and wise, you make nooks and crannies for wretchedness to lodge in. Innocence is Nature's wisdom; knowledge is man's folly.

An hour before noon our patience was rewarded when we saw the Haddon Hall coach drive into the courtyard with Dawson on the box. I tried to make myself believe that I did not wish Lady Crawford were ill. But there is little profit in too close scrutiny of our deep-seated motives, and in this case I found no comfort in self-examination. I really did wish that Aunt Dorothy were ill.

My motive studying, however, was brought to a joyous end when I saw Will Dawson close the coach door after Madge and Dorothy had alighted.

How wondrously beautiful they were! Had we lived in the days when Olympus ruled the world, John surely would have had a god for his rival. Dorothy seemed luminous, so radiant was she with the fire of life. As for Madge, had I beheld a corona hovering over her head I should have thought it in all respects a natural and appropriate phenomenon — so fair and saintlike did she appear to me. Her warm white furs and her clinging gown of soft light-colored woollen stuff seemed to be a saint's robe, and her dainty little hat, fashioned with ermine about the edge of the rim — well, that was the corona, and I was ready to worship.

Dorothy, as befitted her, wore a blaze of harmonious colors and looked like the spirit of life and youth. I wish

I could cease rhapsodizing over those two girls, but I cannot. You may pass over it as you read, if you do not like it.

"Ye gods! did ever a creature so perfect as she tread the earth?" asked John, meaning, of course, Dorothy.

"No," answered I, meaning, of course, Madge.

The girls entered the inn, and John and I descended to the tap-room for the purpose of consulting Will Dawson concerning the state of Aunt Dorothy's health.

When we entered the tap-room Will was standing near the fireplace with a mug of hot punch in his hand. When I touched him, he almost dropped the mug so great was his surprise at seeing me.

"Sir Mal —" he began to say, but I stopped him by a gesture. He instantly recovered his composure and appeared not to recognize me.

I spoke in broken English, for, as you know, I belong more to France than to any other country. "I am Sir François de Lorraine," said I. "I wish to inquire if Lady Crawford is in good health?"

"Her ladyship is ill, sir, I am sorry to say," responded Will, taking off his hat. "Mistress Vernon and Lady Madge Stanley are at the inn. If you wish to inquire more particularly concerning Lady Crawford's health, I will ask them if they wish to receive you. They are in the parlor."

Will was the king of trumps!

"Say to them," said I, "that Sir François de Lorraine — mark the name carefully, please — and his friend desire to make inquiry concerning Lady Crawford's health, and would deem it a great honor should the ladies grant them an interview."

Will's countenance was as expressionless as the face upon the mug from which he had been drinking.

"I shall inform the ladies of your honor's request."

He thereupon placed the half-emptied mug upon the fire-shelf and left the room.

When Will announced his errand to the girls, Dorothy said in surprise : —

"Sir François de Lorraine? That is the name of the Grand Duc de Guise, but surely— Describe him to me, Will."

"He is about your height, Mistress Dorothy, and is very handsome," responded Will.

The latter part of Will's description placed me under obligation to him to the extent of a gold pound sterling.

"Ah, it is John!" thought Dorothy, forgetting the fact that John was a great deal taller than she, but feeling that Will's description of "very handsome" could apply to only one man in the world. "He has taken Malcolm's name." Then she said, "Bring him to us, Will. But who is the friend? Do you know him? Tell me his appearance."

"I did not notice the other gentleman," replied Will, "and I can tell you nothing of him."

"Will, you are a very stupid man. But bring the gentlemen here." Dorothy had taken Will into her confidence to the extent of telling him that a gentleman would arrive at the Royal Arms who would inquire for Lady Crawford's health, and that she, Dorothy, would fully inform the gentleman upon that interesting topic. Will may have had suspicions of his own, but if so, he kept them to himself, and at least did not know that the gentleman whom his mistress expected to see was Sir John Manners. Neither did he suspect that fact. Dawson had never seen Manners, and did not know he was in the neighborhood of Derby. The fact was concealed from Dawson by Dorothy not so much because she doubted him, but for the reason that she wished him to be able truthfully to plead innocence in case trouble should grow out of the Derby-town escapade.

"I wonder why John did not come alone?" thought Dorothy. "This friend of his will be a great hindrance."

Dorothy ran to the mirror and hurriedly gave a few touches to her hair, pressing it lightly with her soft flexible fingers here, and tucking in a stray curl there, which for beauty's sake should have been allowed to hang loose. She was standing at the pier-glass trying to see the back of her head when Will knocked to announce our arrival.

"Come," said Dorothy.

Will opened the door and held it for us to pass in. Madge was seated near the fire. When we entered Dorothy was standing with great dignity in the centre of the floor, not of course intending to make an exhibition of delight over John in the presence of a stranger. But when she saw that I was the stranger, she ran to me with outstretched hands.

"Good morning, Mistress Vernon," said I, in mock ceremoniousness.

"Oh, Malcolm! Malcolm!" cried Madge, quickly rising from her chair. "You are cruel, Dorothy, to surprise me in this fashion."

"I, too, am surprised. I did not know that Malcolm was coming," replied Dorothy, turning to give welcome to John. Then I stepped to Madge's side and took her hands, but all I could say was "Madge! Madge!" and all she said was "Malcolm! Malcolm!" yet we seemed to understand each other.

John and Dorothy were likewise stricken with a paucity of words, but they also doubtless understood each other. After a moment or two there fell upon me a shower of questions from Dorothy.

"Did you not go to France? How happens it that you are in Derby-town? Where did you meet Sir John? What a delightful surprise you have given us! Nothing was wanting to make us happy but your presence."

"I am so happy that it frightens me," said Dorothy in ecstasy. "Trouble will come, I am sure. One extreme always follows another. The pendulum always swings as far back as it goes forward. But we are happy now, aren't we, Madge? I intend to remain so while I can. The pendulum may swing as far backward as it chooses hereafter. Sufficient to the day is the evil thereof. Sometimes the joy is almost sufficient, isn't it, Madge?"

"The evil is more than sufficient some days," answered Madge.

"Come, Madge, don't be foreboding."

"Dorothy, I have not met the other gentleman," said Madge.

"Ah, pardon me. In my surprise I forgot to present you. Lady Madge Stanley, let me present Sir John Manners."

"Sir John Manners!" cried Madge, taking a step backward. Her surprise was so great that she forgot to acknowledge the introduction. "Dorothy, what means this?" she continued.

"It means," replied Dorothy, nervously, "that Sir John is my very dear friend. I will explain it to you at another time."

We stood silently for a few moments, and John said:—

"I hope I may find favor in your heart, Lady Madge. I wish to greet you with my sincere homage."

"Sir John, I am glad to greet you, but I fear the pendulum of which Dorothy spoke will swing very far backward erelong."

"Let it swing as far back as it chooses," answered Dorothy, with a toss of her head, "I am ready to buy and to pay for happiness. That seems to be the only means whereby we may have it. I am ready to buy it with pain any day, and am willing to pay upon demand. Pain passes away; joy lasts forever."

I

"I know," said Sir John, addressing Madge, "I know it is not prudent for Malcolm and me to be here to-day; but imprudent things seem to be the most delightful."

"For men, Sir John," returned Madge. "Upon women they leave their mark."

"I fear you are right," he answered. "I had not thought of my visit in that light. For Mistress Vernon's sake it is better that I do not remain in Derby."

"For Mistress Vernon's sake you shall remain," cried that impetuous young woman, clutching John's arm.

After a time, Dorothy wishing to visit one of the shops to make purchases, it was agreed between us that we should all walk out. Neither Dorothy nor Madge had ever before visited Derby-town. John and I had visited the place but once; that was upon the occasion of our first meeting. No one in the town knew us, and we felt safe in venturing forth into the streets. So we helped Dorothy and Madge to don their furs, and out we went happier and more reckless than four people have any good right to be. But before setting out I went to the tap-room and ordered dinner.

I found the host and directed him to prepare a dozen partridges in a pie, a haunch of venison, a few links of German sausage, and a capon. The host informed me that he had in his pantry a barrel of roots called potatoes which had been sent to him by a sea-captain who had recently returned from the new world. He hurried away and brought a potato for inspection. It was of a gray brown color and near the size of an egg. The landlord assured me that it was delicious when baked, and I ordered four, at the cost of a crown each. I understand that my Lord Raleigh claims to have brought the first potatoes and tobacco into England in '85; but I know that I smoked tobacco in '66, and I saw potatoes at the Royal Arms in Derby-town in '67. I also ordered another new dish for our famous dinner. It was a brown beverage called coffee.

The berries from which the beverage is made mine host showed to me, and said they had been brought to him by a sea-faring man from Arabia. I ordered a pot of the drink at a cost of three crowns. I have heard it said that coffee was not known in Europe or in England till it was introduced by Rawolf in '73, but I saw it at the Royal Arms in '67. In addition to this list, I ordered for our drinking sweet wine from Madeira and red wine from Burgundy. The latter-named wine had begun to grow in favor at the French court when I left France five years before. It was little liked in England. All these dainties were rare at the time of which I write; but they have since grown into considerable use, and I doubt not, as we progress in luxury, they will become common articles of food upon the tables of the rich. Prongs, or forks, as they are called, which by some are used in cutting and eating one's food at table, I also predict will become implements of daily use. It is really a filthy fashion, which we have, of handling food with our fingers. The Italians have used forks for some time, but our preachers speak against them, saying God has given us our fingers with which to eat, and that it is impious to thwart his purposes by the use of forks. The preachers will probably retard the general use of forks among the common people.

After I had given my order for dinner we started out on our ramble through Derby-town.

Shortly after we left the inn we divided into couples for the ostensible reason that we did not wish to attract too much attention — Dorothy and John, Madge and I! Our real reason for separating was — but you understand.

Madge's hand lay like a span of snow upon my arm, and — but this time I will restrain my tendency to rhapsodize.

We walked out through those parts of the town which were little used, and Madge talked freely and happily.

She fairly babbled, and to me her voice was like the murmurings of the rivers that flowed out of paradise.

We had agreed with John and Dorothy to meet them at the Royal Arms in one hour, and that time had almost passed when Madge and I turned our faces toward the inn.

When we were within a short distance of our hostelry we saw a crowd gathered around a young man who was standing on a box. He was speaking in a mournful, lugubrious voice and accompanied his words with violent gesticulations. Out of curiosity we stopped to listen, and learned that religion was our orator's theme.

I turned to a man standing near me and asked : —

"Who is the fellow speaking?"

"The pious man is Robert Brown. He is exhorting in the name of the Lord of Hosts."

"The pious Robert Brown?" I queried, "exhorting in the name of — of the Lord of where, did you say?"

"Hosts," laconically responded my friend, while listening intently to the words of Brown.

"Hosts, say you? Who is he?" I asked of my interesting neighbor. "I know him not."

"Doubtless you know Him not," responded the man, evidently annoyed at my interruption and my flippancy.

After a moment or two I, desiring to know more concerning the orator, asked : —

"Robert Brown, say you?"

"Even he," came the response. "It will be good for your soul if you but listen to him in a prayerful mood. He is a young man upon whom the Spirit hath descended plenteously."

"The Spirit?" I asked.

"Ay," returned my neighbor.

I could not extract another word from him, so I had the worst of the encounter.

We had been standing there but a short time when the young exhorter descended from his improvised pulpit and passed among the crowd for the purpose of collecting money. His harangue had appeared ridiculous to me, but Madge seemed interested in his discourse. She said : —

"He is very earnest, Malcolm," and at once my heart went out to the young enthusiast upon the box. One kind word from Madge, and I was the fellow's friend for life. I would have remained his friend had he permitted me that high privilege. But that he would not do. When he came to me, I dropped into his hat a small silver piece which shone brightly among a few black copper coins. My liberal contribution did not induce him to kindness, but, on the contrary, it attracted his attention to the giver. He looked at the silver coin, and then turning his solemn gaze upon me, eyed me insolently from head to foot. While doing so a look of profound disgust spread over his mournful countenance. After a calm survey of my person, which to me was uncomfortably long, he turned to the bystanders, and in the same high-pitched, lugubrious voice which he had used when exhorting, said : —

"Brethren, here behold ye the type of anti-Christ," and he waved his thin hand toward me much to my amusement and annoyance. "Here," said he, "we find the leading strings to all that is iniquitous — vanity. It is betokened in his velvets, satins, and laces. Think ye, young man," he said, turning to me, "that such vanities are not an abomination in the eyes of the God of Israel?"

"I believe that the God of Israel cares nothing about my apparel," I replied, more amused than angered. He paid no attention to my remark.

"And this young woman," he continued, pointing to Madge, "this young woman, daughter of the Roman harlot, no doubt, she also is arrayed in silks, taffetas, and fine cloth. Look ye, friends, upon this abominable collar of

Satan; this ruff of fine linen, all smeared in the devil's own liquor, starch. Her vanity is an offence in the nostrils of God's people."

As he spoke he stretched forth his hand and caught in his clawlike grasp the dainty white ruff that encircled Madge's neck. When I saw his act, my first impulse was to run him through, and I drew my sword half from its scabbard with that purpose. But he was not the sort of a man upon whom I could use my blade. He was hardly more than a boy — a wild, half-crazed fanatic, whose reason, if he had ever possessed any, had been lost in the Charybdis of his zeal. He honestly thought it was his duty to insult persons who apparently disagreed with him. Such a method of proselyting is really a powerful means of persuasion among certain classes, and it has always been used by men who have successfully founded permanent religious sects. To plant successfully a religious thought or system requires more violent aggression than to conquer a nation.

Since I could not run the fellow through, I drew back my arm, and striking as lightly as possible, I laid our zealous friend sprawling on his back. Thus had I the honor of knocking down the founder of the Brownists.

If I mistake not, the time will come, if these men are allowed to harangue the populace, when the kings of England will be unable to accomplish the feat of knocking down Brown's followers. Heresies, like noxious weeds, grow without cultivation, and thrive best on barren soil. Or shall I say that, like the goodly vine, they bear better fruit when pruned? I cannot fully decide this question for myself; but I admire these sturdy fanatics who so passionately love their own faith, and so bitterly hate all others, and I am almost prepared to say that each new heresy brings to the world a better orthodoxy.

For a little time after my encounter with Brown, all my skill was needed to ward off the frantic hero. He quickly rose to his feet, and, with the help of his friends, seemed determined to spread the gospel by tearing me to pieces. My sword point kept the rabble at a respectful distance for a while, but they crowded closely upon me, and I should have been compelled to kill some of them had I not been reënforced by two men who came to my help and laid about them most joyfully with their quarterstaffs. A few broken heads stemmed for a moment the torrent of religious enthusiasm, and during a pause in the hostilities I hurriedly retreated with Madge, ungratefully leaving my valiant allies to reap the full reward of victory should the fortunes of war favor them.

Madge was terribly frightened, and with her by my side I, of course, would not have remained to fight the redoubtable Bayard himself.

We hurried forward, but before we reached the inn we were overtaken by our allies whom we had abandoned. Our friends were young men. One wore a rich, half-rustic habit, and the other was dressed as a horse boy. Both were intoxicated. I had been thankful for their help; but I did not want their company.

"How now, Cousin Madge?" said our richly dressed ally. "What in the devil's name has brought you into this street broil?"

"Ah, Cousin James, is it you?" replied the trembling girl.

"Yes, but who is your friend that so cleverly unloaded his quarrel upon us? Hell's fires! but they were like a swarm of wasps. Who is your friend, Madge?"

"Sir Malcolm Vernon," replied Madge. "Let me present you, Sir Malcolm, to my cousin, Lord James Stanley."

I offered my hand to his Lordship, and said : —

"I thank you much for your timely help. I should not have deserted you had I not felt that my first duty was to extricate Lady Madge from the disagreeable situation. We must hasten away from here, or the mad rabble will follow us."

"Right you are, my hearty," returned Stanley, slapping me on the shoulder. "Of course you had to get the wench away. Where do you go? We will bear you company."

I longed to pay the fellow for his help by knocking him down; but the possibilities of trouble ahead of us were already too great, and I forced myself to be content with the prowess already achieved.

"But you have not told me what brought you into the broil," asked his Lordship, as we walked toward the inn.

"Sir Malcolm and I were walking out to see the town and —"

"To see the town? By gad, that's good, Cousin Madge. How much of it did you see? You are as blind as an owl at noon," answered his Lordship.

"Alas! I am blind," returned Madge, clinging closely to me, and shrinking from her cousin's terrible jest. I could not think of anything sufficiently holy and sacred upon which to vow my vengeance against this fellow, if the time should ever come when I dared take it.

"Are you alone with this — this gentleman?" asked his Lordship, grasping Madge by the arm.

"No," returned Madge, "Dorothy is with us."

"She is among the shops," I volunteered reluctantly.

"Dorothy? Dorothy Vernon? By gad, Tod, we are in luck. I must see the wench I am to marry," said his Lordship, speaking to his companion, the stable boy. "So Dorothy is with you, is she, cousin? I haven't seen her for years. They say she is a handsome filly now. By gad, she had room to improve, for she was plain enough to frighten rats away from a barn when I last saw her. We will go to the inn and see for ourselves, won't we, Tod? Dad's word won't satisfy us when it comes to the matter of marrying, will it, Tod?"

Tod was the drunken stable boy who had assisted his Lordship and me in our battle with the Brownists.

I was at a loss what course to pursue. I was forced to submit to this fellow's company, and to endure patiently his insolence. But John and Dorothy would soon return, and there is no need that I should explain the dangers of the predicament which would then ensue.

When we were within a few yards of the inn door I looked backward and saw Dorothy and John approaching us. I held up my hand warningly. John caught my meaning, and instantly leaving Dorothy's side, entered an adjacent shop. My movement had attracted Stanley's attention, and he turned in the direction I had been looking. When he saw Dorothy, he turned again to me and asked: —

"Is that Dorothy Vernon?"

"Yes," I replied.

"Look at her, Tod!" exclaimed my lord, "look at her, Tod! The dad was right about her, after all. I thought the old man was hoaxing me when he told me that she was beautiful. Holy Virgin, Tod, did you ever see anything so handsome? I will take her quick enough; I will take her. Dad won't need to tease me. I'm willing."

Dorothy approached to within a few yards of us, and my Lord Stanley stepped forward to meet her.

"Ye don't know me, do ye?" said Stanley.

Dorothy was frightened and quickly stepped to my side.

"I — I believe not," responded Dorothy.

"Lord James Stanley," murmured Madge, who knew of the approaching Stanley marriage.

"Madge is right," returned Stanley, grinning foolishly. "I am your cousin James, but not so much of a cousin that I cannot be more than cousin, heh?" He laughed boisterously, and winking at Tod, thrust his thumb into that worthy's ribs. "Say, Tod, something more than cousin; that's the thing, isn't it, Tod?"

John was standing half-concealed at the door of the shop in which he had sought refuge. Dorothy well knew the peril of the situation, and when I frowned at her warningly, she caught the hint that she should not resent Stanley's words, however insulting and irritating they might become.

"Let us go to the inn," said Dorothy.

"That's the thing to do. Let us go to the inn and have dinner," said Stanley. "It's two hours past dinner time now, and I'm almost famished. We'll have a famous dinner. Come, cousin," said he, addressing Dorothy. "We'll have kidneys and tripe and —"

"We do not want dinner," said Dorothy. "We must return home at once. Sir Malcolm, will you order Dawson to bring out the coach?"

We went to the inn parlor, and I, loath to do so, left the ladies with Stanley and his horse-boy friend while I sought Dawson for the purpose of telling him to fetch the coach with all haste.

"We have not dined," said the forester.

"We shall not dine," I answered. "Fetch the coach with all the haste you can make." The bystanders in the tap-room were listening, and I continued, "A storm is brewing, and we must hasten home."

True enough, a storm was brewing.

When I left Dawson, I hurriedly found John and told him we were preparing to leave the inn, and that we would expect him to overtake us on the road to Rowsley.

I returned to the ladies in the parlor and found them standing near the window. Stanley had tried to kiss Dorothy, and she had slapped his face. Fortunately he had taken the blow good-humoredly, and was pouring into her unwilling ear a fusillade of boorish compliments when I entered the parlor.

I said, " The coach is ready."

The ladies moved toward the door. " I am going to ride with you, my beauty," said his Lordship.

"That you shall not do," retorted Dorothy, with blazing eyes.

"That I will do," he answered. " The roads are free to all, and you cannot keep me from following you."

Dorothy was aware of her predicament, and I too saw it, but could find no way out of it. I was troubled a moment; but my fear was needless, for Dorothy was equal to the occasion.

"We should like your company, Cousin Stanley," replied Dorothy, without a trace of anger in her manner, "but we cannot let you ride with us in the face of the storm that is brewing."

"We won't mind the storm, will we, Tod? We are going with our cousin."

"If you insist upon being so kind to us," said Dorothy, "you may come. But I have changed my mind about dinner. I am very hungry, and we accept your invitation."

"Now you are coming around nicely," said Lord James, joyfully. "We like that, don't we, Tod?"

Tod had been silent under all circumstances.

Dorothy continued: " Madge and I will drive in the coach to one or two of the shops, and we shall return in one hour. Meantime, Cousin Stanley, we wish you to have a fine dinner prepared for us, and we promise to do ample justice to the fare."

"She'll never come back," said silent Tod, without moving a muscle.

"How about it, cousin?" asked Stanley. "Tod says you'll never come back; he means that you are trying to give us the slip."

"Never fear, Cousin Stanley," she returned, "I am too

ager for dinner not to come back. If you fail to have a
well-loaded table for me, I shall never speak to you again."

We then went to the coach, and as the ladies entered it
Dorothy said aloud to Dawson : —

"Drive to Conn's shop."

I heard Tod say to his worthy master : —

"She's a slippin' ye."

"You're a fool, Tod. Don't you see she wants
me more than she wants the dinner, and she's hungry,
too."

"Don't see," retorted his laconic friend.

Of course when the coach was well away from the inn,
Dawson received new instructions, and took the road to
Rowsley. When the ladies had departed, I went to the tap-
room with Stanley, and after paying the host for the coffee,
the potatoes, and the dinner which alas! we had not tasted,
I ordered a great bowl of sack and proceeded to drink with
my allies in the hope that I might make them too drunk to
follow us. Within half an hour I discovered that I was
laboring at a hopeless task. There was great danger that
I would be the first to succumb ; so I, expressing a wish to
sleep off the liquor before the ladies should return, made
my escape from the tap-room, mounted my horse, and
galloped furiously after Dorothy and Madge. John was
riding by the coach when I overtook it.

It was two hours past noon when I came up with John
and the girls. Snow had been falling softly earlier in the
afternoon, but as the day advanced the storm grew in violence. A cold, bleak wind was blowing from the north,
and by reason of the weather and because of the ill condition of the roads, the progress of the coach was so slow
that darkness overtook us before we had finished half of
our journey to Rowsley. Upon the fall of night the storm
increased in violence, and the snow came in piercing, hori-
zontal shafts which stung like the prick of a needle.

At the hour of six — I but guessed the time — John and I, who were riding at the rear of the coach, heard close on our heels the trampling of horses. I rode forward to Dawson, who was in the coach box, and told him to drive with all the speed he could make. I informed him that some one was following us, and that I feared highwaymen were on our track.

Hardly had I finished speaking to Dawson when I heard the report of a hand-fusil, back of the coach, near the spot where I had left John. I quickly drew my sword, though it was a task of no small labor, owing to the numbness of my fingers. I breathed along the blade to warm it, and then I hastened to John, whom I found in a desperate conflict with three ruffians. No better swordsman than John ever drew blade, and he was holding his ground in the darkness right gallantly. When I rode to his rescue, another hand-fusil was discharged, and then another, and I knew that we need have no more fear from bullets, for the three men had discharged their weapons, and they could not reload while John and I were engaging them. I heard the bullets tell upon the coach, and I heard the girls screaming lustily. I feared they had been wounded, but you may be sure I had no leisure to learn the truth. Three against two was terrible odds in the dark, where brute force and luck go for more than skill. We fought desperately for a while, but in the end we succeeded in beating off the highwaymen. When we had finished with the knaves who had attacked us, we quickly overtook our party. We were calling Dawson to stop when we saw the coach, careening with the slant of the hill, topple over, and fall to the bottom of a little precipice five or six feet in height. We at once dismounted and jumped down the declivity to the coach, which lay on its side, almost covered by drifted snow. The pole had broken in the fall, and the horses were standing on the road. We first saw Dawson. He was swearing like a Dutchman, and when we had dragged him from his snowy grave, we opened the coach door, lifted out the ladies, and seated them upon the uppermost side of the coach. They were only slightly bruised, but what they lacked in bruises they made up in fright. In respect to the latter it were needless for me to attempt a description.

We can laugh about it now and speak lightly concerning the adventure, and, as a matter of truth, the humor of the situation appealed to me even then. But imagine yourself in the predicament, and you will save me the trouble of setting forth its real terrors.

The snow was up to our belts, and we did not at first know how we were to extricate the ladies. John and Dawson, however, climbed to the road, and I carried Dorothy and Madge to the little precipice where the two men at the top lifted them from my arms. The coach was broken, and when I climbed to the road, John, Dawson, and myself held a council of war against the storm. Dawson said we were three good miles from Rowsley, and that he knew of no house nearer than the village at which we could find shelter. We could not stand in the road and freeze, so I got the blankets and robes from the coach and made riding pads for Dorothy and Madge. These we strapped upon the broad backs of the coach horses, and then assisted the ladies to mount. I walked by the side of Madge, and John performed the same agreeable duty for Dorothy. Dawson went ahead of us, riding my horse and leading John's; and thus we travelled to Rowsley, half dead and nearly frozen, over the longest three miles in the kingdom.

John left us before entering the village, and took the road to Rutland, intending to stop for the night at a cottage two miles distant, upon his father's estates. I was to follow Sir John when the ladies were safely lodged at The Peacock.

It was agreed between us that nothing should be said concerning the presence of any man save Dawson and myself in our party.

When John left us, I rode to The Peacock with Dorothy and Madge, and while I was bidding them good-by my violent cousin, Sir George, entered the inn. Dorothy ran to her father and briefly related the adventures of the night, dwelling with undeserved emphasis upon the help I had rendered. She told her father — the statement was literally true — that she had met me at the Royal Arms, where I was stopping, and that she had, through fear of the storm and in dread of highwaymen, asked me to ride beside their coach to Rowsley.

When I saw Sir George enter the room, I expected to have trouble with him; but after he had spoken with Dorothy, much to my surprise, he offered me his hand and said:—

"I thank you, Malcolm, for the help you have rendered my girls, and I am glad you have come back to us."

"I have not come back to you, Sir George," said I, withholding my hand. "I met Mistress Vernon and Lady Madge at the Royal Arms, and escorted them to Rowsley for reasons which she has just given to you. I was about to depart when you entered."

"Tut, tut! Malcolm, you will come with us to Haddon Hall."

"To be ordered away again, Sir George?" I asked.

"I did not order you to go. You left in a childish fit of anger. Why in the devil's name did you run away so quickly? Could you not have given a man time to cool off? You treated me very badly, Malcolm."

"Sir George, you certainly know — "

"I know nothing of the sort. Now I want not another word from you. Damme! I say, not another word. If I ever ordered you to leave Haddon Hall, I didn't know what I was doing," cried Sir George, heartily.

"But you may again not know," said I.

"Now, Malcolm, don't be a greater fool than I was. If I say I did not order you to leave Haddon Hall, can't you take me at my word? My age and my love for you should induce you to let me ease my conscience, if I can. If the same illusion should ever come over you again — that is, if you should ever again imagine that I am ordering you to leave Haddon Hall — well, just tell me to go to the devil. I have been punished enough already, man. Come home with us. Here is Dorothy, whom I love better than I love myself. In anger I might say the same thing to her that I said to you, but — Nonsense, Malcolm, don't be a fool. Come home with us. Haddon is your home as freely as it is the home of Dorothy, Madge, and myself."

The old gentleman's voice trembled, and I could not withstand the double force of his kindness and my desire. So it came about that when Madge held out her fair hand appealingly to me, and when Dorothy said, "Please come home with us, Cousin Malcolm," I offered my hand to Sir George, and with feeling said, "Let us make this promise to each other: that nothing hereafter shall come between us."

"I gladly promise," responded the generous, impulsive old man. "Dorothy, Madge, and you are all in this world whom I love. Nothing shall make trouble between us. Whatever happens, we will each forgive."

The old gentleman was in his kindest, softest mood.

"Let us remember the words," said I.

"I give my hand and my word upon it," cried Sir George.

How easy it is to stake the future upon a present impulse. But when the time for reckoning comes, — when the future becomes the present, — it is sometimes hard to pay the priceless present for the squandered past.

Next morning we all rode home to Haddon, — how sweet

the words sound even at this distance of time!—and there was rejoicing in the Hall as if the prodigal had returned.

In the evening I came upon Madge unawares. She was softly singing a plaintive little love song. I did not disturb her, and as I stole away again I said to myself, "God is good." A realization of that great truth had of late been growing upon me. When once we thoroughly learn it, life takes on a different color.

CHAPTER VII

Tribulation in Haddon

AFTER I had left Haddon at Sir George's tempestuous order, he had remained in a state of furious anger against Dorothy and myself for a fortnight or more. But after her adroit conversation with him concerning the Stanley marriage, wherein she neither promised nor refused, and after she learned that she could more easily cajole her father than command him, Dorothy easily ensconced herself again in his warm heart, and took me into that capacious abode along with her.

Then came the trip to Derby, whereby his serene Lordship, James Stanley, had been enabled to see Dorothy and to fall in love with her winsome beauty, and whereby I was brought back to Haddon. Thereafter came events crowding so rapidly one upon the heels of another that I scarce know where to begin the telling of them. I shall not stop to say, "Sir George told me this," or "Madge, Dorothy, or John told me that," but I shall write as if I had personal knowledge of all that happened. After all, the important fact is that I know the truth concerning matters whereof I write, and of that you may rest with surety.

The snow lay upon the ground for a fortnight after the storm in which we rode from Derby, but at the end of that time it melted, and the sun shone with the brilliancy and warmth of springtide. So warm and genial was the weather that the trees, flowers, and shrubs were cozened into budding forth. The buds were withered by a killing frost which came upon us later in the season at a time when the spring should have been abroad in all her graciousness, and that year was called the year of the leafless summer.

One afternoon Sir George received a distinguished guest in the person of the Earl of Derby, and the two old gentle-men remained closeted together for several hours. That night at supper, after the ladies had risen from table, Sir George dismissed the servants saying that he wished to speak to me in private. I feared that he intended again bringing forward the subject of marriage with Dorothy, but he soon relieved my mind.

"The Earl of Derby was here to-day. He has asked for Doll's hand in marriage with his eldest son and heir, Lord James Stanley, and I have granted the request."

"Indeed," I responded, with marvellous intelligence. I could say nothing more, but I thought — in truth I knew— that it did not lie within the power of any man in or out of England to dispose of Dorothy Vernon's hand in marriage to Lord James Stanley. Her father might make a mur-deress out of her, but Countess of Derby, never.

Sir George continued, "The general terms of the mar-riage contract have been agreed upon by the earl and me, and the lawyers will do the rest."

"What is your feeling in the matter?" I asked aim-lessly.

"My feeling?" cried Sir George. "Why, sir, my feel-ing is that the girl shall marry Stanley just as soon as arrangements can be made for the wedding ceremony. The young fellow, it seems, saw Doll at Derby-town the day you came home, and since then he is eager, his father tells me, for the union. He is coming to see her when I give my permission, and I will send him word at as early a date as propriety will admit. I must not let them be seen together too soon, you know. There might be a hitch in the marriage negotiations. The earl is a tight one in business matters, and might drive a hard bargain with me should I allow his son to place Doll in a false position before the marriage contract is signed." He little knew how certainly Dorothy herself would avoid that disaster.

He took a long draught from his mug of toddy and winked knowingly at me, saying, "I am too wise for that."

"Have you told Dorothy?" I asked.

"No," he replied, "I have not exactly told her. I had a talk with her a few days ago on the subject, though the earl and I had not, at that time, entirely agreed upon the terms, and I did not know that we should agree. But I told her of the pending negotiations, because I wished to prepare her for the signing of the contract; and also, by gad, Malcolm, I wanted to make the girl understand at the outset that I will have no trifling with my commands in this matter. I made that feature of the case very plain, you may rest assured. She understands me fully, and although at first she was a little inclined to fight, she soon — she soon — well, she knuckled under gracefully when she found she must."

"Did she consent to the marriage?" I asked, well knowing that even if she had consented in words, she had no thought of doing so in deed.

"Y-e-s," returned Sir George, hesitatingly.

"I congratulate you," I replied.

"I shall grieve to lose Doll," the old man slowly continued with perceptible signs of emotion. "I shall grieve to lose my girl, but I am anxious to have the wedding over. You see, Malcolm, of late I have noticed signs of wilfulness in Doll that can be more easily handled by a husband than by a father. Marriage and children anchor a woman, you know. In truth, I have opened my eyes to the fact that Doll is growing dangerous. I'gad, the other day I thought she was a child, but suddenly I learn she is a woman. I had not before noticed the change. Beauty and wilfulness, such as the girl has of late developed, are powers not to be underestimated by wise men. There is hell in them, Malcolm, I tell you there is hell in them." Sir George meditatively snuffed the candle with his fingers and continued : " If a horse once learns that he can kick — sell him. Only yesterday, as I said, Doll was a child, and now, by Jove, she is a full-blown woman, and I catch myself standing in awe of her and calling her Dorothy. Yes, damme, standing in awe of my own child ! That will never do, you know. What has wrought the change ? And, after all, what is the change ? I can't define it, but there has been a great one."

He was in a revery and spoke more to himself than to me. "Yesterday she was my child — she was a child, and now — and now — she is — she is — Why the devil didn't you take her, Malcolm ? " cried the old man, awakening. " But there, never mind ; that is all past and gone, and the future Earl of Derby will be a great match for her."

" Do you know the future Earl of Derby ? " I asked. " Have you ever seen him ? "

" No," Sir George replied. " I hear he is rather wild and uncouth, but — "

" My dear cousin,' said I, interrupting him, " he is a vulgar, drunken clown, whose associates have always been stable boys, tavern maids, and those who are worse than either."

" What ? " cried Sir George, hotly, the liquor having reached his brain. " You won't have Doll yourself, and you won't consent to another — damme, would you have the girl wither into spinsterhood ? How, sir, dare you interfere ? "

" I withdraw all I said, Sir George," I replied hastily. " I have not a word to say against the match. I thought — "

"Well, damn you, sir, don't think."

"You said you wished to consult me about the affair, and I supposed — "

"Don't suppose either," replied Sir George, sullenly. "Supposing and thinking have hanged many a man. I didn't wish to consult you. I simply wanted to tell you of the projected marriage." Then after a moment of half-maudlin, sullen silence he continued, "Go to bed, Malcolm, go to bed, or we'll be quarrelling again."

I was glad enough to go to bed, for my cousin was growing drunk, and drink made a demon of this man, whose violence when sober was tempered by a heart full of tenderness and love.

Next morning Sir George was feeling irritable from the effects of the brandy he had drunk over night. At breakfast, in the presence of Lady Crawford, Madge, and myself, he abruptly informed Dorothy that he was about to give that young goddess to Lord James Stanley for his wife. He told her of the arrangement he had made the day before with the Earl of Derby. Lady Crawford looked toward her brother in surprise, and Madge pushed her chair a little way back from the table with a startled movement. Dorothy sprang to her feet, her eyes flashing fire and her breast rising and falling like the storm-wrought pulsing of the sea. I coughed warningly and placed my finger on my lips, making the sign of silence to Dorothy. The girl made a wondrous and beautiful struggle against her wrath, and in a moment all signs of ill-temper disappeared, and her face took on an expression of sweet meekness which did not belong there of right. She quietly sat down again, and when I looked at her, I would have sworn that Griselda in the flesh was sitting opposite me. Sir George was right. "Ways such as the girl had of late developed were dangerous." Hell was in them to an extent little dreamed of by her father. Breakfast was

finished in silence.   Dorothy did not come down to dinner
at noon, but Sir George did not mark her absence.   At
supper her place was still vacant.

"Where is Doll?" cried Sir George, angrily.   He had
been drinking heavily during the afternoon.   "Where is
Doll?" he demanded.

"She is on the terrace," answered Madge.   "She said
she did not want supper."

"Tell your mistress to come to supper," said Sir George,
speaking to one of the servants.   "You will find her on
the terrace."

The servant left the room, but soon returned, saying that
Mistress Dorothy wanted no supper.

"Tell her to come to the table whether she wants
supper or not.   Tell her I will put a stop to her moping
about the place like a surly vixen," growled Sir George.

"Don't send such a message by a servant," pleaded
Lady Crawford.

"Then take it to her yourself, Dorothy," exclaimed her
brother.

Dorothy returned with her aunt and meekly took her
place at the table.

"I will have none of your moping and pouting," said
Sir George, as Dorothy was taking her chair.

The girl made no reply, but she did not eat.

"Eat your supper," her father commanded.   "I tell
you I will have no —"

"You would not have me eat if I am not hungry, would
you, father?" she asked softly.

"I'd have you hungry, you perverse wench."

"Then make me an appetite," returned the girl.   I
never heard more ominous tones fall from human lips.
They betokened a mood in which one could easily do
murder in cold blood, and I was surprised that Sir George
did not take warning and remain silent.

"I cannot make an appetite for you, fool," he replied testily.

"Then you cannot make me eat," retorted Dorothy.

"Ah, you would answer me, would you, you brazen, insolent huzzy," cried her father, angrily.

Dorothy held up her hand warningly to Sir George, and uttered the one word, "Father." Her voice sounded like the clear, low ring of steel as I have heard it in the stillness of sunrise during a duel to the death. Madge gently placed her hand in Dorothy's, but the caress met no response.

"Go to your room," answered Sir George.

Dorothy rose to her feet and spoke calmly: "I have not said that I would disobey you in regard to this marriage which you have sought for me; and your harshness, father, grows out of your effort to reconcile your conscience with the outrage you would put upon your own flesh and blood — your only child."

"Suffering God!" cried Sir George, frenzied with anger and drink. "Am I to endure such insolence from my own child? The lawyers will be here to-morrow. The contract will be signed, and, thank God, I shall soon be rid of you. I'll place you in the hands of one who will break your damnable will and curb your vixenish temper." Then he turned to Lady Crawford. "Dorothy, if there is anything to do in the way of gowns and women's trumpery in preparation for the wedding, begin at once, for the ceremony shall come off within a fortnight."

This was beyond Dorothy's power to endure. Madge felt the storm coming and clutched her by the arm in an effort to stop her, but nothing could have done that.

"I marry Lord Stanley?" she asked in low, bell-like tones, full of contempt and disdain. "Marry that creature? Father, you don't know me."

"By God, I know myself," retorted Sir George, "and I say —"

"Now hear me, father," she interrupted in a manner that silenced even him. She bent forward, resting one fair hand upon the table, while she held out her other arm bared to the elbow. "Hear what I say and take it for the truth as if it had come from Holy Writ. I will open the veins in this arm and will strew my blood in a gapless circle around Haddon Hall so that you shall tread upon it whenever you go forth into the day or into the night before I will marry the drunken idiot with whom you would curse me. Ay, I will do more. I will kill you, if need be, should you try to force him on me. Now, father, we understand each other. At least you cannot fail to understand me. For the last time I warn you. Beware of me."

She gently pushed the chair back from the table, quietly adjusted the sleeve which she had drawn upward from her wrist, and slowly walked out of the room, softly humming the refrain of a roundelay. There was no trace of excitement about the girl. Her brain was acting with the ease and precision of a perfectly constructed machine. Sir George, by his violence and cruelty, had made a fiend of this strong, passionate, tender heart. That was all.

The supper, of course, was quickly finished, and the ladies left the room.

Sir George took to his bottle and remained with it till his servants put him to bed. I slipped away from him and smoked a pipe in front of the kitchen fire. Then I went early to my bed in Eagle Tower.

Dorothy went to her apartments. There she lay upon her bed, and for a time her heart was like flint. Soon she thought of her precious golden heart pierced with a silver arrow, and tears came to her eyes as she drew the priceless treasure from her breast and breathed upon it a prayer to the God of love for help. Her heart was soft again, soft only as hers could be, and peace came to her as she pressed John's golden heart to her lips and murmured over and over the words, "My love, my love, my love," and murmuring fell asleep.

I wonder how many of the countless women of this world found peace, comfort, and ecstasy in breathing those magic words yesterday? How many have found them to-day? How many will find them to-morrow? No one can tell; but this I know, they come to every woman at some time in her life, righteously or unrighteously, as surely as her heart pulses.

That evening Jennie Faxton bore a letter to John, informing him of the projected Stanley marriage. It asked him to meet the writer at Bowling Green Gate, and begged him to help her if he could.

The small and intermittent remnants of conscience, sense of duty, and caution which still remained in John's head — I will not say in John's heart, for that was full to overflowing with something else — were quickly banished by the unwelcome news in Dorothy's letter. His first impulse was to kill Stanley; but John Manners was not an assassin, and a duel would make public all he wished to conceal. He wished to conceal, among other things, his presence at Rutland. He had two reasons for so desiring. First in point of time was the urgent purpose with which he had come to Derbyshire. That purpose was to further a plan for the rescue of Mary Stuart and to bring her incognito to Rutland Castle as a refuge until Elizabeth could be persuaded to receive her. Of this plan I knew nothing till after the disastrous attempt to carry it out, of which I shall hereafter tell you. The other reason why John wished his presence at Rutland unknown was that if he were supposed to be in London, no one would suspect him of knowing Dorothy Vernon.

You must remember there had been no overt love-making between John and Dorothy up to that time. The

scene at the gate approached perilously near it, but the
line between concealment and confession had not been
crossed. Mind you, I say there had been no love-making
between them. While Dorothy had gone as far in that
direction as a maiden should dare go — and to tell the
exact truth, a great deal farther — John had remained almost silent for reasons already given you. He also felt
a fear of the girl, and failed to see in her conduct those
signs of intense love which would have been plainly dis-
cernible had not his perceptions been blinded by the fury
of his own infatuation. He had placed a curb on his passion
and did not really know its strength and power until he
learned that another man was soon to possess the girl he
loved. Then life held but one purpose for him. Thus,
you see that when Dorothy was moaning, " My love, my
love," and was kissing the golden heart, she was taking
a great deal for granted. Perhaps, however, she better
understood John's feeling for her than did he himself. A
woman's sixth sense, intuition, is a great help to her in
such cases. Perhaps the girl knew with intuitive confidence that her passion was returned; and perhaps at
first she found John's receptive mode of wooing sweeter
far than an aggressive attack would have been. It may
be also there was more of the serpent's cunning than
of reticence in John's conduct. He knew well the ways
of women, and perhaps he realized that if he would allow
Dorothy to manage the entire affair she would do his wooing for him much better than he could do it for himself.
If you are a man, try the plan upon the next woman whom
you seek to win. If she happens to be one who has full
confidence in her charms, you will be surprised at the
result. Women lacking that confidence are restrained by
fear and doubt. But in no case have I much faith in the
hammer-and-tongs process at the opening of a campaign.
Later on, of course — but you doubtless are quite as well

informed concerning this important subject as I. There
is, however, so much blundering in that branch of science
that I have a mind to endow a college at Oxford or at
Paris in which shall be taught the gentle, universally
needed art of making love. What a noble attendance
such a college would draw. But I have wandered wo-
fully from my story.

I must go back a short time in my narrative. A few
days before my return to Haddon Hall the great iron key
to the gate in the wall east of Bowling Green Hill was
missed from the forester's closet where it had hung for a
century or more. Bowling Green Hill, as you know, is
eastward from Haddon Hall a distance of the fourth part
of a mile, and the gate is east of the hill about the same
distance or less. A wall is built upon the east line of the
Haddon estate, and east of the wall lies a great trackless
forest belonging to the house of Devonshire. In olden
times there had been a road from Bakewell to Rowsley
along the east side of the wall; but before Sir George's
seizin the road had been abandoned and the gate was not
used. It stood in a secluded, unfrequented spot, and Dorothy thought herself very shrewd in choosing it for a trysting-place.

But as I told you, one day the key was missed. It was
of no value or use, and at first nothing was thought of its
loss; but from time to time the fact that it could not be
found was spoken of as curious. All the servants had
been questioned in vain, and the loss of the key to Bowling Green Gate soon took on the dignity of a mystery — a
mystery soon to be solved, alas! to Dorothy's undoing.

The afternoon of the day following the terrible scene
between Sir George and his daughter at the supper table,
Dorothy rode forth alone upon her mare Dolcy. From
the window of my room in Eagle Tower I saw her go
down the west side of the Wye toward Rowsley. I

ascended to the roof of the tower, and from that eleva-
tion I saw her cross the river, and soon she was lost to
sight in the forest. At that time I knew nothing of the
new trysting-place, but I felt sure that Dorothy had gone
out to seek John. The sun shone brightly, and its gentle
warmth enticed me to remain upon the tower battlements,
to muse, and to dream. I fetched my pipe and tobacco
from my room. I had been smoking at intervals for several months, but had not entirely learned to like the weed,
because of a slight nausea which it invariably caused me to
feel. But I thought by practice now and again to inure
myself to the habit, which was then so new and fashionable among modish gentlemen. While I smoked I mused
upon the past and present, and tried to peer into the
future — a fruitless task wherein we waste much valuable
time; a vain striving, like Eve's, after forbidden knowledge, which, should we possess it, would destroy the little
remnant of Eden still existing on earth. Could we look
forward only to our joys, a knowledge of the future might
be good to have; but imagine, if you can, the horror of
anticipating evils to come.

After a short time, a lotuslike dreaminess stole over me,
and past and future seemed to blend in a supreme present
of contentment and rest. Then I knew I had wooed and
won Tobacco and that thenceforth I had at hand an ever
ready solace in time of trouble. At the end of an hour
my dreaming was disturbed by voices, which came distinctly up to me from the base of the tower. I leaned
over the battlements to listen, and what I heard gave me
alarm and concern such as all the tobacco in the world
could not assuage. I looked down the dizzy heights of
Eagle Tower and saw Sir George in conversation with Ben
Shaw, a woodman. I had not heard the words first spoken
between them.

"Ay, ay, Sir George," said Ben, "they be there, by

Bowling Green Gate, now. I saw them twenty minutes since, — Mistress Vernon and a gentleman."

"Perhaps the gentleman is Sir Malcolm," answered my cousin. I drew back from the battlements, and the woodman replied, "Perhaps he be, but I doubt it."

There had been a partial reconciliation — sincere on Sir George's part, but false and hollow on Dorothy's — which Madge had brought about between father and daughter that morning. Sir George, who was sober and repentant of his harshness, was inclined to be tender to Dorothy, though he still insisted in the matter of the Stanley marriage. Dorothy's anger had cooled, and cunning had taken its place. Sir George had asked her to forgive him for the hard words he had spoken, and she had again led him to believe that she would be dutiful and obedient. It is hard to determine, as a question of right and wrong, whether Dorothy is to be condemned or justified in the woful deception she practised upon her father. To use a plain, ugly word, she lied to him without hesitation or pain of conscience. Still, we must remember that, forty years ago, girls were frequently forced, regardless of cries and piteous agony, into marriages to which death would have been preferable. They were flogged into obedience, imprisoned and starved into obedience, and alas! they were sometimes killed in the course of punishment for disobedience by men of Sir George's school and temper. I could give you at least one instance in which a fair girl met her death from punishment inflicted by her father because she would not consent to wed the man of his choice. Can we blame Dorothy if she would lie or rob or do murder to avoid a fate which to her would have been worse than death? When you find yourself condemning her, now or hereafter in this history, if you are a man ask yourself this question: "If I had a sweetheart in Dorothy's sad case, should I not wish her to do

as she did? Should I not wish, if it were possible by
any means, that she should save herself from the worst of
fates, and should save me from the agony of losing her
to such a man as Sir George had selected for Dorothy's
husband? Is it not a sin to disobey the law of self-preservation actively or passively?" Answer these questions as
you choose. As for myself, I say God bless Dorothy for
lying. Perhaps I am in error. Perhaps I am not. I but
tell you the story of Dorothy as it happened, and I am a
poor hand at solving questions of right and wrong where
a beautiful woman is concerned. To my thinking, she
usually is in the right. In any case, she is sure to have the
benefit of the doubt.

When Sir George heard the woodman's story, he started
hurriedly toward Bowling Green Gate.

Now I shall tell you of Dorothy's adventures after I saw
her cross the Wye.

When she reached the gate, John was waiting for her.

"Ah, Sir John, I am so glad you are here. That is, I
am glad you are here before I arrived — good even," said
the girl, confusedly. Her heart again was beating in a
provoking manner, and her breath would not come with
ease and regularity. The rapid progress of the malady
with which she was afflicted or blessed was plainly dis-
cernible since the last meeting with my friend, Sir John.
That is, it would have been plain to any one but John,
whose ailment had taken a fatal turn and had progressed
to the ante-mortem state of blindness. By the help of
the stimulating hope and fear which Dorothy's letter had
brought to him, he had planned an elaborate conversation,
and had determined to speak decisive words. He hoped
to receive from her the answer for which he longed; but
his heart and breath seemed to have conspired with Dorothy
to make intercommunication troublesome.

"I received your gracious letter, Mistress Vernon, and I

thank you. I was — I am — that is, my thanks are more than I — I can express."

"So I see," said the girl, half amused at John's condition, although it was but little worse than her own. This universal malady, love, never takes its blind form in women. It opens their eyes. Under its influence they can see the truth through a millstone. The girl's heart jumped with joy when she saw John's truth-telling manner, and composure quickly came to her relief, though she still feigned confusion because she wished him to see the truth in her as she had seen it in him. She well knew of his blindness, and had almost begun to fear lest she would eventually be compelled to tell him in words that which she so ardently wished him to see for himself. She thought John was the blindest of his sex; but she was, to a certain extent, mistaken. John was blind, as you already know, but his reticence was not all due to a lack of sight. He at least had reached the condition of a well-developed hope. He hoped the girl cared for him. He would have fully believed it had it not been for the difficulty he found in convincing himself that a goddess like Dorothy could care for a man so unworthy as himself. Most modest persons are self-respecting. That was John's condition; he was not vain.

"Jennie brought me your letter also," said the girl, laughing because she was happy, though her merriment somewhat disconcerted John.

"It told me," she continued, "that you would come. I have it here in my pocket — and — and the gate key," She determined this time to introduce the key early in the engagement. "But I feared you might not want to come." The cunning, the boldness, and the humility of the serpent was in the girl. "That is, you know, I thought — perhaps — that is, I feared that you might not come. Your father might have been ill, or you might have changed your mind after you wrote the letter."

"No," answered John, whose face was beaming with joy. Here, truly, was a goddess who could make the blind to see if she were but given a little time.

"Do you mean that your father is not ill, or that you did not change your mind?" asked Dorothy, whose face, as it should have been after such a speech, was bent low while she struggled with the great iron key, entangled in the pocket of her gown.

"I mean that I have not changed my mind," said John, who felt that the time to speak had come. "There has been no change in me other than a new access of eagerness with every hour, and a new longing to see you and to hear your voice."

Dorothy felt a great thrill pass through her breast, and she knew that the reward of her labors was at hand.

"Certainly," said the self-complacent girl, hardly conscious of her words, so great was the joyous tumult in her heart, "I should have known."

There was another pause, devoted to the key, with bended head. "But — but you might have changed your mind," she continued, "and I might not have known it, for, you see, I did not know your former state of mind; you have never told me." Her tongue had led her further than she had intended to go, and she blushed painfully, and I think, considering her words, appropriately.

"My letter told you my state of mind. At least it told you of my intention to come. I — I fear that I do not understand you," said John.

"I mean," she replied, with a saucy, fluttering little laugh as she looked up from her conflict with the entangled key, "I mean that — that you don't know what I mean. But here is the key at last, and — and — you may, if you wish, come to this side of the gate."

She stepped forward to unlock the gate with an air that seemed to say, "Now, John, you shall have a clear field."

L

But to her surprise she found that the lock had been removed. That discovery brought back to John his wandering wits.

"Mistress Dorothy," he cried in tones of alarm, "I must not remain here. We are suspected and are sure to be discovered. Your father has set a trap for us. I care not for myself, but I would not bring upon you the trouble and distress which would surely follow discovery. Let us quickly choose another place and time of meeting. I pray you, sweet lady, meet me to-morrow at this time near the white cliff back of Lathkil mill. I have that to say to you which is the very blood of my heart. I must now leave you at once."

He took her hand, and kissing it, started to leave through the open gate.

The girl caught his arm to detain him. "Say it now, John, say it now. I have dreamed of it by night and by day. You know all, and I know all, and I long to hear from your lips the words that will break down all barriers between us." She had been carried away by the mad onrush of her passion. She was the iron, the seed, the cloud, and the rain, and she spoke because she could not help it.

"I will speak, Dorothy, God help me! God help me, I will speak!" said John, as he caught the girl to his breast in a fierce embrace. "I love you, I love you! God Himself only knows how deeply, how passionately! I do not know. I cannot fathom its depths. With all my heart and soul, with every drop of blood that pulses through my veins, I love you — I adore you. Give me your lips, my beauty, my Aphrodite, my queen!"

"There — they — are, John, — there they are. They are — all yours — all yours — now! Oh, God! my blood is on fire." She buried her face on his breast for shame, that he might not see her burning eyes and her scarlet cheeks. Then after a time she cared not what he saw, and she lifted her lips to his, a voluntary offering. The supreme emotions of the moment drove all other consciousness from their souls.

"Tell me, Dorothy, that you will be my wife. Tell me, tell me!" cried John.

"I will, I will, oh, how gladly, how gladly!"

"Tell me that no power on earth can force you to marry Lord Stanley. Tell me that you will marry no man but me; that you will wait — wait for me till —"

"I will marry no man but you, John, no man but you," said the girl, whisperingly. Her head was thrown back from his breast that she might look into his eyes, and that he might see the truth in hers. "I am all yours. But oh, John, I cannot wait — I cannot! Do not ask me to wait. It would kill me. I wear the golden heart you gave me, John," she continued, as she nestled closer in his embrace. "I wear the golden heart always. It is never from me, even for one little moment. I bear it always upon my heart, John. Here it is." She drew from her breast the golden heart and kissed it. Then she pressed it to his lips, and said: "I kiss it twenty times in the day and in the night; ay, a hundred times. I do not know how often; but now I kiss your real heart, John," and she kissed his breast, and then stood tiptoe to lift her lips to his.

There was no room left now in John's heart for doubt that Dorothy Vernon was his own forever and forever. She had convinced him beyond the reach of fear or doubt. John forgot the lockless gate. He forgot everything but Dorothy, and cruel time passed with a rapidity of which they were unconscious. They were, however, brought back to consciousness by hearing a long blast from the forester's bugle, and John immediately retreated through the gate.

Dorothy then closed the gate and hastily seated herself

upon a stone bench against the Haddon side of the wall. She quickly assumed an attitude of listless repose, and Dolcy, who was nibbling at the grass near by, doubtless supposed that her mistress had come to Bowling Green Gate to rest because it was a secluded place, and because she desired to be alone.

Dorothy's attitude was not assumed one moment too soon, for hardly was her gown arranged with due regard to carelessness when Sir George's form rose above the crest of Bowling Green Hill. In a few minutes he was standing in front of his daughter, red with anger. Dorothy's face wore a look of calm innocence, which I believe would have deceived Solomon himself, notwithstanding that great man's experience with the sex. It did more to throw Sir George off the scent than any words the girl could have spoken.

"Who has been with you?" demanded Sir George, angrily.

"When, father?" queried the girl, listlessly resting her head against the wall.

"Now, this afternoon. Who has been with you? Ben Shaw said that a man was here. He said that he saw a man with you less than half an hour since."

That piece of information was startling to Dorothy, but no trace of surprise was visible in her manner or in her voice. She turned listlessly and brushed a dry leaf from her gown. Then she looked calmly up into her father's face and said laconically, but to the point: —

"Ben lied." To herself she said, "Ben shall also suffer."

"I do not believe that Ben lied," said Sir George. "I, myself, saw a man go away from here."

That was crowding the girl into close quarters, but she did not flinch.

"Which way did he go, father?" she asked, with a fine show of carelessness in her manner, but with a feeling of excruciating fear in her breast. She well knew the wisdom of the maxim, " Never confess."

"He went northward," answered Sir George.

"Inside the wall?" asked Dorothy, beginning again to breathe freely, for she knew that John had ridden southward.

"Inside the wall, of course," her father replied. "Do you suppose I could see him through the stone wall? One should be able to see through a stone wall to keep good watch on you."

"You might have thought you saw him through the wall," answered the girl. "I sometimes think of late, father, that you are losing your mind. You drink too much brandy, my dear father. Oh, wouldn't it be dreadful if you were to lose your mind?" She rose as she spoke, and going to her father began to stroke him gently with her hand. She looked into his face with real affection; for when she deceived him, she loved him best as a partial atonement for her ill-doing.

"Wouldn't that be dreadful?" she continued, while Sir George stood lost in bewilderment. "Wouldn't that be dreadful for my dear old father to lose his mind? But I really think it must be coming to pass. A great change has of late come over you, father. You have for the first time in your life been unkind to me and suspicious. Father, do you realize that you insult your daughter when you accuse her of having been in this secluded place with a man? You would punish another for speaking so against my fair name."

"But, Dorothy," Sir George replied, feeling as if he were in the wrong, "Ben Shaw said that he saw you here with a man, and I saw a man pass toward Bakewell. Who was he? I command you to tell me his name."

Dorothy knew that her father must have seen a man near the gate, but who he was she could not imagine. John surely was beyond the wall and well out of sight on his way to Rowsley before her father reached the crest of Bowling Green Hill. But it was evident that Shaw had seen John. Evidence that a man had been at the gate was too strong to be successfully contradicted. Facts that cannot be successfully contradicted had better be frankly admitted. Dorothy sought through her mind for an admission that would not admit, and soon hit upon a plan which, shrewd as it seemed to be, soon brought her to grief.

"Perhaps you saw Cousin Malcolm," said Dorothy, as the result of her mental search. "He passed here a little time since and stopped for a moment to talk. Perhaps you saw Malcolm, father. You would not find fault with me because he was here, would you?"

"Dorothy, my daughter," said Sir George, hesitatingly, "are you telling me the truth?"

Then the fair girl lifted up her beautiful head, and standing erect at her full height (it pains me to tell you this) said: "Father, I am a Vernon. I would not lie."

Her manner was so truthlike that Sir George was almost convinced.

He said, "I believe you."

Her father's confidence touched her keenly; but not to the point of repentance, I hardly need say.

Dorothy then grew anxious to return to the Hall that she might prepare me to answer whatever idle questions her father should put to me. She took Dolcy's rein, and leading the mare with one hand while she rested the other upon her father's arm, walked gayly across Bowling Green down to the Hall, very happy because of her lucky escape.

But a lie is always full of latent retribution.

I was sitting in the kitchen, dreamily watching the huge fire, when Dorothy and her father entered.

"Ah, Malcolm, are you here?" asked Sir George in a

peculiar tone of surprise for which I could see no reason. " I thought you were walking."

I was smoking. I took my pipe from my lips and said, " No, I am helping old Bess and Jennie with supper."

" Have you not been walking?" asked Sir George.

There was an odd expression on his face when I looked up to him, and I was surprised at his persistent inquiry concerning so trivial a matter. But Sir George's expression, agitated as it was, still was calm when compared with that of Dorothy, who stood a step or two behind her father. Not only was her face expressive, but her hands, her feet, her whole body were convulsed in an effort to express something which, for the life of me, I could not understand. Her wonderful eyes wore an expression, only too readable, of terror and pleading. She moved her hands rapidly and stamped her foot. During this pantomime she was forming words with her lips and nodding her head affirmatively. Her efforts at expression were lost upon me, and I could only respond with a blank stare of astonishment. The expression on my face caused Sir George to turn in the direction of my gaze, and he did so just in time to catch Dorothy in the midst of a mighty pantomimic effort at mute communication.

" Why in the devil's name are you making those grimaces?" demanded Sir George.

" I wasn't making grimaces — I — I think I was about to sneeze," replied Dorothy.

" Do you think I am blind?" stormed Sir George. " Perhaps I am losing my mind? You are trying to tell Malcolm to say that he was with you at Bowling Green Gate. Losing my mind, am I? Damme, I'll show you that if I am losing my mind I have not lost my authority in my own house."

" Now, father, what is all this storming about?" asked the girl, coaxingly, as she boldly put her hands upon her

father's shoulders and turned her face in all its wondrous beauty and childish innocence of expression up to
his. "Ask Malcolm to tell you whatever you wish to
know." She was sure that her father had told me what
she had been so anxious to communicate, and she felt certain that I would not betray her. She knew that I, whose
only virtues were that I loved my friend and despised a
lie, would willingly bear false witness for her sake. She
was right. I had caught the truth of the situation from Sir
George, and I quickly determined to perjure my soul, if
need be, to help Dorothy. I cannot describe the influence
this girl at times exerted over me. When under its spell I
seemed to be a creature of her will, and my power to act
voluntarily was paralyzed by a strange force emanating from
her marvellous vitality. I cannot describe it. I tell you
only the incontestable fact, and you may make out of it
whatever you can. I shall again in the course of this history have occasion to speak of Dorothy's strange power,
and how it was exerted over no less a person than Queen
Elizabeth.

"Ask Malcolm," repeated the girl, leaning coaxingly
upon her father's breast. But I was saved from uttering
the lie I was willing to tell; for, in place of asking me, as
his daughter had desired, Sir George demanded excitedly
of Dorothy, "What have you in your pocket that strikes
against my knee?"

"Mother of Heaven!" exclaimed Dorothy in a whisper,
quickly stepping back from her father and slowly lifting her
skirt while she reached toward her pocket. Her manner
was that of one almost bereft of consciousness by sudden
fright, and an expression of helplessness came over her face
which filled my heart with pity. She stood during a long
tedious moment holding with one hand the uplifted skirt,
while with the other she clutched the key in her pocket.

"What have you in your pocket?" demanded Sir George

with a terrible oath. "Bring it out, girl. Bring it out, I tell you."

Dorothy started to run from the room, but her father caught her by the wrist and violently drew her to him. "Bring it out, huzzy; it's the key to Bowling Green Gate. Ah, I've lost my mind, have I? Blood of Christ! I have not lost my mind yet, but I soon shall lose it at this rate," and he certainly looked as if he would.

Poor frightened Dorothy was trying to take the key from her pocket, but she was too slow to please her angry father, so he grasped the gown and tore a great rent whereby the pocket was opened from top to bottom. Dorothy still held the key in her hand, but upon the floor lay a piece of white paper which had fallen out through the rent Sir George had made in the gown. He divined the truth as if by inspiration. The note, he felt sure, was from Dorothy's unknown lover. He did not move nor speak for a time, and she stood as if paralyzed by fear. She slowly turned her face from her father to me, and in a low tone spoke my name, "Malcolm." Her voice was hardly louder than a whisper, but so piteous a cry for help I have never heard from human lips. Then she stooped, intending to take the letter from the floor, and Sir George drew back his arm as if he would strike her with his clenched hand. She recoiled from him in terror, and he took up the letter, unfolded it, and began to read: —

"Most gracious lady, I thank you for your letter, and with God's help I will meet you at Bowling Green Gate — " The girl could endure no more. She sprang with a scream toward her father and tried to snatch the letter. Sir George drew back, holding firmly to the paper. She followed him frantically, not to be thrown off, and succeeded in clutching the letter. Sir George violently thrust her from him. In the scuffle that ensued the letter was torn, and the lower portion of the sheet remained in Dorothy's hand. She ran

to the fireplace, intending to thrust the fragment into the
fire, but she feared that her father might rescue it from
the ashes. She glanced at the piece of paper, and saw that
the part she had succeeded in snatching from her father
bore John's name. Sir George strode hurriedly across the
room toward her and she ran to me.

"Malcolm! Malcolm!" she cried in terror. The cry was
like a shriek. Then I saw her put the paper in her mouth.
When she reached me she threw herself upon my breast
and clung to me with her arms about my neck. She
trembled as a single leaf among the thousands that deck a
full-leaved tree may tremble upon a still day, moved by a
convulsive force within itself. While she clung to me her
glorious bust rose and fell piteously, and her wondrous
eyes dilated and shone with a marvellous light. The expression was the output of her godlike vitality, strung to
its greatest tension. Her face was pale, but terror domi-
nated all the emotions it expressed. Her fear, however,
was not for herself. The girl, who would have snapped
her fingers at death, saw in the discovery which her father
was trying to make, loss to her of more than life. That
which she had possessed for less than one brief hour was
about to be taken from her. She had not enjoyed even
one little moment alone in which to brood her new-found
love, and to caress the sweet thought of it. The girl had
but a brief instant of rest in my arms till Sir George
dragged her from me by his terrible strength.

"Where is the paper?" he cried in rage. "It contained
the fellow's signature."

"I have swallowed it, father, and you must cut me open
to find it. Doubtless that would be a pleasant task for
you," answered Dorothy, who was comparatively calm now
that she knew her father could not discover John's name.
I believe Sir George in his frenzy would have killed the girl
had he then learned that the letter was from John Manners.

"I command you to tell me this fellow's name," said Sir George, with a calmness born of tempest. Dorothy did not answer, and Sir George continued: "I now understand how you came by the golden heart. You lied to me and told me that Malcolm had given it to you. Lie upon lie. In God's name I swear that I would rather father a thief than a liar."

"I did give her the heart, Sir George," I said, interrupting him. "It was my mother's." I had caught the lying infection. But Sir George, in his violence, was a person to incite lies. He of course had good cause for his anger. Dorothy had lied to him. Of that there could be no doubt; but her deception was provoked by his own conduct and by the masterful love that had come upon her. I truly believe that prior to the time of her meeting with Manners she had never spoken an untruth, nor since that time I also believe, except when driven to do so by the same motive. Dorothy was not a thief, but I am sure she would have stolen for the sake of her lover. She was gentle and tender to a degree that only a woman can attain; but I believe she would have done murder in cold blood for the sake of her love. Some few women there are in whose hearts God has placed so great an ocean of love that when it reaches its flood all other attributes of heart and soul and mind are ingulfed in its mighty flow. Of this rare class was Dorothy.

"God is love," says the Book.

"The universe is God," says the philosopher. "Therefore," as the mathematician would say, "love is the universe." To that proposition Dorothy was a corollary.

The servants were standing open-eyed about us in the kitchen.

"Let us go to the dining hall," I suggested. Sir George led the way by the stone steps to the screens, and from the screens to the small banquet hall, and I followed, leading Dorothy by the hand.

The moment of respite from her father's furious attack gave her time in which to collect her scattered senses.

When we reached the banquet hall, and after I had closed the door, Sir George turned upon his daughter, and with oath upon oath demanded to know the name of her lover. Dorothy stood looking to the floor and said nothing. Sir George strode furiously to and fro across the room.

"Curse the day you were born, you wanton huzzy. Curse you! curse you! Tell me the name of the man who wrote this letter," he cried, holding toward her the fragment of paper. "Tell me his name or, I swear it before God, I swear it upon my knighthood, I will have you flogged in the upper court till you bleed. I would do it if you were fifty times my child."

Then Dorothy awakened. The girl was herself again. Now it was only for herself she had to fear.

Her heart kept saying, "This for his sake, this for his sake." Out of her love came fortitude, and out of her fortitude came action.

Her father's oath had hardly been spoken till the girl tore her bodice from her shoulders. She threw the garment to the floor and said : —

"I am ready for the whip, I am ready. Who is to do the deed, father, you or the butcher? It must be done. You have sworn it, and I swear before God and by my maidenhood that I will not tell you the name of the man who wrote the letter. I love him, and before I will tell you his name or forego his love for me, or before I will abate one jot or tittle of my love for him, I will gladly die by the whip in your hand. I am ready for the whip, father. I am ready. Let us have it over quickly."

The girl, whose shoulders were bare, took a few steps toward the door leading to the upper court, but Sir George did not move. I was deeply affected by the terrible scene, and I determined to prevent the flogging if to do so should cost Sir George's life at my hands. I would have killed him ere he should have laid a single lash of the whip upon Dorothy's back.

"Father," continued the terrible girl, " are you not going to flog me? Remember your oaths. Surely you would not be forsworn before God and upon your knighthood. A forsworn Christian? A forsworn knight? A forsworn Vernon? The lash, father, the lash — I am eager for it."

Sir George stood in silence, and Dorothy continued to move toward the door. Her face was turned backward over her shoulder to her father, and she whispered the words, "Forsworn, forsworn, forsworn!"

As she put her hand on the latch the piteous old man held forth his arms toward her and in a wail of agony cried: "Doll! Doll! My daughter! My child! God help me!"

He covered his face with his hands, his great form shook for a moment as the tree trembles before the fall, and he fell prone to the floor sobbing forth the anguish of which his soul was full.

In an instant Dorothy was by her father's side holding his head upon her lap. She covered his face with her kisses, and while the tears streamed from her eyes she spoke incoherent words of love and repentance.

"I will tell you all, father; I will tell you all. I will give him up; I will see him never again. I will try not to love him. Oh, father, forgive me, forgive me. I will never again deceive you so long as I live."

Truly the fate of an overoath is that it shall be broken. When one swears to do too much, one performs too little.

I helped Sir George rise to his feet.

Dorothy, full of tenderness and in tears, tried to take his hand, but he repulsed her rudely, and uttering terrible oaths coupled with her name quitted the room with tottering steps.

When her father had gone Dorothy stood in revery for

a little time, and then looking toward the door through which her father had just passed, she spoke as if to herself: " He does not know. How fortunate ! "

" But you said you would tell him," I suggested. " You said you would give him up."

Dorothy was in a deep revery. She took her bodice from the floor and mechanically put it on.

"I know I said I would tell my father, and I offered to give — give him up," she replied; " but I will do neither. Father would not meet my love with love. He would not forgive me, nor would he accept my repentance when it was he who should have repented. I was alarmed and grieved for father's sake when I said that I would tell him about — about John, and would give him up." She was silent and thoughtful for a little time. "Give him up?" she cried defiantly. " No, not for my soul; not for ten thousand thousand souls. When my father refused my love, he threw away the only opportunity he shall ever have to learn from me John's name. That I swear, and I shall never be forsworn. I asked father's forgiveness when he should have begged for mine. Whip me in the courtyard, would he, till I should bleed ! Yet I was willing to forgive him, and he would not accept my forgiveness. I was willing to forego John, who is more than life to me; but my father would not accept my sacrifice. Truly will I never be so great a fool the second time. Malcolm, I will not remain here to be the victim of another insult such as my father put upon me to-day. There is no law, human or divine, that gives to a parent the right to treat his daughter as my father has used me. Before this day my conscience smote me when I deceived him, and I suffered pain if I but thought of my father. But now, thanks to his cruelty, I may be happy without remorse. Malcolm, if you betray me, I will — I will kill you if I must follow you over the world to do it."

"Do you think that I deserve that threat from you, Dorothy?" I asked.

"No, no, my dear friend, forgive me. I trust you," and she caught up my hand and kissed it gently.

Dorothy and I remained in the banquet hall, seated upon the stone bench under the blazoned window.

Soon Sir George returned, closely followed by two men, one of whom bore manacles such as were used to secure prisoners in the dungeon. Sir George did not speak. He turned to the men and motioned with his hand toward Dorothy. I sprang to my feet, intending to interfere by force, if need be, to prevent the outrage; but before I could speak Lady Crawford hurriedly entered the hall and ran to Sir George's side.

"Brother," she said, "old Bess has just told me that you have given orders for Dorothy's confinement in the dungeon. I could not believe Bess; but these men with irons lead me to suspect that you really intend —"

"Do not interfere in affairs that do not concern you," replied Sir George, sullenly.

"But this does concern me greatly," said Aunt Dorothy, "and if you send Doll to the dungeon, Madge and I will leave your house and will proclaim your act to all England."

"The girl has disobeyed me and has lied to me, and —"

"I care not what she has done, I shall leave your house and disown you for my brother if you perpetrate this outrage upon my niece. She is dear to me as if she were my own child. Have I not brought her up since babyhood? If you carry out this order, brother, I will leave Haddon Hall forever."

"And I'll go with her," cried old Bess, who stood at the door of the screens.

"And I, too," said Dawson, who was one of the men who had entered with Sir George.

"And I," cried the other man, throwing the manacles to the floor, "I will leave your service."

Sir George took up the manacles and moved toward Dorothy.

"You may all go, every cursed one of you. I rule my own house, and I will have no rebels in it. When I have finished with this perverse wench, I'll not wait for you to go. I'll drive you all out and you may go to —"

He was approaching Dorothy, but I stepped in front of him.

"This must not be, Sir George," said I, sternly. "I shall not leave Haddon Hall, and I fear you not. I shall remain here to protect your daughter and you from your own violence. You cannot put me out of Haddon Hall; I will not go."

"Why cannot I put you out of Haddon Hall?" retorted Sir George, whose rage by that time was frightful to behold.

"Because, sir, I am a better man and a better swordsman than you are, and because you have not on all your estates a servant nor a retainer who will not join me against you when I tell them the cause I champion."

Dawson and his fellow stepped to my side significantly, and Sir George raised the iron manacles as if intending to strike me. I did not move. At the same moment Madge entered the room.

"Where is my uncle?" she asked.

Old Bess led her to Sir George. She spoke not a word, but placed her arms gently about his neck and drew his face down to hers. Then she kissed him softly upon the lips and said: —

"My uncle has never in all his life spoken in aught but kindness to me, and now I beg him to be kind to Dorothy."

The heavy manacles fell clanking to the floor. Sir George placed his hand caressingly upon Madge's head and turned from Dorothy.

Lady Crawford then approached her brother and put her hand upon his arm, saying : —

"Come with me, George, that I may speak to you in private."

She moved toward the door by which she had entered, and Madge quietly took her uncle's hand and led him after Lady Crawford.   Within five minutes Sir George, Aunt Dorothy, and Madge returned to the room.

"Dorothy?" said Madge in a low voice.

"Here I am, Madge," murmured Dorothy, who was sitting on the bench by the blazoned window.   Madge walked gropingly over to her cousin and sat by her side, taking her hand.   Then Lady Crawford spoke to Dorothy : —

"Your father wishes me to say that you must go to your apartments in Entrance Tower, and that you shall not leave them without his consent.   He also insists that I say to you if you make resistance or objection to this decree, or if you attempt to escape, he will cause you to be manacled and confined in the dungeon, and that no persuasion upon our part will lead him from his purpose."

"Which shall it be?" asked Sir George, directing his question to Lady Crawford.

Dorothy lifted her eyebrows, bit the corner of her lip, shrugged her shoulders, and said : —

"Indeed, it makes no difference to me where you send me, father; I am willing to do whatever will give you the greatest happiness.   If you consult my wishes, you will have me whipped in the courtyard till I bleed.   I should enjoy that more than anything else you can do.   Ah, how tender is the love of a father!   It passeth understanding."

"Come to your apartments, Dorothy," said Lady Crawford, anxious to separate the belligerents.   "I have given your father my word of honor that I will guard you and will keep you prisoner in your rooms.   Do you not pity me?   I gave my promise only to save you from the

M

dungeon, and painful as the task will be, I will keep my word to your father."

"Which shall it be, father?" asked Dorothy. "You shall finish the task you began. I shall not help you in your good work by making choice. You shall choose my place of imprisonment. Where shall it be? Shall I go to my rooms or to the dungeon?"

"Go to your rooms," answered Sir George, "and let me never see —" but Sir George did not finish the sentence. He hurriedly left the hall, and Dorothy cheerfully went to imprisonment in Entrance Tower.

CHAPTER VIII

MALCOLM NO. 2

SIR GEORGE had done a bad day's work. He had hardened Dorothy's heart against himself and had made it more tender toward John. Since her father had treated her so cruelly, she felt she was at liberty to give her heart to John without stint. So when once she was alone in her room the flood-gates of her heart were opened, and she poured forth the ineffable tenderness and the passionate longings with which she was filled. With solitude came the memory of John's words and John's kisses. She recalled every movement, every word, every tone, every sensation. She gave her soul unbridled license to feast with joyous ecstasy upon the thrilling memories. All thoughts of her father's cruelty were drowned in a sea of bliss. She forgot him. In truth, she forgot everything but her love and her lover. That evening, after she had assisted Madge to prepare for bed, as was her custom, Dorothy stood before her mirror making her toilet for the night. In the flood of her newly found ecstasy she soon forgot that Madge was in the room.

Dorothy stood before her mirror with her face near to its polished surface, that she might scrutinize every feature, and, if possible, verify John's words.

"He called me 'my beauty' twice," she thought, "and 'my Aphrodite' once." Then her thoughts grew into unconscious words, and she spoke aloud:—

"I wish he could see me now." And she blushed at the thought, as she should have done. "He acted as if he meant all he said," she thought. "I know he meant it. I trust him entirely. But if he should change? Holy Mother, I believe I should die. But I do believe him. He would not lie, even though he is not a Vernon."

With thoughts of the scene between herself and her father at the gate, there came a low laugh, half of amusement, half of contentment, and the laugh meant a great deal that was to be regretted; it showed a sad change in Dorothy's heart. But yesterday the memory of her deceit would have filled her with grief. To-night she laughed at it. Ah, Sir George! Pitiable old man! While your daughter laughs, you sigh and groan and moan, and your heart aches with pain and impotent rage. Even drink fails to bring comfort to you. I say impotent rage, because Dorothy is out of your reach, and as surely as the sun rises in the east she is lost to you forever. The years of protection and tender love which you have given to her go for nothing. Now comes the son of your mortal enemy, and you are but an obstruction in her path. Your existence is forgotten while she revels in the memory of his words, his embraces, and his lips. She laughs while you suffer, in obedience to the fate that Heaven has decreed for those who bring children into this world.

Who is to blame for the pitiable mite which children give in return for a parent's flood of love? I do not know, but of this I am sure: if parents would cease to feel that they own their children in common with their horses, their estates, and their cattle; if they would not, as many do in varying degrees, treat their children as their property, the return of love would be far more adequate than it is.

Dorothy stood before her mirror plaiting her hair. Her head was turned backward a little to one side that she might more easily reach the great red golden skein. In that entrancing attitude the reflection of the nether lip of which John had spoken so fondly came distinctly to Dorothy's notice. She paused in the braiding of her hair and held her face close to the mirror that she might inspect the lip, whose beauty John had so ardently admired. She turned her face from one side to the other that she might view it from all points, and then she thrust it forward with a pouting movement that would have set the soul of a mummy pulsing if he had ever been a man. She stood for a moment in contemplation of the full red lip, and then resting her hands upon the top of the mirror table leaned forward and kissed its reflected image.

Again forgetfulness fell upon her and her thoughts grew into words.

"He was surely right concerning my lower lip," she said, speaking to herself. Then without the least apparent relevance, "He had been smoking." Again her words broke her revery, and she took up the unfinished braid of hair. When she did so, she caught a glimpse of her arm which was as perfectly rounded as the fairest marble of Phidias. She stretched the arm to its full length that the mirror might reflect its entire beauty. Again she thought aloud: "I wish he could see my arm. Perhaps some day —" But the words ceased, and in their place came a flush that spread from her hair to her full white throat, and she quickly turned the mirror away so that even it should not behold her beauty.

You see after all is told Dorothy was modest.

She finished her toilet without the aid of her mirror; but before she extinguished the candle she stole one more fleeting glance at its polished surface, and again came the thought, "Perhaps some day —" Then she covered the candle, and amid enfolding darkness lay down beside Madge, full of thoughts and sensations that made her tremble; for they were strange to her, and she knew not what they meant.

Dorothy thought that Madge was asleep, but after a few minutes the latter said : —

"Tell me, Dorothy, who was on fire?"

"Who was on fire?" asked Dorothy in surprise. "What do you mean, Madge?"

"I hope they have not been trying to burn any one," said Madge.

"What do you mean?" again asked Dorothy.

"You said 'He had been smoking,'" responded Madge.

"Oh," laughed Dorothy, "that is too comical. Of course not, dear one. I was speaking of — of a man who had been smoking tobacco, as Malcolm does." Then she explained the process of tobacco smoking.

"Yes, I know," answered Madge. "I saw Malcolm's pipe. That is, I held it in my hands for a moment while he explained to me its use."

Silence ensued for a moment, and Madge again spoke : —

"What was it he said about your lower lip, and who was he? I did not learn why Uncle George wished to confine you in the dungeon. I am so sorry that this trouble has come upon you."

"Trouble, Madge?" returned Dorothy. "Truly, you do not understand. No trouble has come upon me. The greatest happiness of my life has come to pass. Don't pity me. Envy me. My happiness is so sweet and so great that it frightens me."

"How can you be happy while your father treats you so cruelly?" asked Madge.

"His conduct makes it possible for my happiness to be complete," returned Dorothy. "If he were kind to me, I should be unhappy, but his cruelty leaves me free to be as happy as I may. For my imprisonment in this room I care not a farthing. It does not trouble me, for when I wish to see — see him again, I shall do so. I don't know at this time just how I shall effect it; but be sure, sweet one, I shall find a way." There was no doubt in Madge's mind that Dorothy would find a way.

"Who is he, Dorothy? You may trust me. Is he the gentleman whom we met at Derby-town?"

"Yes," answered Dorothy, "he is Sir John Manners."

"Dorothy!" exclaimed Madge in tones of fear.

"It could not be worse, could it, Madge?" said Dorothy.

"Oh, Dorothy!" was the only response.

"You will not betray me?" asked Dorothy, whose alarm made her suspicious.

"You know whether or not I will betray you," answered Madge.

"Indeed, I know, else I should not have told you my secret. Oh, you should see him, Madge; he is the most beautiful person living. The poor soft beauty of the fairest woman grows pale beside him. You cannot know how wonderfully beautiful a man may be. You have never seen one."

"Yes, I have seen many men, and I well remember their appearance. I was twelve years old, you know, when I lost my sight."

"But, Madge," said Dorothy, out of the fulness of her newly acquired knowledge, "a girl of twelve cannot see a man."

"No woman sees with her eyes the man whom she loves," answered Madge, quietly.

"How does she see him?" queried Dorothy.

"With her heart."

"Have you, too, learned that fact?" asked Dorothy.

Madge hesitated for a moment and murmured "Yes."

"Who is he, dear one?" whispered Dorothy.

"I may not tell even you, Dorothy," replied Madge.

"because it can come to nothing. The love is all on my part."

Dorothy insisted, but Madge begged her not to ask for her secret.

"Please don't even make a guess concerning him," said Madge. "It is my shame and my joy."

It looked as if this malady which had fallen upon Dorothy were like the plague that infects a whole family if one but catch it.

Dorothy, though curious, was generous, and remained content with Madge's promise that she should be the first one to hear the sweet story if ever the time should come to tell it.

"When did you see him?" asked Madge, who was more willing to receive than to impart intelligence concerning affairs of the heart.

"To-day," answered Dorothy. Then she told Madge about the scenes at the gate and described what had happened between her and Sir George in the kitchen and banquet hall.

"How could you tell your father such a falsehood?" asked Madge in consternation.

"It was very easy. You see I had to do it. I never lied until recently. But oh, Madge, this is a terrible thing to come upon a girl!" "This" was somewhat indefinite, but Madge understood, and perhaps it will be clear to you what Dorothy meant. The girl continued: "She forgets all else. It will drive her to do anything, however wicked. For some strange cause, under its influence she does not feel the wrong she does. It acts upon a girl's sense of right and wrong as poppy juice acts on pain. Before it came upon me in — in such terrible force, I believe I should have become ill had I told my father a falsehood. I might have equivocated, or I might have evaded the truth in some slight degree, but I could not have told a lie. But now it is as easy as winking."

"And I fear, Dorothy," responded Madge, "that wink-ing is very easy for you."

"Yes," answered candid Dorothy with a sigh.

"It must be a very great evil," said Madge, deploringly.

"One might well believe so," answered Dorothy, "but it is not. One instinctively knows it to be the essence of all that is good."

Madge asked, "Did Sir John tell you that — that he — "

"Yes," said Dorothy, covering her face even from the flickering rays of the rushlight.

"Did you tell him?"

"Yes," came in reply from under the coverlet.

After a short silence Dorothy uncovered her face.

"Yes," she said boldly, "I told him plainly; nor did I feel shame in so doing. It must be that this strange love makes one brazen. You, Madge, would die with shame had you sought any man as I have sought John. I would not for worlds tell you how bold and over-eager I have been."

"Oh, Dorothy!" was all the answer Madge gave.

"You would say 'Oh, Dorothy,' many times if you knew all." Another pause ensued, after which Madge asked: —

"How did you know he had been smoking?"

"I — I tasted it," responded Dorothy.

"How could you taste it? I hope *you* did not smoke?" returned Madge in wonderment.

Dorothy smothered a little laugh, made two or three vain attempts to explain, tenderly put her arms about Madge's neck and kissed her.

"Oh, Dorothy, that certainly was wrong," returned Madge, although she had some doubts in her own mind upon the point.

"Well, if it is wrong," answered Dorothy, sighing, "I don't care to live."

"Dorothy, I fear you are an immodest girl," said Madge.

"I fear I am, but I don't care — John, John, John!"

"How came he to speak of your lower lip?" asked Madge. "It certainly is very beautiful; but how came he to speak of it?"

"It was after — after — once," responded Dorothy.

"And your arm," continued remorseless Madge, "how came he to speak of it? You surely did not —"

"No, no, Madge; I hope you do not think I would show him my arm. I have not come to that. I have a poor remnant of modesty left; but the Holy Mother only knows how long it will last. No, he did not speak of my arm."

"You spoke of your arm when you were before the mirror," responded Madge, "and you said, 'Perhaps some day —'"

"Oh, don't, Madge. Please spare me. I indeed fear I am very wicked. I will say a little prayer to the Virgin to-night. She will hear me, even if I am wicked; and she will help me to become good and modest again."

The girls went to sleep, and Dorothy dreamed "John, John, John," and slumbered happily.

That part of the building of Haddon Hall which lies to the northward, west of the kitchen, consists of rooms according to the following plan: —

The two rooms in Entrance Tower over the great doors at the northwest corner of Haddon Hall were occupied by Dorothy and Madge. The west room overlooking the Wye was their parlor. The next room to the east was their bedroom. The room next their bedroom was occupied by Lady Crawford. Beyond that was Sir George's bedroom, and east of his room was one occupied by the pages and two retainers. To enter Dorothy's apartments one must pass through all the other rooms I have mentioned. Her windows were twenty-five feet from the ground and were barred with iron. After Dorothy's sentence of imprisonment, Lady Crawford, or some trusted person in her place, was always on guard in Aunt Dorothy's room to prevent Dorothy's escape, and guards were also stationed in the retainer's room for the same purpose. I tell you this that you may understand the difficulties Dorothy would have to overcome before she could see John, as she declared to Madge she would. But my opinion is that there are no limits to the resources of a wilful girl. Dorothy saw Manners. The plan she conceived to bring about the desired end was so seemingly impossible, and her execution of it was so adroit and daring, that I believe it will of itself interest you in the telling, aside from the bearing it has upon this history. No sane man would have deemed it possible, but this wilful girl carried it to fruition. She saw no chance of failure. To her it seemed a simple, easy matter. Therefore she said with confidence and truth, " I will see him when I wish to."

Let me tell you of it.

During Dorothy's imprisonment I spent an hour or two each evening with her and Madge at their parlor in the tower. The windows of the room, as I have told you, faced westward, overlooking the Wye, and disclosed the beautiful, undulating scenery of Overhaddon Hill in the distance.

One afternoon when Madge was not present Dorothy asked me to bring her a complete suit of my garments, — boots, hose, trunks, waistcoat, and doublet. I laughed, and asked her what she wanted with them, but she refused to tell me. She insisted, however, and I promised to fetch the garments to her. Accordingly the next evening I delivered the bundle to her hands. Within a week she returned them all, saving the boots. Those she kept — for what reason I could not guess.

Lady Crawford, by command of Sir George, carried in

her reticule the key of the door which opened from her own room into Sir George's apartments, and the door was always kept locked.

Dorothy had made several attempts to obtain possession of the key, with intent, I believe, of making a bold dash for liberty. But Aunt Dorothy, mindful of Sir George's wrath and fearing him above all men, acted faithfully her part of gaoler. She smiled, half in sadness, when she told me of the girl's simplicity in thinking she could hoodwink a person of Lady Crawford's age, experience, and wisdom. The old lady took great pride in her own acuteness. The distasteful task of gaoler, however, pained good Aunt Dorothy, whose simplicity was, in truth, no match for Dorothy's love-quickened cunning. But Aunt Dorothy's sense of duty and her fear of Sir George impelled her to keep good and conscientious guard.

One afternoon near the hour of sunset I knocked for admission at Lady Crawford's door. When I had entered she locked the door carefully after me, and replaced the key in the reticule which hung at her girdle.

I exchanged a few words with her Ladyship, and entered Dorothy's bedroom, where I left my cloak, hat, and sword. The girls were in the parlor. When I left Lady Crawford she again took her chair near the candle, put on her great bone-rimmed spectacles, and was soon lost to the world in the pages of "Sir Philip de Comynges." The dear old lady was near-sighted and was slightly deaf. Dorothy's bedroom, like Lady Crawford's apartments, was in deep shadow. In it there was no candle.

My two fair friends were seated in one of the west windows watching the sunset. They rose, and each gave me her hand and welcomed me with the rare smiles I had learned to expect from them. I drew a chair near to the window and we talked and laughed together merrily for a few minutes. After a little time Dorothy excused herself, saying that she would leave Madge and me while she went into the bedroom to make a change in her apparel.

Madge and I sat for a few minutes at the window, and I said, " You have not been out to-day for exercise."

I had ridden to Derby with Sir George and had gone directly on my return to see my two young friends. Sir George had not returned.

"Will you walk with me about the room?" I asked.

My real reason for making the suggestion was that I longed to clasp her hand, and to feel its velvety touch, since I should lead her if we walked.

She quickly rose in answer to my invitation and offered me her hand. As we walked to and fro a deep, sweet contentment filled my heart, and I felt that any words my lips could coin would but mar the ineffable silence.

Never shall I forget the soft light of that gloaming as the darkening red rays of the sinking sun shot through the panelled window across the floor and illumined the tapestry upon the opposite wall.

The tapestries of Haddon Hall are among the most beautiful in England, and the picture upon which the sun's rays fell was that of a lover kneeling at the feet of his mistress. Madge and I passed and repassed the illumined scene, and while it was softly fading into shadow a great flood of tender love for the girl whose soft hand I held swept over my heart. It was the noblest motive I had ever felt.

Moved by an impulse I could not resist, I stopped in our walk, and falling to my knee pressed her hand ardently to my lips. Madge did not withdraw her hand, nor did she attempt to raise me. She stood in passive silence. The sun's rays had risen as the sun had sunk, and the light was falling like a holy radiance from the gates of paradise upon the girl's head. I looked upward, and never in my eyes had woman's face appeared so fair and saintlike.

She seemed to see me and to feel the silent outpouring of my affection. I rose to my feet, and clasping both her hands spoke only her name "Madge."

She answered simply, "Malcolm, is it possible?" And her face, illumined by the sunlight and by the love-god, told me all else. Then I gently took her to my arms and kissed her lips again and again and again, and Madge by no sign nor gesture said me nay. She breathed a happy sigh, her head fell upon my breast, and all else of good that the world could offer compared with her was dross to me.

We again took our places by the window, since now I might hold her hand without an excuse. By the window we sat, speaking little, through the happiest hour of my life. How dearly do I love to write about it, and to lave my soul in the sweet aromatic essence of its memory. But my rhapsodies must have an end.

When Dorothy left me with Madge at the window she entered her bedroom and quickly arrayed herself in garments which were facsimiles of those I had lent her. Then she put her feet into my boots and donned my hat and cloak. She drew my gauntleted gloves over her hands, buckled my sword to her slim waist, pulled down the broad rim of my soft beaver hat over her face, and turned up the collar of my cloak. Then she adjusted about her chin and upper lip a black chin beard and moustachio, which she had in some manner contrived to make, and, in short, prepared to enact the rôle of Malcolm Vernon before her watchful gaoler, Aunt Dorothy.

While sitting silently with Madge I heard the clanking of my sword against the oak floor in Dorothy's bedroom. I supposed she had been toying with it and had let it fall. She was much of a child, and nothing could escape her curiosity. Then I heard the door open into Aunt Dorothy's apartments. I whispered to Madge requesting her to remain silently by the window, and then I stepped softly over to the door leading into the bedroom. I noiselessly opened the door and entered. From my dark hiding-place in Dorothy's bedroom I witnessed a scene in Aunt Dorothy's room which filled me with wonder and suppressed laughter. Striding about in the shadow-darkened portions of Lady Crawford's apartment was my other self, Malcolm No. 2, created from the flesh and substance of Dorothy Vernon.

The sunlight was yet abroad, though into Lady Crawford's room its slanting rays but dimly entered at that hour, and the apartment was in deep shadow, save for the light of one flickering candle, close to the flame of which the old lady was holding the pages of the book she was laboriously perusing.

The girl held her hand over her mouth trumpet-wise that her voice might be deepened, and the swagger with which she strode about the room was the most graceful and ludicrous movement I ever beheld. I wondered if she thought she was imitating my walk, and I vowed that if her step were a copy of mine, I would straightway amend my pace.

"What do you read, Lady Crawford?" said my cloak and hat, in tones that certainly were marvellously good imitations of my voice.

"What do you say, Malcolm?" asked the deaf old lady, too gentle to show the ill-humor she felt because of the interruption to her reading.

"I asked what do you read?" repeated Dorothy.

"The 'Chronicle of Sir Philip de Comynges,'" responded Lady Crawford. "Have you read it? It is a rare and interesting history."

"Ah, indeed, it is a rare book, a rare book. I have read it many times." There was no need for that little fabrication, and it nearly brought Dorothy into trouble.

"What part of the 'Chronicle' do you best like?" asked

Aunt Dorothy, perhaps for lack of anything else to say
Here was trouble already for Malcolm No. 2.

"That is hard for me to say. I so well like it all. Perhaps — ah — perhaps I prefer the — the ah — the middle
portion."

"Ah, you like that part which tells the story of Mary of
Burgundy," returned Aunt Dorothy. "Oh, Malcolm, I
know upon what theme you are always thinking — the
ladies, the ladies."

"Can the fair Lady Crawford chide me for that?" my
second self responded in a gallant style of which I was
really proud. "She who has caused so much of that sort
of thought surely must know that a gentleman's mind cannot be better employed than — "

"Malcolm, you are incorrigible. But it is well for a
gentleman to keep in practice in such matters, even though
he have but an old lady to practise on."

"They like it, even if it be only practice, don't they?"
said Dorothy, full of the spirit of mischief.

"I thank you for nothing, Sir Malcom Vernon," retorted
Aunt Dorothy with a toss of her head. "I surely don't
value your practice, as you call it, one little farthing's
worth."

But Malcolm No. 2, though mischievously inclined, was
much quicker of wit than Malcolm No. 1, and she easily
extricated herself.

"I meant that gentlemen like it, Lady Crawford."

"Oh!" replied Lady Crawford, again taking up her
book. "I have been reading Sir Philip's account of the
death of your fair Mary of Burgundy. Do you remember
the cause of her death?"

Malcolm No. 2, who had read Sir Philip so many times,
was compelled to admit that he did not remember the cause
of Mary's death.

"You did not read the book with attention," replied Lady

Crawford. "Sir Philip says that Mary of Burgundy died from an excess of modesty."

"That disease will never depopulate England," was the answer that came from my garments, much to my chagrin.

"Sir Malcolm," exclaimed the old lady, "I never before heard so ungallant a speech from your lips." — "And," thought I, "she never will hear its like from me."

"Modesty," continued Lady Crawford, "may not be valued so highly by young women nowadays as it was in the time of my youth, but — "

"I am sure it is not," interrupted Dorothy.

"But," continued Lady Crawford, "the young women of England are modest and seemly in their conduct, and they do not deserve to be spoken of in ungallant jest."

I trembled lest Dorothy should ruin my reputation for gallantry.

"Do you not," said Lady Crawford, "consider Dorothy and Madge to be modest, well-behaved maidens?"

"Madge! Ah, surely she is all that a maiden should be. She is a saint, but as to Dorothy — well, my dear Lady Crawford, I predict another end for her than death from modesty. I thank Heaven the disease in its mild form does not kill. Dorothy has it mildly," then under her breath, "if at all."

The girl's sense of humor had vanquished her caution, and for the moment it caused her to forget even the reason for her disguise.

"You do not speak fairly of your cousin Dorothy," retorted Lady Crawford. "She is a modest girl, and I love her deeply."

"Her father would not agree with you," replied Dorothy.

"Perhaps not," responded the aunt. "Her father's conduct causes me great pain and grief."

"It also causes me pain," said Dorothy, sighing.

"But, Malcolm," continued the old lady, putting down

her book and turning with quickened interest toward my other self, "who, suppose you, is the man with whom Dorothy has become so strangely entangled?"

"I cannot tell for the life of me," answered Malcolm No. 2. "Surely a modest girl would not act as she does."

"Surely a modest girl would," replied Aunt Dorothy, testily. "Malcolm, you know nothing of women."

"Spoken with truth," thought I.

The old lady continued: "Modesty and love have nothing whatever to do with each other. When love comes in at the door, modesty flies out at the window. I do pity my niece with all my heart, and in good truth I wish I could help her, though of course I would not have her know my feeling. I feign severity toward her, but I do not hesitate to tell you that I am greatly interested in her romance. She surely is deeply in love."

"That is a true word, Aunt Dorothy," said the love-lorn young woman. "I am sure she is fathoms deep in love."

"Nothing," said Lady Crawford, "but a great passion would have impelled her to act as she did. Why, even Mary of Burgundy, with all her modesty, won the husband she wanted, ay, and had him at the cost of half her rich domain."

"I wonder if Dorothy will ever have the man she wants?" said Malcolm, sighing in a manner entirely new to him.

"No," answered the old lady, "I fear there is no hope for Dorothy. I wonder who he is? Her father intends that she shall soon marry Lord Stanley. Sir George told me as much this morning when he started for Derby-town to arrange for the signing of the marriage contract within a day or two. He had a talk yesterday with Dorothy. She, I believe, has surrendered to the inevitable, and again there is good feeling between her and my brother."

Dorothy tossed her head expressively.

"It is a good match," continued Lady Crawford, "a good match, Malcolm. I pity Dorothy; but it is my duty to guard her, and I shall do it faithfully."

"My dear Lady Crawford," said my hat and cloak, "your words and feelings do great credit to your heart. But have you ever thought that your niece is a very wilful girl, and that she is full of disturbing expedients? Now I am willing to wager my beard that she will, sooner than you suspect, see her lover. And I am also willing to lay a wager that she will marry the man of her choice despite all the watchfulness of her father and yourself. Keep close guard over her, my lady, or she will escape."

Lady Crawford laughed. "She shall not escape. Have no fear of that, Malcolm. The key to the door is always safely locked in my reticule. No girl can outwit me. I am too old to be caught unawares by a mere child like Dorothy. It makes me laugh, Malcolm — although I am sore at heart for Dorothy's sake — it makes me laugh, with a touch of tears, when I think of poor simple Dorothy's many little artifices to gain possession of this key. They are amusing and pathetic. Poor child! But I am too old to be duped by a girl, Malcolm. I am too old. She has no chance to escape."

I said to myself: "No one has ever become too old to be duped by a girl who is in love. Her wits grow keen as the otter's fur grows thick for the winter's need. I do not know your niece's plan; but if I mistake not, Aunt Dorothy, you will in one respect, at least, soon be rejuvenated."

"I am sure Lady Crawford is right in what she says," spoke my other self, "and Sir George is fortunate in having for his daughter a guardian who cannot be hoodwinked and who is true to a distasteful trust. I would the trouble were over and that Dorothy were well married."

"So wish I, Malcolm, with all my heart," replied Aunt Dorothy.

After a brief pause in the conversation Malcolm No. 2 said : —

"I must now take my leave. Will you kindly unlock the door and permit me to say good night?"

"If you must go," answered my lady, glad enough to be left alone with her beloved Sir Philip. Then she unlocked the door.

"Keep good watch, my dear aunt," said Malcolm. "I greatly fear that Dorothy —" but the door closed on the remainder of the sentence and on Dorothy Vernon.

"Nonsense!" ejaculated the old lady somewhat impatiently. "Why should he fear for Dorothy? I hope I shall not again be disturbed." And soon she was deep in the pages of her book.

CHAPTER IX

A Tryst at Bowling Green Gate

I WAS at a loss what course to pursue, and I remained for a moment in puzzling thought. I went back to Madge, and after closing the door, told her of all I had seen. She could not advise me, and of course she was deeply troubled and concerned. After deliberating, I determined to speak to Aunt Dorothy that she might know what had happened. So I opened the door and walked into Lady Crawford's presence. After viewing my lady's back for a short time, I said : —

"I cannot find my hat, cloak, and sword. I left them in Dorothy's bedroom. Has any one been here since I entered?"

The old lady turned quickly upon me, "Since you entered?" she cried in wonderment and consternation. "Since you left, you mean. Did you not leave this room a few minutes ago? What means this? How found you entrance without the key?"

"I did not leave this room, Aunt Dorothy; you see I am here," I responded.

"Who did leave? Your wraith? Some one—Dorothy!" screamed the old lady in terror. "That girl!!— Holy Virgin! where is she?"

Lady Crawford hastened to Dorothy's room and returned to me in great agitation.

"Were you in the plot?" she demanded angrily.

" No more than were you, Lady Crawford," I replied, telling the exact truth. If I were accessory to Dorothy's crime, it was only as a witness and Aunt Dorothy had seen as much as I.

I continued: " Dorothy left Lady Madge and me at the window, saying she wished to make a change in her garments. I was watching the sunset and talking with Lady Madge."

Lady Crawford, being full of concern about the main event, — Dorothy's escape, — was easily satisfied that I was not accessory before the fact.

" What shall I do, Malcolm? What shall I do? Help me, quickly. My brother will return in the morning — perhaps he will return to-night — and he will not believe that I have not intentionally permitted Dorothy to leave the Hall. I have of late said so much to him on behalf of the girl that he suspects me already of being in sympathy with her. He will not believe me when I tell him that I have been duped. The ungrateful, selfish girl! How could she so unkindly return my affection! "

The old lady began to weep.

I did not believe that Dorothy intended to leave Haddon Hall permanently. I felt confident she had gone out only to meet John, and was sure she would soon return. On the strength of that opinion I said: " If you fear that Sir George will not believe you — he certainly will blame you — would it not be better to admit Dorothy quietly when she returns and say nothing to any one concerning the escapade? I will remain here in these rooms, and when she returns I will depart, and the guards will never suspect that Dorothy has left the Hall."

" If she will but return," wailed Aunt Dorothy, " I shall be only too glad to admit her and to keep silent."

" I am sure she will," I answered. " Leave orders with the guard at Sir George's door to admit me at any time during the night, and Dorothy will come in without being recognized. Her disguise must be very complete if she could deceive you."

"Indeed, her disguise is complete," replied the tearful old lady.

Dorothy's disguise was so complete and her resemblance to me had been so well contrived that she met with no opposition from the guards in the retainer's room nor from the porter. She walked out upon the terrace where she strolled for a short time. Then she climbed over the wall at the stile back of the terrace and took her way up Bowling Green Hill toward the gate. She sauntered leisurely until she was out of sight of the Hall. Then gathering up her cloak and sword she sped along the steep path to the hill crest and thence to the gate.

Soon after the first day of her imprisonment she had sent a letter to John by the hand of Jennie Faxton, acquainting him with the details of all that had happened. In her letter, among much else, she said: —

"My true love, I beg you to haunt with your presence Bowling Green Gate each day at the hour of sunset. I cannot tell you when I shall be there to meet you, or surely I would do so now. But be there I will. Let no doubt of that disturb your mind. It does not lie in the power of man to keep me from you. That is, it lies in the power of but one man, you, my love and my lord, and I fear not that you will use your power to that end. So it is that I beg you to wait for me at sunset hour each day near by Bowling Green Gate. You may be caused to wait for me a long weary time; but one day, sooner or later, I shall go to you, and then — ah, then, if it be in my power to reward your patience, you shall have no cause for complaint."

When Dorothy reached the gate she found it securely locked. She peered eagerly through the bars, hoping to see John. She tried to shake the heavy iron structure to assure herself that it could not be opened.

"Ah, well," she sighed, "I suppose the reason love laughs at locksmiths is because he — or she — can climb."

Then she climbed the gate and sprang to the ground on the Devonshire side of the wall.

"What will John think when he sees me in this attire?" she said half aloud. "Malcolm's cloak serves but poorly to cover me, and I shall instead be covered with shame and confusion when John comes. I fear he will think I have disgraced myself." Then, with a sigh, "But necessity knows no raiment."

She strode about near the gate for a few minutes, wishing that she were indeed a man, save for one fact: if she were not a woman, John would not love her, and, above all, she could not love John. The fact that she could and did love John appealed to Dorothy as the highest, sweetest privilege that Heaven or earth could offer to a human being.

The sun had sunk in the west, and his faint parting glory was but dimly to be seen upon a few small clouds that floated above Overhaddon Hill. The moon was past its half; and the stars, still yellow and pale from the lingering glare of day, waited eagerly to give their twinkling help in lighting the night. The forest near the gate was dense, and withal the fading light of the sun and the dawning beams of the moon and stars, deep shadow enveloped Dorothy and all the scene about her. The girl was disappointed when she did not see Manners, but she was not vexed. There was but one person in all the world toward whom she held a patient, humble attitude — John. If he, in his greatness, goodness, and condescension, deigned to come and meet so poor a person as Dorothy Vernon, she would be thankful and happy; if he did not come, she would be sorrowful. His will was her will, and she would

come again and again until she should find him waiting for
her, and he should stoop to lift her into heaven.

If there is a place in all the earth where red warm blood
counts for its full value, it is in a pure woman's veins.
Through self-fear it brings to her a proud reserve toward
all mankind till the right one comes.   Toward him it
brings an eager humbleness that is the essence and the
life of Heaven and of love.   Poets may praise snowy
women as they will, but the compelling woman is she of
the warm blood.   The snowy woman is the lifeless seed,
the rainless cloud, the unmagnetic lodestone, the drossful
iron.   The great laws of nature affect her but passively.
If there is aught in the saying of the ancients, "The best
only in nature can survive," the day of her extermination
will come.   Fire is as chaste as snow, and infinitely more
comforting.

Dorothy's patience was not to be tried for long.   Five
minutes after she had climbed the gate she beheld John
riding toward her from the direction of Rowsley, and her
heart beat with thrill upon thrill of joy.   She felt that the
crowning moment of her life was at hand.   By the help
of a subtle sense — familiar spirit to her love perhaps —
she knew that John would ask her to go with him and to
be his wife, despite all the Rutlands and Vernons dead,
living, or to be born.   The thought of refusing him never
entered her mind.   Queen Nature was on the throne in
the fulness of power, and Dorothy, in perfect attune with
her great sovereign, was fulfilling her destiny in accordance with the laws to which her drossless being was entirely amenable.

Many times had the fear come to her that Sir John
Manners, who was heir to the great earldom of Rutland, —
he who was so great, so good, and so beautiful, — might
feel that his duty to his house past, present, and future,
and the obligations of his position among the grand nobles

of the realm, should deter him from a marriage against which so many good reasons could be urged. But this evening her familiar spirit whispered to her that she need not fear, and her heart was filled with joy and certainty.

John dismounted and tethered his horse at a short distance from the gate. He approached Dorothy, but halted when he beheld a man instead of the girl whom he longed to meet. His hesitancy surprised Dorothy, who, in her eagerness, had forgotten her male attire. She soon saw, however, that he did not recognize her, and she determined, in a spirit of mischief, to maintain her incognito till he should penetrate her disguise.

She turned her back on John and sauntered leisurely about, whistling softly. She pretended to be unconscious of his presence, and John, who felt that the field was his by the divine right of love, walked to the gate and looked through the bars toward Bowling Green. He stood at the gate for a short time with indifference in his manner and irritation in his heart. He, too, tried to hum a tune, but failed. Then he tried to whistle, but his musical efforts were abortive. There was no music in him. A moment before his heart had been full of harmony; but when he found a man instead of his sweetheart, the harmony quickly turned to rasping discord.

John was not a patient man, and his impatience was apt to take the form of words and actions. A little aimless stalking about at the gate was more than enough for him, so he stepped toward the intruder and lifted his hat.

"I beg your pardon," he said, "I thought when first I saw you that you were Sir Malcolm Vernon. I fancied you bore resemblance to him. I see that I was in error."

"Yes, in error," answered my beard.

Again the two gentlemen walked around each other with great amusement on the part of one, and with ever increasing vexation on the part of the other.

Soon John said, "May I ask whom have I the honor to address?"

"Certainly, you may ask," was the response.

A silence ensued during which Dorothy again turned her back on John and walked a few paces away from him. John's patience was rapidly oozing, and when the unknown intruder again turned in his direction, John said with all the gentleness then at his command: —

"Well, sir, I do ask."

"Your curiosity is flattering," said the girl.

"Pardon me, sir," returned John. "My curiosity is not intended to be flattering. I —"

"I hope it is not intended to be insulting, sir?" asked my hat and cloak.

"That, sir, all depends upon yourself," retorted John, warmly. Then after an instant of thought, he continued in tones of conciliation: —

"I have an engagement of a private nature at this place. In short, I hope to meet a — a friend here within a few minutes and I feel sure that under the circumstances so gallant a gentleman as yourself will act with due consideration for the feelings of another. I hope and believe that you will do as you would be done by."

"Certainly, certainly," responded the gallant. "I find no fault at all with your presence. Please take no account whatever of me. I assure you I shall not be in the least disturbed."

John was somewhat disconcerted.

"Perhaps you will not be disturbed," replied John, struggling to keep down his temper, "but I fear you do not understand me. I hope to meet a — a lady and —"

"I hope also to meet a — a friend," the fellow said; "but I assure you we shall in no way conflict."

"May I ask," queried John, "if you expect to meet a gentleman or a lady?"

"Certainly you may ask," was the girl's irritating reply.

"Well, well, sir, I do ask," said John. "Furthermore, I demand to know whom you expect to meet at this place."

"That, of course, sir, is no business of yours."

"But I shall make it my affair. I expect to meet a lady here, my sweetheart." The girl's heart jumped with joy. "And if you have any of the feelings of a gentleman, you must know that your presence will be intolerable to me."

"Perhaps it will be, my dear sir, but I have as good a right here as you or any other. If you must know all about my affairs, I tell you I, too, hope to meet my sweetheart at this place. In fact, I know I shall meet my sweetheart, and, my good fellow, I beg to inform you that a stranger's presence would be very annoying to me."

John was at his wit's end. He must quickly do or say something to persuade this stubborn fellow to leave. If Dorothy should come and see two persons at the gate she, of course, would return to the Hall. Jennie Faxton, who knew that the garments were finished, had told Sir John that he might reasonably expect to see Dorothy at the gate on that evening, for Sir George had gone to Derby-town, presumably to remain over night.

In sheer desperation John said, "I was here first, and I claim the ground."

"That is not true," replied the other. "I have been waiting here for you — I mean for the person I am to meet —" Dorothy thought she had betrayed herself, and that John would surely recognize her. "I had been waiting full five minutes before you arrived."

John's blindness in failing to recognize Dorothy is past my understanding. He explained it to me afterward by saying that his eagerness to see Dorothy, and his fear, nay almost certainty, that she could not come, coupled with the hope which Jennie Faxton had given him, had so completely occupied his mind that other subjects received but slight consideration.

"But I — I have been here before this night to meet — "

"And I have been here to meet — quite as often as you, I hope," retorted Dorothy.

They say that love blinds a man. It must also have deafened John, since he did not recognize his sweetheart's voice.

"It may be true that you have been here before this evening," retorted John, angrily; "but you shall not remain here now. If you wish to save yourself trouble, leave at once. If you stalk about in the forest, I will run you through and leave you for the crows to pick."

"I have no intention of leaving, and if I were to do so you would regret it; by my beard, you would regret it," answered the girl, pleased to see John in his overbearing, commanding mood. His stupidity was past comprehension.

"Defend yourself," said John, drawing his sword.

"Now he will surely know the truth," thought Dorothy, but she said: "I am much younger than you, and am not so large and strong. I am unskilled in the use of a sword, and therefore am I no match for Sir John Manners than whom, I have heard, there is no better swordsman, stronger arm, nor braver heart in England."

"You flatter me, my friend," returned John, forced into a good humor against his will; "but you must leave. He who cannot defend himself must yield; it is the law of nature and of men."

John advanced toward Dorothy, who retreated stepping backward, holding her arm over her face.

"I am ready to yield if you wish. In fact, I am eager to yield — more eager than you can know," she cried.

"It is well," answered John, putting his sword in sheath.

"But," continued Dorothy, "I will not go away."

"Then you must fight," said John.

"I tell you again I am willing, nay, eager to yield to you, but I also tell you I cannot fight in the way you would have me. In other ways perhaps I can fight quite as well as anybody. But really, I am ashamed to draw my sword, since to do so would show you how poorly I am equipped to defend myself under your great laws of nature and of man. Again, I wish to assure you that I am more than eager to yield; but I cannot fight you, and I will not go away."

The wonder never ceases that John did not recognize her. She took no pains to hide her identity, and after a few moments of concealment she was anxious that John should discover her under my garments.

"I would know his voice," she thought, "did he wear all the petticoats in Derbyshire."

"What shall I do with you?" cried John, amused and irritated. "I cannot strike you."

"No, of course you would not murder me in cold blood," answered Dorothy, laughing heartily. She was sure her laughter would open John's eyes.

"I cannot carry you away," said John.

"I would come back again, if you did," answered the irrepressible fellow.

"I suppose you would," returned John, sullenly. "In the devil's name, tell me what you will do. Can I not beg you to go?"

"Now, Sir John, you have touched me. I make you this offer: you expect Mistress Vernon to come from the Hall —"

"What do you know about Mistress Vernon?" cried John. "By God, I will —"

"Now don't grow angry, Sir John, and please don't swear in my presence. You expect her, I say, to come from the Hall. What I propose is this: you shall stand by the gate and watch for Doll — oh, I mean Mistress

Vernon — and I will stand here behind the wall where she cannot see me. When she comes in sight — though in truth I don't think she will come, and I believe were she under your very nose you would not see her — you shall tell me and I will leave at once; that is, if you wish me to leave. After you see Dorothy Vernon if you still wish me to go, I pledge my faith no power can keep me. Now is not that fair ? I like you very much, and I want to remain here, if you will permit me, and talk to you for a little time — till you see Doll Vernon."

"Doll Vernon, fellow ? How dare you so speak of her ? " demanded John, hotly.

"Your pardon and her pardon, I beg ; Mistress Vernon, soon to be Countess of Derbyshire. By the way, I wager you a gold pound sterling that by the time you see Doll Vernon — Mistress Vernon, I pray your pardon — you will have grown so fond of me that you will not permit me to leave you." She thought after that speech he could not help but know her; but John's skull was like an oaken board that night. Nothing could penetrate it. He began to fancy that his companion was a simple witless person who had escaped from his keepers.

"Will you take the wager ? " asked Dorothy.

"Nonsense ! " was the only reply John deigned to give to so foolish a proposition.

"Then will you agree that I shall remain at the gate till Doll — Mistress Vernon comes ? "

"I suppose I shall have to make the best terms possible with you," he returned. "You are an amusing fellow and as perverse as a woman."

"I knew you would soon learn to like me," she responded. "The first step toward a man's affection is to amuse him. That old saw which says the road to a man's heart is through his stomach, is a sad mistake. Amusement is the highway to a man's affections."

"It is better that one laugh with us than at us. There is a vast difference in the two methods," answered John, contemptuously.

"You dare to laugh at me," cried Dorothy, grasping the hilt of her sword, and pretending to be angry. John waved her off with his hand, and laughingly said, "Little you know concerning the way to a man's heart, and no doubt less of the way to a woman's."

"I, perhaps, know more about it than you would believe," returned Malcolm No. 2.

"If you know aught of the latter subject, it is more than I would suppose," said John. "It is absurd to say that a woman can love a man who is unable to defend himself."

"A vain man thinks that women care only for men of his own pattern," retorted Dorothy. "Women love a strong arm, it is true, but they also love a strong heart, and you see I am not at all afraid of you, even though you have twice my strength. There are as many sorts of bravery, Sir John, as — as there are hairs in my beard."

"That is not many," interrupted John.

"And," continued the girl, "I believe, John, — Sir John, — you possess all the kinds of bravery that are good."

"You flatter me," said John.

"Yes," returned Dorothy, "that was my intent."

After that unflattering remark there came a pause. Then the girl continued somewhat hesitatingly : "Doubtless many women, Sir John, have seen your virtues more clearly than even I see them. Women have a keener perception of masculine virtues than — than we have."

Dorothy paused, and her heart beat with a quickened throb while she awaited his reply. A new field of discovery was opening up to her and a new use for her disguise.

John made no reply, but the persistent girl pursued her new line of attack.

"Surely Sir John Manners has had many sweethearts,"

said Dorothy, in flattering tones. There were rocks and shoals ahead for John's love barge. "Many, many, I am sure," the girl persisted.

"Ah, a few, a few, I admit," John like a fool replied. Dorothy was accumulating disagreeable information rapidly.

"While you were at London court," said she, " the fine ladies must have sought you in great numbers — I am sure they did."

"Perhaps, oh, perhaps," returned John. "One cannot always remember such affairs." His craft was headed for the rocks. Had he observed Dorothy's face, he would have seen the storm a-brewing.

"To how many women, Sir John, have you lost your heart, and at various times how many have lost their hearts to you ? " asked the persistent girl.— "What a senseless question," returned John. "A dozen times or more; perhaps a score or two score times. I cannot tell the exact number. I did not keep an account."

Dorothy did not know whether she wanted to weep or be angry. Pique and a flash of temper, however, saved her from tears, and she said, "You are so brave and handsome that you must have found it a very easy task — much easier than it would be for me — to convince those confiding ones of your affection ? "

"Yes," replied John, plunging full sail upon the breakers. " I admit that usually they have been quite easy to convince. I am naturally bold, and I suppose that perhaps — that is, I may possibly have a persuasive trick about me."

Shades of good men who have blundered into ruin over the path of petty vanity, save this man ! But no, Dorothy must drink the bitter cup of knowledge to the dregs.

"And you have been false to all of these women ? " she said.

o

"Ah, well, you know — the devil take it! A man can't be true to a score of women," replied John.

"I am sure none of them wished you to be true," the girl answered, restraining her tears with great difficulty.

At that point in the conversation John began to suspect from the manner and shapeliness of his companion that a woman had disguised herself in man's attire. Yet it did not once occur to him that Dorothy's fair form was concealed within the disguise. He attempted to lift my soft beaver hat, the broad rim of which hid Dorothy's face, but to that she made a decided objection, and John continued : "By my soul I believe you are a woman. Your walk " — Dorothy thought she had been swaggering like a veritable swash-buckler — "your voice, the curves of your form, all betray you." Dorothy gathered the cloak closely about her.

"I would know more of you," said John, and he stepped toward the now interesting stranger. But she drew away from him, and told him to keep hands off.

"Oh, I am right. You are a woman," said John.

Dorothy had maintained the disguise longer than she wished, and was willing that John should discover her identity. At first it had been rare sport to dupe him ; but the latter part of her conversation had given her no pleasure. She was angry, jealous, and hurt by what she had learned.

"Yes," she answered, "I admit that I am a — a woman. Now I must go."

"Stay but one moment," pleaded John, whose curiosity and gallantry were aroused. "I will watch for Mistress Vernon, and when she appears, then you may go."

"I told you that you would want me to remain," said the girl with a sigh. She was almost ready to weep. Then she thought : "I little dreamed I was coming here for this. I will carry the disguise a little farther, and will, perhaps, learn enough to — to break my heart."

She was soon to learn all she wanted to know and a great deal more.

"Come sit by me on this stone," said John, coaxingly. The girl complied, and drew the cloak over her knees.

"Tell me why you are here," he asked.

"To meet a gentleman," she replied, with low-bent face.

"Tell me your name," John asked, as he drew my glove from her passive hand. John held the hand in his, and after examining it in the dim light saw that it was a great deal more than good to look upon. Then he lifted it to his lips and said:

"Since our sweethearts have disappointed us, may we not console ourselves with each other?" He placed his arm around the girl's waist and drew her yielding form toward him. Dorothy, unobserved by John, removed the false beard and moustachio, and when John put his arm about her waist and leaned forward to kiss the fair accommodating neighbor she could restrain her tears no longer and said: —

"That would be no consolation for me, John; that would be no consolation for me. How can you? How can you?"

She rose to her feet and covered her face with her hands in a paroxysm of weeping. John, too, sprang to his feet, you may be sure. "Dorothy! God help me! I am the king of fools. Curse this hour in which I have thrown away my heaven. You must hate and despise me, fool, fool that I am."

John knew that it were worse than useless for him to attempt an explanation. The first thought that flashed through his mind was, to tell the girl that he had only pretended not to know her. He thought he would try to make her believe that he had been turning her trick upon herself; but he was wise in his day and generation, and did not seek refuge in that falsehood.

The girl would never have forgiven him for that.

"The only amends I can make," he said, in very dolefulness, "is that I may never let you see my face again."

"That will not help matters," sobbed Dorothy.

"I know it will not," returned John. "Nothing can help me. I can remain here no longer. I must leave you. I cannot even ask you to say farewell. Mistress Vernon, you do not despise me half so bitterly as I despise myself."

Dorothy was one of those rare natures to whom love comes but once. It had come to her and had engulfed her whole being. To part with it would be like parting with life itself. It was her tyrant, her master. It was her ego. She could no more throw it off than she could expel herself from her own existence. All this she knew full well, for she had analyzed her conditions, and her reason had joined with all her other faculties in giving her a clear concept of the truth. She knew she belonged to John Manners for life and for eternity. She also knew that the chance of seeing him soon again was very slight, and to part from him now in aught but kindness would almost kill her.

Before John had recognized Dorothy he certainly had acted like a fool, but with the shock of recognition came wisdom. All the learning of the ancients and all the cunning of the prince of darkness could not have taught him a wiser word with which to make his peace, "I may never let you see my face again." That was more to be feared by Dorothy than even John's inconstancy.

Her heart was full of trouble. "I do not know what I wish," she said simply. "Give me a little time to think."

John's heart leaped with joy, but he remained silent.

Dorothy continued: "Oh, that I had remained at home. I would to God I had never seen Derby-town nor you."

John in the fulness of his wisdom did not interrupt her.

"To think that I have thus made a fool of myself about a man who has given his heart to a score of women."

"This is torture," moaned John, in real pain.

"But," continued Dorothy, "I could not remain away from this place when I had the opportunity to come to you. I felt that I must come. I felt that I should die if I did not. And you are so false. I wish I were dead. A moment ago, had I been another woman, you would have kissed her. You thought I was another woman."

John's wisdom stood by him nobly. He knew he could neither explain successfully nor beg forgiveness. He simply said: "I cannot remain and look you in the face. If I dare make any request, it is that despite all you have heard from my lips you will still believe that I love you, and that in all my life I have never loved any one so dearly. There is no other woman for me."

"You doubtless spoke the same false words to the other two score women," said Dorothy. Tears and sobs were playing sad havoc with her powers of speech.

"Farewell, Mistress Vernon," replied John. "I should be shameless if I dared ask you to believe any word I can utter. Forget, if possible, that I ever existed; forget me that you may not despise me. I am unworthy to dwell even in the smallest of your thoughts. I am altogether base and contemptible."

"N-o-o," sighed Dorothy, poutingly, while she bent low her head and toyed with the gold lace of my cloak.

"Farewell," said John. He took a step or two backward from her.

"You are over-eager to leave, it seems to me," said the girl in an injured tone. "I wonder that you came at all." John's heart was singing hosanna. He, however, maintained his voice at a mournful pitch and said: "I must go. I can no longer endure to remain." While he spoke he moved toward his horse, and his head was bowed with real shame as he thought of the pitiable fool he had made of himself. Dorothy saw him going from her, and she called to him softly and reluctantly, "John."

He did not hear her, or perhaps he thought best to pretend that he did not hear, and as he moved from her the girl became desperate. Modesty, resentment, insulted womanhood and injured pride were all swept away by the stream of her mighty love, and she cried again, this time without hesitancy or reluctance, "John, John." She started to run toward him, but my cloak was in her way, and the sword tripped her feet. In her fear lest John might leave her, she unclasped the sword-belt from her waist and snatched the cloak from her shoulders. Freed from these hindrances, she ran toward John.

"John, do not leave me. Do not leave me." As she spoke, she reached an open space among the trees and John turned toward her. Her hat had fallen off, and the red golden threads of her hair, freed from their fastenings, streamed behind her. Never before had a vision of such exquisite loveliness sped through the moonbeams. So entrancing was her beauty to John that he stood motionless in admiration. He did not go to meet her as he should have done, and perhaps as he would have done had his senses not been wrapped in benumbing wonderment. His eyes were unable to interpret to his brain all her marvellous beauty, and his other senses abandoning their proper functions had hastened to the assistance of his sight. He saw, he heard, he felt her loveliness. Thus occupied he did not move, so Dorothy ran to him and fell upon his breast.

"You did not come to meet me," she sobbed. "You made me come all the way, to forgive you. Cruel, cruel!"

John held the girl in his arms, but he did not dare to kiss her, and his self-denial soon brought its reward. He had not expected that she would come a beggar to him

The most he had dared to hope was that she would listen to his prayer for forgiveness. With all his worldly wisdom John had not learned the fact that inconstancy does not destroy love in the one who suffers by reason of it; nor did he know of the exquisite pain-touched happiness which comes to a gentle, passionate heart such as Dorothy's from the mere act of forgiving.

"Is it possible you can forgive me for the miserable lies I have uttered?" asked John, almost unconscious of the words he was speaking. "Is it possible you can forgive me for uttering those lies, Dorothy?" he repeated.

She laid her head upon his breast, and softly passing her hand over the lace of his doublet, whispered : —

"If I could believe they were lies, I could easily forgive you," she answered between low sobs and soft sighs. Though she was a woman, the sweet essence of childhood was in her heart.

"But you cannot believe me, even when I tell you that I spoke not the truth," answered John, with growing faith in his system of passive repentance. Again came the sighs, and a few struggling, childish sobs.

"It is easy for us to believe that which we long to believe," she said. Then she turned her face upward to him, and John's reward was altogether disproportioned to the self-denial he had exercised a few minutes before. She rewarded him far beyond his deserts; and after a pause she said mischievously : —

"You told me that you were a bold man with women, and I know that at least that part of what you said was untrue, for you are a bashful man, John, you are downright bashful. It is I who have been bold. You were too timid to woo me, and I so longed for you that I — I — was not timid."

"For God's sake, Dorothy, I beg you to have pity and to make no jest of me. Your kindness almost kills me, and your ridicule —"

"There, there, John," whispered the girl, "I will never again make a jest of you if it gives you pain. Tell me, John, tell me truly, was it all false — that which you told me about the other women?"

There had been more truth in John's bragging than he cared to confess. He feared and loathed a lie; so he said evasively, but with perfect truth : —

"You must know, my goddess. If you do not know without the telling that I love you with all my being; if you do not know that there is for me and ever will be no woman but you in all the world; if you do not know that you have stolen my soul and that I live only in your presence, all that I can say will avail nothing toward convincing you. I am almost crazed with love for you, and with pain and torture. For the love of God let me leave you that I may hide my face."

"Never," cried the girl, clasping her hands about his neck and pressing her lips gently upon his. "Never. There, that will soothe you, won't it, John?"

It did soothe him, and in the next moment, John, almost frenzied with joy, hurt the girl by the violence of his embraces ; but she, woman-like, found her heaven in the pain.

They went back to the stone bench beside the gate, and after a little time Dorothy said : —

"But tell me, John, would you have kissed the other woman? Would you really have done it?"

John's honesty certainly was good policy in that instance The adroit girl had set a trap for him.

"I suppose I would," answered John, with a groan.

"It hurts me to hear the fact," said Dorothy, sighing; "but it pleases me to hear the truth. I know all else you tell me is true. I was trying you when I asked the question, for I certainly knew what you intended to do. A woman instinctively knows when a man is going to — to — when anything of that sort is about to happen."

"How does she know?" asked John.

Rocks and breakers ahead for Dorothy.

"I cannot tell you," replied the girl, naïvely, "but she knows."

"Perhaps it is the awakened desire in her own heart which forewarns her" said John, stealthily seeking from Dorothy a truth that would pain him should he learn it.

"I suppose that is partly the source of her knowledge," replied the knowing one, with a great show of innocence in her manner. John was in no position to ask impertinent questions, nor had he any right to grow angry at unpleasant discoveries; but he did both, although for a time he suppressed the latter.

"You believe she is sure to know, do you?" he asked.

"Usually," she replied. "Of course there are times when — when it happens so suddenly that — "

John angrily sprang to his feet, took a few hurried steps in front of Dorothy, who remained demurely seated with her eyes cast down, and then again he took his place beside her on the stone bench. He was trembling with anger and jealousy. The devil was in the girl that night for mischief.

"I suppose you speak from the fulness of your experience," demanded John, in tones that would have been insulting had they not been pleasing to the girl. She had seen the drift of John's questions at an early stage of the conversation, and his easily aroused jealousy was good proof to her of his affection. After all, she was in no danger from rocks and breakers. She well knew the currents, eddies, rocks, and shoals of the sea she was navigating, although she had never before sailed it. Her foremothers, all the way back to Eve, had been making charts of those particular waters for her especial benefit. Why do we, a slow-moving, cumbersome army of men, continue to do battle with the foe at whose hands defeat is always our portion?

"Experience?" queried Dorothy, her head turned to one side in a half-contemplative attitude. "Experience? Of course that is the only way we learn anything."

John again sprang to his feet, and again he sat down beside the girl. He had so recently received forgiveness for his own sins that he dared not be unforgiving toward Dorothy. He did not speak, and she remained silent, willing to allow time for the situation to take its full effect. The wisdom of the serpent is black ignorance compared with the cunning of a girl in Dorothy's situation. God gives her wit for the occasion as He gives the cat soft paws, sharp claws, and nimbleness. She was teaching John a lesson he would never forget. She was binding him to her with hoops of steel.

"I know that I have not the right to ask," said John, suppressing his emotions, "but may I know merely as a matter of trivial information — may I know the name of — of the person — this fellow with whom you have had so full an experience? God curse him! Tell me his name." He caught the girl violently by both arms as if he would shake the truth out of her. He was unconsciously making full amends for the faults he had committed earlier in the evening. The girl made no answer. John's powers of self-restraint, which were not of the strongest order, were exhausted, and he again sprang to his feet and stood towering before her in a passion. "Tell me his name," he said hoarsely. "I demand it. I will not rest till I kill him."

"If you would kill him, I surely will not tell you his name. In truth, I admit I am very fond of him."

"Speak not another word to me till you tell me his name," stormed John. I feel sorry for John when I think of the part he played in this interview; but every man knows well his condition.

"I care not," continued John, "in what manner I have

offended you, nor does my debt of gratitude to you for your generosity in forgiving my sins weigh one scruple against this you have told me. No man, unless he were a poor clown, would endure it; and I tell you now, with all my love for you, I will not — I will not!"

Dorothy was beginning to fear him. She of course did not fear personal violence; but after all, while he was slower than she, he was much stronger every way, and when aroused, his strength imposed itself upon her and she feared to play him any farther.

"Sit beside me, John, and I will tell you his name," said the girl, looking up to him, and then casting down her eyes. A dimpling smile was playing about her lips.

"No, I will not sit by you," replied John, angrily. She partly rose, and taking him by the arm drew him to her side.

"Tell me his name," again demanded John, sitting rigidly by Dorothy. "Tell me his name."

"Will you kill him?" she asked.

"That I will," he answered. "Of that you may rest assured."

"If you kill him, John, it will break my heart; for to do so, you must commit suicide. There is no other man but you, John. With you I had my first, last, and only experience."

John, of course, was speechless. He had received only what he deserved. I freely admit he played the part of a fool during this entire interview with Dorothy, and he was more fully convinced of the fact than either you or I can be. I do not like to have a fool for the hero of my history; but this being a history and not a romance, I must tell you of events just as they happened, and of persons exactly as they were, else my conscience will smite me for untruthfulness. Dorothy's last assault was too much for John. He could neither parry nor thrust.

Her heart was full of mirth and gladness.

"None other but you, John," she repeated, leaning forward in front of him, and looking up into his eyes. A ray of moonlight stealing its way between the forest boughs fell upon her upturned face and caused it to glow with a goddess-like radiance.

"None but you, John. There never has been and there never shall be another."

When John's consciousness returned he said, "Dorothy, can you love such a fool as I?"

"That I can and that I do with all my heart," she returned.

"And can you forgive me for this last fault — for doubting you?"

"That is easily done," she answered softly, "because doubt is the child of love."

"But you do not doubt me?" he replied.

"N-o-o," she answered somewhat haltingly; "but I — I am a woman."

"And a woman's heart is the home of faith," said John, reverentially.

"Y-e-s," she responded, still not quite sure of her ground. "Sometimes it is the home of too much faith, but faith, like virtue, is its own reward. Few persons are false to one who gives a blind, unquestioning faith. Even a poor degree of honor responds to it in kind."

"Dorothy, I am so unworthy of you that I stand abashed in your presence," replied John.

"No, you are not unworthy of me. We don't look for unmixed good in men," said the girl with a mischievous little laugh. Then seriously: "Those virtues you have are so great and so strong, John, that my poor little virtues, while they perhaps are more numerous than yours, are but weak things by comparison. In truth, there are some faults in men which we women do not — do not altogether dislike. They cause us — they make us — oh, I cannot express exactly what I mean. They make us more eager perhaps. A too constant man is like an overstrong sweet: he cloys us. The faults I speak of hurt us; but we thrive on them. Women enjoy pain now and then. Malcolm was telling me the other day that the wise people of the East have a saying: 'Without shadow there can be no light; without death there can be no life; without suffering there can be no joy.' Surely is that saying true of women. She who suffers naught enjoys naught. When a woman becomes passive, John, she is but a clod. Pain gives us a vent — a vent for something, I know not what it is; but this I know, we are happier for it."

"I fear, Dorothy, that I have given you too much 'vent,' as you call it," said John.

"No, no," she replied. "That was nothing. My great vent is that I can pour out my love upon you, John, without stint. Now that I know you are mine, I have some one whom I can deluge with it. Do you know, John, I believe that when God made me He collected together the requisite portions of reason, imagination, and will, — there was a great plenty of will, John, — and all the other ingredients that go to make a human being. But after He had gotten them all together there was still a great space left to be filled, and He just threw in an immensity of love with which to complete me. Therefore, John, am I not in true proportion. There is too much love in me, and it wells up at times and overflows my heart. How thankful I should be that I may pour it upon you and that it will not be wasted. How good you are to give me the sweet privilege."

"How thankful should I be, Dorothy. I have never known you till this night. I am unworthy — "

"Not another word of that sort, John," she interrupted, covering his mouth with her hand.

They stood for a long time talking a deal of celestial nonsense which I shall not give you. I fear I have already given you too much of what John and Dorothy did and said in this very sentimental interview. But in no other way can I so well make you to know the persons of whom I write. I might have said Dorothy was so and so, and John was such and such. I might have analyzed them in long, dull pages of minute description; but it is that which persons do and say that gives us true concept of their characters; what others say about them is little else than a mere statement that black is black and white is white. But to my story again.

Dorothy by her beauty had won John's admiration when first he beheld her. When he met her afterward, her charms of mind and her thousand winsome ways moved him deeply. But upon the evening of which I am now telling you he beheld for the first time her grand burning soul, and he saw her pure heart filled to overflowing with its dangerous burden of love, right from the hands of God Himself, as the girl had said. John was of a coarser fibre than she who had put him up for her idol; but his sensibilities were keen, and at their awakening he saw clearly the worth of the priceless treasure which propitious fate had given him in the love of Dorothy, and he sat humbly at her feet. Yet she knew it not, but sat humbly at John's feet the happiest woman in all the world because of her great good fortune in having a demigod upon whom she could lavish the untold wealth of her heart. If you are a woman, pray God that He may touch your eyes with Dorothy's blessed blindness. There is a heaven in the dark for you, if you can find it.

I must leave the scene, though I am loath to do so. Seldom do we catch a glimpse of a human soul, and more seldom still does it show itself like a gust of God's breath upon the deep of eternity as it did that night in Dorothy.

After a time John said: "I have your promise to be my wife. Do you still wish to keep it?"

"What an absurd question, John," replied the girl, laughing softly and contentedly. "Why else am I here? Tell me, think you, John, should I be here if I were not willing and eager to — to keep that promise?"

"Will you go with me notwithstanding your father's hatred of my house?" he asked.

"Ah, truly that I will, John," she answered; "surely you know I will go with you."

"Let us go at once. Let us lose not a moment. We have already delayed too long," cried John in eager ecstasy.

"Not to-night, John; I cannot go to-night," she pleaded. "Think of my attire," and she drew my cloak more closely about her. "I cannot go with you this time. My father is angry with me because of you, although he does not know who you are. Is it not famous to have a lover in secret of whom nobody knows? Father is angry with me, and as I told you in my letter, he keeps me a prisoner in my rooms. Aunt Dorothy stands guard over me. The dear, simple old soul! She told me, thinking I was Malcolm, that she was too old to be duped by a girl! Oh, it was too comical!" And she threw back her head and gave forth a peal of laughter that John was reluctantly compelled to silence. "I would so delight to tell you of the scene when I was in Aunt Dorothy's room impersonating Malcolm; but I have so much else to say of more importance that I know I shall not tell the half. When you have left me, I shall remember what I most wished to say but forgot."

"No, John," she continued seriously, "my father has been cruel to me, and I try to make myself think I do not love him; but I fail, for I do love him." Tears were welling up in her eyes and stifling her voice. In a moment she continued: "It would kill him, John, were I to go with you now. I *will* go with you soon, — I give you my solemn promise to that — but I cannot go now, — not now. I cannot leave him and the others. With all his cruelty to me, I love him, John, next to you. He will not come to see me nor will he speak to me. Think of that." The tears that had welled up to her eyes fell in a piteous stream over her cheeks. "Aunt Dorothy and Madge," she continued, "are so dear to me that the thought of leaving them is torture. But I will go with you some day, John, some day soon, I promise you. They have always been kind and gentle to me, and I love them and my father and my dear home where I was born and where my sweet mother died — and Dolcy — I love them all so dearly that I must prepare myself to leave them, John, even to go with you. The heart strings of my whole life bind me to them. Forgive me, John, forgive me. You must think of the grief and pain I shall yet pass through to go to you. It is as I told you: we women reach heaven only through purgatory. I must forsake all else I love when I go to you. All, all! All that has been dear to me in life I must forsake for — for that which is dearer to me than life itself. I promise, John, to go with you, but — but forgive me. I cannot go to-night."

"Nor can I ask it of you, Dorothy," said John. "The sacrifice would be all on one side. I should forego nothing, and I should receive all. You would forego everything, and God help me, you would receive nothing worth having. I am unworthy —"

"Not that word, John," cried Dorothy, again covering his mouth with — well, not with her hand. "I shall give up a great deal," she continued, "and I know I shall suffer. I suffer even now when I think of it, for you must remember that I am rooted to my home and to the dear ones it shelters; but I will soon make the exchange,

John; I shall make it gladly when the time comes, because — because I feel that I could not live if I did not make it."

"My father has already consented to our marriage," said John. "I told him to-day all that had passed between you and me. He, of course, was greatly pained at first; but when I told him of your perfections, he said that if you and I were dear to each other, he would offer no opposition, but would welcome you to his heart."

"Is your father that — that sort of a man?" asked Dorothy, half in revery. "I have always heard — " and she hesitated.

"I know," replied John, "that you have heard much evil of my father, but — let us not talk on that theme. You will know him some day, and you may judge him for yourself. When will you go with me, Dorothy?"

"Soon, very soon, John," she answered. "You know father intends that I shall marry Lord Stanley. *I* intend otherwise. The more father hurries this marriage with my beautiful cousin the sooner I shall be — be your — that is, you know, the sooner I shall go with you."

"You will not allow your father to force you to marry Lord Stanley?" asked John, frightened by the thought.

"Ah," cried the girl, softly, "you know I told you that God had put into me a great plenty of will. Father calls it wilfulness; but whichever it is, it stands me in good hand now. You don't know how much I have of it! You never will know until I am your — your — wife." The last word was spoken in a soft, hesitating whisper, and her head sought shamefaced refuge on John's breast. Of course the magic word "wife" on Dorothy's lips aroused John to action, and — but a cloud at that moment passed over the moon and kindly obscured the scene.

"You do not blame me, John," said Dorothy, "because I cannot go with you to-night? You do not blame me?"

"Indeed I do not, my goddess," answered John. "You will soon be mine. I shall await your pleasure and your own time, and when you choose to come to me — ah, then — " And the kindly cloud came back to the moon.

CHAPTER X

THOMAS THE MAN-SERVANT

AFTER a great effort of self-denial John told Dorothy it was time for her to return to the Hall, and he walked with her down Bowling Green Hill to the wall back of the terrace garden.

Dorothy stood for a moment on the stile at the old stone wall, and John, clasping her hand, said : —

"You will perhaps see me sooner than you expect," and then the cloud considerately floated over the moon again, and John hurried away up Bowling Green Hill.

Dorothy crossed the terrace garden, going toward the door since known as "Dorothy's Postern." She had reached the top of the postern steps when she heard her father's voice, beyond the north wall of the terrace garden well up toward Bowling Green Hill. John, she knew, was at that moment climbing the hill. Immediately following the sound of her father's voice she heard another voice — that of her father's retainer, Sir John Guild. Then came the word "Halt!" quickly followed by the report of a fusil, and the sharp clinking of swords upon the hillside. She ran back to the wall, and saw the dimly outlined forms of four men. One of them was John, who was retreating up the hill. The others were following him. Sir George and Sir John Guild had unexpectedly returned from Derby. They had left their horses with the stable boys and were walking toward the kitchen door when Sir George noticed a man pass from behind the corner of the terrace garden wall and proceed up Bowling Green Hill. The man of course was John. Immediately Sir George and Guild, accompanied by a servant who was with them, started in pursuit of the intruder, and a moment afterward Dorothy heard her father's voice and the discharge of the fusil. She climbed to the top of the stile, filled with an agony of fear. Sir George was fifteen or twenty yards in advance of his companion, and when John saw that his pursuers were attacking him singly, he turned and quickly ran back to meet the warlike King of the Peak. By a few adroit turns with his sword John disarmed his antagonist, and rushing in upon him easily threw him to the ground by a wrestler's trick. Guild and the servant by that time were within six yards of Sir George and John.

"Stop!" cried Manners, "your master is on the ground at my feet. My sword point is at his heart. Make but one step toward me and Sir George Vernon will be a dead man."

Guild and the servant halted instantly.

"What are your terms?" cried Guild, speaking with the haste which he well knew was necessary if he would save his master's life.

"My terms are easy," answered John. "All I ask is that you allow me to depart in peace. I am here on no harmful errand, and I demand that I may depart and that I be not followed nor spied upon by any one."

"You may depart in peace," said Guild. "No one will follow you; no one will spy upon you. To this I pledge my knightly word in the name of Christ my Saviour."

John at once took his way unmolested up the hill and rode home with his heart full of fear lest his tryst with Dorothy had been discovered.

Guild and the servant assisted Sir George to rise, and the three started down the hill toward the stile where Dorothy was standing. She was hidden from them, however, by the wall. Jennie Faxton, who had been on guard while John and Dorothy were at the gate, at Dorothy's suggestion stood on top of the stile where she could easily be seen by Sir George when he approached.

"When my father comes here and questions you," said Dorothy to Jennie Faxton, "tell him that the man whom he attacked was your sweetheart."

"Never fear, mistress," responded Jennie. "I will have a fine story for the master."

Dorothy crouched inside the wall under the shadow of a bush, and Jennie waited on the top of the stile. Sir George, thinking the girl was Dorothy, lost no time in approaching her. He caught her roughly by the arm and turned her around that he might see her face.

"By God, Guild," he muttered, "I have made a mistake. I thought the girl was Doll."

He left instantly and followed Guild and the servant to the kitchen door. When Sir George left the stile, Dorothy hastened back to the postern of which she had the key, and hurried toward her room. She reached the door of her father's room just in time to see Sir George and Guild enter it. They saw her, and supposed her to be myself. If she hesitated, she was lost. But Dorothy never hesitated. To think, with her, was to act. She did not of course know that I was still in her apartments. She took the chance, however, and boldly followed Sir John Guild into her father's room. There she paused for a moment that she might not appear to be in too great haste, and then entered Aunt Dorothy's room where I was seated, waiting for her.

"Dorothy, my dear child," exclaimed Lady Crawford, clasping her arms about Dorothy's neck.

"There is no time to waste in sentiment, Aunt Dorothy," responded the girl. "Here are your sword and cloak, Malcolm. I thank you for their use. Don them quickly." I did so, and walked into Sir George's room, where that worthy old gentleman was dressing a slight wound in the hand. I stopped to speak with him; but he seemed disinclined to talk, and I left the room. He soon went to the upper court, and I presently followed him.

Dorothy changed her garments, and she, Lady Crawford, and Madge also came to the upper court. The braziers in the courtyard had been lighted and cast a glare over two score half-clothed men and women who had been aroused from their beds by the commotion of the conflict on the hillside. Upon the upper steps of the court yard stood Sir George and Jennie Faxton.

"Who was the man you were with?" roughly demanded Sir George of the trembling Jennie. Jennie's trembling was assumed for the occasion.

"I will not tell you his name," she replied with tears. "He is my sweetheart, and I will never come to the Hall again. Matters have come to a pretty pass when a maiden cannot speak with her sweetheart at the stile without he is set upon and beaten as if he were a hedgehog. My father is your leal henchman, and his daughter deserves better treatment at your hands than you have given me."

"There, there!" said Sir George, placing his hand upon her head. "I was in the wrong. I did not know you had a sweetheart who wore a sword. When I saw you at the stile, I was sure you were another. I am glad I was wrong." So was Dorothy glad.

"Everybody be off to bed," said Sir George. "Ben Shaw, see that the braziers are all blackened."

Dorothy, Madge, and Lady Crawford returned to the latter's room, and Sir George and I entered after them. He was evidently softened in heart by the night's adventures and by the mistake he supposed he had made.

A selfish man grows hard toward those whom he injures. A generous heart grows tender. Sir George was generous, and the injustice he thought he had done to Dorothy made him eager to offer amends. The active evil in all Sir George's wrong-doing was the fact that he conscientiously thought he was in the right. Many a man has gone to hell backward — with his face honestly toward heaven. Sir George had not spoken to Dorothy since the scene wherein the key to Bowling Green Gate played so important a part.

"Doll," said Sir George, "I thought you were at the stile with a man. I was mistaken. It was the Faxton girl. I beg your pardon, my daughter. I did you wrong."

"You do me wrong in many matters, father," replied Dorothy.

"Perhaps I do," her father returned, "perhaps I do, but I mean for the best. I seek your happiness."

"You take strange measures at times, father, to bring about my happiness," she replied.

"Whom God loveth He chasteneth," replied Sir George, dolefully.

"That manner of loving may be well enough for God," retorted Dorothy with no thought of irreverence, "but for man it is dangerous. Whom man loves he should cherish. A man who has a good, obedient daughter — one who loves him — will not imprison her, and, above all, he will not refuse to speak to her, nor will he cause her to suffer and to weep for lack of that love which is her right. A man has no right to bring a girl into this world and then cause her to suffer as you — as you —"

She ceased speaking and sought refuge in silent feminine eloquence — tears. One would have sworn she had been grievously injured that night.

"But I am older than you, Doll, and I know what is best for your happiness," said Sir George.

"There are some things, father, which a girl knows with

better, surer knowledge than the oldest man living. Solomon was wise because he had so many wives from whom he could absorb wisdom."

"Ah, well!" answered Sir George, smiling in spite of himself, "you will have the last word."

"Confess, father," she retorted quickly, "that you want the last word yourself."

"Perhaps I do want it, but I'll never have it," returned Sir George; "kiss me, Doll, and be my child again."

"That I will right gladly," she answered, throwing her arms about her father's neck and kissing him with real affection. Then Sir George said good night and started to leave. At the door he stopped, and stood for a little time in thought.

"Dorothy," said he, speaking to Lady Crawford, "I relieve you of your duty as a guard over Doll. She may go and come when she chooses."

"I thank you, George," said Aunt Dorothy. "The task has been painful to me."

Dorothy went to her father and kissed him again, and Sir George departed.

When the door was closed, Lady Crawford breathed a great sigh and said: "I thank Heaven, Dorothy, he does not know that you have been out of your room. How could you treat me so cruelly? How could you deceive me?"

"That, Aunt Dorothy," replied the niece, "is because you are not old enough yet to be a match for a girl who is — who is in love."

"Shame upon you, Dorothy!" said Lady Crawford. "Shame upon you, to act as you did, and now to speak so plainly about being in love! Malcolm said you were not a modest girl, and I am beginning to believe him."

"Did Malcolm speak so ill of me?" asked Dorothy, turning toward me with a smile in her eyes.

"My lady aunt," said I, turning to Lady Crawford, " when did I say that Dorothy was an immodest girl?"

"You did not say it," the old lady admitted. "Dorothy herself said it, and she proves her words to be true by speaking so boldly of her feelings toward this — this strange man. And she speaks before Madge, too."

"Perhaps Madge is in the same sort of trouble. Who knows?" cried Dorothy, laughing heartily. Madge blushed painfully. "But," continued Dorothy, seriously, "I am not ashamed of it; I am proud of it. For what else, my dear aunt, was I created but to be in love? Tell me, dear aunt, for what else was I created?"

"Perhaps you are right," returned the old lady, who in fact was sentimentally inclined.

"The chief end of woman, after all, is to love," said Dorothy. "What would become of the human race if it were not?"

"Child, child," cried the aunt, "where learned you such things?"

"They were written upon my mother's breast," continued Dorothy, "and I learned them when I took in my life with her milk. I pray they may be written upon my breast some day, if God in His goodness shall ever bless me with a baby girl. A man child could not read the words."

"Dorothy, Dorothy!" cried Lady Crawford, "you shock me. You pain me."

"Again I ask," responded Dorothy, "for what else was I created? I tell you, Aunt Dorothy, the world decrees that women shall remain in ignorance, or in pretended ignorance — in silence at least — regarding the things concerning which they have the greatest need to be wise and talkative."

"At your age, Dorothy, I did not have half your wisdom on the subject," answered Lady Crawford.

"Tell me, my sweet Aunt Dorothy, were you really in a state of ignorance such as you would have me believe?"

"Well," responded the old lady, hesitatingly, "I did not speak of such matters."

"Why, aunt, did you not?" asked Dorothy. "Were you ashamed of what God had done? Were you ashamed of His great purpose in creating you a woman, and in creating your mother and your mother's mother before you?"

"No, no, child; no, no. But I cannot argue with you. Perhaps you are right," said Aunt Dorothy.

"Then tell me, dear aunt, that I am not immodest and bold when I speak concerning that of which my heart is full to overflowing. God put it there, aunt, not I. Surely I am not immodest by reason of His act."

"No, no, my sweet child," returned Aunt Dorothy, beginning to weep softly. "No, no, you are not immodest. You are worth a thousand weak fools such as I was at your age."

Poor Aunt Dorothy had been forced into a marriage which had wrecked her life. Dorothy's words opened her aunt's eyes to the fact that the girl whom she so dearly loved was being thrust by Sir George into the same wretched fate through which she had dragged her own suffering heart for so many years. From that hour she was Dorothy's ally.

"Good night, Malcolm," said Lady Crawford, offering me her hand. I kissed it tenderly; then I kissed the sweet old lady's cheek and said:—

"I love you with all my heart, Aunt Dorothy."

"I thank you, Malcolm," she returned.

I took my leave, and soon Madge went to her room, leaving Dorothy and Lady Crawford together.

When Madge had gone the two Dorothys, one at each end of life, spanned the long years that separated them, and became one in heart by reason of a heartache common to both.

Lady Crawford seated herself and Dorothy knelt by her chair.

"Tell me, Dorothy," said the old lady, "tell me, do you love this man so tenderly, so passionately that you cannot give him up?"

"Ah, my dear aunt," the girl responded, "words cannot tell. You cannot know what I feel."

"Alas! I know only too well, my child. I, too, loved a man when I was your age, and none but God knows what I suffered when I was forced by my parents and the priests to give him up, and to wed one whom — God help me — I loathed."

"Oh, my sweet aunt!" cried Dorothy softly, throwing her arms about the old lady's neck and kissing her cheek. "How terribly you must have suffered!"

"Yes," responded Lady Crawford, "and I am resolved you shall not endure the same fate. I hope the man who has won your love is worthy of you. Do not tell me his name, for I do not wish to practise greater deception toward your father than I must. But you may tell me of his station in life, and of his person, that I may know he is not unworthy of you."

"His station in life," answered Dorothy, "is far better than mine. In person he is handsome beyond any woman's wildest dream of manly beauty. In character he is noble, generous, and good. He is far beyond my deserts, Aunt Dorothy."

"Then why does he not seek your hand from your father?" asked the aunt.

"That I may not tell you, Aunt Dorothy," returned the girl, "unless you would have me tell you his name, and that I dare not do. Although he is vastly my superior in station, in blood, and in character, still my father would kill me before he would permit me to marry this man of my choice; and I, dear aunt, fear I shall die if I have him not."

Light slowly dawned upon Aunt Dorothy's mind, and she exclaimed in a terrified whisper: —

"My God, child, is it he?"

"Yes," responded the girl, "yes, it is he."

"Do not speak his name, Dorothy," the old lady said. "Do not speak his name. So long as you do not tell me, I cannot know with certainty who he is." After a pause Aunt Dorothy continued, "Perhaps, child, it was his father whom I loved and was compelled to give up."

"May the blessed Virgin pity us, sweet aunt," cried Dorothy, caressingly.

"And help us," returned Lady Crawford. "I, too, shall help you," she continued. "It will be through no fault of mine if your life is wasted as mine has been."

Dorothy kissed her aunt and retired.

Next morning when Dorothy arose a song came from her heart as it comes from the skylark when it sees the sun at dawn — because it cannot help singing. It awakened Aunt Dorothy, and she began to live her life anew, in brightness, as she steeped her soul in the youth and joyousness of Dorothy Vernon's song.

I have spoken before in this chronicle of Will Dawson. He was a Conformer. Possibly it was by reason of his religious faith that he did not share the general enmity that existed in Haddon Hall against the house of Rutland. He did not, at the time of which I speak, know Sir John Manners, and he did not suspect that the heir to Rutland was the man who had of late been causing so much trouble to the house of Vernon. At least, if he did suspect it, no one knew of his suspicions.

Sir George made a great effort to learn who the mysterious interloper was, but he wholly failed to obtain any clew to his identity. He had jumped to the conclusion that Dorothy's mysterious lover was a man of low degree. He had taken for granted that he was an adventurer whose station and person precluded him from openly wooing his daughter. He did not know that the heir to Rutland was in the Derbyshire country; for John, after his first meeting with Dorothy, had carefully concealed his presence from everybody save the inmates of Rutland. In fact, his mission to Rutland required secrecy, and the Rutland servants and retainers were given to understand as much. Even had Sir George known of John's presence at Rutland, the old gentleman's mind could not have compassed the thought that Dorothy, who, he believed, hated the race of Manners with an intensity equalled only by his own feelings, could be induced to exchange a word with a member of the house. His uncertainty was not the least of his troubles; and although Dorothy had full liberty to come and go at will, her father kept constant watch over her. As a matter of fact, Sir George had given Dorothy liberty partly for the purpose of watching her, and he hoped to discover thereby and, if possible, to capture the man who had brought trouble to his household. Sir George had once hanged a man to a tree on Bowling Green Hill by no other authority than his own desire. That execution was the last in England under the old Saxon law of Infangthef and Outfangthef. Sir George had been summoned before Parliament for the deed; but the writ had issued against the King of the Peak, and that being only a sobriquet, was neither Sir George's name nor his title. So the writ was quashed, and the high-handed act of personal justice was not farther investigated by the authorities. Should my cousin capture his daughter's lover, there would certainly be another execution under the old Saxon law. So you see that my friend Manners was tickling death with a straw for Dorothy's sake.

One day Dawson approached Sir George and told him that a man sought employment in the household of Haddon Hall. Sir George placed great confidence in his forester; so he told Dawson to employ the man if his services were needed. The new servant proved to be a fine, strong fellow, having a great shock of carrot-colored hair and a bushy beard of rusty red.

Dawson engaged the newcomer, and assigned to him the duty of kindling the fires in the family apartments of the Hall. The name of the new servant was Thomas Thompson, a name that Dorothy soon abbreviated to Tom-Tom.

One day she said to him, by way of opening the acquaintance, "Thomas, you and I should be good friends; we have so much in common."

"Thank you, my lady," responded Thomas, greatly pleased. "I hope we shall be good friends; indeed, indeed I do, but I cannot tell wherein I am so fortunate as to have anything in common with your Ladyship. What is it, may I ask, of which we have so much in common?"

"So much hair," responded Dorothy, laughing.

"It were blasphemy, lady, to compare my hair with yours," returned Thomas. "Your hair, I make sure, is such as the blessed Virgin had. I ask your pardon for speaking so plainly; but your words put the thought into my mind, and perhaps they gave me license to speak."

Thomas was on his knees, placing wood upon the fire.

"Thomas," returned Dorothy, "you need never apologize to a lady for making so fine a speech. I declare a courtier could not have made a better one."

"Perhaps I have lived among courtiers, lady," said Thomas.

"I doubt not," replied Dorothy, derisively. "You would have me believe you are above your station. It is the way with all new servants. I suppose you have seen fine company and better days."

"I have never seen finer company than now, and I have never known better days than this," responded courtier Thomas. Dorothy thought he was presuming on her condescension, and was about to tell him so when he continued: "The servants at Haddon Hall are gentlefolk compared with servants at other places where I have worked, and I desire nothing more than to find favor in Sir George's eyes. I would do anything to achieve that end."

Dorothy was not entirely reassured by Thomas's closing words; but even if they were presumptuous, she admired his wit in giving them an inoffensive turn. From that day forth the acquaintance grew between the servant and mistress until it reached the point of familiarity at which Dorothy dubbed him Tom-Tom.

Frequently Dorothy was startled by remarks made by Thomas, having in them a strong dash of familiarity; but he always gave to his words a harmless turn before she could resent them. At times, however, she was not quite sure of his intention.

Within a week after Thomas's advent to the hall, Dorothy began to suspect that the new servant looked upon her with eyes of great favor. She frequently caught him watching her, and at such times his eyes, which Dorothy thought were really very fine, would glow with an ardor all too evident. His manner was cause for amusement rather than concern, and since she felt kindly toward the new servant, she thought to create a faithful ally by treating him graciously. She might, she thought, need Thomas's help when the time should come for her to leave Haddon Hall with John, if that happy time should ever come. She did not realize that the most dangerous, watchful enemy to her cherished scheme would be a man who was himself in love with her, even though he were a servant, and she looked on Thomas's evident infatuation with a smile. She did not once think that in the end it might cause her great trouble, so she accepted his mute admiration, and thought to make use of it later on. To Tom, therefore, Dorothy was gracious.

John had sent word to Dorothy, by Jennie Faxton, that he had gone to London, and would be there for a fortnight or more.

Sir George had given permission to his daughter to ride out whenever she wished to do so, but he had ordered that Dawson or I should follow in the capacity of spy, and Dorothy knew of the censorship, though she pretended ignorance of it. So long as John was in London she did not care who followed her; but I well knew that when Manners should return, Dorothy would again begin manœuvring, and that by some cunning trick she would see him.

One afternoon I was temporarily absent from the Hall and Dorothy wished to ride. Dawson was engaged, and when Dorothy had departed, he ordered Tom to ride after his mistress at a respectful distance. Nearly a fortnight had passed since John had gone to London, and when Dorothy rode forth that afternoon she was beginning to hope he might have returned, and that by some delightful possibility he might then be loitering about the old trysting-place at Bowling Green Gate. There was a half-unconscious conviction in her heart that he would be there. She determined, therefore, to ride toward Rowsley, to cross the Wye at her former fording-place, and to go up to Bowling Green Gate on the Devonshire side of the Haddon wall. She had no reason, other than the feeling born of her wishes, to believe that John would be there; but she loved the spot for the sake of the memories which hovered about it. She well knew that some one would follow her from the Hall; but she felt sure that in case the spy proved to be Dawson or myself, she could easily arrange matters to her satisfaction, if by good fortune she should find her lover at the gate.

Tom rode so far behind his mistress that she could not determine who was following her. Whenever she brought Dolcy to a walk, Tom-Tom also walked his horse. When Dorothy galloped, he galloped; but after Dorothy had crossed the Wye and had taken the wall over into the Devonshire lands, Tom also crossed the river and wall and quickly rode to her side. He uncovered and bowed low with a familiarity of manner that startled her. The act of riding up to her and the manner in which he took his place by her side were presumptuous to the point of insolence, and his attitude, although not openly offensive, was slightly alarming. She put Dolcy to a gallop; but the servant who, she thought, was presuming on her former graciousness, kept close at Dolcy's heels. The man was a stranger, and she knew nothing of his character. She was alone in the forest with him, and she did not know to what length his absurd passion for her might lead him. She was alarmed, but she despised cowardice, although she knew herself to be a coward, and she determined to ride to the gate, which was but a short distance ahead of her. She resolved that if the insolent fellow continued his familiarity, she would teach him a lesson he would never forget. When she was within a short distance of the gate she sprang from Dolcy and handed her rein to her servant. John was not there, but she went to the gate in the hope that a letter might be hidden beneath the stone bench where Jennie was wont to find them in times past. Dorothy found no letter, but she could not resist the temptation to sit down upon the bench where he and she had sat, and to dream over the happy moments she had spent there. Tom, instead of holding the horses, hitched them, and walked toward Dorothy. That act on

Q

the part of her servant was effrontery of the most insolent sort. Will Dawson himself would not have dared do such a thing. It filled her with alarm, and as Tom approached she was trying to determine in what manner she would crush him. But when the audacious Thomas, having reached the gate, seated himself beside his mistress on the stone bench, the girl sprang to her feet in fright and indignation. She began to realize the extent of her fool-hardiness in going to that secluded spot with a stranger.

"How dare you approach me in this insolent fashion?" cried Dorothy, breathless with fear.

"Mistress Vernon," responded Thomas, looking boldly up into her pale face, "I wager you a gold pound sterling that if you permit me to remain here by your side ten minutes you will be unwilling —"

"John, John!" cried the girl, exultantly. Tom snatched the red beard from his face, and Dorothy, after one fleeting, luminous look into his eyes, fell upon her knees and buried her face in her hands. She wept, and John, bending over the kneeling girl, kissed her sunlit hair.

"Cruel, cruel," sobbed Dorothy. Then she lifted her head and clasped her hands about his neck. "Is it not strange," she continued, "that I should have felt so sure of seeing you? My reason kept telling me that my hopes were absurd, but a stronger feeling full of the breath of certainty seemed to assure me that you would be here. It impelled me to come, though I feared you after we crossed the wall. But reason, fear, and caution were powerless to keep me away."

"You did not know my voice," said John, "nor did you penetrate my disguise. You once said that you would recognize me though I wore all the petticoats in Derbyshire."

"Please don't jest with me now," pleaded Dorothy. "I cannot bear it. Great joy is harder to endure than great grief. Why did you not reveal yourself to me at the Hall?" she asked plaintively.

"I found no opportunity," returned John, "others were always present."

I shall tell you nothing that followed. It is no affair of yours nor of mine.

They were overjoyed in being together once more. Neither of them seemed to realize that John, while living under Sir George's roof, was facing death every moment. To Dorothy, the fact that John, who was heir to one of England's noblest houses, was willing for her sake to become a servant, to do a servant's work, and to receive the indignities constantly put upon a servant, appealed most powerfully. It added to her feeling for him a tenderness which is not necessarily a part of passionate love.

It is needless for me to tell you that while John performed faithfully the duty of keeping bright the fires in Haddon Hall, he did not neglect the other flame — the one in Dorothy's heart — for the sake of whose warmth he had assumed the leathern garb of servitude and had placed his head in the lion's mouth.

At first he and Dorothy used great caution in exchanging words and glances, but familiarity with danger breeds contempt for it. So they utilized every opportunity that niggard chance offered, and blinded by their great longing soon began to make opportunities for speech with each other, thereby bringing trouble to Dorothy and deadly peril to John. Of that I shall soon tell you.

During the period of John's service in Haddon Hall negotiations for Dorothy's marriage with Lord Stanley were progressing slowly but surely. Arrangements for the marriage settlement by the Stanleys, and for Dorothy's dower to be given by Sir George, were matters that the King of the Peak approached boldly as he would have met any other affair of business. But the Earl of Derby, whose mind moved slowly, desiring that a generous portion of the Vernon wealth should be transferred with Dorothy

to the Stanley holdings without the delay incident to
Sir George's death, put off signing the articles of marriage
in his effort to augment the cash payment. In truth, the
great wealth which Dorothy would bring to the house of
Stanley was the earl's real reason for desiring her marriage
with his son. The earl was heavily in debt, and his estate
stood in dire need of help.

Sir George, though attracted by the high nobility of the
house of Stanley, did not relish the thought that the wealth
he had accumulated by his own efforts, and the Vernon
estates which had come down to him through centuries,
should go to pay Lord Derby's debts. He therefore insisted that Dorothy's dower should be her separate estate,
and demanded that it should remain untouched and un-
touchable by either of the Stanleys. That arrangement
did not suit my lord earl, and although the son since he
had seen Dorothy at Derby-town was eager to possess the
beautiful girl, his father did not share his ardor. Lawyers
were called in who looked expensively wise, but they accomplished the purpose for which they were employed. An
agreement of marriage was made and was drawn up on an
imposing piece of parchment, brave with ribbons, pompous
with seals, and fair in clerkly penmanship.

One day Sir George showed me the copy of the contract
which had been prepared for him. That evening at the
cost of much labor he and I went over the indenture word
for word, and when we had finished Sir George thought it
was very good indeed. He seemed to think that all difficulties in the way of the marriage were overcome when the
agreement that lay before us on the table had been achieved
between him and the earl. I knew Sir George's troubles
had only begun; for I was aware of a fact which it seemed
impossible for him to learn, though of late Dorothy had
given him much teaching thereto. I knew that he had
transmitted to his daughter a large portion of his own

fierce, stubborn, unbreakable will, and that in her it existed in its most deadly form — the feminine. To me after supper that night was assigned the task of reading and rereading many times to Sir George the contents of the beautiful parchment. When I would read a clause that particularly pleased my cousin, he insisted on celebrating the event by drinking a mug of liquor drawn from a huge leather stoup which sat upon the table between us. By the time I had made several readings of the interesting document the characters began to mingle in a way that did not impart ease and clearness to my style. Some of the strange combinations which I and the liquor extracted from amid the seals and ribbons puzzled Sir George not a little. But with each new libation he found new clauses and fresh causes for self-congratulation, though to speak exact truth I more than once married Sir George to the Earl of Derby, and in my profanity gave Lord James Stanley to the devil to have and to hold.

Sir George was rapidly falling before his mighty enemy, drink, and I was not far behind him, though I admit the fault with shame. My cousin for a while was mightily pleased with the contract; but when the liquor had brought him to a point where he was entirely candid with himself, he let slip the fact that after all there was regret at the bottom of the goblet, metaphorically and actually. Before his final surrender to drink he dropped the immediate consideration of the contract and said : —

"Malcolm, I have in my time known many fools, but if you will permit an old man, who loves you dearly, to make a plain statement of his conviction — "

"Certainly," I interrupted.

"It would be a great relief to me," he continued, "to say that I believe you to be the greatest fool the good God ever permitted to live."

"I am sure, Sir George, that your condescending flattery is very pleasing," I said.

Sir George, unmindful of my remark, continued, "Your disease is not usually a deadly malady, as a look about you will easily show; but, Malcolm, if you were one whit more of a fool, you certainly would perish."

I was not offended, for I knew that my cousin meant no offence.

"Then, Sir George, if the time ever comes when I wish to commit suicide, I have always at hand an easy, painless mode of death. I shall become only a little more of a fool." I laughingly said, "I will do my utmost to absorb a little wisdom now and then as a preventive."

"Never a bit of wisdom will you ever absorb. A man who would refuse a girl whose wealth and beauty are as great as Dorothy's, is past all hope. I often awaken in the dark corners of the night when a man's troubles stalk about his bed like livid demons; and when I think that all of this evil which has come up between Dorothy and me, and all of this cursed estrangement which is eating out my heart could have been averted if you had consented to marry her, I cannot but feel—"

"But, Sir George," I interrupted, "it was Dorothy, not I, who refused. She could never have been brought to marry me."

"Don't tell me, Malcolm; don't tell me," cried the old man, angrily. Drink had made Sir George sullen and violent. It made me happy at first; but with liquor in excess there always came to me a sort of frenzy.

"Don't tell me," continued Sir George. "There never lived a Vernon who couldn't win a woman if he would try. But put all that aside. She would have obeyed me. I would have forced her to marry you, and she would have thanked me afterward."

"You could never have forced her to marry me," I replied.

"But that I could and that I would have done," said Sir George. "The like is done every day. Girls in these modern times are all perverse, but they are made to yield. Take the cases of Sir Thomas Mobley, Sir Grant Rhodas, and William Kimm. Their daughters all refused to marry the men chosen for them, but the wenches were made to yield. If I had a daughter who refused to obey me, I would break her; I would break her. Yes, by God, I would break her if I had to kill her," and the old man brought his clenched hand down upon the oak table with a crash. His eyes glared frightfully, and his face bore a forbidding expression which boded no good for Dorothy.

"She will make trouble in this matter," Sir George continued, tapping the parchment with his middle finger. "She will make trouble about this ; but, by God, Malcolm, she shall obey me."

He struck the oaken table another great blow with his fist, and glared fiercely across at me.

"Lord Wyatt had trouble with his daughter when he made the marriage with Devonshire," continued Sir George. "A damned good match it was, too, for the girl. But she had her heart set on young Gillman, and she refused to obey her father. She refused, by God, point blank, to obey her father. She refused to obey the man who had given her life. What did Wyatt do ? He was a man who knew what a child owes to its father, and, by God, Malcolm, after trying every other means to bring the wench to her senses, after he had tried persuasion, after having in two priests and a bishop to show her how badly she was acting, and after he had tried to reason with her, he whipped her; yes, he whipped her till she bled — till she bled, Malcolm, I tell you. Ah, Wyatt knew what is due from a child to its parents. The whipping failed to bring the perverse huzzy to obedience, so Wyatt threw her into a dungeon and starved her till — till — "

"Till she died," I interrupted.

"Yes, till she died," mumbled Sir George, sullenly, " till she died, and it served her right, by God, served her right."

The old man was growing very drunk, and everything was beginning to appear distorted to me. Sir George rose to his feet, leaned toward me with glaring eyes, struck the table a terrible blow with his fist, and said: —

"By the blood of God I swear that if Doll refuses to marry Stanley, and persists in her refusal, I'll whip her. Wyatt is a man after my own heart. I'll starve her. I'll kill her. Ay, if I loved her ten thousand times more than I do, I would kill her or she should obey me."

Then dawned upon me a vision of terrible possibilities. I was sure Sir George could not force Dorothy to marry against her will; but I feared lest he might kill her in his effort to "break her." I do not mean that I feared he would kill her by a direct act, unless he should do so in a moment of frenzy induced by drink and passion, but I did fear for the results of the breaking process. The like had often happened. It had happened in the case of Wyatt's daughter. Dorothy under the intoxicating influence of her passion might become so possessed by the spirit of a martyr that she could calmly take a flogging, but my belief was that should matters proceed to that extreme, should Sir George flog his daughter, the chords of her highly strung nature would snap under the tension, and she would die. I loved Dorothy for the sake of her fierce, passionate, tender heart, and because she loved me; and even in my sober, reflective moments I had resolved that my life, ay, and Sir George's life also, should stand between the girl and the lash. If in calmness I could deliberately form such a resolution, imagine the effect on my liquor-crazed brain of Sir George's words and the vista of horrors they disclosed. I was intoxicated. I was drunk. I say it with shame; and on hearing Sir George's threat my half-frenzied imagination ran riot into the foreboding future.

All the candles, save one tottering wick, were dead in their sockets, and the room was filled with lowering phantom-like shadows from oaken floor to grimy vaulted roof beams. Sir George, hardly conscious of what he did and said, all his evil passions quickened with drink, leaned his hands upon the table and glared across at me. He seemed to be the incarnation of rage and ferocity, to so great a pitch had he wrought himself. The sputtering candle feebly flickered, and seemed to give its dim light only that the darksome shadows might flit and hover about us like vampires on the scent of blood. A cold perspiration induced by a nameless fear came upon me, and in that dark future to which my heated imagination travelled I saw, as if revealed by black magic, fair, sweet, generous Dorothy, standing piteously upon Bowling Green hillside. Over her drooping form there hung in air a monster cloudlike image of her father holding in its hand a deadly bludgeon. So black, so horrid was this shadow-demon that I sprang from my chair with a frightful oath, and shrieked:—

"Hell is made for man because of his cruelty to woman."

Sir George had sunk into his chair. Liquor had finished its work, and the old man, resting his head upon his folded arms, leaned forward on the table. He was drunk — dead to the world. How long I stood in frenzied stupor gazing at shadow-stricken Dorothy upon the hillside I do not know. It must have been several minutes. Blood of Christ, how vividly I remember the vision! The sunny radiance of the girl's hair was darkened and dead. Her bending attitude was one of abject grief. Her hands covered her face, and she was the image of woe. Suddenly she lifted her head with the quick impulsive movement so familiar in her, and with a cry eloquent as a child's wail for its mother called, "John," and held out her arms imploringly toward the dim shadowy form of her lover standing upon the hill crest. Then John's form began to fade, and as its shadowy essence grew dim, despair slowly stole like a mask of death over Dorothy's face. She stood for a moment gazing vacantly into space. Then she fell to the ground, the shadow of her father hovering over her prostrate form, and the words, "Dead, dead, dead," came to me in horrifying whispers from every dancing shadow-demon in the room.

In trying to locate the whispers as they reverberated from floor to oaken rafters, I turned and saw Sir George. He looked as if he were dead.

"Why should you not be dead in fact?" I cried. "You would kill your daughter. Why should I not kill you? That will solve the whole question."

I revelled in the thought; I drank it in; I nursed it; I cuddled it; I kissed it. Nature's brutish love for murder had deluged my soul. I put my hand to my side for the purpose of drawing my sword or my knife. I had neither with me. Then I remember staggering toward the fireplace to get one of the fire-irons with which to kill my cousin. I remember that when I grasped the fire-iron, by the strange working of habit I employed it for the moment in its proper use; and as I began to stir the embers on the hearth, my original purpose was forgotten. That moment of habit-wrought forgetfulness saved me and saved Sir George's life. I remember that I sank into the chair in front of the fireplace, holding the iron, and I thank God that I remember nothing more.

During the night the servants aroused me, and I staggered up the stone stairway of Eagle Tower and clambered into my room.

The next morning I awakened feeling ill. There was a taste in my mouth as if I had been chewing a piece of the devil's boot over night. I wanted no breakfast, so I climbed to the top of the tower, hoping the fresh morning breeze might cool my head and cleanse my mouth. For a moment or two I stood on the tower roof bareheaded and open-mouthed while I drank in the fresh, purifying air. The sweet draught helped me physically; but all the winds of Boreas could not have blown out of my head the vision of the previous night. The question, "Was it prophetic?" kept ringing in my ears, answerless save by a superstitious feeling of fear. Then the horrid thought that I had only by a mere chance missed becoming a murderer came upon me, and again was crowded from my mind by the memory of Dorothy and the hovering spectre which had hung over her head on Bowling Green hillside.

I walked to the north side of the tower and on looking down the first person I saw was our new servant, Thomas, holding two horses at the mounting stand. One of them was Dolcy, and I, feeling that a brisk ride with Dorothy would help me to throw off my wretchedness, quickly descended the tower stairs, stopped at my room for my hat and cloak, and walked around to the mounting block Dorothy was going to ride, and I supposed she would prefer me to the new servant as a companion.

I asked Thomas if his mistress were going out for a ride and he replied affirmatively.

"Who is to accompany her?" I asked.

"She gave orders for me to go with her," he answered.

"Very well," I responded, "take your horse back to the stable and fetch mine." The man hesitated, and twice he began to make reply, but finally he said:—

"Very well, Sir Malcolm."

He hitched Dolcy to the ring in the mounting block and started back toward the stable leading his own horse. At that moment Dorothy came out of the tower gate, dressed for the ride. Surely no woman was ever more beautiful than she that morning.

"Tom-Tom, where are you taking the horse?" she cried.

"To the stable, Mistress," answered the servant. "Sir Malcolm says he will go with you."

Dorothy's joyousness vanished. From radiant brightness her expression changed in the twinkling of an eye to a look of disappointment so sorrowful that I at once knew there was some great reason why she did not wish me to ride with her. I could not divine the reason, neither did I try. I quickly said to Thomas:—

"Do not bring my horse. If Mistress Vernon will excuse me, I shall not ride with her this morning. I forgot for the moment that I had not breakfasted."

Again came to Dorothy's face the radiant look of joy as if to affirm what it had already told me. I looked toward Thomas, and his eyes, too, were alight. I could make nothing of it. Thomas was a fine-looking fellow, notwithstanding his preposterous hair and beard; but I felt sure there could be no understanding between the man and his mistress.

When Thomas and Dorothy had mounted, she timidly ventured to say:—

"We are sorry, Cousin Malcolm, that you cannot ride with us."

She did not give me an opportunity to change my mind, but struck Dolcy a sharp blow with her whip that sent the spirited mare galloping toward the dove-cote, and Thomas quickly followed at a respectful distance. From the dove-cote Dorothy took the path down the Wye toward Rowsley. I, of course, connected her strange conduct with John. When a young woman who is well balanced physically, mentally, and morally acts in a strange, unusual manner, you may depend on it there is a man somewhere behind her motive.

I knew that John was in London. Only the night before I had received word from Rutland Castle that he had not returned, and that he was not expected home for many days.

So I concluded that John could not be behind my fair

cousin's motive. I tried to stop guessing at the riddle
Dorothy had set me, but my effort was useless. I wondered and thought and guessed, but I brought to myself
only the answer, "Great is the mystery of womanhood."

After Dorothy had ridden away I again climbed to the
top of Eagle Tower and saw the riders cross the Wye at
Dorothy's former fording-place, and take the wall. I then
did a thing that fills me with shame when I think of it.
For the only time in my whole life I acted the part of a
spy. I hurried to Bowling Green Gate, and horror upon
horror, there I beheld my cousin Dorothy in the arms of
Thomas, the man-servant. I do not know why the truth
of Thomas's identity did not dawn upon me, but it did not,
and I stole away from the gate, thinking that Dorothy,
after all, was no better than the other women I had known
at various times in my life, and I resolved to tell John
what I had seen. You must remember that the women I
had known were of the courts of Mary Stuart and of Guise,
and the less we say about them the better. God pity
them! Prior to my acquaintance with Dorothy and Madge
I had always considered a man to be a fool who would put
his faith in womankind. To me women were as good as
men, — no better, no worse. But with my knowledge of
those two girls there had grown up in me a faith in woman's
virtue which in my opinion is man's greatest comforter; the
lack of it his greatest torment.

I went back to Eagle Tower and stood at my window
looking down the Wye, hoping soon to see Dorothy returning home. I did not feel jealousy in the sense that a lover
would feel it; but there was a pain in my heart, a mingling
of grief, anger, and resentment because Dorothy had de-
stroyed not only my faith in her, but, alas! my sweet, new-
born faith in womankind. Through her fault I had fallen
again to my old, black belief that virtue was only another
name for the lack of opportunity. It is easy for a man

who has never known virtue in woman to bear and forbear the lack of it; but when once he has known the priceless treasure, doubt becomes excruciating pain.

After an hour or two Dorothy and her servant appeared at the ford and took the path up the Wye toward Haddon. Thomas was riding a short distance behind his accommodating mistress, and as they approached the Hall, I recognized something familiar in his figure. At first, the feeling of recognition was indistinct, but when the riders drew near, something about the man — his poise on the horse, a trick with the rein or a turn with his stirrup, I could not tell what it was — startled me like a flash in the dark, and the word "John!" sprang to my lips. The wonder of the thing drove out of my mind all power to think. I could only feel happy, so I lay down upon my bed and soon dropped off to sleep.

When I awakened I was rapt in peace, for I had again found my treasured faith in womankind. I had hardly dared include Madge in my backsliding, but I had come perilously near doing it, and the thought of my narrow escape from such perfidy frightened me. I have never taken the risk since that day. I would not believe the testimony of my own eyes against the evidence of my faith in Madge.

I knew that Thomas was Sir John Manners, and yet I did not know it certainly. I determined, if possible, to remain in partial ignorance, hoping that I might with some small show of truth be able to plead ignorance should Sir George accuse me of bad faith in having failed to tell him of John's presence in Haddon Hall. That Sir George would sooner or later discover Thomas's identity I had little doubt. That he would kill him should he once have him in his power, I had no doubt at all. Hence, although I had awakened in peace concerning Dorothy, you may understand that I awakened to trouble concerning John.

CHAPTER XI

The Cost Mark of Joy

PEACE had been restored between Dorothy and her father. At least an armistice had been tacitly declared. But, owing to Dorothy's knowledge of her father's intention that she should marry Lord Stanley, and because of Sir George's feeling that Dorothy had determined to do nothing of the sort, the belligerent powers maintained a defensive attitude which rendered an absolute reconciliation impossible. They were ready for war at a moment's notice.

The strangest part of their relation was the failure of each to comprehend and fully to realize the full strength of the other's purpose. Dorothy could not bring herself to believe that her father, who had until within the last few weeks, been kind and indulgent to her, seriously intended to force her into marriage with a creature so despicable as Stanley. In fact, she did not believe that her father could offer lasting resistance to her ardent desire in any matter. Such an untoward happening had never befallen her. Dorothy had learned to believe from agreeable experience that it was a crime in any one, bordering on treason, to thwart her ardent desires. It is true she had in certain events, been compelled to coax and even to weep gently. On a few extreme occasions she had been forced to do a little storming in order to have her own way; but that any presumptuous individuals should resist her will after the storming had been resorted to was an event of such recent happening in her life that she had not grown familiar with the thought of it. Therefore, while she felt that her father might seriously annoy her with the Stanley project, and while she realized that she might be compelled to resort to the storming process in a degree thitherto uncalled for, she believed that the storm she would raise would blow her father entirely out of his absurd and utterly untenable position. On the other hand, while Sir George anticipated trouble with Dorothy, he had never been able to believe that she would absolutely refuse to obey him. In those olden times — now nearly half a century past — filial disobedience was rare. The refusal of a child to obey a parent, and especially the refusal of a daughter to obey her father in the matter of marriage, was then looked upon as a crime and was frequently punished in a way which amounted to barbarous ferocity. Sons, being of the privileged side of humanity, might occasionally disobey with impunity, but woe to the poor girl who dared set up a will of her own. A man who could not compel obedience from his daughter was looked upon as a poor weakling, and contempt was his portion in the eyes of his fellow-men — in the eyes of his fellow-brutes, I should like to say.

Growing out of such conditions was the firm belief on the part of Sir George that Dorothy would in the end obey him ; but if by any hard chance she should be guilty of the high crime of disobedience — Well! Sir George intended to prevent the crime. Perhaps mere stubborness and fear of the contempt in which he would be held by his friends in case he were defeated by his own daughter were no small parts of Sir George's desire to carry through the enterprise in which he had embarked with the Stanleys. Although there was no doubt in Sir George's mind that he would eventually conquer in the conflict with Dorothy, he had a profound respect for the power of his antagonist to do temporary battle, and he did not care to enter into actual hostilities until hostilities should become actually necessary.

Therefore, upon the second day after I had read the beribboned, besealed contract to Sir George, he sent an advance guard toward the enemy's line. He placed the ornamental piece of parchment in Lady Crawford's hands and directed her to give it to Dorothy.

But before I tell you of the parchment I must relate a scene that occurred in Aunt Dorothy's room a few hours after I recognized John as he rode up the Wye with Dorothy. It was late in the afternoon of the day after I read the contract to Sir George and saw the horrid vision on Bowling Green.

I was sitting with Madge at the west window of Dorothy's parlor. We were watching the sun as it sank in splendor beneath Overhaddon Hill.

I should like first to tell you a few words — only a few, I pray you — concerning Madge and myself. I will.

I have just said that Madge and I were watching the sun at the west window, and I told you but the truth, for Madge had learned to see with my eyes. Gladly would I have given them to her outright, and willingly would I have lived in darkness could I have given light to her. She gave light to me — the light of truth, of purity, and of exalted motive. There had been no words spoken by Madge nor me to any one concerning the strange and holy chain that was welding itself about us, save the partial confession which she had whispered to Dorothy. But notwithstanding our silence, our friends in the Hall understood that Madge and I were very dear to each other. I, of course, saw a great deal of her; but it was the evening hour at the west window to which I longingly looked forward all the day. I am no poet, nor do my words and thoughts come with the rhythmic flow and eloquent

R

imagery of one to whom the talent of poesy is given. But during those evening hours it seemed that with the soft touch of Madge's hand there ran through me a current of infectious dreaming which kindled my soul till thoughts of beauty came to my mind and words of music sprang to my lips such as I had always considered not to be in me. It was not I who spoke; it was Madge who saw with my eyes and spoke with my voice. To my vision, swayed by Madge's subtle influence, the landscape became a thing of moving beauty and of life, and the floating clouds became a panorama of ever shifting pictures. I, inspired by her, described so eloquently the wonders I saw that she, too, could see them. Now a flock of white-winged angels rested on the low-hung azure of the sky, watching the glory of Phœbus as he drove his fiery steeds over the western edge of the world. Again, Mount Olympus would grow before my eyes, and I would plainly see Jove sitting upon his burnished throne, while gods and goddesses floated at his feet and revelled on the fleecy mountain sides. Then would mountain, gods, and goddesses dissolve, — as in fact they did dissolve ages ago before the eyes of millions who had thought them real, — and in their places perhaps would come a procession of golden-maned lions, at the description of which would Madge take pretended fright. Again, would I see Madge herself in flowing white robes made of the stuff from which fleecy clouds are wrought. All these wonders would I describe, and when I would come to tell her of the fair cloud image of herself I would seize the joyous chance to make her understand in some faint degree how altogether lovely in my eyes the vision was. Then would she smile and softly press my hand and say : —

"Malcolm, it must be some one else you see in the cloud," though she was pleased.

But when the hour was done then came the crowning

moment of the day, for as I would rise to take my leave, if perchance we were alone, she would give herself to my arms for one fleeting instant and willingly would her lips await—but there are moments too sacred for aught save holy thought. The theme is sweet to me, but I must go back to Dorothy and tell you of the scene I have promised you.

As I have already said, it was the evening following that upon which I had read the marriage contract to Sir George, and had seen the vision on the hillside. Madge and I were sitting at the west window. Dorothy, in kindness to us, was sitting alone by the fireside in Lady Crawford's chamber. Thomas entered the room with an armful of fagots, which he deposited in the fagot-holder. He was about to replenish the fire, but Dorothy thrust him aside, and said :—

"You shall kindle no more fires for me. At least you shall not do so when no one else is by. It pains me that you, at whose feet I am unworthy to kneel, should be my servant."

Thereupon she took in her hands the fagot John had been holding. He offered to prevent her, but she said :—

"Please, John, let me do this."

The doors were open, and we heard all that was said by Dorothy and Tom. Madge grasped my hand in surprise and fear.

"Please, John," said Dorothy, "if it gives me pleasure to be your servant, you should not wish to deny me. There lives but one person whom I would serve. There, John, I will give you another, and you shall let me do as I will."

Dorothy, still holding the fagot in her hands, pressed it against John's breast and gently pushed him backward toward a large armchair, in which she had been sitting by the west side of the fireplace.

"You sit there, John, and we will make believe that this is our house, and that you have just come in very cold from a ride, and that I am making a fine fire to warm you. Isn't it pleasant, John? There, you sit and warm yourself — my — my — husband," she said laughingly. "It is fine sport even to play at. There is one fagot on the fire," she said, as she threw the wood upon the embers, causing them to fly in all directions. John started up to brush the scattered embers back into the fireplace, but Dorothy stopped him.

"I will put them all back," she said. "You know you are cold and very tired. You have been overseeing the tenantry and have been hunting. Will you have a bowl of punch, my — my husband?" and she laughed again and kissed him as she passed to the holder for another fagot.

"I much prefer that to punch," said John, laughing softly. "Have you more?"

"Thousands of them, John, thousands of them." She rippled forth a little laugh and continued: "I occupy my time nowadays in making them that I may always have a great supply when we are — that is, you know, when you — when the time comes that you may require a great many to keep you in good humor." Again came the laugh, merry and clear as the tinkle of sterling silver.

She laughed again within a minute or two; but when the second laugh came, it sounded like a knell.

Dorothy delighted to be dressed in the latest fashion. Upon this occasion she wore a skirt vast in width, of a pattern then much in vogue. The sleeves also were preposterously large, in accordance with the custom of the times. About her neck a beautiful white linen ruff stood out at least the eighth part of an ell. The day had been damp and cold, and the room in which she had been sitting was chilly. For that reason, most fortunately, she had thrown over her shoulders a wide sable cloak broad enough to enfold her many times and long enough to reach nearly to her knees: Dorothy thus arrayed was standing in front of John's chair. She had just spoken the words "good humor," when the door leading to her father's room opened and in walked Sir George. She and her ample skirts and broad sleeves were between John and the door. Not one brief instant did Dorothy waste in thought. Had she paused to put in motion the machinery of reason, John would have been lost. Thomas sitting in Lady Crawford's chair and Dorothy standing beside him would have told Sir George all he needed to know. He might not have discovered John's identity, but a rope and a tree in Bowling Green would quickly have closed the chapter of Dorothy's mysterious love affair. Dorothy, however, did not stop to reason nor to think. She simply acted without preliminary thought. as the rose unfolds or as the lightning strikes. She quietly sat down upon John's knees, leaned closely back against him, spread out the ample folds of her skirt, threw the lower parts of her broad cape over her shoulders and across the back of the chair, and Sir John Manners was invisible to mortal eyes.

"Come in, father," said Dorothy, in dulcet tones that should have betrayed her.

"I heard you laughing and talking," said Sir George, "and I wondered who was with you."

"I was talking to Madge and Malcolm who are in the other room," replied Dorothy.

"Did not Thomas come in with fagots?" asked Sir George.

"I think he is replenishing the fire in the parlor, father, or he may have gone out. I did not notice. Do you want him?"

"I do not especially want him," Sir George answered.

"When he finishes in the parlor I will tell him that you want him," said Dorothy.

"Very well," replied Sir George.

He returned to his room, but he did not close the door.

The moment her father's back was turned Dorothy called : —

"Tom-Tom, father wants you," and instantly Thomas was standing deferentially by her side, and she was seated in the great chair. It was a rapid change, I assure you. But a man's life and his fortune for good or ill often hang upon a tiny peg — a second of time protruding from the wall of eternity. It serves him briefly ; but if he be ready for the vital instant, it may serve him well.

"Yes, mistress," said Thomas, "I go to him at once."

John left the room and closed the door as he passed out. Then it was that Dorothy's laugh sounded like the chilling tones of a knell. It was the laugh of one almost distraught. She came to Madge and me laughing, but the laugh quickly changed to convulsive sobs. The strain of the brief moment during which her father had been in Lady Crawford's room had been too great for even her strong nerves to bear. She tottered and would have fallen had I not caught her. I carried her to the bed, and Madge called Lady Crawford. Dorothy had swooned.

When she wakened she said dreamily : —

"I shall always keep this cloak and gown."

Aunt Dorothy thought the words were but the incoherent utterances of a dimly conscious mind, but I knew they were the deliberate expression of a justly grateful heart.

The following evening trouble came about over the matter of the marriage contract.

You remember I told you that Sir George had sent Lady Crawford as an advance guard to place the parchment in the enemy's hands. But the advance guard feared the enemy and therefore did not deliver the contract directly to Dorothy. She placed it conspicuously upon the table, knowing well that her niece's curiosity would soon prompt an examination.

I was sitting before the fire in Aunt Dorothy's room, talking to Madge when Lady Crawford entered, placed the parchment on the table, and took a chair by my side. Soon Dorothy entered the room. The roll of parchment, brave with ribbons, was lying on the table. It attracted her attention at once, and she took it in her hands.

"What is this?" she asked carelessly. Her action was prompted entirely by idle curiosity. That, by the way, was no small motive with Dorothy. She had the curiosity of a young doe. Receiving no answer, she untied the ribbons and unrolled the parchment to investigate its contents for herself. When the parchment was unrolled, she began to read:—

"In the name of God, amen. This indenture of agreement, looking to union in the holy bonds of marriage between the Right Honorable Lord James Stanley of the first part, and Mistress Dorothy Vernon of Haddon of the second part—"

She read no farther. She crumpled the beautiful parchment in her hands, walked over to the fire, and quietly placed the sacred instrument in the midst of the flames. Then she turned away with a sneer of contempt upon her face and — again I grieve to tell you this — said:—

"In the name of God, amen. May this indenture be damned."

"Dorothy!" exclaimed Lady Crawford, horrified at her niece's profanity. "I feel shame for your impious words."

"I don't care what you feel, aunt," retorted Dorothy, with a dangerous glint in her eyes. "Feel as you wish, I meant what I said, and I will say it again if you would like to hear it. I will say it to father when I see him. Now, Aunt Dorothy, I love you and I love my father, but I give you fair warning there is trouble ahead for any one who crosses me in this matter."

She certainly looked as if she spoke the truth. Then

she hummed a tune under her breath—a dangerous signal in Dorothy at certain times. Soon the humming turned to whistling. Whistling in those olden days was looked upon as a species of crime in a girl.

Dorothy stood by the window for a short time and then taking up an embroidery frame, drew a chair nearer to the light and began to work at her embroidery. In a moment or two she stopped whistling, and we could almost feel the silence in the room. Madge, of course, only partly knew what had happened, and her face wore an expression of expectant, anxious inquiry. Aunt Dorothy looked at me, and I looked at the fire. The parchment burned slowly. Lady Crawford, from a sense of duty to Sir George and perhaps from politic reasons, made two or three attempts to speak, and after five minutes of painful silence she brought herself to say:—

"Dorothy, your father left the contract here for you to read. He will be angry when he learns what you have done. Such disobedience is sure to—"

"Not another word from you," screamed Dorothy, springing like a tigress from her chair. "Not another word from you or I will—I will scratch you. I will kill some one. Don't speak to me. Can't you see that I am trying to calm myself for an interview with father? An angry brain is full of blunders. I want to make none. I will settle this affair with father. No one else, not even you, Aunt Dorothy, shall interfere." The girl turned to the window, stood beating a tattoo upon the glass for a moment or two, then went over to Lady Crawford and knelt by her side. She put her arms about Aunt Dorothy's neck, softly kissed her, and said:—

"Forgive me, dear aunt; forgive me. I am almost crazed with my troubles. I love you dearly indeed, indeed I do."

Madge gropingly went to Dorothy's side and took her hand. Dorothy kissed Madge's hand and rose to her feet.

"Where is my father?" asked Dorothy, to whom a repentant feeling toward Lady Crawford had brought partial calmness. "I will go to him immediately and will have this matter over. We might as well understand each other at once. Father seems very dull at understanding me. But he shall know me better before long."

Sir George may have respected the strength of his adversary, but Dorothy had no respect for the strength of her foe. She was eager for the fray. When she had a disagreeable thing to do, she always wanted to do it quickly.

Dorothy was saved the trouble of seeking her father, for at that moment he entered the room.

"You are welcome, father," said Dorothy in cold, defiant tones. "You have come just in time to see the last flickering flame of your fine marriage contract." She led him to the fireplace. "Does it not make a beautiful smoke and blaze?"

"Did you dare —"

"Ay, that I did," replied Dorothy.

"You dared?" again asked her father, unable to believe the evidence of his eyes.

"Ay, so I said; that I did," again said Dorothy.

"By the death of Christ —" began Sir George.

"Now be careful, father, about your oaths," the girl interrupted. "You must not forget the last batch you made and broke."

Dorothy's words and manner maddened Sir George. The expression of her whole person, from her feet to her hair, breathed defiance. The poise of her body and of her limbs, the wild glint in her eyes, and the turn of her head, all told eloquently that Sir George had no chance to win and that Dorothy was an unconquerable foe. It is a wonder he did not learn in that one moment that he could never bring his daughter to marry Lord Stanley.

"I will imprison you," cried Sir George, gasping with rage.

"Very well," responded Dorothy, smilingly. "You kept me prisoner for a fortnight. I did not ask you to liberate me. I am ready to go back to my apartments."

"But now you shall go to the dungeon," her father said.

"Ah, the dungeon!" cried the girl, as if she were delighted at the thought. "The dungeon! Very well, again. I am ready to go to the dungeon. You may keep me there the remainder of my natural life. I cannot prevent you from doing that, but you cannot force me to marry Lord Stanley."

"I will starve you until you obey me!" retorted her father. "I will starve you!"

"That, again, you may easily do, my dear father; but again I tell you I will never marry Stanley. If you think I fear to die, try to kill me. I do not fear death. You have it not in your power to make me fear you or anything you can do. You may kill me, but I thank God it requires my consent for my marriage to Stanley, and I swear before God that never shall be given."

The girl's terrible will and calm determination staggered Sir George, and by its force beat down even his strong will. The infuriated old man wavered a moment and said: —

"Fool, I seek only your happiness in this marriage. Only your happiness. Why will you not consent to it?

I thought the battle was over, and that Dorothy was the victor. She thought so, too, but was not great enough to bear her triumph silently. She kept on talking and carried her attack too far.

"And I refuse to obey because of my happiness. I refuse because I hate Lord Stanley, and because, as you already know, I love another man."

When she spoke the words "because I love another man," the cold, defiant expression of her face changed to one of ecstasy.

"I will have you to the dungeon this very hour, you brazen huzzy," cried Sir George.

"How often, father, shall I repeat that I am ready to go to the dungeon? I am eager to obey you in all things save one."

"You shall have your wish," returned Sir George. "Would that you had died ere you had disgraced your house with a low-bred dog whose name you are ashamed to utter."

"Father, there has been no disgrace," Dorothy answered, and her words bore the ring of truth.

"You have been meeting the fellow at secluded spots in the forest — how frequently you have met him God only knows — and you lied to me when you were discovered at Bowling Green Gate."

"I would do it again gladly if I but had the chance," answered the girl, who by that time was reckless of consequences.

"But the chance you shall not have," retorted Sir George.

"Do not be too sure, father," replied Dorothy. She was unable to resist the temptation to mystify him. "I may see him before another hour. I will lay you this wager, father, if I do not within one hour see the man — the man whom I love — I will marry Lord Stanley. If I see him within that time you shall permit me to marry him. I have seen him two score times since the day you surprised me at the gate."

That was a dangerous admission for the girl to make, and she soon regretted it with all her heart. Truly she was right. An angry brain is full of blunders.

Of course Dorothy's words, which were so full of meaning to Madge and me, meant little to Sir George. He looked upon them only as irritating insolence on her part. A few minutes later, however, they became full of significance.

Sir George seemed to have forgotten the Stanley marriage and the burning of the contract in his quarrel with Dorothy over her unknown lover.

Conceive, if you can, the situation in Haddon Hall at that time. There was love-drunk Dorothy, proud of the skill which had enabled her to outwit her wrathful father. There was Sir George, whose mental condition, inflamed by constant drinking, bordered on frenzy because he felt that his child, whom he had so tenderly loved from the day of her birth, had disgraced herself with a low-born wretch whom she refused to name. And there, under the same roof, lived the man who was the root and source of all the trouble. A pretty kettle of fish!

"The wager, father, will you take it?" eagerly asked Dorothy.

Sir George, who thought that her words were spoken only to anger him, waved her off with his hands and said: —

"I have reason to believe that I know the wretch for whose sake you have disgraced yourself. You may be sure that I shall soon know him with certainty. When I do, I will quickly have him in my power. Then I will hang him to a tree on Bowling Green, and you shall see the low-born dog die."

"He is better born than any of our house," retorted Dorothy, who had lost all sense of caution. "Ay, he is better born than any with whom we claim kin."

Sir George stood in open-eyed wonder, and Dorothy continued: "You cannot keep him from me. I shall see him, and I will have him despite you. I tell you again, I have seen him two score times since you tried to spy upon us at Bowling Green Gate, and I will see him whenever I choose, and I will wed him when I am ready to do so. You cannot prevent it. You can only be forsworn, oath upon oath; and if I were you, I would stop swearing."

Sir George, as was usual with him in those sad times, was inflamed with drink, and Dorothy's conduct, I must admit, was maddening. In the midst of her taunting Thomas stepped into the room bearing an armful of fagots. Sir George turned to him and said : —

"Go and tell Welch to bring a set of manacles."

"For Mistress Dorothy?" Thomas asked, surprised into the exclamation.

"Curse you, do you mean to bandy words with me, you scum?" cried Sir George.

He snatched a fagot from John and drew back his arm to strike him. John took one step back from Sir George and one step nearer to Dorothy.

"Yes, Thomas," said Dorothy, sneeringly, "bring Welch with the manacles for me. My dear father would put me in the dungeon out of the reach of other men, so that he may keep me safely for my unknown lover. Go, Thomas. Go, else father will again be forsworn before Christ and upon his knighthood."

"This before a servant! I'll gag you, you hellish vixen," cried Sir George. Then I am sure he knew not what he did. "Curse you!" he cried, as he held the fagot upraised and rushed upon Dorothy. John, with his arms full of fagots, could not avert the blow which certainly would have killed the girl, but he could take it. He sprang between Dorothy and her father, the fagot fell upon his head, and he sank to the floor. In his fall John's wig dropped off, and when the blood began to flow from the wound Dorothy kneeled beside his prostrate form. She snatched the great bush of false beard from his face and fell to kissing his lips and his hands in a paroxysm of passionate love and grief. Her kisses she knew to be a panacea for all ills John could be heir to, and she thought they would heal even the wound her father had given, and stop the frightful outpouring of John's

life-blood.   The poor girl, oblivious of all save her wounded
lover, murmured piteously : —

"John, John, speak to me ; 'tis Dorothy."   She placed
her lips near his ear and whispered : " 'Tis Dorothy, John.
Speak to her."   But she received no response.   Then came
a wild light to her eyes and she cried aloud :   "John, 'tis
Dorothy.   Open your eyes.   Speak to me, John ! oh, for
God's sake speak to me !   Give some little sign that you
live," but John was silent.   "My God, my God !   Help,
help !   Will no one help me save this man ?   See you
not that his life is flowing away ?   This agony will kill
me.   John, my lover, my lord, speak to me.   Ah, his
heart, his heart !   I will know."   She tore from his breast
the leathern doublet and placed her ear over his heart.
"Thank God, it beats ! " she cried in a frenzied whisper,
as she kissed his breast and turned her ear again to hear
his heart's welcome throbbing.   Then she tried to lift
him in her arms and succeeded in placing his head
in her lap.   It was a piteous scene.   God save me from
witnessing another like it.

After Dorothy lifted John's head to her lap he began to
breathe perceptibly, and the girl's agitation passed away as
she gently stroked his hair and kissed him over and over
again, softly whispering her love to his unresponsive ear
in a gentle frenzy of ineffable tenderness such as was
never before seen in this world, I do believe.   I wish with
all my heart that I were a maker of pictures so that I
might draw for you the scene which is as clear and vivid
in every detail to my eyes now as it was upon that awful
day in Haddon Hall.   There lay John upon the floor and
by his side knelt Dorothy.   His head was resting in her
lap.   Over them stood Sir George with the murderous
fagot raised, as if he intended again to strike.   I had
sprung to his side and was standing by him, intending to
fell him to the floor should he attempt to repeat the blow

upon either Dorothy or John. Across from Sir George and me, that is, upon the opposite side of Dorothy and John, stood Lady Crawford and Madge, who clung to each other in terror. The silence was heavy, save when broken by Dorothy's sobs and whispered ejaculations to John. Sir George's terrible deed had deprived all of us, including himself, of the power to speak. I feared to move from his side lest he should strike again. After a long agony of silence he angrily threw the fagot away from him and asked : —

"Who is this fellow?   Can any one tell me?"

Only Madge, Dorothy, and I could have given him true answer. By some strange power of divination Madge had learned all that had happened, and she knew as well as I the name of the man who lay upon the floor battling with death. Neither Madge nor I answered.

"Who is this fellow?" again demanded Sir George.

Dorothy lifted her face toward her father.

"He is the man whom you seek, father," she answered, in a low, tearful voice. "He is my lover ; he is my life ; he is my soul, and if you have murdered him in your attempt to kill your own child, all England shall hear of it and you shall hang. He is worth more in the eyes of the queen than we and all our kindred. You know not whom you have killed."

Sir George's act had sobered him.

"I did not intend to kill him — in that manner," said Sir George, dropping his words absent-mindedly. "I hoped to hang him. Where is Dawson? Some one fetch Dawson."

Several of the servants had gathered about the open door in the next room, and in obedience to Sir George's command one of them went to seek the forester. I feared that John would die from the effects of the blow ; but I also knew from experience that a man's head may receive very hard knocks and life still remain. Should John recover and should Sir George learn his name, I was sure that my violent cousin would again attempt the personal administration of justice and would hang him, under the old Saxon law. In that event Parliament would not be so easily pacified as upon the occasion of the former hanging at Haddon; and I knew that if John should die by my cousin's hand, Sir George would pay for the act with his life and his estates. Fearing that Sir George might learn through Dawson of John's identity, I started out in search of Will to have a word with him before he could see his master. I felt sure that for many reasons Will would be inclined to save John; but to what extent his fidelity to the cause of his master might counteract his resentment of Sir George's act, I did not know. I suspected that Dawson was privy to John's presence in Haddon Hall, but I was not sure of it, so I wished to prepare the forester for his interview with Sir George and to give him a hint of my plans for securing John's safety, in the event he should not die in Aunt Dorothy's room.

When I opened the door in the Northwest Tower I saw Dawson coming toward the Hall from the dove-cote, and I hastened forward to meet him. It was pitiful that so good a man as Sir George Vernon was, should have been surrounded in his own house by real friends who were also traitors. That was the condition of affairs in Haddon Hall, and I felt that I was the chief offender. The evil, however, was all of Sir George's making. Tyranny is the father of treason.

When I met Dawson I said: "Will, do you know who Tom-Tom is?"

The forester hesitated for a moment, and said, "Well, Sir Malcolm, I suppose he is Thomas —"

"No, no, Will, tell me the truth. Do you know that he is — or perhaps by this time I should say he was — Sir John Manners?"

"Was?" cried Will. "Great God! Has Sir George discovered — is he dead? If he is dead, it will be a sad day for Sir George and for Haddon Hall. Tell me quickly."

I at once knew Will Dawson was in the secret. I answered: —

"I hope he is not dead. Sir George attempted to strike Dorothy with a fagot, but Thomas stepped in front of her and received the blow. He is lying almost, if not quite, dead in Lady Crawford's room. Sir George knows nothing about him, save that he is Dorothy's lover. But should Thomas revive I feel sure my cousin will hang him in the morning unless steps are taken to prevent the deed."

"Sir Malcolm, if you will stand by me," said Dawson, "Sir George will not hang him."

"I certainly will stand by you, Dawson. Have no doubt on that score. Sir George intends to cast John into the dungeon, and should he do so I want you to send Jennie Faxton to Rutland and have her tell the Rutlanders to rescue John to-night. To-morrow morning I fear will be too late. Be on your guard, Will. Do not allow Sir George to discover that you have any feeling in this matter. Above all, lead him from the possibility of learning that Thomas is Sir John Manners. I will contrive to admit the Rutland men at midnight."

I hastened with Dawson back to the Hall, where we found the situation as I had left it. John's head was lying on Dorothy's lap, and she was trying to dress his wound with pieces of linen torn from her clothing. Sir George was pacing to and fro across the room, breaking forth at times in curses against Dorothy because of her relations with a servant.

When Dawson and I entered the room, Sir George spoke angrily to Will: —

"Who is this fellow? You employed him. Who is he?"

s

"He gave me his name as Thomas Thompson," returned Will, "and he brought me a favorable letter of recommendation from Danford."

Danford was forester to the Duke of Devonshire, and lived at Chatsworth.

"There was naught in the letter save that he was a good servant and an honest man. That is all we can ask of any man."

"But who is he ?" again demanded Sir George.

"Your worship may perhaps learn from Danford more than I can tell you," replied the forester, adroitly avoiding a lie.

"Think of it, Malcolm," said Sir George, speaking to me. "Think of it. My daughter, my only child, seeks for her husband this low-born serving man. I have always been sure that the fellow would prove to be such." Then he turned to Dawson: "Throw the fellow into the dungeon. If he lives till morning, I will have him hanged. To the dungeon with him."

Sir George waved his hand toward Dawson and Tom Welch, and then stepped aside. Will made an effort to hide his feelings, and without a word or gesture that could betray him, he and Welch lifted John to carry him away. Then it was piteous to see Dorothy. She clung to John and begged that he might be left with her. Sir George violently thrust her away from John's side, but she, still upon her knees, grasped her father's hand and cried out in agony : —

"Father, let me remain with him. If you have ever felt love for me, and if my love for you has ever touched one tender spot in your heart, pity me now and leave this man with me, or let me go with him. I beg you, father ; I plead ; I implore. He may be dying. We know not. In this hour of my agony be merciful to me."

But Sir George rudely repulsed her and left the room,

following Welch and Dawson, who bore John's unconscious form between them. Dorothy rose to her feet screaming and tried to follow John. I, fearing that in her frenzy of grief she might divulge John's name, caught her in my arms and detained her by force. She turned upon me savagely and struck me in her effort to escape. She called me traitor, villain, dog, but I lifted her in my arms and carried her struggling to her bedroom. I wanted to tell her of the plans which Dawson and I had made, but I feared to do so, lest she might in some way betray them, so I left her in the room with Lady Crawford and Madge. I told Lady Crawford to detain Dorothy at all hazards, and I whispered to Madge asking her to tell Dorothy that I would look to John's comfort and safety. I then hastily followed Sir George, Dawson, and Welch, and in a few moments I saw them leave John, bleeding and senseless, upon the dungeon floor. When Sir George's back was turned, Dawson by my orders brought the surgeon from the stable where he had been working with the horses. The surgeon bound up the wound in John's head and told me, to my great joy, that it was not fatal. Then he administered a reviving potion and soon consciousness returned. I whispered to John that Dawson and I would not forsake him, and, fearing discovery by Sir George, hurriedly left the dungeon.

I believe there is a certain amount of grief and sorrow which comes with every great joy to give it a cost mark whereby we may always know its value. The love between Dorothy and John indeed was marked in plain figures of high denominations.

CHAPTER XII

THE LEICESTER POSSIBILITY

ON leaving the dungeon I sought Madge, and after I had whispered a word to her from my heart I asked her to tell Dorothy the encouraging words of the surgeon, and also to tell her that she should not be angry with me until she was sure she had good cause. I dared not send a more explicit message, and I dared not go to Dorothy, for Sir George was in a suspicious mood and I feared ruin not only for myself but for John, should my violent cousin suspect me of sympathy with his daughter and her lover.

I also sought Aunt Dorothy and whispered a word to her of which you shall hear more presently.

"Ah, I cannot do it," cried the trembling old lady in response to my whispered request. "I cannot do it."

"But you must, Aunt Dorothy," I responded. "Upon it depend three lives: Sir George's, Dorothy's, and her lover's. You must do it."

"I will try," she replied.

"That assurance will not suit me," I responded. "You must promise upon your salvation that you will not fail me."

"I promise upon my salvation," replied Aunt Dorothy.

That evening of course we did not see the ladies at supper. Sir George and I ate in silence until my cousin became talkative from drink. Then he spoke bitterly of Dorothy's conduct, and bore with emphasis upon the fact that the lover to whom Dorothy had stooped was a low-born serving man.

"But Dorothy declares he is noble," I responded.

"She has lied to me so often that I do not believe a word she says," returned Sir George.

He swore oath upon oath that the wretch should hang in the morning, and for the purpose of carrying into effect his intention he called in Joe the butcher and told him to make all things ready for the execution.

I did not attempt to thwart his purpose by word or gesture, knowing it would be useless, but hoped that John would be out of his reach long ere the cock would crow his first greeting to the morrow's sun.

After Sir George had drunk far into the night the servants helped him to bed, and he carried with him the key to the dungeon together with the keys to all the outer doors and gates of Haddon Hall, as was his custom. The keys were in a bunch, held together by an iron ring, and Sir George always kept them under his pillow at night.

I sought my bed in Eagle Tower and lay down in my clothes to rest and wait. The window of my room was open.

Within an hour after midnight I heard the hooting of an owl. The doleful sound came up to me from the direction of the stone footbridge at the southwest corner of the Hall below the chapel. I went to my window and looked out over the courts and terrace. Haddon Hall and all things in and about it were wrapped in slumbrous silence. I waited, and again I heard the hooting of the owl. Noise-lessly leaving my room I descended the stone steps to an unused apartment in the tower from which a window opened upon the roof of the north wing of the Hall. Along that roof I crept with bared feet, till I reached another roof, the battlements of which at the lowest point were not more than twenty feet from the ground. Thence I clambered down to a window cornice five or six feet lower, and jumped, at the risk of my limbs, the remaining distance of fifteen or sixteen feet to the soft sod beneath. I ran with all haste, took my stand under Aunt Dorothy's window, and whistled softly. The window casing opened and I heard the great bunch of keys jingling and clinking against the stone wall as Aunt Dorothy paid them out to me by means of a cord. After I had secured the keys I called in a whisper to Lady Crawford and directed her to leave the cord hanging from the window. I also told her to remain in readiness to draw up the keys when they should have served their purpose. Then I took them and ran to the stone footbridge where I found four Rutland men who had come in response to the message Dawson had sent by Jennie Faxton. Two of the men went with me, and we entered the lower garden by the southwest postern. Thence we crept noiselessly to the terrace and made our entrance into the Hall by "Dorothy's Postern." I had in my life engaged in many questionable and dangerous enterprises, but this was my first attempt at housebreaking. To say that I was nervous would but poorly define the state of my feelings. Since that day I have respected the high calling of burglary and regard with favor the daring knights of the skeleton key. I was frightened. I, who would feel no fear had I to fight a dozen men, trembled with fright during this adventure. The deathlike silence and the darkness in familiar places seemed uncanny to me. The very chairs and tables appeared to be sleeping, and I was fearful lest they should awaken. I cannot describe to you how I was affected. Whether it was fear or awe or a smiting conscience I cannot say, but my teeth chattered as if they were in the mouth of a fool, and my knees quaked as if they supported a coward. Still I knew I was doing my duty, though one's conscience sometimes smites him when his reason tells him he is acting righteously. It is more dangerous to possess a sensitive conscience which cannot be made to hear reason than to have none at all. But I will make short my account of that night's doings. The two Rutland men and I groped our way to the dungeon and carried forth John, who was weak from loss of blood. I told them to lock the door of the Hall as they passed out and to attach the keys to the cord hanging from Lady Crawford's window. Then I climbed to my room again, feeling in conscience like a criminal because I had done the best act of my life.

Early next morning I was awakened by a great noise in the upper court. When I looked out at my window I beheld Sir George. He was half dressed and was angrily questioning the servants and retainers. I knew that he had discovered John's escape, but I did not know all, nor did I know the worst. I dressed and went to the kitchen, where I bathed my hands and face. There I learned that the keys to the hall had been stolen from under Sir George's pillow, and that the prisoner had escaped from the dungeon. Old Bess, the cook, nodded her head wisely and whispered to me the words, " Good for Mistress Doll."

Bess's unsought confidence alarmed me. I did not relish the thought that Bess nor any one else should believe me to be in sympathy with Dorothy, and I said : —

" If Mistress Vernon had aught to do with last night's affairs, she should be full of shame. I will not believe that she knew of it at all. My opinion is that one of the servants was bribed by some person interested in Tom-Tom's escape."

" Believe nothing of the sort," retorted Bess. " It is the mistress and not the servant who stole the keys and liberated Tom-Tom. But the question is, who may Tom-Tom be ? and the servants' hall is full of it. We are not uncertain as to the manner of his escape. Some of the servants do say that the Earl of Leicester be now visiting the Duke

of Devonshire; and some also do say that his Lordship be
fond of disguises in his gallantry. They do also say that
the queen is in love with him, and that he must disguise
himself when he woos elsewhere, or she be's famously jealous. It would be a pretty mess the master has brought
us all into should Tom-Tom prove to be my lord Earl of
Leicester. We'd all hang and to hell."

"Bess, that tongue of yours will cost you your head one
of these good times," I remarked, while I rubbed my face
with the towel.

"I would sooner lose my head," retorted Bess, "than
have my mouth shut by fear. I know, Sir Malcolm, that
I'll not die till my time comes; but please the good God
when my time does come I will try to die talking."

"That you will," said I.

"True word, Sir Malcolm," she answered, and I left her
in possession of the field.

I went into the courtyard, and when Sir George saw me
he said, "Malcolm, come with me to my room; I want a
word with you."

We went to his room.

"I suppose you know of the fellow's escape last night?"
he said.

"Yes," I replied, "Bess told me about it in the kitchen."
It seemed to me that my words said, "I did it."

"Not only was the fellow liberated," said my cousin,
"but the keys to all the outer gates and doors of the Hall
have been stolen and carried away. Can you help me
unravel this affair?"

"Do you suspect any one of having stolen the keys?" I
asked.

"I know, of course, that Dorothy did it. Who her
accomplices were, if any she had, I do not know. I have
catechized the servants, but the question is bottomless to
me."

"Have you spoken to Dorothy on the subject?" I asked.

"No," he replied, "but I have sent word to her by the Faxton girl that I am going to see her at once. Come with me."

We went into Lady Crawford's room. She was ill and in bed. I did not wonder that she was ill after the experiences of the previous night. Sir George asked her if she had heard or seen Dorothy pass through her room during the night. She said: —

"Dorothy did not pass through this room last night. I did not once close my eyes in sleep, and I should have seen her had she been here at all."

Sir George entered Dorothy's bedroom, and Lady Crawford beckoned me to go to her side.

"I waited till sunrise," she said, "that I might draw up the keys."

"Hush!" said I, "the cord?"

"I burned it," she replied.

Then I followed Sir George into Dorothy's room. Madge was dressed for the day, and Dorothy, who had been helping her, was making her own toilet. Her hair hung loose and fell like a cataract of sunshine over her bare shoulders. But no words that I can write would give you a conception of her wondrous beauty, and I shall not waste them in the attempt. When we entered the room she was standing at the mirror. She turned, comb in hand, toward Sir George and said: —

"I suppose, father, you will accuse me of liberating Thomas."

"You must know that I will accuse you," replied Sir George.

"Then, father, for once you will accuse me falsely. I am overjoyed that he has escaped, and I certainly should have tried to liberate him had I thought it possible to do so.

But I did not do it, though to tell you the truth I am sorry I did not."

"I do not believe you," her father replied.

"I knew you would not believe me," answered Dorothy. "Had I liberated him I should probably have lied to you about it; therefore, I wonder not that you should disbelieve me. But I tell you again upon my salvation that I know nothing of the stealing of the keys nor of Tom-Tom's escape. Believe me or not, I shall deny it no more."

Madge gropingly went to Sir George's side, and he tenderly put his arms about her, saying:—

"I would that you were my daughter." Madge took his hand caressingly.

"Uncle, I want to tell you that Dorothy speaks the truth," she said. "I have been with her every moment since the terrible scene of yesterday evening. Neither Dorothy nor I closed our eyes in sleep all night long. She lay through the dark hours moaning, and I tried to comfort her. Our door was locked, and it was opened only by your messenger who brought the good news of Tom-Tom's escape. I say good news, uncle, because his escape has saved you from the stain of murder. You are too brave a man to do murder, uncle."

"How dare you," said Sir George, taking his arm from Madge's waist, "how dare you defend—"

"Now, uncle, I beg you pause and take a moment's thought," said Madge, interrupting him. "You have never spoken unkindly to me."

"Nor will I, Madge, so long as I live. I know there is not a lie in you, and I am sure you believe to be true all you tell me, but Dorothy has deceived you by some adroit trick."

"If she deceived me, she is a witch," retorted Madge, laughing softly.

"That I am almost ready to believe is the case," said Sir

George. Dorothy, who was combing her hair at the mirror, laughed softly and said : —

"My broomstick is under the bed, father."

Sir George went into Lady Crawford's room and shut the door, leaving me with the girls.

When her father had left, Dorothy turned upon me with fire in her eyes : —

"Malcolm Vernon, if you ever lay hands upon me again as you did last night, I will — I will scratch you. You pretended to be his friend and mine, but for a cowardly fear of my father you came between us and you carried me to this room by force. Then you locked the door and — and " —

"Did not Madge give you my message?" I asked, interrupting her.

"Yes, but did you not force me away from him when, through my fault, he was almost at death's door?"

"Have your own way, Dorothy," I said. "There lives not, I hope, another woman in the world so unreasoning and perverse as you."

She tossed her head contemptuously and continued to comb her hair.

"How, suppose you," I asked, addressing Dorothy's back, as if I were seeking information, "how, suppose you, the Rutland people learned that John was confined in the Haddon dungeon, and how did they come by the keys?"

The girl turned for a moment, and a light came to her anger-clouded face as the rainbow steals across the blackened sky.

"Malcolm, Malcolm," she cried, and she ran to me with her bare arms outstretched.

"Did you liberate him?" she asked. "How did you get the keys?"

"I know nothing of it, Dorothy, nothing," I replied.

"Swear it, Malcolm, swear it," she said.

"I will swear to nothing," I said, unclasping her arms from my neck.

"Then I will kiss you," she answered, "for you are my dear good brother, and never so long as I iive will I again doubt you."

But she did before long doubt me again, and with good cause.

Dorothy being in a gentle humor, I took advantage of the opportunity to warn her against betraying John's name to her father. I also told her to ask her father's forgiveness, and advised her to feign consent to the Stanley marriage. Matters had reached a point where some remedy, however desperate, must be applied.

Many persons, I fear, will condemn me for advising Dorothy to deceive her father; but what would you have had me do? Should I have told her to marry Stanley? Certainly not. Had I done so, my advice would have availed nothing. Should I have advised her to antagonize her father, thereby keeping alive his wrath, bringing trouble to herself and bitter regret to him? Certainly not The only course left for me to advise was the least of three evils — a lie. Three evils must be very great indeed when a lie is the least of them. In the vast army of evils with which this world swarms the lie usually occupies a proud position in the front rank. But at times conditions arise when, coward-like, he slinks to the rear and evils greater than he take precedence. In such sad case I found Dorothy, and I sought help from my old enemy, the lie. Dorothy agreed with me and consented to do all in her power to deceive her father, and what she could not do to that end was not worth doing.

Dorothy was anxious about John's condition, and sent Jennie Faxton to Bowling Green, hoping a letter would be there for her. Jennie soon returned with a letter, and

Dorothy once more was full of song, for John's letter told her that he was fairly well and that he would by some means see her soon again despite all opposition.

"At our next meeting, my fair mistress," John said in the letter, "you must be ready to come with me. I will wait no longer for you. In fairness to me and to yourself you shall not ask me to wait. I will accept no more excuses. You must come with me when next we meet."

"Ah, well," said Dorothy to Madge, "if I must go with him, I must. Why did he not talk in that fashion when we rode out together the last time? I like to be made to do what I want to do. He was foolish not to make me consent, or better still would it have been had he taken the reins of my horse and ridden off with me, with or against my will. I might have screamed, and I might have fought him, but I could not have hurt him, and he would have had his way, and — and," with a sigh, "I should have had my way."

After a brief pause devoted to thought, she continued: —

"If I were a man and were wooing a woman, I would first learn what she wanted to do and then — and then, by my word, I would make her do it."

I went from Dorothy's room to breakfast, where I found Sir George. I took my seat at the table and he said: —

"Who, in God's name, suppose you, could have taken the keys from my pillow?"

"Is there any one whom you suspect?" I asked for lack of anything else to say.

"I at first thought, of course, that Dorothy had taken them," he answered. "But Madge would not lie, neither would my sister. Dorothy would not hesitate to lie herself blue in the face, but for some reason I believed her when she told me she knew nothing of the affair. Her words sounded like truth for once."

"I think, Sir George," said I, "you should have left off 'for once.' Dorothy is not a liar. She has spoken falsely to you only because she fears you. I am sure that a lie is hateful to her."

"Malcolm, I wish I could have your faith," he responded. "By the way, Malcolm, have you ever seen the Earl of Leicester?"

"I saw him only once. He visited Scotland during the ceremonies at Queen Mary's return from France. I saw him once, and then but briefly. Why do you ask?"

"It is whispered among the servants," said Sir George, "that Leicester is at Chatsworth in disguise."

Chatsworth was the home of the Duke of Devonshire, and was but a short distance from Haddon. After Sir George spoke, I remembered the words of old Bess.

"Still, I do not know why you ask." I said.

"My reason is this," replied Sir George; "Dorothy declared the fellow was of noble blood. It is said that Leicester loves gallant adventure incognito. He fears her Majesty's jealousy if in such matters he acts openly. You remember the sad case of Mistress Robsart. I wonder what became of the girl? He made way with her in some murderous fashion, I am sure." Sir George remained in revery for a moment, and then the poor old man cried in tones of distress: "Malcolm, if that fellow whom I struck last night was Leicester, and if he has been trying his hellish tricks on my Doll I — I should pity her; I should not abuse her. I may have been wrong. If he has wronged Doll — if he has wronged my girl, I will pursue him to the ends of the earth for vengeance. That is why I ask if you have ever seen the Earl of Leicester. Was the man who lay upon the floor last night Robert Dudley? If it were he, and if I had known it, I would have beaten him to death then and there. Poor Doll!"

Any one hearing the old man speak would easily have

known that Doll was all that life held for him to love.

"I do not distinctly remember Leicester's face," I answered, "but since you speak of it, I believe there is a resemblance between him and the man we called Thomas. But even were it he, Sir George, you need have no fear for Dorothy. She of all women is able and willing to protect herself."

"I will go to Dorothy and ask her to tell me the truth. Come with me."

We again went to Dorothy's room. She had, since I last saw her, received the letter from John of which I have spoken, and when we entered her parlor where she and Madge were eating breakfast we found her very happy. As a result she was willing and eager to act upon my advice.

She rose and turned toward her father.

"You told me, Doll, that the fellow was of noble blood. Did you speak the truth?"

"Yes, father, I spoke the truth. There is no nobler blood in England than his, save that of our royal queen. In that you may believe me, father, for I speak the truth."

Sir George remained silent for a moment and then said: —

"If the man is he whom I believe him to be he can have no true purpose with you. Tell me, my child — the truth will bring no reproaches from me — tell me, has he misused you in any way?"

"No, father, before God, he has been a true gentleman to me."

The poor old man struggled for a moment with his emotions; then tears came to his eyes and he covered his face with his hands as he started to leave the room.

Dorothy ran to him and clasped her arms about his

neck. Those two, father and child, were surely of one blood as shown in the storms of violence and tenderness by which their natures were alternately swept.

"Father, you may believe me; you do believe me," said Dorothy. "Furthermore, I tell you that this man has treated me with all courtesy, nay, more : he has treated me with all the reverence he would have shown our queen."

"He can have no true purpose with you, Doll," said Sir George, who felt sure that Leicester was the man.

"But he has, father, a true purpose with me. He would make me his wife to-day would I consent."

"Why then does he not seek you openly ? "

"That he cannot do," Dorothy responded hesitatingly.

"Tell me, Doll, who is the man ? " asked Sir George.

I was standing behind him and Dorothy's face was turned toward me. She hesitated, and I knew by her expression that she was about to tell all. Sir George, I believe, would have killed her had she done so. I placed my finger on my lips and shook my head.

Dorothy said : "That I cannot tell you, father. You are wasting words in asking me."

"Is it because of his wish that you refuse to tell me his name ? " asked Sir George. I nodded my head.

"Yes, father," softly responded Dorothy in the old dangerous, dulcet tones.

"That is enough ; I know who the man is."

Dorothy kissed her father. He returned the caress, much to my surprise, and left the room.

When I turned to follow Sir George I glanced toward Dorothy. Her eyes were like two moons, so full were they of wonderment and inquiry.

I stopped with Sir George in his room. He was meditative and sad.

"I believe my Doll has told me the truth," he said.

"Have no doubt of it, Sir George," I replied.

"But what good intent can Leicester have toward my girl?" he asked.

"Of that I cannot say," I replied; "but my dear cousin, of this fact be sure: if he have evil intent toward Dorothy, he will fail."

"But there was the Robsart girl," he replied.

"Ay," said I, "but Dorothy Vernon is not Amy Robsart. Have no fear of your daughter. She is proof against both villany and craft. Had she been in Mistress Robsart's place, Leicester would not have deserted her. Dorothy is the sort of woman men do not desert. What say you to the fact that Leicester might wish to make her his wife?"

"He may purpose to do so secretly, as in the case of the Robsart girl," returned Sir George. "Go, Malcolm, and ask her if he is willing to make her his wife before the world."

I was glad of an opportunity for a word with Dorothy, so I hastily went to her. I told her of the Leicester phase of the situation, and I also told her that her father had asked me if the man whom she loved was willing to make her his wife before the world.

"Tell my father," said she, "that I will be no man's wife save before all the world. A man who will not acknowledge me never shall possess me."

I went back to Sir George and delivered the message word for word.

"She is a strange, strong girl, isn't she, Malcolm?" said her father.

"She is her father's child," I replied.

"By my spurs she is. She should have been a man," said Sir George, with a twinkle of admiration in his eyes. He admired a good fight even though he were beaten in it.

T

It is easy to be good when we are happy. Dorothy, the great disturber, was both. Therefore, peace reigned once more in Haddon Hall.

Letters frequently passed between John and Dorothy by the hand of Jennie Faxton, but John made no attempt to meet his sweetheart. He and Dorothy were biding their time.

A fortnight passed during which Cupid confined his operations to Madge and myself. For her sweet sake he was gracious and strewed our path with roses. I should delight to tell you of our wooing. She a fair young creature of eighteen, I a palpitating youth of thirty-five. I should love to tell you of Madge's promise to be my wife, and of the announcement in the Hall of our betrothal; but there was little of interest in it to any one save ourselves, and I fear lest you should find it very sentimental and dull indeed. I should love to tell you also of the delightful walks which Madge and I took together along the sweet old Wye and upon the crest of Bowling Green; but above all would I love to tell you of the delicate rose tints that came to her cheek, and how most curiously at times, when my sweetheart's health was bounding, the blessed light of day would penetrate the darkened windows of her eyes, and how upon such occasions she would cry out joyously, "Oh, Malcolm, I can dimly see." I say I should love to tell you about all those joyous happenings, but after all I fear I should shrink from doing so in detail, for the feelings and sayings of our own hearts are sacred to us. It is much easier to tell of the love affairs of others.

A fortnight or three weeks passed quietly in Haddon Hall. Sir George had the notion firmly fixed in his head that the man whom Dorothy had been meeting held honorable intentions toward the girl. He did her the justice to believe that by reason of her strength and purity she would tolerate none other. At times he felt sure that the man was Leicester, and again he flouted the thought as impossible. If it were Leicester, and if he wished to marry Dorothy, Sir George thought the match certainly would be illustrious. Halting between the questions, " Is he Leicester?" and "Is he not Leicester?" Sir George did not press the Stanley nuptials, nor did he insist upon the signing of the contract. Dorothy received from her father full permission to go where and when she wished. But her father's willingness to give her liberty excited her suspicions. She knew he would permit her to leave the Hall only that he might watch her, and, if possible, entrap her and John. Therefore, she rode out only with Madge and me, and sought no opportunity to see her lover. It may be that her passiveness was partly due to the fact that she knew her next meeting with John would mean farewell to Haddon Hall. She well knew she was void of resistance when in John's hands. And his letter had told her frankly what he would expect from her when next they should meet. She was eager to go to him; but the old habit of love for home and its sweet associations and her returning affection for her father, now that he was kind to her, were strong cords entwining her tender heart, which she could not break suddenly even for the sake of the greater joy.

One day Dorothy received from John a letter telling her he would on the following morning start for the Scottish border with the purpose of meeting the queen of Scotland. A plan had been formed among Mary's friends in Scotland to rescue her from Lochleven Castle, where she was a prisoner, and to bring her incognito to Rutland. John had been chosen to escort her from the English border to his father's castle. From thence, when the opportunity should arise, she was to escape to France, or make her peace with Elizabeth. The adventure was full of peril both for her Scottish and English friends. The Scottish regent Murray surely would hang all the conspirators whom he might capture, and Elizabeth would probably inflict summary punishment upon any of her subjects whom she could convict of complicity in the plot.

In connection with this scheme to rescue Mary it was said there was also another conspiracy. There appeared to be a plot within a plot which had for its end the enthronement of Mary in Elizabeth's stead.

The Rutlands knew nothing of this subplot.

Elizabeth had once or twice expressed sympathy with her Scottish cousin. She had said in John's presence that while she could not for reasons of state *invite* Mary to seek refuge in England, still if Mary would come uninvited she would be welcomed. Therefore, John thought he was acting in accord with the English queen's secret wish when he went to Rutland with the purpose of being in readiness to meet Mary at the Scottish border.

There were two elements in Elizabeth's character on which John had not counted. One was her royal prerogative to speak words she did not mean; and the other was the universal feminine privilege to change her mind. Our queen did not want Mary to visit England, nor had she any knowledge of the plot to induce that event. She did, however, fear that Mary's unwise friends among the Catholics cherished the purpose of making Mary queen of England. Although John had heard faint rumors of such a plot, he had been given to understand that Mary had no share in it, and he believed that the adventure in which he was about to embark had for its only purpose her liberation from a cruel and unjust imprisonment. Her cause appealed to John's chivalrous nature as it appealed to so many other good though mistaken men who sought to give help to the Scottish queen, and brought only grief to her and ruin to themselves.

Dorothy had heard at various times just enough of these

plots to fill her heart with alarm when she learned that John was about to be engaged in them. Her trouble was twofold. She feared lest personal injury or death might befall John; and jealousy, that shame of love, gnawed at her heart despite her efforts to drive it away.

"Is she so marvellously beautiful?" Dorothy asked of me over and over again, referring to Mary Stuart. "Is she such a marvel of beauty and fascination that all men fall before her?"

"That usually is the result," I replied. "I have never known her to smile upon a man who did not at once respond by falling upon his knees to her."

My reply certainly was not comforting.

"Ah, then, I am lost," she responded, with a tremulous sigh. "Is — is she prone to smile on men and — and — to grow fond of them?"

"I should say, Dorothy, that both the smiling and the fondness have become a habit with her."

"Then she will be sure to choose John from among all men. He is so glorious and perfect and beautiful that she will be eager to — to — O God! I wish he had not gone to fetch her."

"You need have no fear," I said reassuringly. "While Mary Stuart is marvellously beautiful and fascinating, there is at least one woman who excels her. Above all, that woman is pure and chaste."

"Who is she, that one woman, Malcolm? Who is she?" asked the girl, leaning forward in her chair and looking at me eagerly with burning eyes.

"You are already a vain girl, Dorothy, and I shall not tell you who that one woman is," I answered laughingly.

"No, no, Malcolm, I am not vain in this matter. It is of too great moment to me for the petty vice of vanity to have any part in it. You do not understand me. I care not for my beauty, save for his sake. I long to be more beautiful, more fascinating, and more attractive than she — than any woman living — only because I long to hold John — to keep him from her, from all others. I have seen so little of the world that I must be sadly lacking in those arts which please men, and I long to possess the beauty of the angels, and the fascinations of Satan that I may hold John, hold him, hold him, hold him. That I may hold him so sure and fast that it will be impossible for him to break from me. At times, I almost wish he were blind; then he could see no other woman. Ah, am I not a wicked, selfish girl? But I will not allow myself to become jealous. He is all mine, isn't he, Malcolm?" She spoke with nervous energy, and tears were ready to spring from her eyes.

"He is all yours, Dorothy," I answered, "all yours, as surely as that death will some day come to all of us. Promise me, Dorothy, that you will never again allow a jealous thought to enter your heart. You have no cause for jealousy, nor will you ever have. If you permit that hateful passion to take possession of you, it will bring ruin in its wake."

"It was, indeed, foolish in me," cried Dorothy, springing to her feet and clasping her hands tightly; "and I promise never again to feel jealousy. Malcolm, its faintest touch tears and gnaws at my heart and racks me with agony. But I will drive it out of me. Under its influence I am not responsible for my acts. It would quickly turn me mad. I promise, oh, I swear, that I never will allow it to come to me again."

Poor Dorothy's time of madness was not far distant nor was the evil that was to follow in its wake.

John in writing to Dorothy concerning his journey to Scotland had unhesitatingly intrusted to her keeping his honor, and, unwittingly, his life. It did not once occur to him that she could, under any conditions, betray him. I trusted her as John did until I saw her vivid flash of burning jealousy. But by the light of that flash I saw that should the girl, with or without reason, become convinced that Mary Stuart was her rival, she would quickly make Derby-shire the warmest locality in Christendom, and John's life might pay the cost of her folly. Dorothy would brook no rival — no, not for a single hour. Should she become jealous she would at once be swept beyond the influence of reason or the care for consequences. It were safer to arouse a sleeping devil than Dorothy Vernon's jealousy.

Now about the time of John's journey to the Scottish border, two matters of importance arose at Haddon Hall. One bore directly upon Dorothy, namely, the renewal by the Stanleys of their suit for her hand. The other was the announcement by the queen that she would soon do Sir George Vernon the honor of spending a fortnight under the roof of Haddon Hall. Each event was of great importance to the King of the Peak. He had concluded that Thomas, the man-servant, was not the Earl of Leicester in disguise, and when the Earl of Derby again came forward with his marriage project, Sir George fell back into his old hardness toward Dorothy, and she prepared her armament, offensive and defensive, for instant use if need should arise. I again began my machinations, since I can call my double dealing by no other name. I induced Dorothy to agree to meet the earl and his son James. Without promising positively to marry Lord Stanley, she, at my suggestion, led her father to believe she was ready to yield to his wishes. By this course she gained time and liberty, and kept peace with her father. Since you have seen the evils that war brought to Haddon, you well know how desirable peace was. In time of war all Haddon was a field of carnage and unrest. In time of peace the dear old Hall was an ideal home. I persuaded Sir George not to insist on a positive promise from Dorothy, and I advised him to allow her yielding mood to grow upon her. I assured him evasively that she would eventually succumb to his paternal authority and love.

What an inherent love we all have for meddling in the affairs of others, and what a delicious zest we find in faithfully applying our surplus energies to business that is not strictly our own! I had become a part of the Sir George-Dorothy-John affair, and I was like the man who caught the bear: I could not loose my hold.

CHAPTER XIII

PROUD DAYS FOR THE OLD HALL

OF course the queen's approaching visit threw Haddon Hall into a frenzy of scrubbing and furbishing. Aunt Dorothy was the busiest woman in England. Floors were newly polished. Draperies were taken down and were carefully washed with mysterious concoctions warranted to remove dirt without injury to color. Superfine wax was bought in great boxes, and candles were made for all the chandeliers and candelabra in the house. Perfumed oil was purchased for the lamp in the state bedroom. Elizabeth, by the way, when she came, did not like the odor of the oil, and with an oath tossed both the oil and the lamp out of the window. The fattest sheep, kine, and hogs were chosen from the flocks and were brought in to be stall-fed in such numbers that one might have supposed we were expecting an ogress who could eat an ox at a meal. Pipers and dancers were engaged, and a merry fool was brought down from London. At last the eventful day came and with it came our queen. She brought with her a hundred yeomen of her guard and a score of ladies and gentlemen. Among the latter was the Earl of Leicester, who was the queen's prime favorite.

Prior to the queen's announcement of her intention to visit Haddon Sir George had, with Dorothy's tacit consent, fixed a day upon which the Earl of Derby and his son, Lord James, should be received at the Hall for the

purpose of signing the marriage contract.   Dorothy, of
course, had no intention of signing the contract, but she
put off the evil hour of refusal as far as possible, hoping
something might occur in the meantime to help her out
of the dilemma.   Something did occur at the last moment.
I am eager to tell you about it, but it must wait its turn.
Truly would the story of this ingenious girl's life make
a romance if it were written by a poet.   In her Guinevere
and Elaine were moulded into one person with the tenderness, purity, and fierceness of each.

To postpone further the time of the Stanley visit, Dorothy suggested that the betrothal should take place in the
presence of the queen.   Sir George acquiesced, and in his
heart grew less eager for the Stanley match as Dorothy apparently became more tractable.   He was, however,
engaged with the earl to an extent that forbade withdrawal,
even had he been sure that he wished to withdraw.

At the time of which I speak the Earl of Leicester was
the most exalted subject of the realm.   He was ardently
devoted to the cause of the ladies, and, although he had fixed
his hope on Elizabeth and longed for a seat beside her on
the throne, his inflammable heart was constantly catching
fire from other eyes.   He, of course, made desperate efforts
to conceal these manifold conflagrations from the queen,
but the inflammable tow of his heart was always bringing
him into trouble with his fiery mistress.

The earl's first glance toward Dorothy was full of admiration.   The second glance was full of conflagration.   The
second day of the queen's residence in Haddon I was
astonished, grieved, and angered to see that our girl had
turned her powerful batteries upon the earl with the evident purpose of conquest.   At times her long lashes would
fall before him, and again her great luminous eyes would
open wide, shedding a soft radiance which no man could
withstand.   Once I saw her walking alone with him upon

the terrace. Her head was drooped shamelessly, and the earl was ardent though restless, being fearful of the queen. I boiled with rage against Dorothy, but by a strong effort I did not boil over until I had better cause. The better cause came later.

I failed to tell you of a brief conversation which occurred between Sir George and me after my cousin first saw the Earl of Leicester. Sir George had gallantly led the queen to her apartments, and I had conducted Leicester and several of the gentlemen to their various rooms. Sir George and I met at the staircase after we had quitted our guests.

He said: "Malcolm, that fellow Thomas whom I knocked in the head looked no more like Leicester than I do. Why did you tell me there was resemblance?"

"I do not know," I answered. "Perhaps your words suggested the thought of a resemblance. Perhaps I had lost all memory of Leicester's features. I cannot answer your question."

Then an expression of anger came to Sir George's face, and he said : —

"I believe Dorothy lied to me when she said that the fellow Thomas was of noble blood."

The next day a servant reported that Thomas had been seen loitering near Bowling Green Gate, and Sir George ordered Dorothy not to leave the Hall without his permission.

Dorothy replied to her father's command, "I shall obey you, father."

To me there was a note of danger in her voice. Such docile submissiveness was not natural to the girl. Of course all appearance of harshness toward Dorothy was suppressed by Sir George during the queen's visit to the Hall. In truth, he had no reason to be harsh, for Dorothy was a meek, submissive, and obedient daughter.

Her meekness, however, as you may well surmise, was but the forerunner of dire rebellion.

The fourth day of the queen's presence at Haddon Hall was the one appointed for the visit of the Stanleys, and Sir George thought to make a great event of the betrothal by having the queen act as a witness to the marriage contract. As the day approached Sir George became thoughtful, while Dorothy grew gleeful. The girl was frequently seen with Leicester, and Sir George could not help noticing that nobleman's pronounced admiration for his daughter. These exhibitions of gallantry were never made in the presence of the queen. The morning of the day when the Stanleys were expected Sir George called me to his room for a private consultation. The old gentleman was in a state of excitement, not unmixed with perplexity and trouble.

He said, " I have great and good news to impart to you, Malcolm; yet I am in a dilemma growing out of it."

"Tell me the good news first, Sir George," I replied. " The dilemma may wait."

"Is Doll a very beautiful girl?" he asked eagerly.

"I believe she is the most beautiful woman in the world," I answered.

"Good, good," he replied, rubbing his hands. "Is she so fascinating, brilliant, and attractive, think you — of course I speak in jest — but think you she might vie with the court ladies for beauty, and think you she might attract — for the sake of illustration I will say — might she attract a man like Leicester?"

"Unless I am much mistaken," I answered, "Leicester is over his ears in love with the girl now."

"Ah, do you believe so, Malcolm?" replied Sir George, laughing and slapping his thigh, as he walked to and fro across the room. "You have seen so much of that sort of thing that you should know it when it comes under your nose. Eh, Malcolm, eh?"

"I should suppose that any one, however inexperienced in such matters, could easily see Leicester's infatuation for Dorothy. If you wish me to tell you what I really believe —"

"I do, I do," interrupted Sir George.

"I should say," I continued, "that Dorothy has deliberately gone in for conquest. Leave the girl to herself, Sir George. She can conduct the campaign without help from any one. She understands the art of such warfare as well as if she were a veteran."

"Gad, but she does, but she does. I believe she could give Venus herself some good points in the matter. But let me tell you, Malcolm," — the old man dropped his voice to a whisper, — "I questioned Doll this morning, and she confessed that Leicester had spoken words of love to her. Would it not be a great match for our house?"

He said "our house," mind you, not "our Doll." I might call his condition of mind patrimonial selfishness. Simple old man! He did not know that words of love are not necessarily words of marriage.

"Has Leicester spoken to you?" I asked in alarm for John's sake.

"No, no, he has not spoken," returned my cousin; "for that, of course, he must have the queen's consent. But he will speak, I am sure, all in good time, Malcolm, all in good time."

"How about the Stanleys?" I asked. "They will be here this afternoon."

"That's the devil's finger in the matter," cried Sir George. "That's where my dilemma lies. How shall I put them off, and still retain them in case nothing should come from Leicester? Besides, I am in honor bound to the earl."

"I have a plan," I replied. "You carry out your part of the agreement with the earl, but let Dorothy, at the last moment, refuse to give her consent. Let her ask for more time, on the plea that she does not know her mind. I will suggest to her, if you wish, the part she is to play; but I will conceal from her the fact that you are a party to it."

"No," said the old man, "that would be bad faith toward the earl." After a pause he continued doubtingly: "No, do not speak to Doll. I believe she needs no suggestions in the matter. I fear that mischief is in her mind already. Her easy acquiescence in my wishes have of late had a suspicious appearance. No, don't speak to her, Malcolm. If ever there lived a girl who could be perverse and wilful on her own account, without help from any one, it is my girl Doll. God bless you, man, if she but knew that I wanted her to reject Stanley, she would have him in spite of hell itself. I wonder what she means by her docility and obedience? No, don't speak a word to her on the subject. Let her believe I am serious regarding this marriage, and she will have some plan of her own to raise the devil. I have been expecting signs of it every day. I had determined not to bear with her perversity, but now that the Leicester possibility has come up we'll leave Doll to work out her own salvation, Malcolm. Don't interfere. No man living can teach that girl a new trick in deviltry. Gods, Malcolm! I am curious to know what she will be doing, for she certainly will be doing something rather than sign that contract of betrothal."

"But suppose out of obedience to you she should sign the contract?" I asked.

"Malcolm, you don't know Doll," he replied. Then, after a pause, "Neither do I. I wish she were well married."

When I left Sir George, I found Dorothy in close con-

sultation with the queen and two of her ladies. I heard
the name of Lord James Stanley spoken amid suppressed
laughter, and I suspected Dorothy had on foot some prank
touching that young man, to which her Majesty was a
party.

After dinner the Stanleys came a-wooing. The party
consisted of father, son, and four retainers, who looked as
if they had been preserved in alcohol for the occasion, so
red were their faces.

The Earl of Derby was a fine old gentleman of the rural
type. His noble son was an uncouth rustic, who had no
thought above a stable boy or tavern maid, nor any ambition
above horse trading. His attire was a wonder to behold.
He wore a ruff of stupendous proportions. His trunks
were so puffed out and preposterous in size that they looked
like a great painted knot on a tree ; and the many-colored
splendors of his sleeves, his hat, his hose, and his shoes
were dazzling to the eye. Add to this wondrous raiment
feet and hands that could not be satisfactorily disposed of,
and an unrest of manner painful to behold, and you may possibly conceive the grandiose absurdity of Dorothy's wooer.
The sight of him almost made Sir George ill; and his
entrance into the long gallery, where the queen was seated
with her ladies and gentlemen, and Sir George and his
friends standing about her, was a signal for laughter in
which her Majesty openly joined.

I shall not lead you through the tedious ceremony of
presentation and introduction, nor shall I tell you of the
pompous manner in which one of the earl's retinue, a
lawyer, read the marriage contract. The fact that the
contract was read without the presence of Dorothy, whom
it so nearly concerned, was significant of the small consideration which at that time was given to a girl's consent. When all was ready for the signing, Dorothy was
summoned.

Sir George stood beside the Stanleys, and his nervous-
ness was painfully apparent. Two servants opened the
great doors at the end of the long gallery, and Dorothy,
holding up the skirt of her gown, bounded into the room.
She kneeled to the queen, and turned toward her uncle
Stanley and her lover-cousin with a low bow. Then she
courtesied and said : —

"Good even, uncle, and how do you do, cousin. Have
you come to inspect me, and, perchance, to buy ? "

Sir George's face bore an expression of mingled shame,
wonder, and alarm, and the queen and her suite laughed
behind their fans.

"It is well," continued Dorothy. "Here am I, ready
for inspection." Thereupon she began to disrobe herself
before the entire company. Leicester laughed outright,
and the queen and her ladies suppressed their merriment
for a moment, and then sent forth peals of laughter without restraint. Sir George stepped toward the girl and
raised his hand warningly, but the queen interposed : —

"Silence, Sir George, I command you;" and Sir George
retreated to his former place beside the Earl of Derby.
Dorothy first removed her bodice, showing her shoulders
and a part of her arms, clothed in the fashion of a tavern
maid.

Leicester, who stood by me, whispered, "God never made
anything more beautiful than Mistress Vernon's arms."

Sir George again spoke angrily, "Doll, what are you
doing ? " But the queen by a wave of her hand commanded silence. Then the girl put her hands behind her,
and loosened the belt which held her skirt in place. The
skirt fell to the floor, and out of it bounded Dorothy in
the short gown of a maid.

"You will be better able to judge of me in this costume,
cousin," said Dorothy. "It will be more familiar to you
than the gowns which ladies wear."

"I will retract," said Leicester, whispering to me, and gazing ardently at Dorothy's ankles. "God has made something more beautiful than Mistress Vernon's arms. By Venus! I suppose that in His omnipotence He might be able to create something more beautiful than her ankles, but up to this time He has not vouchsafed to me a vision of it. Ah! did any one ever behold such strength, such perfect symmetry, such— St. George! the gypsy doesn't live who can dance like that."

Sure enough, Dorothy was dancing. The pipers in the balcony had burst forth in a ribald jig of a tune, and the girl was whirling in a wild, weird, and wondrous dance before her lover-cousin. Sir George ordered the pipers to cease playing; but again Elizabeth, who was filled with mirth, interrupted, and the music pealed forth in wanton volumes which flooded the gallery. Dorothy danced like an elfin gypsy to the inspiring strains. Soon her dance changed to wondrous imitations of the movements of a horse. She walked sedately around in an ever increasing circle; she trotted and paced; she gave the single foot and racked; she galloped, slowly for a while, and then the gallop merged into a furious run which sent the blood of her audience thrilling through their veins with delight. The wondrous ease and grace, and the marvellous strength and quickness of her movements, cannot be described. I had never before thought the human body capable of such grace and agility as she displayed.

After her dance was finished she stepped in front of her cousin and delivered herself as follows:—

"I am sound from ear tip to fetlock. There is not a blemish in me."

"No, by my faith, I will swear there is not!" cried the Earl of Leicester.

"I have good wind," continued Dorothy, "two good eyes. By night or by day I can see everything within

U

the range of my vision, and a great deal that is not. I shy, at times, when an uncouth object suddenly comes upon me. I am warranted gentle if properly handled, but otherwise it is unsafe to curry my heels."

Sir George could no longer restrain himself, and again tried to prevent Dorothy from proceeding with her terrible insult to the Stanleys. The queen, however, was determined to see the end of the frolic, and she said : —

"Proceed, Mistress Vernon, proceed."

Dorothy, nothing loath, continued : "As for my disposition, it might be better. It probably will improve with age, if it doesn't grow worse. I have all the gaits a horse should have. I am four years old, I have never been trained to work double, and I think I never shall be. What think you? Now what have you to offer in exchange? Step out and let me see you move."

She took the poor youth by the hand and led him to the middle of the floor.

"How old are you? Show me your teeth," she said. The heir to Derby smiled uneasily, and drew his hand across his nose.

"Ah, you have a touch of the distemper, I see. Are you subject to it?"

Stanley smiled, and the earl said : —

"Sir George, this insult has gone far enough."

"Stand back, my Lord Derby," said the queen. "Do not interfere with this interesting barter."

The earl reluctantly lapsed into silence. He remembered the insult of her Majesty's words all his life.

"Now step off," said Dorothy to Lord James.

The young man stood in helpless confusion. Dorothy took a step backward from him, and after watching Stanley a moment said : —

"What! You can neither trot, pace, nor gallop? I don't believe you can even walk alone." Then she turned toward Sir George. A smile was on her lips, but a look from hell was in her eyes as she said : —

"Father, take a lesson from this day. I gave you fair warning. Bring me no more scurvy cobs for barter nor trade." Then she turned to the Earl of Derby and to her cousin Lord James, made a deep courtesy, and said : —

"You can have no barter with me. Good day."

She ran from the room, and a great peal of laughter from all save Sir George and the Stanleys followed her as she passed out through the double door. When the laughter had subsided, the Earl of Derby turned to Sir George and said : —

"Sir George, this insult is unbearable, and I shall expect satisfaction for it." Then he turned to the queen : "I beg that your Majesty will give me leave to depart with my son."

"Granted," answered Elizabeth, and father and son started to leave the room, moving backward toward the great doors. Sir George asked the earl and Lord Stanley to remain, and in the presence of the company who had witnessed the insult, he in the humblest manner made abject apology for the treatment his distinguished guests had received at the hands of his daughter. He very honestly and in all truth disclaimed any sympathy with Dorothy's conduct, and offered, as the only reparation he could make, to punish her in some way befitting the offence. Then he conducted the guests to the mounting block near the entrance tower and saw them depart. Dorothy had solved her father's dilemma with a vengeance.

Sir George was not sure that he wanted to be angry at Dorothy, though he felt it was a duty he owed to himself and to the Stanleys. He had wished that the girl would in some manner defer the signing of the contract, but he had not wanted her to refuse young Stanley's hand in a manner so insulting that the match would be broken off altogether.

As the day progressed, and as Sir George pondered over Dorothy's conduct, he grew more inclined to anger; but during the afternoon she kept well under the queen's wing, and he found no opportunity to give vent to his ill-temper.

Late that night he called me to his room. He had been drinking during the evening and was poised between good-humored hilarity and ill-tempered ferocity. The latter condition was usually the result of his libations. When I entered the room it was evident he was amused.

"Did you ever hear or see such brazen effrontery?" he asked, referring to Dorothy's treatment of the Stanleys. "Is there another girl on earth who would have conceived the absurd thought, or, having conceived it, would have dared to carry it out?"

I took a chair and replied, "I think there is not another."

"I hope not," continued Sir George. He sat in thought for a moment, and then broke forth into a great laugh. When he had finished laughing he said: "I admit it was laughable and — and pretty — beautiful. Damme, I didn't know the girl could do it, Malcolm! I didn't know she had it in her. There is not another girl living could have carried the frolic through." Then he spoke seriously, "But I will make her smart for it when the queen leaves Haddon."

"Sir George, if you will allow me to suggest what I feel on the subject, I would say that you have no reason whatever for desiring to make Dorothy smart. She may have deeper designs than we can see."

"What designs do you suppose she can have? Tell me, Malcolm," asked Sir George.

I remained silent for a moment, hardly knowing how to express my thought. "Certainly she could not have appeared to a better advantage than in her tavern maid's costume," I said.

"That is true," answered Sir George. "Though she is my own daughter, I must admit that I have never seen any woman so beautiful as she." The old gentleman laughed softly for a moment and said: "But wasn't it brazen? Wasn't it shameless? I have always given the girl credit for modesty, but — damme, damme — "

"Her beauty in the tavern maid's costume fired Leicester's heart as nothing else could have done," I said. "He stood by my side, and was in raptures over her charms."

Sir George mused a moment and said something about the "Leicester possibility," which I knew to be an impossibility, and before I left him he had determined to allow the matter to drop for the present. "I am making a damned pretty mess of the whole affair, I fear, Malcolm," he said.

"You don't seem to be clearing it up, Sir George," I responded.

After talking over some arrangements for the queen's entertainment, I said good night, and left my cousin brooding over as complicated a problem as man ever tried to solve.

The next morning I told Dorothy how her father felt with respect to the "Leicester possibility." She laughed and said : —

"I will encourage father in that matter, and," with a saucy twinkle in her eye, "incidentally I will not discourage my proud lord of Leicester. I will make the most of the situation, fear not, Malcolm."

"I do not fear," said I, emphatically.

There it was: the full-blown spirit of conquest, strong even in a love-full heart. God breathed into Adam the breath of life; but into Eve he breathed the love of conquest, and it has been growing stronger in the hearts of her daughters with each recurring generation.

"How about John?" I asked.

"Oh, John?" she answered, throwing her head contemplatively to one side. "He is amply able to protect his own interests. I could not be really untrue to him if I wished to be. It is I who am troubled on the score of infidelity. John will be with the most beautiful queen—" She broke off in the midst of her sentence, and her face became clouded with an expression of anger and hatred. "God curse her! I wish she were dead, dead, dead. There! you know how I feel toward your English-French-Scottish beauty. Curse the mongrel—" She halted before the ugly word she was about to use; but her eyes were like glowing embers, and her cheeks were flushed by the heat of anger.

"Did you not promise me, Dorothy, that you would not again allow yourself to become jealous of Queen Mary?" I asked.

"Yes, I promised, but I cannot prevent the jealousy, and I do not intend to try. I hate her, and I love to hate her."

"Why should you hate her?" I asked. "If John remains true to you, there is certainly no cause for you to hate any one. If he should be untrue to you, you should hate him."

"Hate him?" she exclaimed. "That, indeed, is pretty reasoning. If he should be untrue to me, I should of course hate her. I could not hate him. I did not make myself love him. I would never have been so great a fool as to bring that pain upon myself intentionally. I suppose no girl would deliberately make herself love a man and bring into her heart so great an agony. I feel toward John as I do, because I must; and I hate your Scottish mongrel because I must. I tell you, Malcolm, when she comes to Rutland, if I hear of her trying any of her wanton tricks on John there will be trouble—mark my words!"

"I ask you to promise me this, Dorothy: that you will

do nothing concerning John and Queen Mary without first speaking to me."

She paced across the room angrily. " I promise you nothing, Malcolm, save that I shall not allow that woman to come between John and me. That I promise you, on my oath."

Dorothy continued to shed her luminous smiles on Leicester, though she was careful not to shine in the queen's presence. My lord was dazzled by the smiles, and continually sought opportunities to bask in their dangerous light. As a result of this smiling and basking the great London heart-breaker was soon helplessly caught in the toils of Doll, the country maiden. She played him as an angler plays a trout. The most experienced court coquette could not have done the part better than did this girl, whose knowledge of the subject was wholly intuitive, for her life had all been spent amid the green hills and groves of Derbyshire. She so managed the affair that her father should see enough of Leicester's preference to keep alive in Sir George's mind the hope for the " Leicester possibility." Those words had become with her a phrase slyly to play upon.

One afternoon when the sun was graciously warm and bright, I induced Madge to walk with me upon the terrace, that I might for a few moments feel the touch of her hand and hear her whispered words. We took a seat by a large holly bush, which effectually concealed us from view. We had been there but a few moments when we heard footsteps approaching. Looking between the branches of the holly bush I saw Dorothy and Leicester coming toward us from the north end of the terrace. Dorothy's eyes were cast down demurely, and her head hung in the attitude of a shy, modest girl, who listens timidly to words that are music in her ears. Never have I seen an attitude more indicative of the receptive mood than that which Dorothy assumed toward Leicester.

"Ah," thought I, "poor John has given his heart and has risked his life for the sake of Doll, and Doll is a miserable coquette."

But there was conduct still more objectionable to come from Dorothy.

Unconscious of our presence, Leicester said, "My fair beauty, my Venus, here is a settle under this holly bush, well hidden from prying eyes. It invites us. Will you sit here with me for one happy moment, and give me a taste of Paradise?"

"I fear I should not sit with you, my lord, however much I — may — may wish to do so. My father or the queen might observe us." The black lashes fell upon the fair cheek, and the red golden head with its crown of glory hung forward convincingly.

"You false jade," thought I.

"I ask for but one moment," pleaded Leicester. "The queen sleeps at this time after dinner, and perhaps your father would not object if you were to grant this little favor to the first nobleman of the realm."

"You do not know my father, my lord. He is very strict regarding my conduct," murmured the drooping head.

"I ask for but one little moment," continued the earl, "in which to tell you that you have filled my heart with adoration and love."

"I should not listen to you, my lord. Were I mindful of my happiness, I should return to the Hall at once," said the drooping lashes and hanging head.

"You lying wench," thought I. By that time I was thoroughly angered.

"Only one little moment on the settle," pleaded Leicester, "that I may speak to you that which I wish so ardently to say."

"Can you not speak while we walk, my lord?" asked Dorothy.

I felt a bitter desire to curse the girl.

"It is difficult for me to speak while we walk," said Leicester, cautiously taking the girl's hand; so she permitted him to lead her to the settle under the holly bush, on the opposite side of which Madge and I were sitting.

The earl retained the hand for a moment after he and Dorothy were seated, but she gently drew it away and moved a little distance from his Lordship. Still, her eyes were drooped, her head hung low, and her bosom actually heaved as if with emotion.

"I will tell John of your shamelessness," I said to myself. "He shall feel no more heartaches for you — you wanton huzzy."

Then Leicester poured forth his passion most eloquently. Poesy, verse, and rhetoric all came to help him in his wooing. Now and then the girl would respond to his ardor with "Please, my lord," or "I pray you, my lord," and when he would try to take her hand she would say, "I beg you, my lord, do not." But Leicester evidently thought that the "do not" meant "do," for soon he began to steal his arm about her waist, and she was so slow in stopping him that I thought she was going to submit. She, however, arose gently to her feet and said : —

"My lord, I must return to the Hall. I may not longer remain here with you."

The earl caught her hand and endeavored to kiss it, but she adroitly prevented him, and stepping out into the path, started slowly toward the Hall. She turned her head slightly toward Leicester in a mute but eloquent invitation, and he quickly followed her.

I watched the pair walk up the terrace. They descended the steps to the garden, and from thence they entered the Hall by way of the porch.

"Was it not very wicked in Dorothy to listen to such

words from Leicester?" asked Madge. "I do not at all understand her."

Madge, of course, knew only a part of what had happened, and a very small part at that, for she had not seen Dorothy. Madge and I returned to the Hall, and we went at once to Dorothy's room, hoping to see her, and intending to tell her our opinion of the shameless manner in which she had acted.

Dorothy was in her room alone when we entered. She clapped her hands, ran to the door, bolted it, and bounded back toward us.

"I have the greatest news to tell you," she cried laughingly, — "the greatest news and the greatest sport of which you ever heard. My lord Leicester is in love with me."

"Indeed, that is very fine," I responded; but my irony met its usual fate. She did not see it.

"Yes," continued Dorothy, brimming over with mirth, "you should have heard him pleading with me a few moments since upon the terrace."

"We did hear him," said Madge.

"You heard him? Where? How?" Her eyes were wide with wonder.

"We were on the opposite side of the holly bush from you," I answered. "We heard him and we saw you."

"Did you? Good. I am glad of it," said Dorothy.

"Yes, we saw and we heard all, and we think that your conduct was shameless," I responded severely.

"Shameless?" demanded Dorothy. "Now pray tell me what I did or said that was shameless."

I was at a loss to define the wrong in her conduct, for it had been of an intangible quality which in itself was nothing, but notwithstanding meant a great deal.

"You permitted him to hold your hand," I said, trying to fix on something real with which to accuse her.

"I did nothing of the sort," said Dorothy, laughingly.

"He caught my hand several times, but I withdrew it from him."

I knew she spoke the truth regarding her hand, so I tried again.

"You — you hung your head and kept your eyes cast down, and you looked — "

"Oh, I hung my head, I cast down my eyes, and I looked?" she answered, laughing heartily. "Pray let me ask you, Master Fault-finder, for what use else are heads and eyes made?"

I was not prepared to say that the uses to which Dorothy had put her head and eyes were not some of the purposes for which they were created. They are good purposes, too, I admit, although I would not have conceded as much to Dorothy. I knew the girl would soon wheedle me into her way of thinking, so I took a bold stand and said: —

"It is my intention to tell John about your conduct with Leicester, and I shall learn for what purpose he thinks eyes and heads are created."

"Tell John?" cried Dorothy. "Of course you may tell John. He well knows the purposes of heads and eyes, and their proper uses. He has told me many times his opinion on the subject." She laughed for a moment, and then continued: "I, too, shall tell John all that happened or shall happen between Lord Leicester and me. I wish I could tell him now. How I wish I could tell him now." A soft light came to her eyes, and she repeated huskily: "If I might tell him now; if I might tell him now. Why, Malcolm, I despise Leicester. He is a poor, weak fool. He has no more force nor strength than I have. He is not a man. He is no more attractive than a woman. He wanted to kiss me. He begged me to give him but one. It is but a poor kiss which a man gets by begging. Think you I would give him one? Had he but touched my lips, think you I would ever allow John to soil himself again by kissing them? Fear not, Malcolm.

Fear not for John nor for me. No man will ever receive from me a favor, the granting of which would make me unfit to be John's — John's wife. I have paid too dearly for him to throw him away for a penny whistle that I do not want." Then she grew earnest, with a touch of anger: "Leicester! What reason, suppose you, Malcolm, have I for treating him as I do? Think you I act from sheer wantonness? If there were one little spot of that fault upon my soul, I would tear myself from John, though I should die for it."

Her laughing mood had passed away, and I feared to say that I could see no reason other than coquetry for her conduct. I feared the red-haired tigress would scratch my eyes out.

"I have wanted to see you," she continued, "that I might tell you of my plans and of the way they are working out, but now since you have spoken to me in this manner, Sir Malcolm François de Lorraine Vernon, I shall tell you nothing. You suspect me. Therefore, you shall wait with the rest of the world to learn my purposes. You may tell John all you have seen and heard. I care not how quickly you do it." Then with a sigh: "I pray God it may be very soon. He will wish for no explanation, and he shall one day have in me a rich reward for his faith."

"Do you trust him as he trusts you?" I asked, "and would you demand an explanation were he to act toward Mary Stuart as you have acted toward Leicester?"

"He could not act toward her as I did toward Lord Leicester," she said thoughtfully. Then after a moment she laughingly continued: "John can't — he can't hang his head and — droop his eyes and look."

"But if —" I began.

"I want no more of your hellish 'ifs,'" cried the girl in sudden fury. "If John were to — to look at that Scottish mongrel as I looked at Leicester, I would — I would kill the royal wanton. I would kill her if it cost my life.

Now, for God's sake, leave me. You see the state into which you have wrought me." I left Madge with Dorothy and walked out upon Bowling Green to ponder on the events that were passing before me.

From the time we learned that John had gone to fetch the Scottish queen I had fears lest Dorothy's inflammable jealousy might cause trouble, and now those fears were rapidly transforming themselves into a feeling of certainty. There is nothing in life so sweet and so dangerous as the love of a hot-blooded woman.

I soon saw Dorothy again. "Tell me," said I, in conciliation, "tell me, please, what is your reason for acting as you do toward Leicester, and why should you look differently upon similar conduct on John's part?"

"I will not tell you my plans," she responded, — "not now, at least. Perhaps I shall do so when I have recovered from my ill-temper. It is hard for me to give my reasons for feeling differently about like conduct on John's part. Perhaps I feel as I do because — because — It is this way: While I might do little things — mere nothings — such as I have done — it would be impossible for me to do any act of unfaithfulness to John. Oh, it could not be. But with him, he — he — well, he is a man and — and — oh, don't talk to me! Don't talk to me! You are driving me mad. Out of my sight! Out of my room! Holy Virgin! I shall die before I have him; I know I shall."

There it was again. The thought of Mary Stuart drove her wild. Dorothy threw herself on her face upon the bed, and Madge went over and sat by her side to soothe her. I, with a feeling of guilt, so adroit had been Dorothy's defence, left the girls and went to my room in the tower to unravel, by the help of my pipe, the tangled web of woman's incomprehensibility. I failed, as many another man had failed before me, and as men will continue to fail to the end of time.

CHAPTER XIV

MARY STUART

AND now I come to an event in this history which I find difficult to place before you in its true light. For Dorothy's sake I wish I might omit it altogether. But in true justice to her and for the purpose of making you see clearly the enormity of her fault and the palliating excuses therefor, if any there were, I shall pause briefly to show the condition of affairs at the time of which I am about to write — a time when Dorothy's madness brought us to the most terrible straits and plunged us into deepest tribulations.

Although I have been unable to show you as much of John as I have wished you to see, you nevertheless must know that he, whose nature was not like the shallow brook but was rather of the quality of a deep, slow-moving river, had caught from Dorothy an infection of love from which he would never recover. His soul was steeped in the delicious essence of the girl. I would also call your attention to the conditions under which his passion for Dorothy had arisen. It is true he received the shaft when first he saw her at the Royal Arms in Derby-town, but the shaft had come from Dorothy's eyes. Afterward she certainly had done her full part in the wooing. It was for her sake, after she had drawn him on to love her, that he became a servant in Haddon Hall. For her sake he faced death at the hands of her father. And it was through her mad fault that the evil came upon him of which I shall now tell you. That she paid for her fault in suffering does not excuse her, since pain is but the latter half of evil.

During the term of Elizabeth's residence in Haddon Hall John returned to Rutland with Queen Mary Stuart, whose escape from Lochleven had excited all England. The country was full of rumors that Mary was coming to England not so much for sanctuary as to be on the ground ready to accept the English crown when her opportunity to do so should occur. The Catholics, a large and powerful party, flushed with their triumphs under the " Bloody Queen," were believed to sympathize with Mary's cause. Although Elizabeth said little on the subject, she felt deeply, and she feared trouble should the Scottish queen enter her dominion. Another cause of annoyance to Elizabeth was the memory that Leicester had once been deeply impressed with Mary's charms, and had sought her hand in marriage. Elizabeth's prohibition alone had prevented the match. That thought rankled in Elizabeth's heart, and she hated Mary, although her hatred, as in all other cases, was tempered with justice and mercy. This great queen had the brain of a man with its motives, and the heart of a woman with its emotions.

When news of Mary's escape reached London, Cecil came in great haste to Haddon. During a consultation with Elizabeth he advised her to seize Mary, should she enter England, and to check the plots made in Mary's behalf by executing the principal friends of the Scottish queen. He insistently demanded that Elizabeth should keep Mary under lock and key, should she be so fortunate as to obtain possession of her person, and that the men who were instrumental in bringing her into England should be arraigned for high treason.

John certainly had been instrumental in bringing her into England, and if Cecil's advice were taken by the queen, John's head would pay the forfeit for his chivalric help to Mary.

Elizabeth was loath to act on this advice, but Cecil worked upon her fears and jealousies until her mind and her heart were in accord, and she gave secret orders that his advice should be carried out. Troops were sent to the Scottish border to watch for the coming of the fugitive queen. But Mary was already ensconced, safely, as she thought, in Rutland Castle under the assumed name of Lady Blanche. Her presence at Rutland was, of course, guarded as a great secret.

Dorothy's mind dwelt frequently upon the fact that John and the beautiful young Scottish queen lived under the same roof, for John had written to Dorothy immediately after his return. Nothing so propagates itself as jealousy. There were in Haddon Hall two hearts in which this self-propagating process was rapidly progressing — Elizabeth's and Dorothy's. Each had for the cause of her jealousy the same woman.

One night, soon after Cecil had obtained from Elizabeth the order for Mary's arrest, Dorothy, on retiring to her room at a late hour found Jennie Faxton waiting for her with a precious letter from John. Dorothy drank in the tenderness of John's letter as the thirsty earth absorbs the rain; but her joy was neutralized by frequent references to the woman who she feared might become her rival. One-half of what she feared, she was sure had been accomplished: that is, Mary's half. She knew in her heart that the young queen would certainly grow fond of John. That was a foregone conclusion. No woman could be with him and escape that fate, thought Dorothy. Her hope as to the other half — John's part — rested solely upon her faith in John, which was really great, and her confidence in her own charms and in her own power to hold him, which in truth, and with good reason, was not small.

Dorothy went to bed, and Jennie, following her usual custom, when at Haddon, lay upon the floor in the same room. John's letter, with all its tenderness, had thrown Dorothy into an inquisitive frame of mind. After an hour or two of restless tossing upon the bed she fell asleep, but soon after midnight she awakened, and in her drowsy condition the devil himself played upon the strings of her dream-charged imagination. After a time she sprang from the bed, lighted a candle at the rushlight, and read John's letter in a tremor of dream-wrought fear. Then she aroused Jennie Faxton and asked : —

"When were you at Rutland ?"

"I spent yesterday and to-day there, mistress," answered Jennie.

"Did you see a strange lady ?" asked Dorothy.

"Oh, yes, mistress, I did see her three or four times," answered Jennie. "Lady Blanche is her name, and she be a cousin of Sir John's. She do come, they say, from France, and do speak only in the tongue of that country."

"I — I suppose that this — this Lady Blanche and — and Sir John are very good friends? Did you — did you — often see them together?" asked Dorothy. She felt guilty in questioning Jennie for the purpose of spying upon her lover. She knew that John would not pry into her conduct.

"Indeed, yes, mistress," returned Jennie, who admired John greatly from her lowly sphere, and who for her own sake as well as Dorothy's was jealous of Queen Mary. "They do walk together a great deal on the ramparts, and the white snaky lady do look up into Sir John's face like this" — here Jennie assumed a lovelorn expression. "And — and once, mistress, I thought — I thought — "

"Yes, yes, Jesu !" hissed Dorothy, clutching Jennie by the arm, "you thought, you thought. Tell me ! Tell me ! What in hell's name did you think ? Speak quickly, wench."

x

"I be not sure, mistress, but I thought I saw his arm about her waist one evening on the ramparts. It was dark, and for sure I could not tell, but—"

"God's curse upon the white huzzy!" screamed Dorothy. "God's curse upon her! She is stealing him from me, and I am helpless."

She clasped her hands over the top of her head and ran to and fro across the room uttering inarticulate cries of agony. Then she sat upon the bedside and threw herself into Madge's arms, crying under her breath: "My God! My God! Think of it, Madge. I have given him my heart, my soul, O merciful God, my love — all that I have worth giving, and now comes this white wretch, and because she is a queen and was sired in hell she tries to steal him from me and coaxes him to put his arm around her waist."

"Don't feel that way about it, Dorothy," said Madge, soothingly. "I know Sir John can explain it all to you when you see him. He is true to you, I am sure."

"True to me, Madge! How can he be true to me if she coaxes him to woo her and if he puts his arm — I am losing him; I know it. I — I — O God, Madge, I am smothering; I am strangling! Holy Virgin! I believe I am about to die." She threw herself upon the bed by Madge's side, clutching her throat and breast, and her grand woman's form tossed and struggled as if she were in convulsions.

"Holy mother!" she cried, "take this frightful agony from my breast. Snatch this terrible love from my heart. God! If you have pity, give it now. Help me! Help me! Ah, how deeply I love. I never loved him so much as I do at this awful moment. Save me from doing that which is in my heart. If I could have him for only one little portion of a minute. But that is denied me whose right it is, and is given to her who has no right. Ah, God is not just. If he were he would strike her dead. I hate her and I hate — hate him."

She arose to a sitting posture on the edge of the bed and held out her arms toward Madge.

"Madge," she continued, frenzied by the thought, "his arm was around her waist. That was early in the evening. Holy Virgin! What may be happening now?"

Dorothy sprang from the bed and staggered about the room with her hands upon her throbbing temples.

"I cannot bear this agony. God give me strength." Soon she began to gasp for breath. "I can — see — them now — together, together. I hate her; I hate him. My love has turned bitter. What can I do? What can I do? I will do it. I will. I will disturb their sweet rest. If I cannot have him, she shall not. I'll tell the queen, I'll tell the queen."

Dorothy acted on her resolution the moment it was taken, and at once began to unbolt the door.

"Stay, Dorothy, stay!" cried Madge. "Think on what you are about to do. It will cost John his life. Come to me for one moment, Dorothy, I pray you." Madge arose from the bed and began groping her way toward Dorothy, who was unbolting the door.

Madge could have calmed the tempest-tossed sea as easily as she could have induced Dorothy to pause in her mad frenzy. Jennie Faxton, almost paralyzed by fear of the storm she had raised, stood in the corner of the room trembling and speechless. Dorothy was out of the room before poor blind Madge could reach her. The frenzied girl was dressed only in her night robes and her glorious hair hung dishevelled down to her waist. She ran through the rooms of Lady Crawford and those occupied by her father and the retainers. Then she sped down the long gallery and up the steps to Elizabeth's apartment.

She knocked violently at the queen's door.

"Who comes?" demanded one of her Majesty's ladies.

"I, Dorothy," was the response. "I wish to speak to her Majesty at once upon a matter of great importance to her."

Elizabeth ordered her ladies to admit Dorothy, and the girl ran to the queen, who had half arisen in her bed.

"You must have affairs of great moment, indeed," cried Elizabeth, testily, "if they induce you to disturb me in this manner."

"Of great moment, indeed, your Majesty," replied Dorothy, endeavoring to be calm, "of moment to you and to me. Mary Stuart is in England at this instant trying to steal your crown and my lover. She is now sleeping within five leagues of this place. God only knows what she is doing. Let us waste no time, your Majesty."

The girl was growing wilder every second.

"Let us go—you and I—and seize this wanton creature. You to save your crown; I to save my lover and—my life."

"Where is she?" demanded Elizabeth, sharply. "Cease prattling about your lover. She would steal both my lover and my crown if she could. Where is she?"

"She is at Rutland Castle, your Majesty," answered Dorothy.

"Ah, the Duke of Rutland and his son John," said Elizabeth. "I have been warned of them. Send for my Lord Cecil and Sir William St. Loe."

Sir William was in command of the yeoman guards.

"Is Sir John Manners your lover?" asked Elizabeth, turning to Dorothy.

"Yes," answered the girl.

"You may soon seek another," replied the queen, significantly.

Her Majesty's words seemed to awaken Dorothy from her stupor of frenzy, and she foresaw the result of her act. Then came upon her a reaction worse than death.

"You may depart," said the queen to Dorothy, and the girl went back to her room hardly conscious that she was moving.

At times we cannot help feeling that love came to the human breast through a drop of venom shot from the serpent's tongue into the heart of Eve. Again we believe it to be a spark from God's own soul. Who will solve me this riddle?

Soon the hard, cold ringing of arms, and the tramp of mailed feet resounded through Haddon Hall, and the doom-like din reached Dorothy's room in the tones of a clanging knell. There seemed to be a frightful rhythm in the chaos of sounds which repeated over and over again the words: "John will die, John will die," though the full import of her act and its results did nor for a little time entirely penetrate her consciousness. She remembered the queen's words, "You may soon seek another." Elizabeth plainly meant that John was a traitor, and that John would die for his treason. The clanking words, "John will die, John will die," bore upon the girl's ears in ever increasing volume until the agony she suffered deadened her power to think. She wandered aimlessly about the room, trying to collect her senses, but her mind was a blank. After a few minutes she ran back to the queen, having an undefined purpose of doing something to avert the consequences of her mad act. She at first thought to tell the queen that the information she had given concerning Mary Stuart's presence in Rutland was false, but she well knew that a lie seldom succeeds; and in this case, even through her clouded mentality, she could see that a lie would surely fail. She determined to beg the queen to spare John's life. She did not know exactly what she would do, but she hoped by the time she should reach the queen's room to hit upon some plan that would save him. When she knocked at Elizabeth's door it was locked against her. Her Majesty was in consultation with Cecil, Sir William St. Loe, and a few other gentlemen, among whom was Sir George Vernon.

Dorothy well knew there was no help for John if her father were of the queen's council. She insisted upon seeing the queen, but was rudely repulsed. By the time she again reached her room full consciousness had returned, and agony such as she had never before dreamed of overwhelmed her soul. Many of us have felt the same sort of pain when awakened suddenly to the fact that words we have spoken easily may not, by our utmost efforts, be recalled, though we would gladly give our life itself to have them back. If suffering can atone for sin, Dorothy bought her indulgence within one hour after sinning. But suffering cannot atone for sin; it is only a part of it — the result.

"Arise, Madge, and dress," said Dorothy, gently. "I have made a terrible mistake. I have committed a frightful crime. I have betrayed John to death. Ah, help me, Madge, if you can. Pray God to help me. He will listen to you. I fear to pray to Him. He would turn my prayers to curses. I am lost." She fell for a moment upon the bed and placed her head on Madge's breast murmuring, "If I could but die."

"All may turn out better than it now appears," said Madge. "Quiet yourself and let us consider what may be done to arrest the evil of your — your act."

"Nothing can be done, nothing," wailed Dorothy, as she arose from the bed and began to dress. "Please arise, Madge, and dress yourself. Here are your garments and your gown."

They hastily dressed without speaking, and Dorothy began again to pace the floor.

"He will die hating me," said Dorothy. "If he could live I willingly would give him to the — the Scottish woman. Then I could die and my suffering would cease. I must have been mad when I went to the queen. He trusted me with his honor and his life, and I, traitress that I am, have betrayed both. Ah, well, when he dies I also shall die. There is comfort at least in that thought. How helpless I am."

She could not weep. It seemed as if there were not a tear in her. All was hard, dry, burning agony. She again fell upon the bed and moaned piteously for a little time, wringing her hands and uttering frantic ejaculatory prayers for help.

"My mind seems to have forsaken me," she said hoarsely to Madge. "I cannot think. What noise is that?"

She paused and listened for a moment. Then she went to the north window and opened the casement.

"The yeoman guards from Bakewell are coming," she said. "I recognize them by the light of their flambeaux. They are entering the gate at the dove-cote."

A part of the queen's guard had been quartered in the village of Bakewell.

Dorothy stood at the window for a moment and said: "The other guards are here under our window and are ready to march to Rutland. There is Lord Cecil, and Sir William St. Loe, and Malcolm, and there is my father. Now they are off to meet the other yeomen at the dove-cote. The stable boys are lighting their torches and flambeaux. They are going to murder John, and I have sent them."

Dorothy covered her face with her hands and slowly walked to and fro across the room.

"Call Malcolm," said Madge. "Perhaps he can help us. Lead me to the window, Dorothy, and I will call him."

Dorothy led Madge to the window, and above the din of arms I heard her soft voice calling, "Malcolm, Malcolm."

The order to march had been given before Madge called, but I sought Sir William and told him I would return to the Hall to get another sword and would soon overtake him on the road to Rutland.

I then hastened to Dorothy's room. I was ignorant of the means whereby Elizabeth had learned of Mary's presence at Rutland. The queen had told no one how the information reached her. The fact that Mary was in England was all sufficient for Cecil, and he proceeded to execute the order Elizabeth had given for Mary's arrest, without asking or desiring any explanation. I, of course, was in great distress for John's sake, since I knew that he would be attainted of treason. I had sought in vain some plan whereby I might help him, but found none. I, myself, being a Scottish refugee, occupied no safe position, and my slightest act toward helping John or Mary would be construed against me.

When I entered Dorothy's room, she ran to me and said: "Can you help me, Malcolm? Can you help me save him from this terrible evil which I have brought upon him?"

"How did you bring the evil upon him?" I asked, in astonishment. "It was not your fault that he brought Mary Stuart to—"

"No, no," she answered; "but I told the queen she was at Rutland."

"You told the queen?" I exclaimed, unwilling to believe my ears. "You told— How—why—why did you tell her?"

"I do not know why I told her," she replied. "I was mad with—with jealousy. You warned me against it, but I did not heed you. Jennie Faxton told me that she saw John and—but all that does not matter now. I will tell you hereafter if I live. What we must now do is to save him—to save him if we can. Try to devise some plan. Think—think, Malcolm."

My first thought was to ride to Rutland Castle and give the alarm. Sir George would lead the yeomen thither by the shortest route — the road by way of Rowsley. There was another route leading up the Lathkil through the dale, and thence by a road turning southward to Rutland. That road was longer by a league than the one Sir George would take, but I could put my horse to his greatest speed, and I might be able to reach the castle in time to enable John and Mary to escape. I considered the question a moment. My own life certainly would pay the forfeit in case of failure; but my love for John and, I confess it with shame, the memory of my old tenderness for Mary impelled me to take the risk. I explained the plan upon which I was thinking, and told them of my determination. When I did so, Madge grasped me by the arm to detain me, and Dorothy fell upon her knees and kissed my hand.

I said, "I must start at once; for, ride as I may, I fear the yeomen will reach Rutland gates before I can get there."

"But if the guards should be at the gates when you arrive, or if you should be missed by Cecil, you, a Scottish refugee and a friend of Queen Mary, would be suspected of treason, and you would lose your life," said Madge, who was filled with alarm for my sake.

"That is true," I replied; "but I can think of no other way whereby John can possibly be saved."

Dorothy stood for a moment in deep thought, and said : —

"I will ride to Rutland by way of Lathkil Dale — I will ride in place of you, Malcolm. It is my duty and my privilege to do this if I can."

I saw the truth of her words, and felt that since Dorothy had wrought the evil, it was clearly her duty to remedy it if she could. If she should fail, no evil consequences would fall upon her. If I should fail, it would cost me my life; and while I desired to save John, still I wished to save myself. Though my conduct may not have been chivalric, still I was willing that Dorothy should go in my place, and I told her so. I offered to ride with her as far as a certain cross-road a league distant from Rutland Castle. There I would leave her, and go across the country to meet the yeomen on the road they had taken. I could join them before they reached Rutland, and my absence during the earlier portion of the march would not be remarked, or if noticed it could easily be explained.

This plan was agreed upon, and after the guards had passed out at Dove-cote Gate and were well down toward Rowsley, I rode out from the Hall, and waited for Dorothy at an appointed spot near Overhaddon.

Immediately after my departure Dolcy was saddled, and soon Dorothy rode furiously up to me. Away we sped, Dorothy and I, by Yulegrave church, down into the dale, and up the river. Never shall I forget that mad ride. Heavy rains had recently fallen, and the road in places was almost impassable. The rivers were in flood, but when Dorothy and I reached the ford, the girl did not stop to consider the danger ahead of her. I heard her whisper, "On, Dolcy, on," and I heard the sharp "whisp" of the whip as she struck the trembling, fearful mare, and urged her into the dark flood. Dolcy hesitated, but Dorothy struck her again and again with the whip and softly cried, "On, Dolcy, on." Then mare and rider plunged into the swollen river, and I, of course, followed them. The water was so deep that our horses were compelled to swim, and when we reached the opposite side of the river we had drifted with the current a distance of at least three hundred yards below the road. We climbed the cliff by a sheep path. How Dorothy did it I do not know; and how I succeeded in following her I know even less. When we reached the top of the cliff, Dorothy started off at full gallop, leading the way, and again I followed. The sheep path leading up the river to the road followed close the edge of the cliff, where a false step by the horse would mean death to both horse and rider. But Dorothy feared not, or knew not, the danger, and I caught her ever whispered cry,—"On, Dolcy, on; on, Dolcy, on." Ashamed to fall behind, yet fearing to ride at such a pace on such a path, I urged my horse forward. He was a fine, strong, mettlesome brute, and I succeeded in keeping the girl's dim form in sight. The moon, which was rapidly sinking westward, still gave us light through rifts in the black bank of floating clouds, else that ride over the sheep path by the cliff would have been our last journey in the flesh.

Soon we reached the main road turning southward. It was a series of rough rocks and mudholes, and Dorothy and Dolcy shot forward upon it with the speed of the tempest, to undo, if possible, the evil which a dozen words, untimely spoken, had wrought. I urged my horse until his head was close by Dolcy's tail, and ever and anon could I hear the whispered cry,—"On, Dolcy, on; on, Dolcy, sweet Dolcy, good Dolcy; on, my pet, on."

No word was spoken between Dorothy and me; but I could hear Dolcy panting with her mighty effort, and amid the noise of splashing water and the thud, thud, thud of our horses' hoofs came always back to me from Dorothy's lips the sad, sad cry, full of agony and longing, — "On, Dolcy, on; on Dolcy, on."

The road we took led us over steep hills and down through dark, shadow-crowded ravines; but up hill, down hill, and on the level the terrible girl before me plunged forward with unabated headlong fury until I thought surely the flesh of horse, man, and woman could endure the strain not one moment longer. But the horses, the woman, and—though I say it who should not—the man were of God's best handiwork, and the cords of our lives did not snap. One thought, and only one, held possession of the girl, and the matter of her own life or death had no place in her mind.

When we reached the cross-road where I was to leave her, we halted while I instructed Dorothy concerning the road she should follow from that point to Rutland, and directed her how to proceed when she should arrive at the castle gate. She eagerly listened for a moment or two, then grew impatient, and told me to hasten in my speech, since there was no time to lose. Then she fearlessly dashed away alone into the black night; and as I watched her fair form fade into the shadows, the haunting cry came faintly back to me, — "On, Dolcy, on; on, Dolcy on," and I was sick at heart. I was loath to leave her thus in the inky gloom. The moon had sunk for the night, and the clouds had banked up without a rift against the hidden stars; but I could give her no further help, and my life would pay the forfeit should I accompany her. She had brought the evil upon herself. She was the iron, the seed, the cloud, and the rain. She was fulfilling her destiny. She was doing that which she must do: nothing more, nothing less. She was filling her little niche in the universal moment. She was a part of the infinite kaleidoscope — a fate-charged, fate-moved, fragile piece of glass which might be crushed to atoms in the twinkling of an eye, in the sounding of a trump.

After leaving Dorothy I rode across the country and soon overtook the yeoman guard whom I joined unobserved. Then I marched with them, all too rapidly to suit me, to Rutland. The little army had travelled with greater speed than I had expected, and I soon began to fear that Dorothy would not reach Rutland Castle in time to enable its inmates to escape.

Within half an hour from the time I joined the yeomen we saw the dim outlines of the castle, and Sir William

St. Loe gave the command to hurry forward. Cecil, Sir William, Sir George, and myself rode in advance of the column. As we approached the castle by the road leading directly to the gate from the north, I saw for a moment upon the top of the hill west of the castle gate the forms of Dorothy and Dolcy in dim silhouette against the sky. Then I saw them plunge madly down the hill toward the gate. I fancied I could hear the girl whispering in frenzied hoarseness, — "On, Dolcy, on," and I thought I could catch the panting of the mare. At the foot of the hill, less than one hundred yards from the gate, poor Dolcy, unable to take another step, dropped to the ground. Dolcy had gone on to her death. She had filled *her* little niche in the universe and had died at her post. Dorothy plunged forward over the mare's head, and a cry of alarm came from my lips despite me. I was sure the girl had been killed. She, however, instantly sprang to her feet. Her hair was flying behind her and she ran toward the gate crying: "John, John, fly for your life!" And then she fell prone upon the ground and did not rise.

We had all seen the mare fall, and had seen the girl run forward toward the gates and fall before reaching them. Cecil and Sir William rode to the spot where Dorothy lay, and dismounted.

In a moment Sir William called to Sir George: —

"The lady is your daughter, Mistress Dorothy."

"What in hell's name brings her here?" cried Sir George, hurriedly riding forward, "and how came she?"

I followed speedily, and the piteous sight filled my eyes with tears. I cannot describe it adequately to you, though I shall see it vividly to the end of my days. Dorothy had received a slight wound upon the temple, and blood was trickling down her face upon her neck and ruff. Her hair had fallen from its fastenings. She had lost her hat, and her gown was torn in shreds and covered with mud.

I lifted the half-conscious girl to her feet and supported her; then with my kerchief I bound up the wound upon her temple.

"Poor Dolcy," she said, almost incoherently, "I have killed her and I have failed — I have failed. Now I am ready to die. Would that I had died with Dolcy. Let me lie down here, Malcolm, — let me lie down."

I still held her in my arms and supported her half-fainting form.

"Why are you here?" demanded Sir George.

"To die," responded Dorothy.

"To die? Damned nonsense!" returned her father. "How came you here, you fool?"

"On Dolcy. She is dead," returned Dorothy.

"Were you not at Haddon when we left there?" asked her father.

"Yes," she replied.

"Did you pass us on the road?" he asked.

"No."

"How came you here?" Sir George insisted.

"Oh, I flew hither. I am a witch. Don't question me, father. I am in no temper to listen to you. I warn you once and for all, keep away from me; beware of me. I have a dagger in my bosom. Go and do the work you came to do; but remember this, father, if harm comes to him I will take my own life, and my blood shall be upon your soul."

"My God, Malcolm, what does she mean?" asked Sir George, touched with fear by the strength of his daughter's threat. "Has she lost her wits?"

"No," the girl quickly responded, "I have only just found them."

Sir George continued to question Dorothy, but he received no further response from her. She simply held up the palm of her hand warningly toward him, and the gesture was as eloquent as an oration. She leaned against me, and covered her face with her hands, while her form shook and trembled as if with a palsy.

Cecil and Sir William St. Loe then went toward the gate, and Sir George said to me : —

"I must go with them. You remain with Doll, and see that she is taken home. Procure a horse for her. If she is unable to ride, make a litter, or perhaps there is a coach in the castle; if so, take possession of it. Take her home by some means when we return. What, think you, could have brought her here?"

I evaded the question by replying, "I will probably be able to get a coach in the castle, Sir George. Leave Dorothy with me."

Soon, by the command of Sir William, the yeomen rode to the right and to the left for the purpose of surrounding the castle, and then I heard Cecil at the gates demanding : —

"Open in the name of the queen."

"Let us go to the gates," said Dorothy, "that we may hear what they say and see what they do. Will they kill him here, think you?" she asked, looking wildly into my face.

The flambeaux on the castle gate and those which the link-boys had brought with them from Haddon were lighted, and the scene in front of the gate was all aglow.

"No, no, my sweet one," I answered, "perhaps they will not kill him at all. Certainly they will not kill him now. They must try him first."

I tried to dissuade her from going to the gates, but she insisted, and I helped her to walk forward.

When Dorothy and I reached the gates, we found that Cecil and Lord Rutland were holding a consultation through the parley-window. The portcullis was still down, and the gates were closed; but soon the portcullis was raised, a postern was opened from within, and Sir William entered the castle with two score of the yeomen guards.

Sir George approached and again plied Dorothy with questions, but she would not speak. One would have thought from her attitude that she was deaf and dumb. She seemed unconscious of her father's presence.

"She has lost her mind," said Sir George, in tones of deep trouble, "and I know not what to do."

"Leave her with me for a time, cousin. I am sure she will be better if we do not question her now."

Then Dorothy seemed to awaken. "Malcolm is right, father. Leave me for a time, I pray you."

Sir George left us, and waited with a party of yeomen a short distance from the gate for the return of Sir William with his prisoners.

Dorothy and I sat upon a stone bench, near the postern through which Sir William and the guardsmen had entered, but neither of us spoke.

After a long, weary time of waiting Sir William came out of the castle through the postern, and with him came Mary Stuart. My heart jumped when I saw her in the glare of the flambeaux, and the spirit of my dead love for her came begging admission to my heart. I cannot describe my sensations when I beheld her, but this I knew, that my love for her was dead past resurrection.

Following Mary came Lord Rutland, and immediately following his Lordship walked John. When he stepped through the postern, Dorothy sprang to her feet and ran to him with a cry, "John, John!"

He looked at her in surprise, and stepped toward her with evident intent to embrace her. His act was probably the result of an involuntary impulse, for he stopped before he reached the girl.

Sir George had gone at Sir William's request to arrange the guards for the return march.

Dorothy and John were standing within two yards of each other.

"Do not touch me," cried Dorothy, "save to strike me if you will. The evil which has come upon you is of my doing. I betrayed you to the queen."

I saw Mary turn quickly toward the girl when she uttered those words.

"I was insane when I did it," continued Dorothy. "They will take your life, John. But when you die I also shall die. It is a poor reparation, I know, but it is the only one I can make."

"I do not understand you, Dorothy," said John. "Why should you betray me?"

"I cannot tell you," she answered. "All I know is that I did betray you and I hardly know how I did it. It all seems like a dream — like a fearful monster of the night. There is no need for me to explain. I betrayed you and now I suffer for it, more a thousand-fold than you can possibly suffer. I offer no excuse. I have none. I simply betrayed you, and ask only that I may die with you."

Then was manifest in John's heart the noblest quality which God has given to man — charity, strengthened by reason. His face glowed with a light that seemed saint-like, and a grand look of ineffable love and pity came to his eyes. He seemed as if by inspiration to understand all that Dorothy had felt and done, and he knew that if she had betrayed him she had done it at a time when she was not responsible for her acts. He stepped quickly to the girl's side, and caring naught that we all should see him, caught her to his breast. He held her in his arms, and the light of the flambeaux fell upon her upturned face.

"Dorothy," he said, "it matters not what you have done; you are my only love. I ask no explanation. If you have betrayed me to death, though I hope it will not come to that evil, you did not do it because you did not love me."

"No, no, John, you know that," sobbed the girl.

"I do know it, Dorothy; I know all that I wish to know. You would not intentionally bring evil upon me while you love me."

"Ah, that I do, John; only God knows how deeply, how desperately. My love was the cause — my love was my curse — it was your curse."

"Do not weep, Dorothy," said John, interrupting her. "I would that I could take all your suffering upon myself. Do not weep."

Dorothy buried her face upon his breast and tears came to her relief. She was not alone in her weeping, for there stood I like a very woman, and by my side stood rough old Sir William. Tears were coursing down the bronzed cheek of the grand old warrior like drops of glistening dew upon the harrowed face of a mountain rock. When I saw Sir William's tears, I could no longer restrain my emotions, and I frankly tell you that I made a spectacle of myself in full view of the queen's yeoman guard.

Sir George approached our little group, and when he saw Dorothy in John's arms, he broke forth into oaths and stepped toward her intending to force her away. But John held up the palm of his free hand warningly toward Sir George, and drawing the girl's drooping form close to his breast he spoke calmly: —

"Old man, if you but lay a finger on this girl, I will kill you where you stand. No power on earth can save you."

There was a tone in John's voice that forced even Sir George to pause. Then Sir George turned to me.

"This is the man who was in my house. He is the man who called himself Thomas. Do you know him?"

Dorothy saved me from the humiliation of an answer. She took one step from John's side and held him by the hand while she spoke.

"Father," she said, "this man is Sir John Manners. Now you may understand why he could not seek my hand openly, and you also know why I could not tell you his name." She again turned to John, and he put his arm about her. You can imagine much better that I can describe Sir George's fury. He snatched a halberd from the hands of a yeoman who was standing near by and started toward John and Dorothy. Thereupon the hard old warrior, Sir William St. Loe, whose heart one would surely say was the last place where sentiment could dwell, performed a little act of virtue which will balance many a page on the debtor side of his ledger of life. He lifted his sword and scabbard and struck Sir George's outstretched hand, causing the halberd to fall to the ground.

"Don't touch the girl," cried Sir William, hoarsely.

"She is my daughter," retorted Sir George, who was stunned mentally as well as physically by Sir William's blow.

"I care not whose daughter she is," returned Sir William. "You shall not touch her. If you make but one other attempt, I will use my blade upon you."

Sir William and John had been warm friends at London court, and the old captain of the guards quickly guessed the true situation when he saw Dorothy run to John's arms.

"Sir, you shall answer for this," said Sir George, angrily, to Sir William.

"With pleasure," returned Sir William. "I will give you satisfaction whenever you wish it, save this present time. I am too busy now."

Blessed old Sir William! You have been dead these many winters; and were I a priest, I would say a mass for your soul gratis every day in the year.

"Did the girl betray us?" asked Queen Mary.

No one answered her question. Then she turned toward Sir John and touched him upon the shoulder. He turned his face toward her, signifying that he was listening.

"Who is this girl?" Mary demanded.

"My sweetheart, my affianced wife," John answered.

"She says she betrayed us," the queen responded.

"Yes," said John.

"Did you trust her with knowledge of our presence in Rutland?" Mary demanded angrily.

"I did," he answered.

"You were a fool," said Mary.

"I know it," responded John.

"You certainly bear her no resentment for her treason," said Mary.

"I certainly do not," quietly answered John. "Her suffering is greater than mine. Can you not see that it is?"

"It is your privilege," said Mary, scornfully, "to intrust your own secrets to whomsoever you may choose for your confidant, and it is quite saintlike in you to forgive this person for betraying you; but what think you of the hard case in which her treason and your folly have placed me?"

"That is my greatest grief, save for Dorothy," answered John, softly. Lived there ever a man possessed of broader charity or deeper love than John? God surely made him of gold dust, not of common clay.

Queen Mary stepped away from John in disgust, and when she turned she saw me for the first time. She started and was about to speak, but I placed my fingers warningly upon my lips and she remained silent.

"Where do you take us, Sir William?" asked John.

"To Haddon Hall. There you will await the commands of the queen."

"How came you here?" John asked gently of Dorothy.

"I rode Dolcy," she whispered. "She dropped dead at the foot of the hill. Yonder she lies. I came up the Lathkil by the long road, and I hoped that I might reach you in time to give warning. When the guard left Haddon I realized the evil that would come upon you by reason of my base betrayal." Here she broke down and for a moment could not proceed in the narrative. She soon recovered and continued: "Then I mounted Dolcy, and tried to reach here by way of the long road. Poor Dolcy seemed to understand my trouble and my despair, and she brought me with all the speed that a horse could make; but the road was too long and too rough; and she failed, and I failed. Would that I could have died in her place. She gave her life in trying to remedy my fault."

Dorothy again began to weep, and John tenderly whispered: —

"All will yet come right." Then he kissed her before us all, and handed her to me saying, "Care for her, I pray you, sir."

John spoke a few words to Sir William, and in a moment they both went back to the castle.

In a short time the gates were opened, and the Rutland coach drawn by four horses emerged from the castle grounds. Sir William then directed Mary and Dorothy to enter the coach and requested me to ride with them to Haddon Hall.

The yeoman guards were in marching order, and I took my seat in the coach. The fates surely were in a humorous mood when they threw Dorothy, Queen Mary, and myself together. Pause for a moment and consider the situation. You know all the facts and you can analyze it as well as I. I could not help laughing at the fantastic trick of destiny.

Soon after I entered the coach Sir William gave the

word, and the yeomen with Lord Rutland and John moved forward on the road to Haddon.

The coach at once followed the guard and a score of yeomen followed us.

Queen Mary occupied the back seat of the coach, and Dorothy and I sat upon the front seat facing her.

Dorothy was exhausted, and her head lay upon my shoulder. Now and again she would softly moan and sob, but she said nothing. After a few minutes of silence Queen Mary spoke: —

"Why did you betray me, you miserable wretch? Why did you betray me?"

Dorothy did not answer. Mary continued: —

"Have I ever injured you in any manner? Have I ever harmed you by thought, word, or deed?"

Dorothy's only answer was a sob.

"Perhaps you are a canting fanatic, and it may be that you hate me for the sake of that which you call the love of God?"

"No, no, madam," I said, "that was not the reason."

"Do you know the reason, Malcolm?" asked Mary, addressing me for the first time. My name upon her lips had a strange effect on me. It was like the wafting to my nostrils of a sweet forgotten odor, or the falling upon my ears of a tender refrain of bygone days. Her voice in uttering my name thrilled me, and I hated myself for my weakness.

I told Mary that I did not know Dorothy's reasons, and she continued: —

"Malcolm, you were not a party to my betrayal for the sake of revenging yourself on me?"

"God forbid!" I answered. "Sir John Manners will assure you of my innocence. I rode with Mistress Vernon to a cross-road within a league of Rutland, hoping thereby to assist her to give you and Sir John the alarm."

My admission soon brought me into trouble.

"I alone am to blame," said Dorothy, faintly.

"I can easily believe you," said Mary, sharply. "Did you expect to injure me?"

No answer came from Dorothy.

"If you expect to injure me," Mary continued, "you will be disappointed. I am a queen, and my Cousin Elizabeth would not dare to harm me, even though she might wish to do so. We are of the same blood, and she will not wish to do me injury. Your doting lover will probably lose his head for bringing me to England without his queen's consent. He is her subject. I am not. I wish you joy of the trouble you have brought upon him and upon yourself."

"Upon him!" cried Dorothy.

"Yes, upon him," continued Mary, relishing the torture she was inflicting. "You will enjoy seeing him beheaded, will you not, you fool, you huzzy, you wretch? I hope his death will haunt you till the end of your days."

Poor Dorothy, leaning against me, said faintly:—

"It will—it will. You—you devil."

The girl was almost dead from exhaustion and anguish, but she would have been dead indeed had she lacked the power to strike back. I believe had it not been for Dorothy's physical weakness she would have silenced Mary with her hands.

After a little time Dorothy's heavy breathing indicated that she had fallen asleep. Her head rested upon my shoulder, and the delicious perfume of her hair and the sweet warm breath from her lips were almost intoxicating even to me, though I was not in love with her. How great must their effect have been coming upon John hot from her intense young soul!

As the link-boys passed the coach some and some with their flambeaux I could see Dorothy's sweet pale face, almost hidden in the tangled golden red hair which fell in floods about her. The perfect oval of her cheek, the long wet lashes, the arched eyebrows, the low broad forehead, the straight nose, the saucy chin — all presented a picture of beauty and pathos sufficient to soften a heart of stone. Mary had no heart of any sort, therefore she was not moved to pity. That emotion, I am sure, she never felt from the first to the last day of her life. She continued to probe Dorothy's wound until I told her the girl was asleep. I changed Dorothy's position and placed her head against the corner cushion of the coach that she might rest more comfortably. She did not awaken when I moved her. She slept and looked like a child. For a little time after I had changed Dorothy's position Mary and I sat in silence. She was the first to speak. She leaned forward and placing her hands upon mine, whispered my name: —

"Malcolm!"

After a brief silence I said: —

"What would you, your Majesty?"

"Not 'your Majesty'" said Mary, softly, "but Mary, as of old."

She remained for a moment with her hand upon my knee, and then whispered: —

"Will you not sit by me, Malcolm?"

I believe that Mary Stuart's voice was the charm wherewith she fascinated men. I resisted to my utmost strength, but that seemed to be little more than utter weakness; so I took a seat by her side, and she gently placed her hand in mine. The warm touch of her strong, delicate fingers gave me a familiar thrill. She asked me to tell her of my wanderings since I had left Scotland, and I briefly related all my adventures. I told her of my home at Haddon Hall and of the welcome given me by my cousin, Sir George.

"Malcolm, have you forgotten?" she whispered, leaning

gently against me. "Have you forgotten our old-time vows and love? Have you forgotten all that passed between us in the dear old château, when I gave to you my virgin love, fresh from my virgin heart?" I sighed and tried to harden my heart to her blandishments, for I knew she wished to use me and was tempting me to that end.

She continued, "I was then only fourteen years old — ten years ago. You said that you loved me and I believed you. You could not doubt, after the proof I gave to you, that my heart was all yours. We were happy, oh, so happy. Do you remember, Malcolm?"

She brought her face close to mine while she spoke, and pressed my hand upon her breast.

My reason told me that it was but the song of the siren she was singing to my ears. My memory told me that she had been false to me twice two score times, and I knew full well she would again be false to me, or to any other man whom she could use for her purposes, and that she cared not the price at which she purchased him. Bear in mind, you who would blame me for my fall, that this woman not only was transcendently beautiful and fatally fascinating, but she was a queen and had held undisputed sway over my heart for more years than I could accurately number. As I said, added to all her beauty, she was a queen. If you have never known royalty, you cannot understand its enthralling power.

"I remember it all, madam," I replied, trying to hold myself away from her. "It is fresh to me as if it all had happened yesterday." The queen drew my arm closely to her side and nestled her cheek for an instant upon my shoulder.

"I remember also," I continued, "your marriage with Darnley when I had your promise that you would marry me; and, shame upon shame, I remember your marriage with Darnley's murderer, Bothwell."

"Cruel, cruel, Malcolm," she said. "You well know the overpowering reasons of state which impelled me to sacrifice my own happiness by marrying Darnley. I told you at the time that I hated the marriage more than I dreaded death. But I longed to quiet the factions in Scotland, and I hoped to save my poor bleeding people from the evils of war. You know I hated Darnley. You know I loved you. You knew then and you know now that you are the only man who has ever possessed my heart. You know that my words are true. You know that you, alone, have had my love since the time when I was a child."

"And Rizzio?" I asked.

"Ah, Malcolm," she answered tearfully, "I hope you, of all men, do not believe that I ever gave a thought of love to Rizzio. He was to me like my pet monkey or my favorite falcon. He was a beautiful, gentle, harmless soul. I loved him for his music. He worshipped me as did my spaniel."

Still I was determined that her blandishments should not move me.

"And Bothwell?" I asked.

"That is past endurance from you, Malcolm," she said, beginning to weep. "You know I was brutally abducted and was forced into marriage with him. He was an outlaw, an outcast. He was an uncouth brute whom any woman would loathe. I was in his power, and I feigned acquiescence only that I might escape and achieve vengeance upon him. Tell me, Malcolm, tell me," continued Mary, placing her arms about my neck and clinging to me, "tell me, you, to whom I gave my maiden's love, you who have my woman's heart, tell me, do you believe that I could willingly have married Bothwell, even though my heart had not been filled with the image of you, who are strong, gentle, and beautiful?"

You, if you are a man, may think that in my place you would have resisted the attack of this beautiful queen, but if so you think — pardon me, my friend — you are a fool. Under the spell of her magic influence I wavered in the conviction which had long since come upon me, that I had for years been her fool and her dupe. I forgot the former lessons I had learned from her perfidy. I forgot my manhood. I forgot all of good that had of late grown up in me. God help me, I forgot even Madge.

"If I could only believe you, Mary," I answered, growing insane under the influence of her fascinations, "if I could only believe you."

"Give me your lips, Malcolm," she whispered, "give me your lips.—Again, my Malcolm.—Ah, now you believe me."

The lying logic of a wanton kiss is irresistible. I was drunk and, alas! I was convinced. When I think of that time, Samson is my only comfort — Samson and a few hundred million other fools, who like Samson and me have been wheedled, kissed, and duped into misery and ruin.

I said: "I do believe you, Mary. I beg you to forgive me for having doubted you. You have been traduced and brutally misused."

"It is sweet to hear you speak those words. But it is better to think that at last we have come together with nothing to part us save that I am a prisoner in the hands of my vindictive, jealous cousin. I thank God that my kingdom of Scotland has been taken from me. I ever hated the Scots. They are an ignorant, unkempt, wry-necked, stubborn, filthy race. But, above all, my crown stood between you and me. I may now be a woman, and were it not for Elizabeth, you and I could yet find solace in each other for all our past sufferings. Malcolm, I have a sweet thought. If I could escape to fair, beautiful France, all would be happiness for us. You could claim your mother's estates in the balmy south, and we might

live upon them. Help me, my Malcolm, to escape, and
your reward shall be greater and sweeter than man ever
before received from woman."

I struggled against her blandishments for a moment,
but I was lost.

"You shall escape and I will go with you," said I.

Man needs to make but one little prayer to God, "Lead
me not into temptation." That prayer answered, all else
of good will follow.

The morning sun had just begun to rise over Bowling
Green Hill and the shadows of the night were fleeing before his lances, when our cavalcade entered the grounds of
Haddon at the dove-cote. If there were two suns revolving about the earth, one to shine upon us by night and
one by day, much evil would be averted. Men do evil in
the dark because others cannot see them; they think evil
in the dark because they cannot see themselves.

With the first faint gray of dawn there came to me
thoughts of Madge. I had forgotten her, but her familiar
spirit, the light, brought me back to its fair mistress.

When our coach reached the stone bridge I looked up
to the Hall and saw Madge standing at the open casement
of the tower window. She had been watching there all
night, I learned, hoping for our speedy and safe return,
and had been warned of our approach by the noise of the
tramping guard. I drew back from the coach window,
feeling that I was an evil shade slinking away before the
spirit of light.

DOROTHY VERNON

CHAPTER XV

LIGHT

DOROTHY had awakened while we were entering Rowsley, and I was glad that Mary could not touch me again.

When our coach reached the stone steps of the entrance tower we found Sir George, Lady Crawford, and Madge waiting to receive us. The steps and the path leading to them had been carpeted with soft rugs, and Mary, although a prisoner, was received with ceremonies befitting her rank. It was a proud day for Sir George when the roof of his beautiful Hall sheltered the two most famous queens of christendom.

Sir George assisted Mary from the coach most graciously, and in knightly fashion led her to Lady Crawford and Madge, who were standing at the foot of the tower steps. Due presentations were made, and the ladies of Haddon having kissed the queen's hand, Mary went into the Hall upon the arm of his Majesty, the King of the Peak, who stepped forward most proudly.

His resentment against Dorothy was for the moment neutralized by the great honor of which his house and himself were the recipients.

John and Lord Rutland were taken to the dungeon.

I assisted Dorothy from the coach and led her to Madge, who was waiting for us upon the lowest of the steps leading to the entrance tower doorway. Dorothy took Madge's outstretched hand; but Madge, by some strange instinct, knowing of my presence, turned her face toward me. I could not lift my eyes to her face, nor could I endure to remain in her presence. While we were ascending the steps she held out her hand to me and said:—

"Is all well with you, Malcolm?" Her voice was full of tender concern, and it pained me to the heart to hear her speak kindly to me, who was so unworthy of her smallest thought.

"Yes, Lady—yes, Madge," I responded; but she knew from the tones of my voice that all was not right with me.

"I fear, Malcolm, that you do not tell me the truth. You will come to me soon?" she asked.

"I may not be able to go to you soon," I answered, "but I will do so at the first opportunity."

The torture of her kindness was almost unbearable to me. One touch of her hand, one tone of her rare voice, had made me loathe myself. The powers of evil cannot stand for one moment in a fair conflict with the powers of good. I felt that I, alone, was to blame for my treason to Madge; but despite my effort at self-condemnation there was an under-consciousness that Mary Stuart was to blame, and I hated her accordingly. Although Madge's presence hurt me, it was not because I wished to conceal my conduct from her. I knew that I could be happy again only after I had confessed to her and had received forgiveness.

Madge, who was blind of sight, led Dorothy, who was piteously blind of soul, and the two girls went to their apartments.

Curiosity is not foreign even to the royal female breast, and while Mary Stuart was entering Haddon Hall, I saw the luminous head of the Virgin Queen peeked out at a casement on the second floor watching her rival with all the curiosity of a Dutch woman sitting by her window mirror.

I went to my room in Eagle Tower, fell upon my bed, and abandoned myself to an anguish of soul which was almost luxurious. I shall not tease you with the details of my mental and moral processes. I hung in the balance a long time undetermined what course I should pursue. The difference between the influence of Mary and the effect wrought by Madge was the difference between the intoxication and the exhilaration of wine. Following the intoxication of Mary's presence ever came a torturing reaction, while the exhilarating influence of Madge gave health and strength. I chose the latter. I have always been glad I reached that determination without the aid of any impulse outside of myself; for events soon happened which again drove all faith in Mary from my heart forever. Those events would have forced me to abandon my trust in her; but mind you, I took my good resolve from inclination rather than necessity before I learned of Mary's perfidy.

The events of the night had exhausted Dorothy, and she was confined to her bed by illness for the first time in her life. She believed that she was dying, and she did not want to live. I did not go to her apartments. Madge remained with her, and I, coward-like, feared to face the girl to whom I had been untrue.

Dorothy's one and only desire, of course, was to see John, but that desire for a time seemed impossible of accomplishment.

Elizabeth, Cecil, Leicester, and Sir William St. Loe were in secret consultation many times during three or four days and nights. Occasionally Sir George was called into their councils, and that flattering attention so wrought upon the old man's pride that he was a slave to the queen's slightest wish, and was more tyrannical and dictatorial than ever before to all the rest of mankind. There were, however, two persons besides the queen before whom Sir George was gracious: one of these was Mary Stuart, whose powers of fascination had been brought to bear upon the King of the Peak most effectively. The other was Leicester, to whom, as my cousin expressed it, he hoped to dispose of that troublesome and disturbing body — Dorothy. These influences, together with the fact that his enemies of Rutland were in the Haddon dungeon, had given Sir George a spleen-vent, and Dorothy, even in the face of her father's discovery that Manners was her mysterious lover, had for once a respite from Sir George's just and mighty wrath.

The purpose of Elizabeth's many councils of war was to devise some means of obtaining from John and his father, information concerning the plot which had resulted in bringing Mary Stuart into England. The ultimate purpose of Mary's visit, Elizabeth's counsellors firmly believed to be the dethronement of the English queen and the enthronement of her Scottish cousin. Elizabeth, in her heart, felt confident that John and his father were not parties to the treasonable plot, although she had been warned against each of them. Cecil and Sir William St. Loe also secretly held to that opinion, though neither of them expressed it. Elizabeth was conscious of having given to John while at London court an intimation that she would be willing that Mary should visit England. Of such intimation Cecil and Sir William had no knowledge, though they, together with many persons of the court, believed that Elizabeth was not entirely averse to Mary's presence.

Lord Rutland and John were questioned by Cecil in the hope of obtaining some hints which might lead to the detection of those concerned in the chief plot, provided such plot existed. But Lord Rutland knew nothing of the affair except that John had brought the Scottish queen from Scotland, and John persisted in the statement that he had no confederate and that he knew nothing of any plot to place Mary upon the English throne.

John said: "I received from Queen Mary's friends in Scotland letters asking me to meet her on the border, and requesting me to conduct her to my father's castle. Those letters mentioned no Englishman but myself, and they stated that Queen Mary's flight to England was to be undertaken with the tacit consent of our gracious queen. That fact, the letters told me, our queen wished should not be known. There were reasons of state, the letters said, which made it impolitic for our queen openly to invite Queen Mary to seek sanctuary in England. I received those letters before I left Westminster. Upon the day when I received them, I heard our gracious queen say that she would gladly invite Queen Mary to England, were it not for the fact that such an invitation would cause trouble between her and the regent, Murray. Her Majesty at the same time intimated that she would be glad if Mary Stuart should come to England uninvited." John turned to Elizabeth, "I beg your Majesty, in justice, to ratify my words."

Elizabeth hesitated for a moment after John's appeal; but her love of justice came to her rescue and she hung her head as she said, "You are right, Sir John." Then she looked her counsellors in the face and said, "I well remember that I so expressed myself."

"In truth," said John, "I having only an hour before received the letter from Scotland, believed that your Majesty's words were meant for my ear. I felt that your Majesty knew of the letters, and I thought that I should be carrying out your royal wishes should I bring Queen Mary into England without your knowledge."

The queen responded: "I then felt that I wished Queen

Mary to seek refuge in my kingdom, but so many untoward events have transpired since I spoke on the subject
at Westminster that I have good cause to change my mind,
though I easily understand how you might have been mis-
led by my words."

"I am sure," replied John, "that your Majesty has had
good cause to change your mind; but I protest in all sin-
cerity that I considered the Scottish letters to be a command from my queen."

Elizabeth was a strange combination of paradoxes. No
one could be truer than she to a fixed determination once
taken. No one could be swayed by doubt so easily as she
to change her mind sixty times in the space of a minute.
During one moment she was minded to liberate John and
Lord Rutland; in the next she determined to hold them in
prison, hoping to learn from them some substantial fact
concerning the plot which, since Mary's arrival in England,
had become a nightmare to her. But, with all her va-
garies the Virgin Queen surely loved justice. That quality,
alone, makes a sovereign great. Elizabeth, like her mother,
Anne Boleyn, had great faith in her personal beauty; like
her father, she had unbounded confidence in her powers of
mind. She took great pride in the ease with which she
controlled persons. She believed that no one was so adroit
as Elizabeth Tudor in extracting secrets from others, and
in unravelling mysterious situations, nor so cunning in
hunting out plots and in running down plotters. In all
such matters she delighted to act secretly and alone.

During the numerous councils held at Haddon, Elizabeth
allowed Cecil to question John to his heart's content; but
while she listened she formulated a plan of her own which
she was sure would be effective in extracting all the truth
from John, if all the truth had not already been extracted.

Elizabeth kept her cherished plan to herself. It was
this: —

She would visit Dorothy, whom she knew to be ill, and would by her subtle art steal from John's sweetheart all that the girl knew of the case. If John had told Dorothy part of the affair concerning Mary Stuart, he had probably told her all, and Elizabeth felt confident that she could easily pump the girl dry. She did not know Dorothy.

Accordingly our queen, Elizabeth, the adroit, went to Dorothy's room under the pretence of paying the girl a gracious visit. Dorothy wished to arise and receive her royal guest, but Elizabeth said gently: —

"Do not arise, Dorothy; rest quietly, and I will sit here beside you on the bed. I have come to tell you that you must recover your health at once. We miss you greatly in the Hall."

No one could be more gracious than Elizabeth when the humor was upon her; though, in truth, the humor was often lacking.

"Let us send all save you and me from the room," said the queen, "that we may have a quiet little chat together."

All who were in the room save Dorothy and Elizabeth of course departed at once.

When the door was closed, the queen said: "I wish to thank you for telling me of the presence of her Scottish Majesty at Rutland. You know there is a plot on foot to steal my throne from me."

"God forbid that there should be such a plot," replied Dorothy, resting upon her elbow in the bed.

"I fear it is only too true that there is such a plot," returned Elizabeth, "and I owe you a great debt of gratitude for warning me of the Scottish queen's presence in my kingdom."

"I hope the danger will be averted from your Majesty," said Dorothy; "but that which I did will cause my death — it will kill me. No human being ever before has lived through the agony I have suffered since that terrible night. I was a traitress. I betrayed the man who is dearer to me than my immortal soul. He says that he forgives me, but your Majesty knows that my fault is beyond forgiveness."

"Sir John is a noble gentleman, child," said the queen. "I hope that he is loyal to me, but I fear—I fear."

"Do not doubt, do not fear, my queen," returned Dorothy, eagerly; "there is nothing false in him."

"Do you love him deeply, little one?" asked the queen.

"No words can tell you my love for him," answered the girl. "I feel shame to say that he has taken even the holy God's place in my heart. Perhaps it is for that sin that God now punishes me."

"Fear not on that score, Dorothy," replied the queen. "God will not punish you for feeling the love which He Himself has put into your heart. I would willingly give my crown could I feel such love for a worthy man who would in return love me for myself. But I cannot feel, nor can I have faith. Self-interest, which is so dominant in all men, frightens me, and I doubt their vows."

"Surely, any man would love you for your own sake," said Dorothy, tenderly.

"It may be that you speak truly, child; but I cannot know when men's vows are true nor when they are false. The real trouble is within myself. If I could but feel truly, I could interpret truthfully."

"Ah, your Majesty," interrupted Dorothy, "you do not know the thing for which you are wishing; it is a torture worse than death; it is an ecstasy sweeter than heaven. It is killing me. I pity you, though you are a queen, if you have never felt it."

"Would you do anything I might ask of you, if you could thereby save Sir John's life?" asked the queen.

"Ah, I would gladly give my soul to save him," responded

Dorothy, with tears in her eyes and eagerness in her voice.
" Oh, my queen, do not lead me to hope, and then plunge
me again into despair. Give me no encouragement unless
you mean to free him. As for my part, take my life and
spare John's. Kill me by torture, burn me at the stake,
stretch me upon the rack till my joints are severed and
my flesh is torn asunder. Let me die by inches, my queen ;
but spare him, oh, spare him, and do with me as you will.
Ask from me what you wish. Gladly will I do all that you
may demand ; gladly will I welcome death and call it sweet,
if I can thereby save him. The faint hope your Majesty's
words hold out makes me strong again. Come, come, take
my life ; take all that I can give. Give me him."

" Do you believe that I am an ogress thirsting for blood,
Dorothy, that you offer me your life for his ? You can
purchase Sir John's life at a much smaller cost." Dorothy
rose to the queen with a cry, and put her arms about her
neck. " You may purchase his freedom," continued the
queen, " and you may serve your loving queen at one and
the same time, if you wish to do so."

Dorothy had sunk back into the bed, and Elizabeth was
sitting close by her side ; but when the queen spoke she
turned her head on the pillow and kissed the royal hand
which was resting upon the coverlid.

" Ah, you are so good, so true, and so beautiful," said
Dorothy.

Her familiarity toward the queen was sweet to the
woman, to whom it was new.

Dorothy did not thank the queen for her graciousness.
She did not reply directly to her offer. She simply
said : —

" John has told me many times that he was first attracted
to me because I resembled you."

The girl had ample faith in her own beauty, and knew
full well the subtle flattery which lay in her words. " He

said," she continued, "that my hair in some faint degree
resembled yours, but he said it was not of so beautiful a
hue. I have loved my hair ever since the day he told me
that it resembled your Majesty's." The girl leaned forward
toward the queen and gently kissed the royal locks. They
no more resembled Dorothy's hair than brick dust resembles
the sheen of gold.

The queen glanced at the reflection of her hair in the
mirror and it flatly contradicted Dorothy. But the girl's
words were backed by Elizabeth's vanity, and the adroit
flattery went home.

"Ah, my child," exclaimed her Majesty softly, as she
leaned forward and kissed Dorothy's fair cheek.

Dorothy wept gently for a moment and familiarly rested
her face upon the queen's breast. Then she entwined
her white arms about Elizabeth's neck and turned her
glorious eyes up to the queen's face that her Majesty
might behold their wondrous beauty and feel the flattery
of the words she was about to utter.

"He said also," continued Dorothy, "that my eyes in
some slight degree resembled your Majesty's, but he quali-
fied his compliment by telling me — he did not exactly tell
me that my eyes were not so large and brilliant as your
Majesty's, for he was making love to me, and of course he
would not have dared to say that my eyes were not the
most perfect on earth; but he did say that — at least I
know that he meant — that my eyes, while they resembled
yours, were hardly so glorious, and — and I am very
jealous of your Majesty. John will be leaving me to
worship at your feet."

Elizabeth's eyes were good enough. The French called
them "marcassin," that is, wild boar's eyes. They were
little and sparkling; they were not luminous and large
like Dorothy's, and the girl's flattery was rank. Elizabeth,
however, saw Dorothy's eyes and believed her words rather

than the reply of the lying mirror, and her Majesty's heart was soft from the girl's kneading. Consider, I pray you, the serpent-like wisdom displayed by Dorothy's method of attack upon the queen. She did not ask for John's liberty. She did not seek it. She sought only to place John softly on Elizabeth's heart. Some natures absorb flattery as the desert sands absorb the unfrequent rain, and Elizabeth — but I will speak no ill of her. She is the greatest and the best sovereign England has ever had. May God send to my beloved country others like her. She had many small shortcomings; but I have noticed that those persons who spend their evil energies in little faults have less force left for greater ones. I will show you a mystery: Little faults are personally more disagreeable and rasping to us than great ones. Like flying grains of sand upon a windy day, they vex us constantly. Great faults come like an avalanche, but they come less frequently, and we often admire their possessor, who sooner or later is apt to become our destroyer.

"I can hardly tell you," said Dorothy in response to a question by Elizabeth, "I can hardly tell you why I informed your Majesty of Queen Mary's presence at Rutland. I did it partly for love of your Majesty and partly because I was jealous of that white, plain woman from Scotland."

"She is not a plain woman, is she?" said Elizabeth, delighted to hear Mary of Scotland so spoken of for once. One way to flatter some women is to berate those whom they despise or fear. Elizabeth loved Dorothy better for the hatred which the girl bore to Mary. Both stood upon a broad plane of mutual sympathy — jealousy of the same woman. It united the queen and the maiden in a common heart-touching cause.

Dorothy's confidence grew apace. "She is plain," replied Dorothy, poutingly. "She appears plain, colorless, and repulsive by the side of your Majesty."

"No, no, Dorothy, that cannot be," returned Queen Elizabeth, gently patting Dorothy's cheek and glancing stealthily at the reflection of her own face in the mirror. At this point Dorothy considered that the time had come for a direct attack.

"Your Majesty need have no fear of a plot to place Queen Mary upon your throne. The English people would not endure her wicked pale face for a moment."

"But there is such a plot in existence," said Elizabeth.

"What you say may be true," returned Dorothy; "but, your Majesty, John is not in the plot, and he knows nothing of it."

"I hope — I believe — he is not in the plot," said Elizabeth, "but I fear — "

The girl kissed the sleeve of Elizabeth's gown, and then she drew the queen closer to her and kissed her hair and her face.

"Ah, my beauteous queen," said Dorothy, "I thank you for those words. You must know that John loves you, and is your loyal subject. Take pity upon me. Help me. Hold out your gracious hand and lift me from my despair."

Dorothy slipped from the bed and fell on her knees, burying her face in the queen's lap.

Elizabeth was touched by the girl's appeal, and caressingly stroked her hair, as she said: "I believe he is innocent, but I fear he knows or suspects others who harbor treasonable designs. Tell me, Dorothy, do you know of any such persons? If you can tell me their names, you will serve your queen, and will save your lover. No harm shall come to Sir John, and no one save myself shall have knowledge of any word that you may speak. If I do not learn the names of the traitors through you or through Sir John, I may be compelled to hold him a prisoner until I discover them. If through you I learn them, Sir John shall go free at once."

"Gladly, for your Majesty's sake alone would I tell you the names of such traitorous men, did I know them;" replied Dorothy, "and thrice gladly would I do so if I might thereby liberate John. Your Majesty must see that these motives are strong enough to induce me to speak if I knew aught to tell you. I would betray the whole world to save him, of that you may be sure. But alas! I know no man whom I can betray. John told me nothing of his expedition to the Scottish border save what was in two letters which he sent to me. One of these I received before he left Rutland, and the other after his return."

She fetched the letters to the queen, who read them carefully.

"Perhaps if I were to see him, he might, upon my importunity, tell me all he knows concerning the affair and those connected with it if he knows anything more than he has already told," said Dorothy, by a great effort suppressing her eagerness. "I am sure, your Majesty, he would tell me all. Should he tell me the names of any persons connected with any treasonable plot, I will certainly tell you. It would be base in me again to betray John's confidence; but your Majesty has promised me his life and liberty, and to obtain those I would do anything, however evil it might be. If I may see John, I promise to learn all that he knows, if he knows anything; and I also promise to tell you word for word all that he says."

The girl felt safe in making these promises, since she was sure that John knew nothing of a treasonable character.

The queen, thinking that she had adroitly led Dorothy up to making the offer, said, "I accept the conditions. Be in readiness to visit Sir John, upon my command."

Thus the compact was sealed, and the queen, who thought herself wise, was used by the girl, who thought herself simple.

For the purpose of hiding her exultation, Dorothy appeared to be ill, but when the queen passed out at the door and closed it behind her, the girl sprang from the bed and danced around the room as if she were a bear-baiter. From the depths of despair she flew to the pinnacle of hope. She knew, however, that she must conceal her happiness; therefore she went back to bed and waited impatiently the summons of Elizabeth requiring her to go to John.

But now I must pause to tell you of my troubles which followed so swiftly upon the heels of my fault that I was fairly stunned by them. My narrative will be brief, and I shall soon bring you back again to Dorothy.

Queen Mary had no sooner arrived at Haddon Hall than she opened an attack upon Leicester, somewhat after the same plan, I suppose, which she had followed with me in the coach. She could no more easily resist inviting homage from men than a swallow can refrain from flying. Thus, from inclination and policy, she sought Leicester and endeavored by the pleasant paths of her blandishments to lead him to her cause. There can be no doubt concerning Leicester's wishes in the premises. Had Mary's cause held elements of success, he would have joined her; but he feared Elizabeth, and he hoped some day to share her throne. He would, however, prefer to share the throne with Mary.

Mary told him of her plans and hopes. She told him that I had ridden with Dorothy for the purpose of rescuing John and herself, and that I had promised to help her to escape to France. She told him she would use me for her tool in making her escape, and would discard me when once she should be safe out of England. Then would come Leicester's turn. Then should my lord have his recompense, and together they would regain the Scottish crown.

How deeply Leicester became engaged in the plot I cannot say, but this I know: through fear of Elizabeth, or for the purpose of winning her favor, he unfolded to our queen all the details of Mary's scheme, together with the full story of my ride with Dorothy to Rutland, and my return with Dorothy and Mary in the coach. Thereupon Mary was placed under strict guard. The story spread quickly through the Hall, and Dawson brought it to me. On hearing it, my first thought was of Madge. I knew it would soon reach her. Therefore I determined to go to her at once and make a clean breast of all my perfidy. Had I done so sooner, I should at least have had the benefit of an honest, voluntary confession; but my conscience had made a coward of me, and the woman who had been my curse for years had so completely disturbed my mind that I should have been quite as well off without any at all. It led me from one mistake into another.

After Dawson told me that my miserable story was known throughout the Hall, I sought Madge, and found her with Aunt Dorothy. She was weeping, and I at once knew that I was too late with my confession. I spoke her name, "Madge," and stood by her side awaiting her reply.

"Is it true, Malcolm?" she asked. "I cannot believe it till I hear it from your lips."

"It was true," I responded. "I promised to help Queen Mary escape, and I promised to go with her; but within one hour of the time when I gave my word I regretted it as I have never regretted anything else in all my life. I resolved that, while I should, according to my promise, help the Scottish queen escape, I would not go with her. I resolved to wait here at Haddon to tell all to you and to our queen, and then I would patiently take my just punishment from each. My doom from the queen, I believed, would probably be death; but I feared more your — God help me! It is useless for me to speak." Here I broke down and fell upon my knees, crying, " Madge, Madge, pity me, pity me! Forgive me if you can, and, if our queen decrees it, I shall die happy."

In my desperation I caught the girl's hand, but she drew it quickly from me, and said : —

" Do not touch me ! "

She arose to her feet, and groped her way to her bed-room. We were in Aunt Dorothy's room. I watched Madge as she sought with her outstretched hand the door-way ; and when she passed slowly through it, the sun of my life seemed to turn black. Just as Madge passed from the room, Sir William St. Loe, with two yeomen, entered by Sir George's door and placed irons upon my wrist and ankles. I was led by Sir William to the dungeon, and no word was spoken by either of us.

I had never in my life feared death, and now I felt that I would welcome it. When a man is convinced that his life is useless, through the dire disaster that he is a fool, he values it little, and is even more than willing to lose it.

Then there were three of us in the dungeon, — John, Lord Rutland, and myself ; and we were all there because we had meddled in the affairs of others, and because Doro-thy had inherited from Eve a capacity for insane, unreason-ing jealousy.

Lord Rutland was sitting on the ground in a corner of the dungeon. John, by the help of a projecting stone in the masonry, had climbed to the small grated opening which served to admit a few straggling rays of light into the dungeon's gloom. He was gazing out upon the fair day, whose beauty he feared would soon fade away from him forever.

Elizabeth's coldness had given him no hope. It had taken all hope from his father.

The opening of the door attracted John's attention, and he turned his face toward me when I entered. He had been looking toward the light, and his eyes, unaccustomed for the moment to the darkness, failed at first to recognize of me. When the dungeon door had closed behind me, he sprang down from his perch by the window, and came toward me with outstretched hands. He said sorrowfully:—

"Malcolm, have I brought you here, too? Why are you in irons? It seems that I am destined to bring calamity upon all whom I love."

"It is a long story," I replied laughingly. "I will tell it to you when the time begins to drag; but I tell you now it is through no fault of yours that I am here. No one is to blame for my misfortune but myself." Then I continued bitterly, "Unless it be the good God who created me a fool."

John went to his father's side and said:—

"Sir Malcolm is here, father. Will you not rise and greet him?"

John's voice aroused his father, and the old lord came to the little patch of light in which I was standing and said: "A terrible evil has fallen upon us, Sir Malcolm, and without our fault. I grieve to learn that you also are entangled in the web. The future looks very dark."

"Cheer up, father," said John, taking the old man's hand. "Light will soon come; I am sure it will."

"I have tried all my life to be a just man," said Lord Rutland. "I have failed at times, I fear, but I have tried. That is all any man can do. I pray that God in His mercy will soon send light to you, John, whatever of darkness there may be in store for me."

I thought, "He will surely answer this just man's prayer," and almost before the thought was completed the dungeon door turned upon its hinges and a great light came with glorious refulgence through the open portal — Dorothy.

"John!"

Never before did one word express so much of mingled

joy and grief.   Fear and confidence, and, greater than all, love unutterable were blended in its eloquent tones.   She sprang to John as the lightning leaps from cloud to cloud, and he caught her to his heart.   He gently kissed her hair, her face being hidden in the folds of his doublet.

"Let me kneel, John, let me kneel," she murmured.

"No, Dorothy, no," he responded, holding her closely in his arms.

"But one moment, John," she pleaded.

"No, no; let me see your eyes, sweet one," said John, trying to turn her face upward toward his own.

"I cannot yet, John, I cannot.   Please let me kneel for one little moment at your feet."

John saw that the girl would find relief in self-abasement, so he relaxed his arms, and she sank to her knees upon the dungeon floor.   She wept softly for a moment, and then throwing back her head with her old impulsive manner looked up into his face.

"Oh, forgive me, John!   Forgive me!   Not that I deserve your forgiveness, but because you pity me."

"I forgave you long ago, Dorothy.   You had my full forgiveness before you asked it."

He lifted the weeping girl to her feet and the two clung together in silence.   After a pause Dorothy spoke : —

"You have not asked me, John, why I betrayed you."

"I want to know nothing, Dorothy, save that you love me."

"That you already know.   But you cannot know how much I love you.   I myself don't know.   John, I seem to have turned all to love.   However much there is of me, that much there is of love for you.   As the salt is in every drop of the sea, so love is in every part of my being; but John," she continued, drooping her head and speaking regretfully, "the salt in the sea is not unmixed with many things hurtful." Her face blushed with shame and she continued limpingly: "And my love is not — is not without evil. Oh, John, I feel deep shame in telling you, but my love is terribly jealous. At times a jealousy comes over me so fierce and so distracting that under its influence I am mad, John, mad. I then see nothing in its true light; my eyes seem filled with — with blood, and all things appear red or black and — and — oh! John, I pray you never again cause me jealousy. It makes a demon of me."

You may well know that John was nonplussed.

"I cause you jealousy?" he asked in surprise. "When did I — " But Dorothy interrupted him, her eyes flashing darkly and a note of fierceness in her voice. He saw for himself the effects of jealousy upon her.

"That white — white Scottish wanton! God's curse be upon her! She tried to steal you from me."

"Perhaps she did," replied John, smilingly, "of that I do not know. But this I do know, and you, Dorothy, must know it too henceforth and for all time to come. No woman can steal my love from you. Since I gave you my troth I have been true to you; I have not been false even in one little thought."

"I feel sure, John, that you have not been untrue to me," said the girl with a faint smile playing about her lips; "but — but you remember the strange woman at Bowling Green Gate whom you would have — "

"Dorothy, I hope you have not come to my dungeon for the purpose of making me more wretched than I already am?"

"No, no, John, forgive me," she cried softly; "but John, I hate her, I hate her! and I want you to promise that you too will hate her."

"I promise," said John, "though, you have had no cause for jealousy of Queen Mary."

"Perhaps — not," she replied hesitatingly. "I have

never thought," the girl continued poutingly, "that *you*
did anything of which I should be jealous; but she — she
— oh, I hate her! Let us not talk about her. Jennie
Faxton told me — I will talk about her, and you shall not
stop me — Jennie Faxton told me that the white woman
made love to you and caused you to put your arm about
her waist one evening on the battlements and — "

"Jennie told you a lie," said John.

"Now don't interrupt me," the girl cried nervously,
almost ready for tears, "and I will try to tell you all.
Jennie told me the — the white woman looked up to you
this fashion," and the languishing look she gave John in
imitation of Queen Mary was so beautiful and comical that
he could do nothing but laugh and cover her face with
kisses, then laugh again and love the girl more deeply and
yet more deeply with each new breath he drew. Dorothy
was not sure whether she wanted to laugh or to cry, so
she did both.

"Jennie told me in the middle of the night," continued
Dorothy, "when all things seem so vivid and appear so
distorted and — and that terrible blinding jealousy of
which I told you came upon me and drove me mad. I
really thought, John, that I should die of the agony. Oh,
John, if you could know the anguish I suffered that night
you would pity me; you would not blame me."

"I do not blame you, Dorothy."

"No, no, there — " she kissed him softly, and quickly
continued: "I felt that I must separate her from you at
all cost. I would have done murder to accomplish my
purpose. Some demon whispered to me, 'Tell Queen
Elizabeth,' and — and oh, John, let me kneel again."

"No, no, Dorothy, let us talk of something else," said
John, soothingly.

"In one moment, John. I thought only of the evil that
would come to her — her of Scotland. I did not think of

the trouble I would bring to you, John, until the queen, after asking me if you were my lover, said angrily: ' You may soon seek another.' Then, John, I knew that I had also brought evil upon you. Then I *did* suffer. I tried to reach Rutland, and you know all else that happened on that terrible night. Now John, you know all — all. I have withheld nothing. I have confessed all, and I feel that a great weight is taken from my heart. You will not hate me, will you, John?"

He caught the girl to his breast and tried to turn her face toward his.

"I could not hate you if I would," he replied, with quick-coming breath, "and God knows I would not. To love you is the sweetest joy in life," and he softly kissed the great lustrous eyes till they closed as if in sleep. Then he fiercely sought the rich red lips, waiting soft and passive for his caresses, while the fair head fell back upon the bend of his elbow in a languorous, half-conscious sweet surrender to his will. Lord Rutland and I had turned our backs on the shameless pair, and were busily discussing the prospect for the coming season's crops.

Remember, please, that Dorothy spoke to John of Jennie Faxton. Her doing so soon bore bitter fruit for me.

Dorothy had been too busy with John to notice any one else, but he soon presented her to his father. After the old lord had gallantly kissed her hand, she turned scornfully to me and said: —

"So you fell a victim to her wanton wiles? If it were not for Madge's sake, I could wish you might hang."

"You need not balk your kindly desire for Madge's sake," I answered. "She cares little about my fate. I fear she will never forgive me."

"One cannot tell what a woman will do," Dorothy replied. "She is apt to make a great fool of herself when it comes to forgiving the man she loves."

24

"Men at times have something to forgive," I retorted, looking with a smile toward John. The girl made no reply, but took John's hand and looked at him as if to say, "John, please don't let this horrid man abuse me."

"But Madge no longer cares for me," I continued, wishing to talk upon the theme, "and your words do not apply to her."

The girl turned her back disdainfully on me and said, "You seem to be quite as easily duped by the woman who loves you and says she doesn't as by the one who does not care for you but says she does."

"Damn that girl's tongue!" thought I; but her words, though biting, carried joy to my heart and light to my soul.

After exchanging a few words with Lord Rutland, Dorothy turned to John and said: —

"Tell me upon your knightly honor, John, do you know aught of a wicked, treasonable plot to put the Scottish woman on the English throne?"

I quickly placed my finger on my lips and touched my ear to indicate that their words would be overheard; for a listening-tube connected the dungeon with Sir George's closet.

"Before the holy God, upon my knighthood, by the sacred love we bear each other, I swear I know of no such plot," answered John. "I would be the first to tell our good queen did I suspect its existence."

Dorothy and John continued talking upon the subject of the plot, but were soon interrupted by a warning knock upon the dungeon door.

Lord Rutland, whose heart was like twenty-two carat gold, soft, pure, and precious, kissed Dorothy's hand when she was about to leave, and said: "Dear lady, grieve not for our sake. I can easily see that more pain has come to you than to us. I thank you for the great fearless love you bear my son. It has brought him trouble, but it is worth its cost. You have my forgiveness freely, and I pray God's choicest benediction may be with you."

She kissed the old lord and said, "I hope some day to make you love me."

"That will be an easy task," said his Lordship, gallantly.

Dorothy was about to leave. Just at the doorway she remembered the chief purpose of her visit; so she ran back to John, put her hand over his mouth to insure silence, and whispered in his ear.

On hearing Dorothy's whispered words, signs of joy were so apparent in John's face that they could not be mistaken. He said nothing, but kissed her hand and she hurriedly left the dungeon.

After the dungeon door closed upon Dorothy, John went to his father and whispered a few words to him. Then he came to me, and in the same secretive manner said : —

"The queen has promised Dorothy our liberty."

I was not at all sure that "our liberty" included me, — I greatly doubted it, — but I was glad for the sake of my friends, and, in truth, cared little for myself.

Dorothy went from our dungeon to the queen, and that afternoon, according to promise, Elizabeth gave orders for the release of John and his father. Sir George, of course, was greatly chagrined when his enemies slipped from his grasp; but he dared not show his ill-humor in the presence of the queen nor to any one who would be apt to enlighten her Majesty on the subject.

Dorothy did not know the hour when her lover would leave Haddon; but she sat patiently at her window till at last John and Lord Rutland appeared. She called to Madge, telling her of the joyous event, and Madge, asked : —

"Is Malcolm with them?"

"No," replied Dorothy, "he has been left in the dungeon, where he deserves to remain."

After a short pause, Madge said : —

"If John had acted toward the Scottish queen as Malcolm did, would you forgive him?"

"Yes, of course. I would forgive him anything."

"Then why shall we not forgive Malcolm?" asked Madge.

"Because he is not John," was the absurd reply.

"No," said Madge, promptly; "but he is 'John' to me."

"That is true," responded Dorothy, "and I will forgive him if you will."

"I don't believe it makes much difference to Malcolm whether or not you forgive him," said Madge, who was provoked at Dorothy's condescending offer. "My forgiveness, I hope, is what he desires."

"That is true, Madge," replied Dorothy, laughingly; "but may not I, also, forgive him?"

"If you choose," responded Madge, quietly; "as for me, I know not what I wish to do."

You remember that Dorothy during her visit to the dungeon spoke of Jennie Faxton. The girl's name reached Sir George's ear through the listening-tube and she was at once brought in and put to the question.

Jennie, contrary to her wont, became frightened and told all she knew concerning John and Dorothy, including my part in their affairs. In Sir George's mind, my bad faith to him was a greater crime than my treason to Elizabeth, and he at once went to the queen with his tale of woe.

Elizabeth, the most sentimental of women, had heard from Dorothy the story of her tempestuous love, and also of mine, and the queen was greatly interested in the situation.

I will try to be brief.

Through the influence of Dorothy and Madge, as I afterward learned, and by the help of a good word from Cecil, the queen was induced to order my liberation on condition that I should thenceforth reside in France. So one morning, three days after John's departure from Haddon, I was overjoyed to hear the words, "You are free."

I did not know that Jennie Faxton had given Sir George her large stock of disturbing information concerning my connection with the affairs of Dorothy and John. So when I left the dungeon, I, supposing that my stormy cousin would be glad to forgive me if Queen Elizabeth would, sought and found him in Aunt Dorothy's room. Lady Crawford and Sir George were sitting near the fire and Madge was standing near the door in the next room beyond. When I entered, Sir George sprang to his feet and cried out angrily : —

"You traitorous dog, the queen has seen fit to liberate you, and I cannot interfere with her orders ; but if you do not leave my Hall at once I shall set the hounds on you. Your effects will be sent to The Peacock, and the sooner you quit England the safer you will be." There was of course nothing for me to do but to go.

"You once told me, Sir George — you remember our interview at The Peacock — that if you should ever again order me to leave Haddon, I should tell you to go to the devil. I now take advantage of your kind permission, and will also say farewell."

I kissed Aunt Dorothy's cheek, took my leave, and sought Cecil, from whom I obtained a passport to France. Then I asked Dawson to fetch my horse.

I longed to see Madge before I left Haddon, but I knew that my desire could not be gratified ; so I determined to stop at Rowsley and send back a letter to her which Dawson undertook to deliver. In my letter I would ask Madge's permission to return for her from France and to take her home with me as my wife. After I had despatched my letter I would wait at The Peacock for an answer.

Sore at heart, I bade good-by to Dawson, mounted my horse, and turned his head toward the Dove-cote Gate. As I rode under Dorothy's window she was sitting there. The casement was open, for the day was mild, although the season was little past midwinter. I heard her call to Madge, and then she called to me : —

"Farewell, Malcolm! Forgive me for what I said to you in the dungeon. I was wrong, as usual. Forgive me, and God bless you. Farewell!"

While Dorothy was speaking, and before I replied, Madge came to the open casement and called : —

"Wait for me, Malcolm, I am going down to you."

Great joy is a wonderful purifier, and Madge's cry finished the work of the past few months and made a good man of me, who all my life before had known little else than evil.

Soon Madge's horse was led by a groom to the mounting block, and in a few minutes she emerged gropingly from the great door of Entrance Tower. Dorothy was again a prisoner in her rooms and could not come down to bid me farewell. Madge mounted, and the groom led her horse to me and placed the reins in my hands.

"Is it you, Malcolm?" asked Madge.

"Yes," I responded, in a voice husky with emotion. "I cannot thank you enough for coming to say farewell. You have forgiven me?"

"Yes," responded Madge, almost in tears, "but I have not come to say farewell."

I did not understand her meaning.

"Are you going to ride part of the way with me — perhaps to Rowsley?" I asked, hardly daring to hope for so much.

"To France, Malcolm, if you wish to take me," she responded murmuringly.

For a little time I could not feel the happiness that had come upon me in so great a flood. But when I had collected my scattered senses, I said: —

"I thank God that He has turned your heart again to me. May I feel His righteous anger if ever I give you cause to regret the step you are taking."

"I shall never regret it, Malcolm," she answered softly, as she held out her hand to me.

Then we rode by the dove-cote, out from Haddon Hall, never to see its walls again.

We went to Rutland, whence after a fortnight we journeyed to France. There I received my mother's estates, and never for one moment, to my knowledge, has Madge regretted having intrusted her life and happiness to me. I need not speak for myself.

Our home is among the warm, sunlit, vine-covered hills of southern France, and we care not for the joys of golden streets so long as God in His goodness vouchsafes to us our earthly paradise. Age, with the heart at peace, is the fairest season of life; and love, leavened of God, robs even approaching death of his sting and makes for us a broad flower-strewn path from the tempestuous sea of time to the calm, sweet ocean of eternity.

CHAPTER XVI

LEICESTER WAITS AT THE STILE

I SHALL now tell you of the happenings in Haddon Hall during the fortnight we spent at Rutland before our departure for France.

We left Dorothy, you will remember, a prisoner in her rooms.

After John had gone Sir George's wrath began to gather, and Dorothy was not permitted to depart from the Hall for even a walk upon the terrace, nor could she leave her own apartments save when the queen requested her presence.

A few days after my departure from Haddon, Sir George sent Dawson out through the adjoining country to invite the nobility and gentry to a grand ball to be given at the Hall in honor of Queen Elizabeth. Queen Mary had been sent a prisoner to Chatsworth.

Tom Shaw, the most famous piper of his times, and a choice company of musicians to play with him were hired for the occasion, and, in short, the event was so glorious that its wonders have been sung in minstrelsy throughout Derbyshire ever since.

Dorothy's imprisonment saddened Leicester's heart, and he longed to see her, for her beauty had touched him nearly. Accordingly, the earl one day intimated to Sir George his wish in terms that almost bespoke an intention to ask for the girl's hand when upon proper opportunity the queen's consent might be sought and perchance obtained. His equivocal words did not induce Sir George to grant a meeting by which Dorothy might be compromised; but a robust hope for the ultimate accomplishment of the "Leicester possibility" was aroused in the breast of the King of the Peak, and from hope he could, and soon did, easily step to faith. He saw that the earl was a handsome man, and he believed, at least he hoped, that the fascinating lord might, if he were given an opportunity, woo Dorothy's heart away from the hated scion of a hated race. Sir George, therefore, after several interviews with the earl, grew anxious to give his Lordship an opportunity to win her. But both Sir George and my lord feared Elizabeth's displeasure, and the meeting between Leicester and the girl seemed difficult to contrive. Sir George felt confident that Dorothy could, if she would, easily capture the great lord in a few private interviews; but would she? Dorothy gave her father no encouragement in the matter, and took pains to shun Leicester rather than to seek him.

As Dorothy grew unwilling, Leicester and Sir George grew eager, until at length the latter felt that it was almost time to exert his parental authority. He told Aunt Dorothy his feeling on the subject, and she told her niece. It was impossible to know from what source Dorothy might draw inspiration for mischief. It came to her with her father's half-command regarding Leicester.

Winter had again asserted itself. The weather was bitter cold and snow covered the ground to the depth of a horse's fetlock.

The eventful night of the grand ball arrived, and Dorothy's heart throbbed till she thought surely it would burst.

At nightfall guests began to arrive, and Sir George, hospitable soul that he was, grew boisterous with good humor and delight.

The rare old battlements of Haddon were ablaze with

flambeaux, and inside the rooms were alight with waxen tapers. The long gallery was brilliant with the smiles of bejewelled beauty, and laughter, song, and merriment filled the grand old Hall from terrace to Entrance Tower. Dorothy, of course, was brought down from her prison to grace the occasion with a beauty which none could rival. Her garments were of soft, clinging, bright-colored silks and snowy laces, and all who saw her agreed that a creature more radiant never greeted the eye of man.

When the guests had all arrived, the pipers in the balcony burst forth in heart-swelling strains of music, and every foot in the room longed for the dance to begin.

I should like to tell you how Elizabeth most graciously opened the ball with his Majesty, the King of the Peak, amid the plaudits of worshipping subjects, and I should enjoy describing the riotous glory which followed, — for although I was not there, I know intimately all that happened, — but I will balk my desire and tell you only of those things which touched Dorothy.

Leicester, of course, danced with her, and during a pause in the figure, the girl in response to pleadings which she had adroitly incited, reluctantly promised to grant the earl the private interview he so much desired if he could suggest some means for bringing it about. Leicester was in raptures over her complaisance and glowed with triumph and delightful anticipation. But he could think of no satisfactory plan whereby his hopes might be brought to a happy fruition. He proposed several, but all seemed impracticable to the coy girl, and she rejected them. After many futile attempts he said : —

"I can suggest no good plan, mistress. I pray you, gracious lady, therefore, make full to overflowing the measure of your generosity, and tell me how it may be accomplished."

Dorothy hung her head as if in great shame and said :

"I fear, my lord, we had better abandon the project for a time. Upon another occasion perhaps —"

"No, no," interrupted the earl, pleadingly, "do not so grievously disappoint me. My heart yearns to have you to myself for one little moment where spying eyes cannot see nor prying ears hear. It is cruel in you to raise my hopes only to cast them down. I beg you, tell me if you know in what manner I may meet you privately."

After a long pause, Dorothy with downcast eyes said, "I am full of shame, my lord, to consent to this meeting, and then find the way to it, but — but — " ("Yes, yes, my Venus, my gracious one," interrupted the earl) — "but if my father would permit me to — to leave the Hall for a few minutes, I might — oh, it is impossible, my lord. I must not think of it."

"I pray you, I beg you," pleaded Leicester. "Tell me, at least, what you might do if your father would permit you to leave the Hall. I would gladly fall to my knees, were it not for the assembled company."

With reluctance in her manner and gladness in her heart, the girl said : —

"If my father would permit me to leave the Hall, I might — only for a moment, meet you at the stile, in the northeast corner of the garden back of the terrace half an hour hence. But he would not permit me, and — and, my lord, I ought not to go even should father consent."

"I will ask your father's permission for you. I will seek him at once," said the eager earl.

"No, no, my lord, I pray you, do not," murmured Dorothy, with distracting little troubled wrinkles in her forehead. Her trouble was more for fear lest he would not than for dread that he would.

"I will, I will," cried his Lordship, softly; "I insist, and you shall not gainsay me."

The girl's only assent was silence, but that was sufficient

for so enterprising a gallant as the noble Robert Dudley, Earl of Leicester. So he at once went to seek Sir George.

The old gentleman, although anxious to give Leicester a chance to press his suit with Dorothy, at first refused, but Leicester said : —

"My intentions are honorable, Sir George. If I can win your daughter's heart, it is my wish, if the queen's consent can be obtained, to ask Mistress Vernon's hand in marriage."

Sir George's breast swelled with pride and satisfaction, for Leicester's words were as near an offer of marriage as it was in his power to make. So the earl received, for Dorothy, permission to leave the Hall, and eagerly carried it to her.

"Your father consents gladly," said the earl. "Will you meet me half an hour hence at the stile?"

"Yes," murmured the girl, with shamelessly cast down eyes and drooping head. Leicester bowed himself away, and fully fifteen minutes before the appointed time left the Hall to wait in the cold at the stile for Dorothy.

Before the expiration of the tedious half hour our meek maiden went to her father and with deep modesty and affected shame said : —

"Father, is it your wish that I go out of the Hall for a few minutes to meet — to meet — " She apparently could not finish the sentence, so modest and shame-faced was she.

"Yes, Doll, I wish you to go on this condition : if Leicester asks you to marry him, you shall consent to be his wife."

"I promise, father," replied the dutiful girl, "if Lord Leicester asks me this night, I will be his wife."

"That is well, child, that is well. Once more you are my good, obedient daughter, and I love you. Wear your sable cloak, Doll; the weather is very cold out of doors."

Her father's solicitude touched her nearly, and she

gently led him to a secluded alcove near by, threw her arms about his neck, and kissed him passionately. The girl's affection was sweet to the old man who had been without it so long, and his eyes grew moist as he returned her caresses. Dorothy's eyes also were filled with tears. Her throat was choked with sobs, and her heart was sore with pain. Poor young heart! Poor old man!

Soon after Dorothy had spoken with her father she left the Hall by Dorothy's Postern. She was wrapped in her sable cloak — the one that had saved John's life in Aunt Dorothy's room; but instead of going across the garden to the stile where Lord Leicester was waiting, which was north and east of the terrace, she sped southward down the terrace and did not stop till she reached the steps which led westward to the lower garden. She stood on the terrace till she saw a man running toward her from the postern in the southwest corner of the lower garden. Then down the steps she sped with winged feet, and outstretching her arms, fell upon the man's breast, whispering: "John, my love! John, my love!"

As for the man — well, during the first minute or two he wasted no time in speech.

When he spoke he said: —

"We must not tarry here. Horses are waiting at the south end of the footbridge. Let us hasten away at once."

Then happened the strangest of all the strange things I have had to record of this strange, fierce, tender, and at times almost half-savage girl.

Dorothy for months had longed for that moment. Her heart had almost burst with joy when a new-born hope for it was suggested by the opportunities of the ball and her father's desire touching my lord of Leicester. But now that the longed-for moment was at hand, the tender heart, which had so anxiously awaited it, failed, and the girl broke down weeping hysterically.

"Oh, John, you have forgiven so many faults in me," she said between sobs, "that I know you will forgive me when I tell you I cannot go with you to-night. I thought I could and I so intended when I came out here to meet you. But oh, John, my dearest love, I cannot go; I cannot go. Another time I will go with you, John. I promise that I will go with you soon, very soon, John; but I cannot go now, oh, I cannot. You will forgive me, won't you, John? You will forgive me?"

"No," cried John in no uncertain tones, "I will not forgive you. I will take you. If you cry out, I will silence you." Thereupon he rudely took the girl in his arms and ran with her toward the garden gate near the north end of the stone footbridge.

"John, John!" she cried in terror. But he placed his hand over her mouth and forced her to remain silent till they were past the south wall. Then he removed his hand and she screamed and struggled against him with all her might. Strong as she was, her strength was no match for John's, and her struggles were in vain.

John, with his stolen bride, hurriedly crossed the footbridge and ran to the men who were holding the horses. There he placed Dorothy on her feet and said with a touch of anger:—

"Will you mount of your own will or shall I put you in the saddle?"

"I'll mount of my own will, John," she replied submissively, "and John, I — I thank you, I thank you for — for — " she stopped speaking and toyed with the tufts of fur that hung from the edges of her cloak.

"For what, my love? For what do you thank me?" asked John after a little pause.

"For making — me — do — what I — I longed to do. My conscience would not let me do it of my own free will."

Then tears came from her eyes in a great flood, and throwing her arms about John's neck she gave him herself and her heart to keep forever and forever.

And Leicester was shivering at the stile! The girl had forgotten even the existence of the greatest lord in the realm.

My wife, Lord Rutland, and I waited in the watch-room above the castle gates for the coming of Dorothy and John; and when they came — but I will not try to describe the scene. It were a vain effort. Tears and laughter well compounded make the sweetest joy; grief and joy the truest happiness; happiness and pain the grandest soul, and none of these may be described. We may analyze them, and may take them part from part; but, like love, they cannot be compounded. We may know all the component parts, but when we try to create these great emotions in description, we lack the subtle compounding flux to unite the ingredients, and after all is done, we have simply said that black is black and that white is white.

Next day, in the morning, Madge and I started for our new home in France. We rode up the hill down which poor Dolcy took her last fatal plunge, and when we reached the crest, we paused to look back. Standing on the battlements, waving a kerchief in farewell to us, was the golden-crowned form of a girl. Soon she covered her face with her kerchief, and we knew she was weeping. Then we, also, wept as we turned away from the fair picture; and since that far-off morning — forty long, long years ago — we have not seen the face nor heard the voice of our sweet, tender friend. Forty years! What an eternity it is if we tear it into minutes!

L'ENVOI

The fire ceases to burn; the flames are sucked back into the earth; the doe's blood has boiled away; the caldron cools, and my shadowy friends — so real to me — whom I love with a passionate tenderness beyond my power to express, have sunk into the dread black bank of the past, and my poor, weak wand is powerless to recall them for the space of even one fleeting moment. So I must say farewell to them; but all my life I shall carry a heart full of tender love and pain for the fairest, fiercest, gentlest, weakest, strongest of them all — Dorothy Vernon.

MALCOLM POSSIBLY IN ERROR

MALCOLM VERNON is the only writer on the life of Dorothy Vernon who speaks of Rutland Castle. All others writing on the subject say that Belvoir Castle was the home of the Earl of Rutland.

No other writer mentions the proposed marriage, spoken of by Malcolm, between Dorothy and Lord Derby's son. They do, however, say that Dorothy had an elder sister who married a Stanley, but died childless, leaving Dorothy sole heiress to Sir George Vernon's vast estate.

All writers agree with Malcolm upon the main fact that brave Dorothy eloped with John Manners and brought to him the fair estate of Haddon, which their descendant, the present Duke of Rutland, now possesses.

No other writer speaks of Mary Stuart having been at Haddon, and many chroniclers disagree with Malcolm as to the exact date of her imprisonment in Lochleven and her escape.

In all other essential respects the history of Dorothy Vernon as told by Malcolm agrees with other accounts of her life.

I do not pretend to reconcile the differences between these great historical authorities, but I confess to considerable faith in Malcolm.